CRITICS PRAISE
BEDLAM, BATH AND BEYOND!

"Told in breezy chick-lit style, this is a very well-done fae tale....A lighthearted, fun read."

—*RT BOOKreviews*

"*Bedlam, Bath and Beyond* is a fresh story filled with humor. The premise is unique and the action is non-stop....*Bedlam, Bath and Beyond* is a fun start to what promises to be an interesting series."

—Romance Reviews Today

"From the cover, you'll expect a snappy comedy, but there's more to this story than that. Yes, there is humor, but the emphasis is more on action, danger, and a touch of romance than on tossing out random witticisms. It's Tam Lin meets a caper movie, but only the good parts of one."

—Huntress Reviews

AFTER THE STORM

I tried to pull away, but Azimuth was much stronger. I found myself restrained by both of his hands as he pulled me against him. Our two wet bodies met, back to front. "Cor!" I cried, my throat raw and ragged. I felt as if I'd swallowed a mouthful of glass.

From the confusion of wings, a single Storm Raven separated itself and swooped down. My eyes caught the iridescent sheen of its dark, feathered body before it began to transform. From the haze and confusion of light, Cor rose. He was shirtless and barefoot, his lank hair dripping, his body glistening with rain. I gasped to see his body peppered with spots of red; a bloody cut, long but not deep, arched from the center of his flat stomach to his upper chest. "Oh, my baby!" I whispered, trying to reach for him. "Are you all right?"

Cor stared at the man restraining me, his head moving up and down as he inspected my captor before looking me dead in the eyes. Then finally he spoke. "Who the devil is your friend?"

J. D. WARREN

Crate & Peril

LOVE SPELL NEW YORK CITY

LOVE SPELL®

October 2008

Published by

Dorchester Publishing Co., Inc.
200 Madison Avenue
New York, NY 10016

ISBN 10: 0-505-52699-9
ISBN 13: 978-0-505-52699-1

The name "Love Spell" and its logo are trademarks of Dorchester Publishing Co., Inc.

Printed in the United States of America.

10 9 8 7 6 5 4 3 2 1

Visit us on the web at www.dorchesterpub.com.

ACKNOWLEDGMENTS

I must thank Michelle Grajkowski for being the best and most upbeat agent a writer could have. Not a writing day goes by that I'm not grateful to have her positive influence in my life! I also owe a big bucket of thanks to Andrew Wright for the title and for being my general funny-name-go-to-guy, and to Patty Woodwell for her superior continuity and proofreading skills, as well as for having the patience of a saint.

Crate & Peril

Chapter One

"Let's get down to business, bucko," I suggested, withdrawing an envelope from my bag. The rubber band surrounding it was the only thing that kept the stack of hundred-dollar bills within from spilling out. "You've got what I asked for, right?"

Lunchtime at the Baby Blues BBQ, one of Venice's more prominent home-grown eateries, was as crowded as ever. The hunched-over man known as Rooster and I had gotten one of the last tables in the joint. "Jeez, Samantha," he growled. "You get more hardboiled every time I see you. Was there some Sam Spade film festival on TCM last night, or what? Why not let a guy get a few bites in before you grill him?"

"It's hot," said one of the restaurant's two bald-headed owners as he dropped a blue Fiestaware dish covered with lunch in front of my companion. "And here's your take-out order," he added for my benefit, sliding a box my way before ambling back behind the counter. The fellow sitting opposite me ignored the warning and grabbed for the buttery, cheese-encrusted cob of corn sitting on the side of his plate. Immediately he swore, yanked his hands back and blew furiously on his reddening fingertips. "Told you it was hot!" the owner called back, without even looking over his brawny shoulder.

"I don't know why I keep coming here," he growled, flipping off the owner's back.

I looked at the man and shook my head. And when I say *man*, I mean it in the most generic of senses, because although he looked normal enough, genetically, he wasn't at all human. "From what Cor tells me, just about anyone from your race immigrating to California comes to the Baby Blues," I reminded him. "It's practically the first tourist stop outside the gates of Resht for any self-respecting Peri, isn't it?"

"It used to be," grumbled Rooster. How he'd gotten that nickname, I had no idea. Perhaps it was his red face or the flap of jowl hanging beneath his chin. "Then Venice got gentrified and the prices shot up. Freakin' Los Angeles, man. I keep saying I should move to San Diego."

"Yeah, well, lunch is on me, remember?" I tossed him a couple of the wet naps from the little bowl at my side. "Provided you've got the goods."

"You don't trust me?"

I shrugged. Trust is for crazy folk. That's my motto. I believe what my eyes see.

"I've got them, I've got them." At the sight of my expectant, raised eyebrows, Rooster sighed and reached into his sport coat to pull out a packet of papers stuffed into an oversized manila envelope that had seen better days. It looked like an artifact from the crash site of a small craft midair collision. With dirty fingertips, Rooster pushed the envelope across the table, so that it slid next to my takeout container. I used the salt shaker to gently move it to a less contagious position. "All my notes. Everything I remember them saying."

"And how good is your memory these days, exactly?" He seemed offended by my question, but I pressed on. "The last time that I used your services . . ."

"Yeah, and I gave you a refund for that, didn't I?" he said, stuffing three of the large-cut French fries into his piehole at once.

"The *last* time," I emphasized, "Cor went flying into what he thought was going to be a cabal of border smugglers and ended up busting the Venice United Methodist

Church Crafty Ladies Annual Crochet Challenge." I crossed my arms and dared him to dispute that one.

Through a mouth full of potato, he added, "Okay. I *might* have gotten the street number of that one wrong. My bad. No trust, Samantha! No trust at all! It's not like I can carry a pen and paper with me when I'm on recon, is it? No," he said, answering his own question before I could half-heartedly agree. "I have to keep it all up here. In my noggin." The fellow rapped the knuckles of one hand on his skull—I half-expected it to make a hollow sound—while he nibbled intently on his corn with another. "In my brain."

Honestly, from the way he chowed down while he spoke, I would've guessed Rooster hadn't eaten in a week. "Yes, but it's a rodent-sized brain. No offense."

"None taken," he granted. How could he mind? I hadn't meant it as an insult. Rooster was of the Kin, as his race informally termed it. Officially, they were known as the Peri, shape-shifters with whom I'd become entangled six months before. It was because of some nasty Peri that I'd lost three years of my life. With the help of some of their nicer representatives, however—and with especial thanks to the sexiest individual I'd ever met—I'd managed to get back on track. Rooster's ability was to shift into a rat, giving him an opportunity to infiltrate spaces ordinary people couldn't, and to eavesdrop.

"But it's not like my head fits less stuff when I'm smaller, you know," he added.

I'd never seen my hired informant in his vermin form. I wasn't really sure I wanted to. Rodents and I just don't get along—something about those pink-ringed tails really creeps me out. Since my first encounter with the Peri, though, I'd taken up a career sniffing out little criminal irregularities affecting both their sphere and my own. Having a plant among the dirty underbelly of a race to which I didn't belong helped pay the bills. If Rooster's ratty self in any way resembled his humanoid form when he ate, particularly in the way his nose twitched and his oversized front teeth gnawed away at the cob of corn he held between his quivering fingers . . . well, I could do without witnessing his particular transformation.

"So what's in here?" I asked. Much as I disliked doing it, I picked up the envelope by the corners and looked inside. True to form, all of Rooster's notes had been written on torn scraps of paper, rolled into a wad and fastened with rubber bands that looked on the verge of snapping. Poring over them was going to be a bacterial bloodbath. "This is all the information about the border crossings?"

"The deals I overheard, yeah. Couple of Kin making promises to a crazy-rich Hollywood type about smuggling humans through the gate into Resht, telling them they'll live forever once they're in the Kinlands, that kind of crap." He put down the corn and began chomping away at a glistening beef rib with relish. "Making them pay up front all kinds of money for a shot at the fountain of youth, eternal life, all that bull. Hell's bells if they don't buy it, too. Two million, this agent guy has paid. Four installments of five hundred thou, for some guy on basic cable." He jabbed at the envelope with his index finger, adding a fresh, dark stain to it. "And that's just the cash he's put out so far. When the Kin who's selling him lies disappears—either because you and Corydonais pick him up or because he decides to move on to the next mark—the Hollywood guy is just going to start looking for a new contact."

"Fantastic." I grimaced. "And there's nothing we can do about Mr. Hollywood, because there're no human laws against throwing away your money to stay young forever. If there were, there'd be no Rodeo Drive." Persian lore had it that the Peri came to earth as fallen angels—or at least so said my mom, a professor in the classics and an ordinary (if slightly screwy) woman as far removed from this crazy business of mine as I could possibly leave her. Persian lore would also probably have it that the Kin were mythical, but here I was, neck-deep in their schemes and dirty dealings. Not that they were any worse than we humans were, really. Some were better. The one I lived with, for example. He was good. Very, very good.

As if reading my mind, Rooster raised his head from his frantic gorging to ask, "So how is ol' Corydonais? Haven't seen him for a while. Yeah, yeah, I know," he added, before I could answer. "He's too recognizable to make his own social calls. Besides, you're his lapdog now."

Oh, that was beyond the pale. "I am *not* his lapdog." I made little air quotes around that terrible phrase. "Cor and his Storm Ravens deal with investigations of the royal Peri court. I sniff out the little stuff for them to follow up on." Did I sound discontent with that arrangement? In case I did, I added, "And that's fine. It's a living."

When an inexperienced youth fresh out of Resht, the capital city of the Kinlands, fell in love and talked too much about the Kin to a homegrown California mall rat, I was the one who appeared with a settlement and a binding nondisclosure contract for the girl to sign. When a group of adolescent Peri (and the Kin had an adolescence that lasted roughly well into the third century of their lifespan) snuck through the hidden portal leading from Resht to Venice to go on an all-night bender, I was the one visiting the bars the next morning to get descriptions and settle the skipped tabs and bills for damages. Before I'd run into these people— this race that lived among us but weren't of us—I'd been an insurance investigator. My current job wasn't much different, though the pay was better.

And, I had to admit as I thought about Cor, the benefits were glorious. "I like it," I finished, lamely.

"Uh-huh." Rooster simply studied me as he picked up the cup of coleslaw at the plate's side and let some of the contents slide into the black hole he called his mouth. "I didn't know he went for dishwater blondes. His last lapdog was a redhead. What happened there? He ditch her?"

"If you're talking about Ginger . . . Jinjurnaturnia," I said, hastily amending my sobriquet for Cor's second-in-command to her actual name, "she's still very much in the picture."

"Kinky." The single word managed to conjure up an entire room of bound editions of *Penthouse Forum*.

"You are disgusting." I couldn't take the gorging anymore; it was too much like a feeding frenzy in the shark tank. I grabbed my take-out container with one hand and my bag in the other so I could stuff the notes inside. "Enjoy your lunch."

"Hold, hold, hold on there, lady." Rooster's expression of enjoyment at my discomfort couldn't have been more obvious; he wore it as plainly as the smear of barbecue sauce across the lower half of his face. "We're not done here."

"Oh, yes we are. You've got your cash, I've got my information, and I'm not paying extra for the abuse. Later, gator."

I was halfway to my feet when Rooster's hands shot out and grabbed my wrist. I recoiled at his touch, mostly because he kept his fingernails sharp and long. "You aren't going yet," he said, his nose twitching with amusement. When I wrenched my arm out of his grasp, he yanked back his own hands, seeming to know he'd gone too far. They hung, limp and twitching, in front of his chest. "I mean, there's more. I have a message for you."

"A message?" I cocked my head. "If it's about more money, forget it."

Rooster rolled his eyes. That mischievous grin crept back onto his face. "Open your mind, wouldja? It's not about money. Sheesh. Give me a little credit. This is about a message someone told me to give you."

"Someone?" I asked, raising my eyebrows. Being around Rooster made me uncomfortable enough as it was. I liked keeping our meetings short and sweet, leaning to the short side. "Someone like . . . who?"

The Peri shrugged and resumed eating. "I don't know him. He said he had a message for Samantha of the DeRengiers."

When I was a little girl, I used to have a toy marionette that I took an unholy pleasure in making crumple to the ground by keeping the strings slack. Suddenly, I knew exactly how that marionette felt. I slid back into my just-vacated seat, letting gravity drag me down. "DeRengier?" I said, repeating the word. "You know my last name is Dorringer, right?"

The question was a test. He simply shrugged. "Can't say I ever really thought about your last name." Now it was my turn to twitch. Shortly before he'd died, one of the Peris who had abducted me and taken away three years of my life, all in the name of the death cult known as the Order of the Crow, had called me a DeRengier. I'd found out from my mother that it was her family's original name before they'd emigrated to the U.S., but other than a cursory look in the White Pages to see if there were any DeRengiers in the greater Los Angeles area, I hadn't investigated it further. To hear the name coming from the mouth of yet another of the Kin left me sagging. Rooster cocked his head at my silence. "Maybe it's not for you, then?"

"Just give me the message!" I snapped, impatient and, weirdly, more than a little frightened. Of all the places to feel apprehensive, too—the Baby Blues BBQ couldn't have been any more everyday. But just the merest reminder of the night I'd had to confront my mortal enemy and nearly lose the man I'd begun to love gave me an unshakeable case of the creeps.

"Fine, fine." Rooster still seemed to be relishing his hold over me. In his tiny little head, it was probably some kind of revenge for all the times Cor and I had asked him to scuttle into out-of-the-way places in rat form to do a little reconnaissance. "He wants to meet you."

"Who wants to meet me?"

"This guy."

"What guy?"

"The guy who wants to meet you."

It is a pity that God gave me sturdy, strong hands, yet conscience enough to prevent me from strangling anyone. My voice gargled in my throat as I intoned, "Who is this guy . . . who wants to . . . meet me?"

For some people, a little bit of power is an ugly thing. Rooster shrugged again, grinning. "I told you, I don't know him."

I made a quick decision. If he wanted to play some variation of a seventh-grade guessing game, bully for him. I'd had enough, though. I raised my right hand and flipped the fingers in a definite farewell.

"I know you're not gonna walk away," he called out to my back, but I was already smiling at the second of the restaurant's brawny, bald-headed owners as I handed over the tab along with a couple of bills. "You're bluffing," Rooster shouted, oblivious to the stares from the other midday diners. I continued to ignore him as I received my change. "Aw, come on," he groaned when I made a beeline for the door. "Come back, already!"

I paused at the exit, hands on the glass, waiting a moment. The question I meant to ask was expressed in my eyebrows arching toward the ceiling when I turned.

"Fine, I'll tell you," he called. Now it was my turn to enjoy the irritation on his face as I marched back to the table. I rested my hands on its edge, leaned forward, and waited. "Whatever. You win!"

"I always do," I commented, trying not to sound smug. "Now, who is this guy?"

"I don't know." Before I could make another dramatic exit, he waved his hands and stopped me. "I honestly don't. All I know is that he said his name was Azimuth, and that he had a message for Samantha of the DeRengiers. He wants to talk to you."

One of the things I'd picked up from working in the field of insurance claims investigations for a few years before my abduction was a good sense of who was lying to me. Rooster wasn't—at least, not now. His eyes weren't shifty. When he talked, he didn't stare at the saltshaker or anywhere else other than me. "So this human. . . ."

"He was of the Kin," Rooster corrected.

"Ah. So this Peri just approached you and said he wanted to talk to me. And out of the goodness of your heart. . . ."

"Please. He gave me *money*." My informant looked pained that I'd suggested otherwise. "What do I look like, a chump? I don't do diddly for charity, Sam. The fellow wants to talk to you."

"Just wants to talk, huh?" I didn't buy it. "What'd this guy look like?"

I was expecting a description of a shadowy figure in a cowl and robe, face obscured by dark alley shadows, but instead Rooster replied, "Oh, you'll recognize him."

The comment was about as unhelpful as I could have gotten, really. "All right, great," I replied, fishing in my bag for my keys. "Get him to give you a phone number or something and I'll call sometime during the week."

I noticed Rooster was munching on a French fry and shaking his head at me. "He didn't seem that type of guy. If you agree to meet, he'll find *you*."

I'd become accustomed to the otherworldly activities of the Kin over the previous few months, but I still didn't like the sound of Rooster's promise. Knowing that my hometown of Venice, California was the absolute epicenter of Peri activity on this continent didn't bother me. In fact, it more than amply explained why the boardwalk was littered with freaks. Hanging out with Corydonais and the Order of the Storm Ravens meant that many times I'd watched them transform and fly off to fight evildoers, like a troop of feathered superheroes. It might have been a little disconcerting the first few times. I coped, though. I was even used to it now.

Agreeing that some shape-shifting stalker type could simply appear out of nowhere to visit me, however, sounded like the kind of thing I typically advised against in the self-defense classes my mom had roped me into teaching down at the local senior center. Yet I'd be fibbing if I didn't admit to some intrigue. What if this Azimuth guy was on the up-and-up? What if he had some kind of information I could use? "Let me talk to Cor about it."

"Nuh-uh." Rooster shook his head. "That was the other thing. He forbids you to tell Corydonais."

Well. If that was the condition, I'd had enough. "*Forbids* me? You've got to be kidding! Cor and I don't keep secrets." I picked up my take-out box again. This time, I wouldn't be persuaded to come back.

"Oh, don't you?"

I didn't like the tone of slimy insinuation Rooster used. He really was a repulsive little creature, and the fact that I had to deal with him at all rubbed me the wrong way. After today, though, I might cut the ties completely. There had to be other among the Kin who could do what he did with less back talk and familiarity. "No, we don't," I told him. "He knows everything there is to know about me, and I know all about him." Or at least what portions of his multi-century lifespan I'd been able to learn about in six months. There were definite disadvantages to dating an older man, even if he looked only thirty. "That's the way we roll."

"Oh, that's the way you roll, huh?" The echoing thing was getting on my nerves, particularly since he did it so mockingly. "So that's why he told you all about his dame? And his great-dame?"

"What about them?" I asked, shrugging. I didn't know what his mother and grandmother had to do with anything. True, I hadn't met them, nor did I necessarily think I ever would, given how uncommon a Peri/human romance was. Our worlds colliding seemed unlikely. "I mean, there's nothing unusual, is there?"

Rooster's reply was a snort. He regarded me levelly while he continued to down his lunch. "Is there? I don't know. If you and Corydonais don't have any *secrets* from each other, any, you know, unspoken *confidences* that you shouldn't be keeping, it shouldn't be hard to ask. Right?" His sharp incisors loosened another hunk of meat from a rib bone. "Isn't that what Dr. Phil says about good relationships? What's that look for? I like Dr. Phil."

My eyes narrowed. "Tell your friend I'm not interested." I stood up straight once more so I could pretend to have missed his low blow. This exit would be the last.

"Oh, he'll be waiting around," Rooster said while I stomped toward the door again. "Probably where you least expect it." He raised his voice as I reached the door. "A pleasure doing business with you, Sam!"

After being inside the dim Baby Blues BBQ with an even dimmer personality, the California sun was so dazzling that I had to don my shades. Once my vision was properly adjusted to the polarized lenses and I'd dug out my car keys, I tucked my bag beneath my arm, hefted the take-out order I'd been clinging to for the last several minutes, and began walking to my Mini Cooper parked down the street. Ridiculous, the notion that I would agree to meet some perfect stranger—one of the Kin, no less—on command. I wasn't any Peri's to direct or forbid; even Cor had learned, the hard way, that I responded to suggestions better than to outright directions.

Still. I marched along the pavement, passing some of the odd strays of Venice and trying out my fledgling Kin-dar to attempt to figure out exactly to which race they might belong. Blue eyes were often a tip-off, but not a guarantee. Many of the Kin clans wore elaborate tattoos on their backs and shoulders, but this was Venice, where every storefront that wasn't a coffeehouse was a tattoo parlor. No, the only guaranteed way to tell one of the Kin was to look at his midriff. He wouldn't have a navel.

I couldn't help wondering what anyone named Azimuth might want from me. No one else had ever called me a DeRengier. Maybe he'd know something about the Order of the Crow and its one remaining leader, the woman I once knew as Agnes Jones. Cor and his followers had been looking for leads in that direction.

But still! The high-handed attitude of this Azimuth guy would have to change if he wanted to meet. He'd find me? People didn't find me. They made appointments, like civilized beings. They called. Sometimes they sent letters. They didn't just *find*. . . .

It was at that moment, a mere twenty feet from my little black Mini Cooper, that from the corner of my eyes I saw movement from the alleyway behind the restaurant. A masculine hand shot out and clutched my arm. Before I could yell, it was yanking me off the sidewalk into the shadows.

Chapter Two

Did I panic, when I felt that strong grip on my wrist?

You bet your bippy I did! Panic is the natural human re-action when things go bump in the dark. Like I told my self-defense students at the senior center every other Tues-day night, nature's taken thousands of years to perfect that scalding flush of adrenaline that makes the spine tingle and the heart pound. Thousands of years of saber-toothed tiger attacks and fleeing from mastodons and Vikings and Huns and flashbulb-clicking paparazzi have whetted our defenses into a paranoid bundle of nerves so sensitive that the slight-est out-of-place cracking of a twig is enough to set us run-ning. Usually with good reason. I tell my ladies to honor their instincts, because they're probably right.

Of course, I'd also cautioned them not to let the fear be-come too overwhelming. If it does, you won't be able use that rush of energy to pull off the moves necessary to ensure your safety. Moves like the stomp-kick I lifted my knee to begin now, knowing that my foot would land squarely atop his instep, crippling my attacker and making him hobble off in pain. Or moves like the way I jerked my left arm forward, so I could use every ounce of my strength to jam it back into my assailant's ribs and send him breathless and reeling. Oh, I had a whole arsenal of dodges like that, trotted out twice monthly before a collection of women my grandmother's age who were worried about how to conduct themselves should their purses be snatched while walking back to their cars from the Venice Farmer's Market.

All I needed now were two basic tricks, though—the foot stomp and the ribcage assault, enough to leave my attacker wheezing and limping so I could make a getaway to the sidewalk and daylight and safety. I needed to yell, too. That's what I always told my ladies. Yell like crazy . . . something assertive and powerful meant to scare and intimidate. And yet, even with all that practical information coursing through my head, the best that I could come up with when I opened my mouth was a gargled, *"Aaaaaooooooof!"*

It was followed very quickly by my cry of *"Arrrgh!"* when I brought my foot down onto what I thought was going to be my assailant's instep, but was instead a bent length of thick rebar lying flat on the ground near the alley Dumpster. Even worse, it morphed into a grunt of displeasure and an outright curse of "Crap-beans!" when my elbow—my poor pointy elbow, intended to deliver the coup de grace to the guy's ribcage—jerked back and swung into empty space. The tip grazed the cinderblock wall at the top of its arc, the mild scrape prompting a few stray tears.

"What in the devil are you doing?" I heard a familiar, baffled male voice ask when I stumbled backward, free from the grasp that had sent me into action. There was no hulking thug looming in the shadows. Only a dark silhouette, lanky and long-haired, that I knew all too well. "Are you trying to kill me?"

"Cor! You *idiot!*" I gasped, whipping around and clutching my hurt arm. The act of wrenching my thoughts into something coherent was a chore, with all the conflicting energies coursing through me. First and foremost, I was grateful to see my lover standing in the shadows instead of a purse-snatcher or gang member. Secondly, I was happy I hadn't broken the arch of his foot or damaged his solar plexus, assuming I'd actually reached them. Lastly, of course, I wanted to murder the bum. "You don't do that!" The bag

I'd been clutching under my arm tumbled onto the pavement as I lunged at him and slapped both hands on his chest. "Never *do that!*"

"Do what?" he asked, genuinely puzzled.

"Grab a girl and pull her into a dark alley!" I was aware that my voice was still raised to the maximum volume I could maintain without actually screeching like a fishwife, but I didn't care. Hot adrenaline still pumped through my veins, and I couldn't calm down. Not yet. "You scared the Depends off me! Depends are adult diapers," I added, seeing the incomprehension in his blue eyes. "No, I don't wear diapers. It's an expression."

"Adult diapers?" he asked. Over the last few months I'd learned that I shouldn't expect Cor or any of his Peri friends to get my casual references. Their race might spend a lot of time occupying the same world we humans did, and they might even have learned to dress like us and to blend in, but they seemed to believe, by and large, that the less time they spent wallowing in our popular culture, the better. And frankly, I could understand the impulse. If I had a lifespan of hundreds of years, why would I want to invest any of that time trying to remember which Baldwin brother was on Hollywood's hot seat at any given moment?

Sometimes it made me feel as if I was having a conversation with an orthodox Amish elder, though. "I'm trying to tell you that I nearly wet myself." The racing of my heart had subsided from overdrive into a mere frantic pounding, but I was still panting from fright. "I'm trying to get through your . . . thick . . . skull . . . that you nearly made me lose my bodily functions with that scare! I could have decked you!"

"To deck is to hit? Ah." Finally he seemed to understand. I could tell by the grin that suddenly transformed him. I loved that smile. Whenever it appeared, it softened Cor's brooding and angular features, making him seem less stern. That smile made me feel as if he understood everything I always laid so nakedly before him. "I didn't mean to alarm

you," he explained. "I know that Rooster doesn't like dealing with me, so I thought I'd wait out of sight."

"Yeah, well, Rooster's still in the restaurant eating his
lunch." My last word made me remember something. "Oh
no! Lunch!"

The take-out box from the barbecue joint lay on the
pavement, its latch sprung. My cry of dismay made Cor
kneel down to examine the remains. His face was grave.
One of the many things I loved about Corydonais was how
seriously he took me, even when I was mourning a ruined
order of ribs like a lost pet. "Lunch is fine," he reassured me,
retrieving the carton and plucking a fry from inside. He
munched on it with an air of contemplation, studying me as
I smoothed my clothing and attempted to regain my dignity
by retrieving my purse. "I'm sorry if I scared you."

"It's all right." I'd have to chalk it up to one of those cul-
tural differences between us. I supposed it could be worse. I
could have fallen for a guy who wanted me to wear a yash-
mak. "Just don't do it again."

"All right." He munched slowly on the French fry, still
looking me up and down. I thought I noticed a gleam in his
eyes. Then, out of the blue, he patted the enormous green
trash container beside us and asked, "So. Have you ever done
it against one of these? What are they called? Dumpsters?"

"Oh my God!"

"Come on," he urged, grabbing one of my hands and
swinging me toward him. "How much fun would that be?"

"You're a pervert!" I exclaimed, keeping a firmer hold on
my bag and the papers within than he seemed to be on the
take-out container. "You're just as bad as human men!"

"And you love it." He grinned. His hands rested on my
hips as he knelt to set our lunch on the ground once again.
Bricks scraped through the cotton of my blouse as he pushed
me against the wall. As usual, he was dressed in black from
head to toe; two of the buttons on his crisp linen shirt were

already undone, but his head cocked and his jaw jutted out as he unbuttoned another. "Deny it."

When he further loosened his shirt, I could see traces of the marks that spilled over his neck and shoulders. They swirled in broad strokes, like modern tribal tattoos, but close examination proved them more ornate and detailed. I could have traced from memory the intricate, almost Celtic knots from where they seemed to originate between his shoulder blades, around the firm muscles of his upper back, across his biceps, and then up and over his shoulders and down to the base of his spine. "You are not going to get me to admit that I like making out behind a Dumpster." I tried to keep my voice stern.

I can't really say it came out with much conviction, however. Cor picked up my weakness and moved in for the kill. "You never know," he whispered, his words barely more than breath against my collarbone, my neck, the lobe of my ear. "You might like it."

Oh, how tempting it was to give in. The warmth of his hands against my middle, the insistent rhythm of his hips as they gyrated enticingly against mine . . . the temptation was almost too much. "You are *awful*," I said, battering at him helplessly. "Stop it. No, don't stop. Yes, wait, stop. We can't do this here." While he grinned at me with half-slitted bedroom eyes, I swatted him away. "Seriously! Quit doing that thing you do."

"What thing is that?"

"That thing," I insisted. He shrugged, pretending innocence so that I would have to explain. Although the light in the alley wasn't the best, I rearranged my features to imitate his Casanova come-hither expression, from the narrowed lids and the slightly pursed lips to the come-hither tilt of the head. "The *thing*."

"It's working on me," he said, moving in for a kiss.

I ducked out of his way and began walking back to my

car. So kill me; I couldn't help it. No one could ever say that Samantha Dorringer had been raised to be an easy Dumpster chick. "We can continue this discussion at home," I insisted, "over lunch." The direct sunshine was almost too bright when I stepped out of the alley and closed the short distance between it and my car.

"Fantastic." Cor rubbed his hands together, glee animating his sharp features. "I'll go get things ready."

With a single leap he took to the air. Despite the months I'd known him, I'd never gotten over the astonishment of witnessing him shift his shape. One moment he was a tall, lean man, to any other eyes the well-dressed leader of some minor indie band with long hair tucked behind his ears and a day's growth of stubble on his cheeks. Then, when he would spring upward on the balls of his feet, his form would erupt into confusion of both light and darkness, of gray smoke and sparks from some unseen fire. Less than a second later, a glossy black bird would emerge from the vapor, its strong wings launching him into California's wide and perpetually blue yonder. I covered my eyes as I watched Cor disappear, knowing that in the five minutes it would take me to find my Mini Cooper and drive home, he would have tidied our little apartment, pulled down the shades to keep out the midday sun, and turned down the sheets on our bed.

My head shook as I called after his black-blue raven form, "One-track minds!" It didn't matter if he heard. Males of either species—that was all they seemed to have. Cor had been right, though: with him, I didn't give a hoot.

Right as I folded myself into the driver's seat of the Mini, I realized Cor had shifted his shape in the middle of broad daylight. That'd been careless. What if someone had seen it? He'd gotten lucky; no one was around. We'd have to have a talk about that. I mean, when I drove off, I saw a whole slew of people who might easily have gotten an eyeful of his transformation. One of them was even leaning against the building's corner. One step, one little pace forward, and he would have. . . .

I had to look quickly over my shoulder. The man on the corner seemed to be watching me. His head definitely turned as the car drove by. I caught an impression of tan, finely chiseled features framed by impossibly white hair, and then I had to turn my attention back to the road. When I'd oriented myself enough to take another glance in the rearview mirror, he was gone.

Yes, Cor and I definitely were going to have to have that talk later. Venice already had more than its fair share of freaks, but they were more of the garden-variety hippies and crazies. Shape-shifters weren't quite as common. The last thing I needed was a modern-day witch hunt starting in my own backyard.

Chapter Three

"So what have we got?" To say we were a little disheveled would have been an understatement. Cor hunched over the little kitchen's table, wearing only a pair of boxer shorts. White, covered with tiny monkeys. They were a Christmas gift to him from my mother, the month before. Yeah, I know. I didn't want to ask why, either.

I, in the meantime, had my short little legs poking out of an oversized and much-distressed oxford shirt that several years ago had belonged, if the truth be known, to my big brute of a former boyfriend. Hand-me-down nightshirts had turned out to be the only thing he'd been good for. He surely hadn't been anywhere near as expert at the exercise that had gone on upstairs only a few minutes before. Not even close. "You'll be interested in this one. Here are Rooster's transcriptions of the conversations he snuck into," I said, gesturing to a pile I'd spilled out from the manila envelope. "And these look like photographs. How did he smuggle in a Polaroid?"

"These pictures were taken from a distance," Cor pointed out. He studied one of the fuzzy pictures of a man with a bald head hustling someone into a black Town Car. The guy wore Hollywood power shades and that style of casual sportswear unique to the Rodeo Drive set; over the series of shots, it appeared as if he were looking wildly around to see if he was being watched. "It looks like Rooster was probably in his normal form with a camera. Behind a bush." His index finger tapped the last shot, a fuzzy rendering of greenery and a blurry foot. "So who is this guy?"

"Marcus Grant of Bel Air," I read from the crumpled sheet of notes. Since the both of us were idly consuming the now-cold lunch I'd brought home and I wanted to keep my hands clean, I was trying not to touch anything. "Don't know the name. Take a cold shower, you big horndog!" I said when I felt his foot caress the inside of my thigh. "You're like a fifteen-year-old who's found a copy of *Playboy* under his dad's mattress. Stop it!" I hoisted my own foot between his knees, hoping I could apply some persuasive pressure on his family jewels.

"You stop it." For a moment we had a brief battle of flailing feet beneath the diner-style table, until I accidentally rammed my pinkie toe against one of the cold metal legs, nearly spilling the contents of Rooster's envelope. "Fine," he said, planting both feet back onto the floor. "Truce."

"We had our fun not twenty minutes ago, mister." Keeping my voice stern wasn't easy. My last relationship had been nothing like this—it had been a constant struggle to keep my ex-boyfriend's eyes planted firmly on me instead of all the other women of Las Vegas, where I'd been living at the time. Being with Cor was like . . . oh gee, how to describe it? Like slipping into an outdoor hot tub on a crisp winter's night, knowing that everything was blissfully cozy where we were, despite how cold it might be everywhere else. I wallowed in the easy playfulness of the love I felt for him; I luxuriated in its simplest elements, like spooning up beside him at night like a contented cat or playing with his toes on lazy Sunday mornings. "All right. Marcus Grant. Occupation . . . Rooster said he was a Hollywood-type, so let's see." Cor watched while I brought up the movie database I kept bookmarked on my laptop browser. "Forty-five years old. Manager/Agent, it says." I clicked the link and blinked when I saw the mini-biography that followed. "Oh man. Manager to the stars. Lookit all these *names*." I whistled at the list. "There's not a D-Lister on here. There's not a *B-Lister* on here."

"Are they famous?"

"Are they famous? Are you kidding me?" I jabbed my finger at the celebrity at the top.

He shook his head. "Do I know him?"

"Yes, you know him. We saw the movie together. Where he and his daughters are trying to escape from aliens? And *he* used to date Madonna before she turned British," I said, pointing to another on Grant's list of clients. "Oh my gosh, I see one, two, three, four, five Oscar winners on here."

"Huh." Cor seemed neither appalled nor impressed at the news.

I, on the other hand, had to grapple with my jealousy. It's difficult to live in L.A. and not know someone who knows someone who *knows* someone, but in the small universe of Hollywood, this Marcus Grant guy seemed to be one of the brighter suns around whom lesser, multimillion-dollar salaried, award-winning heavenly bodies revolved. So Cor would get to poke his nose in their business, while I went back to sniffing out Peri bar brawls in Encino? It scarcely seemed fair. Strangling down any sourness in my voice, I sighed. "Now it's back to work for you, I guess."

"For me?"

"Yes, for you." I pushed the papers toward him with one hand and the remnants of lunch with the other. I was done with both. Cor regarded me with what seemed like mild surprise. "What? My contact got the information for you. It was a simple information-gathering job, right? I funnel some money from your high court's funds into Rooster's greedy little paws, he eavesdrops, I get the facts, and now you get to order your storm troopers to swoop in and clean up, right? My part's over." Bitterly did I regret it, too, though I wouldn't say anything.

"Storm Ravens," he corrected. Cor had been the leader of

the group for so long that he was automatically protective of it. I didn't dare joke about the Order of the Storm Ravens—not for long, anyway. "You wouldn't want to come along on a cleanup operation, anyway. It's not that interesting."

Many had been the times he'd returned from one of those operations at two in the morning covered with bruises or small cuts, and had barely been able to wake up the next day. I couldn't even begin to add up in my head all the confidential meetings between Cor and Ginger I hadn't been able to listen in on. "You're right. Intrigue involving famous Hollywood superstars doesn't sound interesting at all. Dull as dishwater, in fact." Boy, did I ever itch for a shot of that brand of being bored.

He laughed. "Sweetheart, I think you're inflating in your head how exciting it is. It's not like that television show you enjoy. The one about opera singers."

"For the hundredth time, *The Sopranos* isn't about musicians."

Cor shrugged. I'd never been able to convince him to watch the DVDs with me. He simply couldn't work up much interest in television.

"We don't strong-arm anyone. We talk to them in a reasonable manner, we remind them of the laws of the crown and of the penalties if they don't comply, and maintain surveillance on—"

"Yadda, yadda, yadda," I interrupted. Once a gal has a little adventure running through her veins, apparently, it's tough for her to settle for a life of what amounted to coffee-shop chats and dispensing cash to informants like some kind of Bank of Peri automated teller. "Fine. You're right. It sounds awful." I'd seen Cor's troops in battle with the enemy before. I hoped never to have to witness that much blood and carnage again. It must have been some remnant of my past as an insurance fraud investigator, though, making me itch to get back out into the field. "Besides, I can't fly. I'm not one of your Storm Ravens."

"Sweetheart," he said, leaning forward and taking my hands. We were quite the pair of opposites, Cor and I—he was so wiry and tall and dark, and I was just a California-bred blonde so much smaller that even my hands were like a doll's between his. "You are not of the Kin and you may never again have wings, but you're one of the Storm Ravens."

His words, so sweet and solemn, almost felt like an official blessing. "Really?" I said, feeling shy.

"You know what it is to fly and what it means to search for justice." His eyes bore into mine. "You stood by us in one of the darkest hours the group has seen in centuries." I felt a faint blush rising at those words. "You'll always be a Storm Raven. They respect you."

"Only because we're seeing each other."

"Don't you trust what I'm telling you?"

Of course I did, but I suppose I wanted some kind of impossible proof. Plus, I was hoping he'd follow up my assertion with a flat denial. I should've known better than to try to engage Cor in any of the human-style neediness I'd picked up in my three decades in this world. Still. His words tickled at a memory of what Rooster had said earlier. I tilted my head and raised my eyebrows to let him know how ridiculous his question was, but then I paused before I said more. "We don't have secrets, right?"

"Of course not."

His reaction was so straightforward and frank that I felt a little bit ashamed at even having asked the question. "I didn't think so," I hastened to assure him, before he could guess what was bothering me.

Too late, though. "Why would you even ask?"

A moment ago I'd relished the way he was leaning comfortably close; now it made me feel slightly ill at ease. "There're just some things you never talk about," I stammered.

"Like?"

"Nothing big. Like, you know. Your family."

"You know my sister better than almost anyone," he reminded me.

I nodded, though I hadn't seen Nikki in over a month. She'd only recently grown into her own shape-shifting; for the last six weeks she'd been back in the Kin's capital city of Resht, honing her new dolphin-form abilities. I'd been more than a little bummed about the loss, too. Having her around had always made me feel like Diana Prince trying to get her hidden superhero duties accomplished with Wonder Girl in tow, but I'd always appreciated her positivity and sense of adventure.

"And you know enough about my sire," Cor said.

Touchy subject, that, considering that during the course of his court career, one of Cor's unpleasant duties had been to incarcerate his father. It had happened roughly back in the days when much of America was still doing the Lindy Hop, but in the terms of an average Peri lifespan, it hadn't been that long ago at all. "I was thinking about the rest of your family." Did my voice sound casual enough? I certainly hoped so. "You know. Other brothers and sisters . . . your mother. . . ."

He gazed steadily at me for a moment before replying. "There's nothing remarkable about my dame."

I decided to make a weak joke of it. "It's not as if I'm really trying to meet the future in-laws or anything. I don't even know if that's a custom with you guys. You know—forget I said anything."

Cor still stared at me with that impassive, unyielding expression. "Why are you so curious all of a sudden? That's not like you."

"I'm always curious!" I protested. If the truth be known, though, I'd always been content with what Cor offered to explain about the customs of the Kin. In a way I suppose that I'd always known if I started asking too many questions, I might not be able to stop.

"Curious about the world around you, yes. About the past? Not so much."

Something about his demeanor told me that I'd trodden onto uninvited territory. Hastily, I tried to backtrack. "This isn't about the past. It's about. . . ."

Before I could even figure out for myself exactly what it was about, I hear the outside door open in our living room. "Hello!" called a familiar voice. One of the advantages of our two-story, nine-hundred-and-eighty-square-foot piece of real estate on the famed Venice canals was that it came rent-free. I know, my real estate sounds absolutely fabulous—until you consider that it's in a converted carriage house-turned-garage on my mother's property, not twenty paces from her back door. "Are you kids awake yet? Are you decent?" Cor sat up in his chair and tightly crossed his legs, while I buttoned up the undone buttons on my shirt. "Oh, don't be silly, Mr. Landemann. Of course they don't mind. Hello? Samantha, dear? Are you awake?"

I sighed. "It's two thirty in the afternoon, Mom," I yelled across the first floor. "Of course we're up. And decent. Jeez." All the same, I pulled my knees discreetly together. "Oh, sorry!" I added to Cor, when I saw him standing up and looking around desperately for something, anything to cover his near-nakedness. When he grabbed an oversized oven mitt from the counter, holding it in front of his goodies, I shook my head. The thumb was just *so* unfortunately placed. "Mom, I know it's your old garage we're living in, but you can't just come bursting in here without knocking," I called, trying to buy him some time.

My mother bustled into the room, looking at me over the tops of her reading glasses. She wore a pair of much-faded jeans and a sweater to which had been appliquéd the outlines of several cats, all with bristly wool whiskers and pink noses. She carried a stack of red-covered booklets in her arms. "Why, there you are," she announced, ignoring me.

"Mom!" Behind her trailed two other familiar faces. Cor's portly sometime bodyguard was one of them. As always, Landemann's Ray-Bans were firmly in place, obscuring his eyes. Yet judging by the pair of lime green shorts, the flip-flops, and the T-shirt proclaiming *Ragdoll Wuv* over the photo of one of my mother's favorite cats, I was guessing he might be off-duty. "We've talked about this."

"I didn't think you'd mind," she said mildly. "Why, hello, Cory!" Mom looked him up and down. "How are you?"

"Fine, Mrs. Nea . . . Barbara," he amended, before she could remind him for the hundredth time that they were supposed to be on a first-name basis. "Thank you for asking." When I turned, I saw that he'd found the yellow apron hanging on the back door and slung it around his midsection, like he'd been inspired by *The Naked Chef* on TV. "I hope you're well?"

"Quite well, thank you. I see you're wearing the boxer shorts I bought you for Christmas! I love those monkeys. Don't you?"

"Um. Oh. Yes."

I interrupted. It had to be done, before she started to ask about the fit. "Mom, is there a reason you brought an entire fleet of people to gawk at us, or is this just a random anti-nooky check of the sort you used to perform when I was fifteen and had boys over for study groups?" In addition to Landemann, standing behind my mother was Gin. She'd trailed into the room behind my mother with a surprisingly bashful air for someone decked out in tough-looking army surplus boots and camouflage fatigues. The sinuous markings on her shoulders and back weren't as extensive as Cor's, but they were still large enough to spill out from the straps on her tank top. The sight of Cor in his improvised getup made her flush slightly and almost lose her grip on the hefty stack of bound papers in her grasp. Seeing the unflappable Ginger blush was something I'd never expected.

"Anti-nooky check!" Mom batted away the idea. To Cor she added, "Samantha was always so sensitive as an adolescent.

And isn't she darling, pretending she actually studied. I never knew *what* kind of boy she'd be bringing home. No, really. There wasn't a one of them who didn't look like he needed a good disinfecting."

"Mom . . ."

"And what with her father's wild blood in her . . ."

"Mom!" My dad had run off to be with some other woman when I was twelve. We'd never heard from him again. His blood was the kind I could do without.

"I'm only saying . . ."

"Just leave it," I ordered, feeling cross. If it hadn't meant exposing that my shirt barely covered my bare butt cheeks, I would have gotten up and physically escorted her from the room. "What did you want, anyway?"

"Well, I saw your poor friend Ginger skulking around your door earlier," she explained, pulling the Peri forward as if she were a shy wallflower instead of a fierce warrior. "And since you kids didn't seem to be around, of course I invited her in so we could really get to know each other." When she squeezed Ginger's forearm, the redhead's eyes grew wide with alarm. "She even assisted Mr. Landemann and me in assembling the external readings for my upcoming class next semester. So much collating!" To Cor, she added, "I'm teaching a special upper-level seminar on Hesiod and the Homeric Hymns. You might be interested. See, I have a theory that any attribution of the authorship of *The Catalogue of Women* to Hesiod is correct only in part, because anyone who looks at the linguistic analysis of the extant text can see . . ."

Ginger's intense blue eyes, wild and wide, darted between me and Cor. Her mouth formed two words I'd often been tempted to use while under the thrall of my mom: *Help me.*

It was up to me to take action. Despite the fact that a good portion of my butt was suddenly exposed to the cool air, I stood up and leaned over to take the course packs from Ginger's helpless arms. "Well, if that's all, Cor and I were in the middle of something." The normally silent Landemann let out a short guffaw. He attempted to cover it up by pretending to cough. I cocked my head and glared in his direction, adding, "One of our cases, thank you."

Mom added her armful of paper to the top of mine. I staggered backward to dump them on the kitchen table. "If you and Cory were going out, I was just wondering if you might drop these by my office. To save me a trip, now that I've gone green."

"Driving you places, Miss Daisy, does not make you green." My mother's office on the Occidental campus wasn't exactly on our way to anywhere and wouldn't spare anyone any gasoline or the environment the emissions, but to get her out of my metaphorical hair I agreed. Pushing her and her boyfriend Landemann from the room, I said, "But fine. Just . . . we're in the middle of looking over some documents for a very important case, and I'm sure that Ginger needs to talk to Cor as well."

"She's such a nice girl," Mom interjected, as I propelled them through the little living area. Once we were out of Ginger's earshot, she added, "Only . . ."

"Only you really shouldn't be coercing Cor's employees into doing your collating for you!"

My scolding didn't have any effect. "She didn't mind! Only I think it's a pity she's single. Don't you? She's such a pretty thing. You young people think you'll have your looks for years and years, but it doesn't last forever, you know."

Perhaps not, but it certainly would last longer for Ginger and her race than it would for me. Mom just didn't *know.* I opened up the door that led into my mother's backyard and tried to shoo her toward her own house, not ten yards away. "I'll be sure to tell her."

The door was in midswing when she added, "If you think she'd be receptive, I know a very nice girl—an assistant professor in French—who might be interested in, you know, a blind date."

Despite every instinct telling me to finish what I'd started, I resisted completing the door's slam and peeked out instead. "Girl? Did you say girl?"

"Of course. Ginger's a follower of Sappho, isn't she?" When I only blinked, my mom tried to explain. "It's a euphemism for 'lesbian.' Sappho was a lyric poet born on the island of Lesbos circa 600 B.C., you see, and it's from the island that the term. . . ."

"Yes, yes, I know who Sappho is," I said, trying to hurry her along. "What in the *world* made you think that Ginger is a lesbian? The way she dresses? Her short hair? Honestly, Mom!" Truth be told, if I'd seen the Peri stomping down the street in her paramilitary gear, I might have assumed the same thing. I couldn't stop the impulse to lash back a little, though, after the interruption. "Try to open your mind a little!"

"Certainly not, Samantha Dorringer," she started to say, her words heated. "Have I ever been the kind of woman who reduced groups to cardboard stereotypes? And at least I wear panties in the middle of the day!"

"What's that have to do with . . . ?" I looked down. My parts were still covered. "You didn't see anything."

"I *might* have seen your cookie without trying very hard."

"My cookie?" I repeated, trying not to guffaw.

I was too late, and unsuccessful. From the way she drew herself up, I could tell I'd taken a swipe at my mother's dignity. "If you are trying to be some kind of . . . Britney . . . Lohan . . . then all I can tell you is that she is not fashionable and going 'commando,' as they call it, is not sanitary. Come on, Mr. Landemann. Let's go for our walk."

It was such a bizarre non sequitur that all I could do was watch, jaw slack, as my mother whipped around, grabbed Landemann's beefy arm, and stalked off to her cat-filled house. Proximity to the Venice canals be damned. Cor and I were seriously going to have to consider getting our own place in the future.

CRATE & PERIL, 31

While I'd been absent, Cor had managed to scare up a black T-shirt and a pair of equally dark lounge pants; he leaned over the kitchen table in consultation with his second-in-command. Any traces of embarrassment either of them might have had earlier had vanished the moment my mother left the room. On my return, though, I noticed that Ginger stood up and seemed to avoid my eyes. "Sorry about that," I said to them both.

"No need to apologize." Cor's tone was amiable enough. Ginger, however, averted her gaze. "We were just making plans to visit this Marcus Grant fellow."

"Oh. Okay." I couldn't help feeling a little down at the announcement. Time for me to split, then. I liked feeling useful. After all the badness that had happened to me at the hands of the Order of the Crow, I'd wanted to keep my hand in the battle against them and their like. Maybe it was a little taste for revenge—I didn't know. But one of the reasons I'd decided to delve into supernatural territory rather than take up insurance fraud investigations again, or any job that might have actually given me dental, was because I enjoyed working side by side with Cor. Yet there he was, with Ginger hanging over his shoulder the way she'd done for over a century. They didn't need me. "All right, then."

I had turned and was heading for the staircase when Cor spoke. "Where are you going?"

"I thought I'd put on some clothes, for one," I said, trying to sound livelier than I felt. "My mother accused me of trying to pull a Britney cookie flash. Besides, you two don't need me." Ginger had already looked back down at the papers scattered on the table. Dismissing me again, probably. Well, you know what? I'd had enough of that. "Wait," I said suddenly, standing my ground. "Yes you do."

"What?"

I put my hands on my hips and answered Cor with a glare. "You fairies don't know a thing about how this town works. Oh, smooth down your ruffled male ego," I ordered.

He absolutely hated that word; in his mind, *fairy* reduced his proud and noble race to the level of Smurfs, Hello Kitty, and My Little Pony. "You didn't even know to look up Marcus Grant in The Internet Movie Database, did you? That was my idea. This whole case is only on your table now because of my spadework, isn't it?"

"Samantha," he said, shaking his head.

Who did he think he was? My father? That schmuck had left my life long ago, thank you very much. "No, seriously. You've got a pretty sweet operation set up here, fighting crime with your fleet of shape-shifting ravens in their army surplus store getups." Luckily, Ginger was too busy looking at the table to see that I was gesturing at her. "But you're used to rounding up refugees in seedy hotels near LAX. Bel Air's an entirely different world."

Ginger opened her mouth to speak. "What I think . . ."

"I'm not interested in what either of you think," I snapped, letting it all tumble out. Boy, I was really letting them have it—all the pent-up itchiness I'd been feeling lately came tumbling out. "I'm *telling* you. And what I'm saying is that this case is just as much mine as yours. Either we do it as a team, or not at all." To make my point, I lunged forward, scrabbled the papers together, and stuffed the semi-tidy stack back into the envelope. "Your choice."

To my surprise, Cor grinned. The sight of his curving lips and those straight white teeth automatically diffused the cloud of moodiness that had been enveloping me in its gray clutches. "You're so . . . so *you,*" he told me.

"What do you mean?"

"What I think we've been trying to say is that we'd already been talking about asking you to help on this one." What? Surely I'd heard wrong. From side to side I looked at both of them, blinking rapidly. "If we'd been able to get in a word edgewise during your tongue-lashing."

"My tongue . . . ? What?" What he'd just told me suddenly sunk in. I couldn't believe it. My heart began to beat twice as quickly, from excitement. "You mean, actually go out with you on a case?" I stepped back into the room. "On this case? With the movie stars? Keep working on it with you and meet the famous movie stars? Together? Really?"

Cor's big grin widened. "Of course, sweetheart. We wouldn't have gotten this far without you."

For the first time, Ginger's eyes flickered to mine. "This area's a little out of our usual realm. You might be helpful," she admitted.

I started to bounce on my toes. "Well, yeah!" I practically shouted. "I'd love that! Thank you! Thank you both!" I said, including Ginger in my happiness. "That would be fantastic. But you know . . ." I tried to sound more sober, though I'd already blown all my cool points by reacting like a twelve-year-old getting a puppy for her birthday. "It was still my find."

All graciousness, Cor nodded. "Of course."

"So long as that's established." I cleared my throat, feeling as cool as a Jell-O shot on a summer's evening. "After all, I'm a professional."

"One suggestion, Ms. Professional?"

I'd been so excited that I didn't notice Cor gazing downward. Ginger had shied her face away. "Anything!" I promised.

He cleared his throat. "How about putting on some real clothes if you're going to jump up and down again?"

"Please?" begged Ginger, her fair face now beet red.

Oh, like I cared at that point. A little cookie never hurt anyone. Besides, I was going out on a big girl case and flying beside the Storm Ravens once again. Nothing in the world could have brought me down to earth.

Chapter Four

"Wow." Something about the convertible's seats made me keep stroking them. Maybe it was the white leather, still supple under the California afternoon sun. Perhaps it was the fact that they were spotless compared to the benches in the battered van the Storm Ravens kept for their operations. "It's so clean! Can we keep it?"

"You've said that about a hundred times." Ginger sighed loudly enough to be heard over the traffic of West Sunset Boulevard. She ignored the appreciative whistle from a shirtless skateboarder weaving his way through the pedestrians nearby. "And definitely no. It's on loan."

I'd called shotgun the minute I'd seen the 1965 300L in all its peach-colored glory, but I'd since reconsidered. "Can we swap at the next light?" I asked, craning my neck and wheedling.

"That's an even more definite no." Ginger, occupying the back by herself, wore the largest pair of dark sunglasses she'd been able to find at the drugstore near my mother's house. Over her short hair she'd draped a colorful floral scarf, crossing it at her neck and tossing the ends over her shoulder. In her retro white dress, with her arms stretched out across the Chevy's backseat, she had somehow managed to look like Tinseltown royalty, circa 1950—utterly feminine and glamorous. Only the dark, Celtic tattoos spilling from her covered shoulders onto the upper inches of her biceps made her seem more modern.

As Cor watched the light turn from red to green and made the convertible purr into action with a gentle thrust of his toes, I resumed my face-forward position in my seat and crossed my arms. "Whatever. Someone obviously had an Audrey Hepburn fixation, back in the day."

"And what's wrong with looking a little like Audrey Hepburn?" I heard from behind me. Ginger was enjoying herself, I could tell. "They say she had Kin blood in her, you know."

"Oh, fine, *now* you think miscegenation's a good thing," I grumped, still put out. When Cor and Ginger had suggested I dress appropriately for this mission, I hadn't realized that they intended to get themselves up in full Hollywood drag. Whereas I had donned a demure sundress that had seen quite a lot of weddings back in my post-graduation days, tied back my hair, and had called it a day, Ginger and Cor had gone all Hepburn and Cary Grant on me. Or maybe, I considered while I took in the sight of Cor's nautical captain's hat once more, it was more along the lines of Mr. and Mrs. Thurston Howell III. I'd started to mention that all he was missing was the ascot, until I realized mentioning it might prompt him to want one. "A few months ago you were acting like half-breeds were anathema to the Kin." In the rearview mirror I could see Ginger turn her head away, ashamed of having said any such thing.

"Ladies," Cor said, by way of a reminder to keep it civil. He turned the car onto one of the north-running streets leading into fashionable Bel Air.

"Fine. I was just joking, anyway." It had been unfair to use that past confrontation against Ginger, I realized. We'd settled those differences long ago. Besides, even if she had agreed to switch spots with me, I suspected I'd find the backseat less luxurious than I imagined, what with her scarf flapping in my yapper. "So what's the plan, Stan?" I asked cheerfully, to show there were no hard feelings.

"Our plan is to drive up to Marcus Grant's house and ask to see him." Cor looked both ways as he pulled through an intersection marked by a stop sign. "What?" he asked, catching the incredulous look I shot him.

"That's it? That's your plan in its outlined, well-thought-out entirety?" I gawped, incredulous, at them both.

"What more do we have to do?" asked Ginger, catching her head covering before it could fly away in a sudden cross-breeze.

"You can't just *walk up* there. 'Hi there, Number Three on this year's *Entertainment Weekly's* Power List, how's tricks? Bought any fountain-of-youth potions from a shady fairy lately?' It won't work."

"*Already with the objections.*" To my ears, Ginger's complaint seemed to sparkle with an unexpected reverberation, almost as if tiny, invisible bells played in the background. I'd learned to recognize that when I heard the unusual chiming overtones, the Peri were talking in their own tongue. None of us was exactly sure how I came to understand the language—maybe it was in my genes, maybe somewhere in the three years the Peri had kidnapped me, maybe something else entirely.

"*That's why we want her with us, remember?*" I didn't bother pointing out that I could hear and understand every word they spoke. They knew. In plain English Cor added, "What do you suggest?"

"Well." I didn't want to get off to a bad start as the person in the group who objects to every single detail with an eye to disclaiming responsibility if the whole thing falls apart at some point. I'd learned from *The Apprentice* that nobody likes that person. Unfortunately, I didn't have any better suggestion to offer. Instead, I waved my hands at the modest houses around us. "Just keep in mind we're not near the country club yet. It'll be different from what you're used to. You'll see."

Not two minutes down the road, they both saw what I meant. As we descended the hillside into lower Bel Air, the front yards began to deepen. The homes grew taller, and wider, and grander in every way. By the time we reached Marcus Grant's address, the houses had given way to outright estates, many of them surrounded by iron fences or brick enclosures a dozen feet tall. Grant's domicile was the most ostentatious of the street. It occupied a choice chunk of real estate on the street's west side, and its multiple roofs were the highest, its front gates were the spikiest, its barricades the thickest. I could have sworn that the twin stone lions relaxing on each side of the driveway had been ripped from the front steps of the New York Public Library. "Subtle, it ain't," I commented.

Now, I didn't know what the royal courts of the Kin looked like, to which Cor was a frequent visitor. The phrase "royal court," though, didn't exactly conjure images of shantytowns. Even he and Ginger seemed impressed by the sheer scale of the place. She peered over the tops of her shades, mouth slightly agape, as our convertible idled from one house down. Cor rubbed his jaw, tipped back his captain's hat to scratch his head, and finally agreed. "I see what you meant, earlier," he said, taking in the multiple security cameras posted around the high enclosure wall. There were even a pair of them installed in the lions' mouths, I now noticed.

He thought for a moment, then sighed, cut the ignition, and reached around to open the car's door from the outside. "Wait, what are you going to do?" I asked, scrambling out from my side.

"Just . . . be honest, I suppose."

When he shrugged, I felt a rush of affection. Cor could be so simple sometimes. Not *stupid*. I didn't mean that at all. Just uncomplicated. Despite all the dark deeds he and the Ravens worked constantly to uncover, it was as if he still believed that he could appeal to the good in the heart of all creatures, man and Kin alike. It was a little sad I was going to have to disabuse him of his idealism. "This is Hollywood," I explained, waving my hands at the displays of conspicuous consumption surrounding us. "Honesty's like the x in an advanced algebra equation. Nobody here knows what it is, and they're sure as heck not going to take the time to puzzle it out."

"I think Samantha might be right." Ginger had not quite abandoned her Audrey Hepburn position in the car, but she had hoisted herself up so that her trim little tuckus perched on the top of the backseat. "After all, this guy's breaking laws."

"The lawbreakers are the Kin trying to sell his clients passports into the Kinlands," Cor corrected, tucking the convertible's keys in his pocket. "Grant's not under our jurisdiction. He's not breaking any law of man."

"That we're concerned with, anyway," I muttered in a dark tone.

"Exactly." Cor smoothed the front of his navy blue jacket and plucked imaginary dust from his lapel. His voice was confident and assertive—a commander's tone that no one would dare disobey. "So we'll try my way first. Stay back here."

"Take off the silly hat, at least," I said, grabbing it from his head and tossing it onto the driver's seat. He looked mildly offended, but then, with a grin, he straightened his rumpled mane and began walking to Grant's front gate.

Cor's way was indeed the exact thing I'd feared. While Ginger and I leaned against the sandstone barricade, trying to stay out of the range of the cameras focused on the compound's entrance, Cor simply strode up to the battery of electronics perched on the driveway, bent over to peer into the camera erected at approximately an SUV driver's height, and pushed a button. Though I couldn't hear the bell or buzzer it activated, what I did hear from somewhere on the other side of the barricade was a series of high-pitched, excited yapping from two or more dogs. Small dogs, by the sound of it. Small, annoying, yippy purebred trophy dogs. Nothing against Chihuahua owners, but give me a big-eared, deep-voiced mongrel any day of the week.

We couldn't hear what Cor was saying, but it was hard not to admire his bright smile or the way his hair flopped down to either side of his face as he spoke. He wasn't re-buffed immediately, which I found encouraging. When he finally did stand up straight, though, he began walking back in our direction. Once he was in earshot, I asked, "So?"

The smile that Cor had been wearing all through the conversation was intact. "So I told the person that I wanted to see Marcus Grant on a matter of grave importance."

"And he said. . . . ?"

Cor's amiable smile grew a little grim. "He told me to shove off, basically." Ginger's shoulders slumped. At the sight of her disappointment, he tried to rally our spirits. "It's not over!" he said, rubbing me between my shoulder blades. "We'll move on to Plan B."

"There's a Plan B?"

Over the wall, the miniature hounds of hell were still yapping wildly. Perhaps the irritation of it gave my innocent question a little bit of a skeptical edge. "Of course there's a Plan B," he replied, seeming hurt. "Do you think I'd leave the house without a Plan B?"

"Plan B," Ginger announced with sudden determination. By the way she leaned on the 300L with her hands firmly planted on its peach-colored loveliness, legs akimbo in a military stance that was definitely at odds with her Holly Golightly getup, I could tell she was making it up on the spot. "Cor and I fly over the wall, wait until Grant's alone, and then . . ."

"And then swoop down and get yourselves turned into Swiss cheese by the fleet of personal bodyguards with the strict orders to shoot any crazies that might invade the sanctity of Hollywood's most famous talent agent's bazillion-dollar home," I concluded for her, my arms crossed. "No." When she continued to look skeptical, I added, "You don't want to take that kind of chance this early. But you need to give him some kind of incentive to want to meet you. He's a big, important guy. You could go on and on about having something urgent to talk to him about, but you won't register on his radar. You'll be about as inconsequential to him as two-bit would-be actors who try to slip headshots and resumés to him under the men's room stalls in L.A.'s swankiest restaurants." I had their attention, and I could tell they knew I was right. Over the sound of the yippy puppies, who seemed to be caroming around the yard beyond the barricade like pool balls after a particularly brutal break, I raised my voice a little. "To get his attention, you've got to have something he wants."

Cor munched thoughtfully on the ball of his thumb. Ginger, her voice quiet, asked, "What could we possibly have that he wants, though?"

"We know that the Kin who are promising his clients refuge in the Kinlands are probably never intending to follow through on their promise," Cor said. "That's important information. Either that or the Storm Ravens are likely to find them out and send his clients home. Shouldn't he want to know that?"

"Of course he should," I said. "That's ultimately what you want to say to him! But that kind of doom and gloom isn't going to get his attention, no matter how loudly you shout it. He won't want to believe it. Who wants to hear a poohpooher when someone else is being slick and selling eternal life or something damned close to it? You could write a scientific piece directly connecting Botox to Alzheimer's Disease or cancer or what have you, and all of Hollywood's over-thirties would still be shooting their faces frozen with the stuff. Just because they think it makes them look that much younger."

"Crazy," Ginger said, shaking her head.

"Yeah, well, you're going to look the same in another ten years, chickie," I said, not meaning to sound as sharp as I did. "We humans age a lot faster than you. We're a little more desperate for the stuff that's going to keep the wrinkles at bay. Anyway, I'm just trying to say that if you want to get into that compound, you need to be bringing something Marcus Grant wants to see. Something he'll be happy to open those gates for. *Then* you can do your strong-arm stuff. Know what I mean?"

Cor had been listening closely. "But where do we start?" he wondered, nodding.

For a moment there, Grant's dogs had sounded as if they might give their tiny little jaws a rest, but an answering, disinterested *wuff* from a neighbor's mastiff sent them back into convulsions of yappy ecstasy. "This is one of those times when we have to think outside the box."

"What box?" Cor wanted to know.

"It means . . . Well, it means that you can't have a pat solution," I explained to the Kin. "Something wildly creative," I said, raising my voice over the barking once again. "Something that won't—my *God*, won't someone take pity on my misery and do something about those *damned dogs*? Oh. Wait." Thanks to my burgeoning headache, I'd had a scathingly brilliant idea. When I looked at Cor, it seemed as if he might be thinking along similar lines. "I think my brain is evil. Wicked, in fact."

"Then mine is too." Cor peered through the sun and leaves at the metal spikes projecting atop the sandstone barrier, then grinned at me.

"Can you do something like that?" I wondered, sure that the two of us were on the same wavelength. I knew that when Cor shape-shifted, his form was unnaturally strong in comparison to a normal raven's. Yet it would seem there'd been some laws of aerodynamics that still had to apply.

"Oh, I think so. Jinjurnaturnia, you and I could manage a few pounds between us, couldn't we?"

Plainly baffled, she said, "I suppose. Depending. What are we talking about? *You forget I'm not a mind reader.*" Her last sentence she spoke in their language, almost with a little jealousy.

Cor slithered out of his sports jacket, shucking it onto the car's front seat. "I'm talking about the two of us flying to get something. Something that Marcus Grant will be sure to want." Ginger still wasn't following. "Come on," he told her, rolling up the sleeves of his blue striped shirt until they bunched around his muscular biceps. "You'll see. Don't worry." With a final assurance to me, he pecked me on the cheek. "We won't be seen."

Ginger crouched and sprang into the air behind her leader. Both of them emerged from the clouds of confusion as sleek black ravens. Cor, the larger of the two, let out a piercing cry as he broke through the canopy of leaves. Ginger twisted and followed. Then they flew over the barricade's top to soar over the estate.

I backed up into the quiet street to try to watch them, but they were already out of sight. Once, when Cor had been imprisoned in a Peri construct designed by the Order of the Crow and their leader, Mrs. Jones, I'd been given the gift of feathers—and more importantly, of flight. I'd glided beside him once, light as air and happier than I'd ever been. Though my feet were a little more firmly on the ground these days, I'd never forgotten what it was like to feel the currents of air beneath my wings, or to let myself be buoyed by a sudden change in warmth in the atmosphere around me. Sure, I was a little jealous that Ginger and the other Storm Ravens would be the ones up there with him in these situations. What girl wouldn't be?

I'd reached the opposite curb before I'd realized it. I leaned on one of the trees that lent the street its shade. It was a little difficult not to fret. After all, there were a hundred things that might go wrong. Grant might have a zealous gardener with a pellet gun or, worse, a rifle. The backyard might not be empty . . . there could be dozens of super-models camped around the pool. (All those moguls had their own pools, didn't they?) The dogs might have bites worse than their barks. When I remembered Cor's last words, though, I knew that I shouldn't expect his return too quickly.

I was still thinking of more things that could go wrong when mere inches away from my ear, I heard a deep voice intone, "Greetings."

"What the—?" I felt the vivid mental sensation of jumping out of my skin back across the street where I'd started. Was I trespassing? Alert and ready to administer one of my self-defense moves if I had to, I spun around.

I found myself mesmerized by the deepest blue eyes I'd ever seen, eyes that didn't waver as they bore into mine, framed on each side by long hair so pale it was almost white. The man who had snuck up on me smiled, creating parentheses on each side of his mouth. "I didn't mean to startle you . . . Samantha Dorringer. Or is that DeRengier?"

Chapter Five

"I know you," I responded immediately. I couldn't place where, or when, I'd seen the man, but I knew in that niggling, back-of-the-mind way that he and I had met somewhere. Still startled, I quickly followed up with, "Who the hell are you? And why are you creeping up on me like some kind of . . . freaky stalker guy?"

"I am flattered." My potential mugger friend inclined his head slightly as he bowed. He wore clothes that were in no way out of the ordinary for typical California warm weather—a retro-fifties camp shirt with bowling pins and the words *Lucky strike!* embroidered above his heart, board shorts, and sandals. With his long platinum hair that fell down to his shoulders, his tanned skin, and his broad shoulders, he looked like an investment banker, retired and turned surfer boy. Yet his somewhat ceremonial air somehow made him seem as if he'd be far more comfortable in formal evening attire. And a cape. Like some kind of maître d'. Or albino vampire. "I apologize if I gave you a jolt."

I took his statement in for a moment and decided against it. "You're not sorry," I finally asserted. "You meant to do it." My defense-class instincts told me that I should have been running for the hills. Good sense still made my skin prickle, telling me to keep my distance, but honestly, what was the guy going to do right here in the most opulent depths of scenic Bel Air in broad daylight? Landscape me to death and flip me for three hundred times my actual real estate market value? I'd contemplated worse fates. "In fact," I said, taking a couple of steps away from him until I stood in the street again, "I think you intended to startle me."

The man placed his palms together, fingers pointed outward, and tapped together his thumbs. "Not at all."

The way his voice sounded, so calm, so reassuring, only maddened me. "Oh, totally 'at all,' Lucius Malfoy," I snapped. "Who are you? And where have I seen you before?"

"You don't know me. As to where you've seen me before . . . well, I couldn't really say."

Too late, though. I'd been digging madly through my memory, knowing I'd spotted him within the last week or so. "Wait!" I nearly had it. I stabbed my finger at him like it was a fireplace poker and he was a late-night intruder I was confronting in my living room. "It was outside. Only for a couple of seconds. I was in my car. You were standing somewhere. On the street! You were standing on the street, and I was driving by . . . near the Baby Blues BBQ! That day. . . ." Instantly I shut my mouth. It had been that day I'd been worrying someone might have seen Cor and Ginger take wing. He'd been staring at me in my Mini Cooper. I remembered it all too well now. "Who are you?" I growled, on edge.

"You do not know me, but I come to you with nothing but the best of intentions."

I recognized the bell-like overtones of that language. "Best of intentions, my Aunt Fanny." Already I'd warned myself not to let the guy see any fear I might be having. Despite the fact that my heart was pounding like an overworked generator pumping out too much wattage, I didn't want it to show. If that meant sounding contentious, so be it. I'd rather that than be a whimpering little ninny, any day.

"So it's true. You do understand our tongue."

"Keep your tongue to yourself, thank you. And you know what, smarty-pants? I'm on to you." All the adrenaline racing through my body had sent my mind into overdrive as well. "I am totally on to you, appearing out of nowhere like that. You're that guy. Azimuth. The one who was going to *find* me." The pleasant, vaguely bland expression on the stranger's face didn't change. I knew I was right. "What have you been doing, stalking me? Waiting for the perfect moment to accost me when I was alone?" The sudden realization that he'd probably been doing just that made me shiver.

"I seize opportunities where I can," Azimuth replied, nodding a little. "But stalk you? Hardly, Samantha. Grant me some credit."

"Ye gods!" I exclaimed, wishing that someone else was around to witness this. Maybe, I thought, I should run over to Marcus Grant's driveway, so at least I'd be in view of the cameras there, in case . . . in case of what? In case he man-handled me? In case he threw a glowing ball of light at me and I lost another chunk of my life to some Kin construct? I guess any of the above. The security guards inside Grant's house wouldn't want a publicity scandal on their hands, would they? *VENICE GIRL KIDNAPPED BY MYTHICAL FAIRY ON MEGA-MANAGER'S DOORSTEP* just wouldn't look right splayed across newspaper front pages on a million doorsteps. "How long have you been following me? Weeks? Months?"

The Peri laughed, exposing perfectly straight teeth. Despite my expectations to the contrary, the canines weren't any sharper or more pronounced than my own. "Dramatic, much?"

The remark took me aback. Strangely, it also made me feel less at risk. "Jeez," I said, "sinister *and* snide. Quite the irresistible combo there. I bet the chicks flock to you, mister." Taking into account his good looks, I reconsidered that remark. "Or wait. Maybe I meant run from you."

"You're not running."

"I'm leaving my options open."

"If you run, you won't have the pleasure of meeting me."

"Oh, you're dead certain it's a pleasure, are you?" At least now I felt sure he wasn't going to abduct me. My experience with evil fairies had taught me that they tended to kidnap first, then run off at the mouth later.

He shrugged. "Why shouldn't it be? Life's so full of ugliness as it is. Don't you find?" He talked on, seemingly unaware at how bizarre the situation was. "So little courtesy. So few of the graces. So many lies."

"So many people popping out of thin air to make a girl streak her shorts," I concluded. The surfer Peri wrinkled his nose slightly at that, giving me satisfaction at having slightly ruffled his feathers. In the excitement, I'd almost forgotten about Cor. I looked over my shoulder at the barricade and branches behind me, hoping he'd returned.

"If you're so repulsed by lies, let's have some truths." Azimuth inclined his head so that his long, Nelson brothers–styled locks bobbed forward in a liquid way that would have made most hair-conditioner actresses seethe with jealousy. "You've been following me?"

"Not as much as you fear," he said. "I haven't been shadowing you, though I did follow you here this morning." He watched me grapple with that information for a minute before adding, "If I'd wanted to introduce myself to you at your home, I could have. I thought, though, that these circumstances would be more . . . neutral."

I stared at his outstretched hands with distrust. "What do you mean? You know where I live?" When he nodded, I demanded, "How?"

"Samantha," he said with mild reproach. "If you saw dozens of police vehicles parked around a building, wouldn't you and everyone else assume it was their headquarters?" Somehow I got his point. If the Kin could recognize one another, the dozens of Ravens regularly patrolling my mom's neighborhood and posted at her home would be a tipoff to any of their race.

"Okay, fine. Whatever. So why all the mystery?" Once again I looked over my shoulder to see if Ginger and Cor had yet returned, only to be disappointed. "Why'd you tell Rooster you needed to see me?" Before he could respond, I interrupted myself. "And what do you know about the DeRengiers?"

"Nothing," he said, presumably in response to my last question. "I only know that in Resht, it's been said in many circles that Corydonais of the Storm Crows had taken up with a mortal woman named Samantha of the DeRengiers."

"Oh, you heard that, did you? Kind of like the Kinlands equivalent of Page Six, huh?" He only smiled, perhaps not understanding what a gossip column was. "You still haven't explained why you wanted to see me."

"Of course you're curious." His voice was soothing, calm—the kind of tone a father would use with an unruly child to defuse a tantrum. Then again, it would be, wouldn't it, if he were trying to snow me? "I discovered our mutual acquaintance. . . ."

"Rooster."

"Yes, Rooster, as you so piquantly call him. His interest in colorful personalities is not known only to you and Corydonais."

I summed up the rigmarole succinctly. "You mean, everybody knows what a slime he is." Azimuth shrugged. Much as I hated to admit it, now that my unease was subsiding some, I could admit he shrugged a charming shrug. "So, what, you're using Rooster too? For . . . ?"

"I'm a businessman, Samantha." His stance relaxed slightly; perhaps he was as nervous of me as I was of him. "My services cater to those of my race who have decided, for one reason or another, to leave Resht to seek greener pastures outside the Kinlands."

"Dropouts, you mean." Cor and his little sister had a certain degree of disrespect for those Peri who traded their extended lifespans to live permanently in the human world. Without revisiting the Kinlands, they eventually grew old and died, almost at the same pace as we did. "So, services like what? You're the fairy apartment finder?"

"Actually, yes." He didn't seem at all offended by my frank tone. "That's one of the many things my associates and I will do. Kin dissociating themselves from an existence they feel is sterile and joyless is a serious business. And one that is not, I might add, without its lucrative side. There are passports to provide, driver's licenses to obtain, vital documents to supply that you take for granted. We help them find homes, point them toward enclaves of similar expatriates where they can find a nurturing and encouraging environment. . . ."

"Support groups," I interrupted. "You mean you help them find dropout support groups. Kin-Anon."

He inclined his head once more, after thinking it over. "Something like that. But from time to time, Samantha, I—and my associates, of course—feel as if some of our customers might not be telling me the entire truth about themselves. For example, someone might be obtaining documents for members of the Kin of whom the court and its enforcer. . . ." He made a formal bow in the direction of the convertible, obviously intending to bring Cor to mind. ". . . might disapprove. Rooster can often provide information that helps me avoid catering to the wrong element. Naturally, I wouldn't want to find myself on the wrong side of the law."

"Naturally." It sounded plausible. Smooth. Almost slick, really. "I'm sure if I asked Corydonais about it, he'd assure me your little business was on the up and up?"

"I'd prefer you didn't."

A-ha! "Didn't what?"

"Didn't mention me to him." Before I could crow about my instincts being right, he began to explain, leaning forward and murmuring confidentially, "You see, he wouldn't know my name. We've never had the pleasure of a formal acquaintance. I've never moved much among the higher echelons of the Kin."

"I see. And that's all you use Rooster for?"

The Peri shrugged his broad shoulders again. "Occasionally he helps me identify competitors. Adversaries, if you will. Then I can move to neutralize them."

"Neutralize them, huh? Which you do in an aboveboard manner, of course."

His smile was almost ironic. "Would you ever suspect me of anything but?"

Azimuth certainly had a gift for florid language when he wanted. His well-formed, roundabout sentences were making my head spin a little. I found myself wanting to believe him. "You're pretty," I blurted out, ashamed of myself the moment I heard the words aloud. "What is it with you Kin? Is it because you're descended from fallen angels that you're all obscenely good looking? Because, you know, experience has taught me not to trust someone just because of a pretty face and pretty words."

"Wise woman," said Azimuth, not bothering to look any less attractive. "I'd still prefer you didn't mention me to your lover."

"Why?"

"Does he tell you everything?"

Rooster had already used that argument with me. I decided to try a different tack. "What is it you want from me?"

"Can't someone merely be interested in meeting the mortal woman who caught the heart of the leader of the Storm Ravens? It's a romantic story, after all." He couldn't have overlooked my eyes narrowing. My patience for his flatteries was wearing thin. "Fine," he admitted, when I stonewalled a response. "I'm intrigued by *your* interest in Marcus Grant." I raised an eyebrow, waiting for more. "I'm the one who suggested his special case, shall we say, to your friend Rooster. I'd heard through the grapevine that he was actively seeking malfeasants willing to hide his clients in the

Kinlands, and I naturally thought of you and Corydonais. It is the kind of thing you investigate, yes?"

My mere presence at the estate answered that question, I supposed. "And what do you *want?*" I repeated.

"Information about the progress of your case."

"Why?"

"I cannot divulge the reasons." It felt a bit odd to hear such lovely sentences from someone of whom, due to sheer appearance, I might suspect of having a limited vocabulary consisting solely of *dude*, *bro*, and *where's my styling product?* "Let me say that if your investigations proceed in the direction I anticipate, the results may provide me with a personal satisfaction that will satisfy—well, my thirst for vengeance, let us say. You understand a thirst for vengeance, do you not, Ms. Dorringer?"

"I see you've done your research," I grumbled, reminded of how I'd never regain those years I'd lost. "But if you expect me to tell you the details of a confidential investigation, I'm afraid I can't . . ."

"Nothing confidential. Not at all," he hastened to reassure me. "I would never ask such a thing!" At the sight of the wry button of doubt my mouth had worked itself into, he folded his hands and bowed slightly, like Mr. Miyagi in *The Karate Kid*. Had we just finished a sparring match? "Only such information that you feel would be appropriate to share, that would break no secrets. And in return, perhaps I could find out . . ." His voice grew softer, forcing me to take a step forward to hear what he said. "More about your family surname."

Damn him. Despite my best reservations, he'd intrigued me. I wasn't going to make any promises, however. Instead, I thought about it a moment, jutted out my jaw, and asked what immediately had come to mind. "You *know* who's behind this?"

"Not at all."

"Because if you do and you're not saying . . ."

"I don't. Although I will say that from what I know of Mr. Grant, it may be to your advantage for your friends not to hide their race from him."

"Whatever. Because if you *did* know who's behind this . . ."

Back in my old days of insurance fraud investigation, I'd learned a particular interrogation technique that involved pulling my face into a bulldog snarl and verbally bullying my way with question after question until my subject gave in and admitted that they hadn't really seen a doctor and that the neck brace they'd been wearing had really been left over from their sister's disk fusion in 1997. Barely had I squinched all my facial features together, though, than I heard a mighty flutter of wings overhead as something burst through the canopy of leaves. I turned in time to see both Cor and Ginger landing on the sidewalk with nearly identical whuffs, shifting and expanding back into human form. Each of them picked up from the sidewalk identical dogs, tiny, lean, black, and with heads of crazy hair. They looked like the Liza Minnellis of pooches, actually, and both seemed stunned to have been scooped up by their collars and deposited outside the limits of their little worlds.

"You're back," I said, relieved and delighted at the same time.

"We're back," Cor echoed. His dog sniffed at his hands greedily, as if he'd never smelled anything like him before. Perhaps he hadn't. "Were you worried?"

"I was just—"

When I whirled around to where Azimuth had been standing moments before, I found myself facing nothing but the hefty tree trunk he'd been leaning on. I looked up to the sky to see if he had shifted into a bird form and flown away, and along the sidewalk to see if he'd escaped as a cat or squirrel. How he'd managed to disappear, though, was a mystery. He'd been there one moment, and gone the next.

"Just what?"

I felt Cor's hand on my shoulder. When I swiveled, he was next to me. "Nothing," I said. I'd tell Cor about the encounter later, I decided. Definitely later, but not now.

His canine captive stopped inhaling his foreign scent and gingerly licked my own fingertips before letting loose with a peal of barks. "Squirmy little creatures," Cor commented, trying to calm the pup down. "Want one for Christmas?"

"Good lord, no." I retrieved my fingers before they became Snausages, tried to settle my mind and get back to business. "I'd rather have a pair of pet alligators."

"I don't know where to get alligators," Cor said, tickling his demon hound's tummy with the tip of a finger. "But I do know where to get a baby hydra, if you had a hankering."

"A baby . . . ? Nope. Never mind," I said, striding back to the convertible. I didn't want to know. Besides, I had a task at hand, and I needed the props. I strode over to Ginger, who had just retrieved her headgear from the convertible's backseat, and held out my hand.

"What?" she asked, sounding apprehensive.

I'd show her who wore the scarf in this outfit.

Chapter Six

"You look like a dragon queen," Ginger was still complaining when we pulled the convertible up to the driveway. Her dog was nestled comfortably in the crook of her arm, panting contentedly as he gazed at her with canine adoration.

It was tough to frame an answer, when in the passenger seat I was attempting to lend myself a semblance of Bel Air elegance while wrestling seven pounds of squirming pooch more interested in kissing the driver on his lips than in sitting on my lap. "Dragon queen?" I asked. "You mean, like an evil villainess in a Charlie Chan movie or something?"

"No, like a man in woman's clothing."

After an internal struggle, I decided to let that one pass.

"This is a private residence." I could picture the man behind the buzz that issued from the speaker sitting slightly above Cor's head level. Bored, wary, and overpaid. Next to the grille, behind a layer of what I was fairly certain had to be bulletproof glass, light caught the camera lens as it swiveled to focus upon our motley little group. "Please back up your car and vacate the property, sir."

Cor looked at me helplessly. No, not helplessly. How can a descendant of generations of fallen angels, especially one with wings of his own and with more courage than I'd ever known, really be helpless? It was pretty obvious, though, that he was looking to me for some guidance. After all, wasn't this why they'd brought me along? "One moment," he said.

My idea had been fairly simple, up to a point. What I hadn't yet considered, during that uncomfortable interview with Azimuth, was exactly what we needed to do after our impromptu dognapping. I had to stall while I considered our options. Leaning over so that I could be better seen, I smiled brightly and found myself saying, to my horror, "I'll have a Big Mac, medium fries, and an extra-large chocolate shake."

After a long silence, the speaker buzzed with weary irritation. "Sir. Please put the car into reverse and vacate the premises."

"We have something of yours." Cor's intonation was so dire that in my head I had an instant vision of one of the ways this scene could end—it involved a SWAT team, helicopters, and me yelling, *Don't tase me, bro!* "Something you want."

My false cheer shot into overdrive as I tried to rescue what was sounding like a ransom demand, before it was too late. "That's right, honey," I said, laughing lightly as I leaned over. I peered over the tops of Ginger's sunglasses. "My husband and I . . . we're neighbors of Mr. Grant's, naturally. And we were driving down the street a moment ago, just the two of us. And our . . . nanny." I could hear Ginger bristling in the back at the role I'd assigned her, but my jaw and imagination were too busy working overtime to assuage her hurt feelings. "And we saw these *adorable* little dogs running down the street. I mean, simply *adorable.*" The adorable dog in my lap opened its mouth and dug its teeth into the back of my hand, bringing tears to my eyes. "So what could we do but pick them up?"

"Lady. . . ." said the annoyed baritone voice. I knew that if I looked around, I'd see every camera along the enclosure wall pointed directly at me, probably cross-referencing my face with FBI files.

"Such sweet things," I said, dragging my tasty flesh from the awful dog's mouth, afraid to look at the wound in case my arm had been reduced to a bloody stump. My immediate

goal had been to pass on the slavering beast to Cor; the moment he touched the dog, it started to dote on him, panting
happily and rubbing its face against his neck. Okay, save for
the wagging tail, Cor had the same effect on me, but now
wasn't the time to be jealous. I reached over and played with
the dog's collar. "We couldn't let them run around in the
street now, could we? After all, there are all kinds of terrible
things that could happen to such cuddly-wuddly. . . ." I had
to rear back as the dog bared its teeth and did a quick Cujo
on me before returning to being Cor's fluffy baby bunny.
Little bastard. "Anyway, we looked on their tags and saw that
it said its name was . . . Ghengis." I flipped over the little
metal tag and read it aloud.

"And Attila," said Ginger from the back, reading the
name from her dog's collar.

Nice names for a dog breed so fluffy that even the makers of Beanie Babies would have dismissed them as trivial.
"Attila and Ghengis! Isn't that cute? Of course, as a neighbor, I felt it was our *duty* to return them."

Cor thrust his dog at the camera, and as if we'd rehearsed
it, we both leaned in to frame Ghengis with our friendly,
smiling faces. In the back, Ginger held up Attilla—and really, when saddled with names like that, who wouldn't expect a pair of dogs to have gone to the dark side?—so that
we could all be seen in the camera's lens. I was still trying to
maintain a frantic smile when the speaker crackled to life
and a dispassionate voice intoned, "We'll send someone out
to pick them up, ma'am."

"No!" With lightning-quick mental reflexes, I tried to
think of a thousand reasons why this faceoff shouldn't end
with a security guard poking his head through the bolted
door to the driveway's right, grabbing the dogs from us, and
sending our troupe on its merry way. "I wouldn't hear of it!
It wouldn't be neighborly. Right, honey?" I asked, dabbing
at Cor's forearm and taking the dog back, against my better
judgment.

"Absolutely," he said, heartily as possible. I had to give him credit for trying, especially since this method wasn't exactly his style. "Besides, we'd like to meet Mr. Grant."

"Since we're such close neighbors and everything now," I interjected. "I couldn't go back home without seeing the look on his face when he saw his precious puppies come home." Precious puppy number one began squirming in my arms again, trying to escape my iron grasp for the sanctuary of Cor's lap, but I clamped down and refused to let him lunge. "I work with a local animal shelter, you know. Do you know how many animals we're asked to take in on a daily basis? Why, you'd be shocked. Animals from homes of all incomes are at risk of wandering and being lost when they're allowed to roam without supervision. It's a national crime. Why," I said, madly improvising, "not two weeks ago, we had PETA asking our shelter if we knew of any high-profile names who had been cited for mistreatment of their pets, for some kind of public. . . ."

"Flogging," Ginger interjected, attempting (I suppose) to be helpful from the backseat. Either that, or she was trying to get even with me for appropriating her scarf.

"Protest," I finished uneasily. "You know. Signs and chanting and, of course, tons of press. Of course, I had to say I couldn't help them, because I didn't *know* any highly placed individuals within the entertainment industry who mistreated their pets. Most of them treat their animals as if they were their children! Oh, but not in a *Mommie Dearest* kind of way, of course. You know how the press can be when they get ahold of the slightest whiff of scandal. I think Greenpeace was involved, too. Was Greenpeace part of it, sweetie? It's—"

My crazed monologue came to an abrupt end, cut short by the groaning of motors. The giant, opaque wooden gates were parting, opening inward inch by inch with a mighty whir of machinery. Maybe the specter of hundreds of PETA and Greenpeace protesters crowding the sidewalk raised a red flag in someone's head. Whatever made them change their minds in there, I wasn't going to complain.

"Follow the drive to the right and park in the visitor's lot," said the voice on the speaker. I could have sworn I heard a sigh. "Someone will meet you."

While we waited for the gates to open wide enough to admit the convertible, Cor looked over at me, eyebrows raised. The slightest smile played across his lips, though he kept them pressed together as we exchanged expressions of barely suppressed surprise. There was something more in his eyes, though. If the two of us had been alone, unobserved by either Cor's right-hand Kinswoman or the cameras watching our every move, I might have been tempted to move in closer and press my lips against his to find out what it was.

But no. We had a task at hand. It was with an entirely different kind of excitement that we looked at the landscape beyond the thick wooden entryway. For the first time in my life, I seemed to know how Dorothy and crew felt at the opening of the Emerald City gates. Not that the Grant estate was as opulent, mind you. There were fewer actual gemstones studding the driveway. I did notice, however, that the geometrically sculpted topiary just inside the gates was probably honed with a laser level and that the sundial erected in the middle of the miniature Greek temple marking the point where the driveway split appeared to be made of solid gold. Or so I was guessing. I wasn't going to get out of the convertible and bite it or anything.

The visitor parking lot, as was called a broad space designed to hold twenty cars, seemed to have been patterned on the Hollywood Walk of Fame, minus the streetside Scientologists, junkies, and tourists. Stars limned with gold had been set into the stone pavement there, each framing the name of a screen luminary. When I wrestled open the convertible door to step out after we pulled to a stop, I couldn't help wondering whether the message that Grant wanted to convey was that the stars upon which he'd built his estate and career were fit only for parking cars upon. Or maybe he wanted to imply he'd hacked up the celebrities with a chainsaw and held a mass burial on his grounds. A winding path of red granite edged with Japanese lanterns led up a slope to the estate itself, a grand old Hollywood home straight from the champagne dreams of *Lifestyles of the Rich and Famous*. The cool white exterior held vast arrays of windows designed to maximize the view of the water on the home's far side. Sometime in the last couple of decades an addition had been constructed that dwarfed the original house in breadth; it was all crisp modern lines, angles, and dark glass to keep out the sun. It was as if a tastefully appointed minor asteroid had made impact and affixed itself in the Hollywood hills, leaving instead of destruction in its wake a broad swath of imported boxwood, shady gazebos, and more burbling water features than witnessed since the inception of HGTV. Chez Grant was the kind of house that most of us poor schmucks see on the cover of *Architectural Digest*, then wonder to whom the owner sold his soul in order to get it.

"We've got company," Cor said from the car's other side. He flipped the keys into the air and tucked them into his pocket. Ginger, I noticed, didn't seem to be having any of the problems with Attila that Genghis was giving me. I should've just handed the pooch over to Cor, since that was obviously where he wanted to go.

Somehow, though, I felt more in control with one of Grant's dogs in my hands. Right now, I felt a little bit safer, too, given that a small squadron of men in sports jackets and black pants had emerged from one of the house's side entrances and were heading our way. "Well, crud." I could barely keep the disappointment from my voice. We weren't being received by Grant. We were going to be taken care of by his thugs.

"We can take them," Ginger announced, the toughness in her voice belying her uncharacteristically feminine exterior.

"We are not taking them," I announced, walking around the convertible to join my friends. "There will be no *taking*." I glared at Ginger, whose legs had adopted a poised fight-or-flight stance. She looked as if she intended to wield Attila as some kind of weapon of yap destruction. "Don't even think about it."

"You're just going to let them grab the dogs and throw us out?" Ginger retorted, lowering her voice. We were still out of earshot, but I didn't blame her for speaking more softly. "When we've gotten this far?"

We weren't going to be able to make our way this far into the Grant estate ever again. It wasn't as if I kept a bottomless barrel full of *I Love Lucy*-grade disguises in my trunk, ready to fool the bad guys into thinking we were hillbillies or glamour gals. "We are not going to let them just throw us out," I growled, feeling like a mastiff with my hackles rising.

Ginger didn't seem very convinced, though. Cor merely seemed wary, as if concentrating more on our circumstances than on my lame reassurances. I was letting them down, I realized with a sinking heart. They'd had every confidence that the Venice-born-and-bred girl could finagle her way into the Grant compound, and here on my very first big assignment I was already showing my limitations. I felt sick in the pit of my stomach.

One of the security guards, a burly, bald man in sunglasses and Ferragamos, slowly reached for something at his side. It was him that Cor watched warily as he held up his hands slightly and said, "Hello, fellas."

"There's really no need . . ." I began, sounding spooked instead of confident. I decided to start again, this time back in the persona I'd adopted. "It's so good to see that these precious babies are loved, isn't it? Such a big welcoming committee!" I appealed to the others for a help I suspected would never come. They were as on edge as I. "Listen, boys, we really don't need to . . ."

Just then, right as my level of hope had reached its nadir, a door slammed from the estate above. "Oh my gosh!" I heard someone call out. A woman's voice, sweet and shrill. Seconds later, a figure began tripping down the rocky path. *Tripping* being the operative word here, because the female in question was attempting to navigate the stone path right edge without getting the spikes of her stilettos caught in the cracks. She was wearing some kind of swimsuit, leg-warmers, and a man's ballooning white shirt, making her either an aerobics instructor circa 1985, or else someone so visionary that her fashion-behind had turned into fashion-forward. Apparently she had graduated *summa cum laude* from the Victoria Beckham School for Hair Lightening, as well. Her hands waved in the air, tipped with long, polished talons painted in deep colors. Her gestures grew more and more manic with every step. "Oh my gosh!" she said, in the voice of someone who had been sucking helium from toy balloons. "Oh my gosh, oh my gosh, ohmygosh!"

"Hello?" If there was any hope in the situation, it lay in our platinum-bobbed friend. I didn't know who she was, or where she came from, but she was the one person in our immediate vicinity not scowling. "Hi. I'm . . ."

"Oh, my precious babies!" The girl—woman? It was tough to tell how old she was, given that everyone in Hollywood seemed to bask in the same ageless glow of youth. She could have been anywhere from twenty-five to fifty, for all I could tell as she sped by in Ginger's direction. "Where have you been? Are you okay? Oh!"

Ginger seemed taken aback at having Attila wrestled away by someone whose nails were longer than her eyelashes. Cor, in the meantime, allowed a smile to cross his lips. "I hope you didn't miss them too much," he said, managing to sound both smooth and charming. Too smooth and too charming for my tastes, but I was hardly going to let petty jealousy get in my way when we had a job to do. Much, anyway.

Thankfully, the woman didn't even seem to notice him from where she was kneeling on the grass. "Oh, my precious babies," she repeated, making smoochies on the dog's snout. It seemed used to the treatment and responded with a long, wide lick at her face with its floppy tongue. "How did you get out?"

"You know how dogs are," I said, moving closer in case she wanted to take Ghengis from me as well. I hoped she did. I would feel much more comfortable with two arms again. "Little scamps."

"Widdle scamps!" The woman rubbed her own nose against the dog's, parroting my words in a baby voice. I would have felt embarrassed for her if it weren't evident that her shoes alone probably cost more than my entire gross income for the previous year. "Are you widdle scamps? Play dead!" she cried. "Play dead!" Without warning, she rolled onto her side, hands curled in a playful pouncing position just below her chin. Attila promptly flopped over on his back and remained motionless. Ghengis, not surprisingly, didn't deign to join them. "Good boy!"

"Yes, they are," Cor said, reaching out a hand to help the woman up.

She rolled to her feet, Attila in her arms. Just when I thought all hope for adult conversation might be lost, she cuddled the dog to her ample (of course) breasts and asked, looking around at all of us, "Are you the Greenpeace people?"

Cor and I stared at each other, both of us trying not to betray the panic in our eyes. "There must be some misunderstanding," he said at last, measuring out his words carefully.

"We're not from Greenpeace," I said with a light laugh. "How funny, dear. They think we're from Greenpeace."

"Hilarious," Cor agreed, bubbling with false mirth. Even Ginger managed to squeeze out a few uncomfortable giggles, while the blonde looked at us with dubious eyes over the top of Attila's black fringe.

"We're neighbors of yours," I explained.

"From the neighborhood," said Cor, rather unnecessarily. Realizing that, he added, "I'm Cor . . . y. Cory. And this is my wife, Sam."

"Samantha," I explained, wishing I'd given him a primer on the modern fondness for pseudonyms during the execution of fraudulent schemes. "And our nanny." Ginger bristled again, but I'd already been through this story once, and I was sticking to it. "As I tried explaining, we were driving down the street and saw these darling . . . well, I don't know what breed they are. . . ." I had been smiling pleasantly in an attempt to keep the facade going, because the spandex God-mama had been keeping the security guards at bay, but my words trailed off at the sight of her expression. She regarded me with her jaw slightly slack, not taking her eyes from mine. "And we couldn't let them run around, you see."

"*Affenpinscher!*" she said.

"Gesundheit!" I responded automatically.

"No, they're Affenpinschers." She'd spoken dreamily, though, her attention elsewhere. Slowly she put Attila on the ground; the dog automatically began running on its wee little legs for the safety of the house, and the woman didn't even watch it go. She was too busy taking careful steps in my direction. "From Germany. Do I—?" Her hands reached out in my direction. "Do I know you?"

"I don't think so," I said, quite honestly.

"I . . . do you mind?" Before I could answer, the blonde had closed the distance between us and grabbed my head in her hands. Alarmed, I looked over at Cor, but he seemed just as amazed as I. Was she going to kiss me? Maybe as thanks for bringing the dogs back? Was this one of those weird Bel Air customs that none of the guidebooks covered? Or did she maybe simply find me hot? No, she wasn't kissing me. She was trying to squeeze my noggin like a lemon—or at least that was what it felt like as she smoothed down the hair on either side of my head as if to make it disappear. "Oh. My. Gosh."

"What?" Part of me panicked at the way she enunciated each word separately, as if it were its own sentence. "Um. Hi."

"Oh my gosh." This chick liked to repeat herself a lot, that was for sure. She continued to clamp her hands on either side of my face, jerking my skull from side to side as she performed some kind of inspection. "Your hair used to be black."

"No." My hair had always been the same plain sandy color, except for one brief period in . . . oh dear.

"High school," she announced, shocking me by reading my mind. "You had black hair in high school. You've gone blond since."

"This is my natural color." Cor raised his scarred eyebrow in my direction. "It *is*! Why are you asking?"

My psychic friends network companion still scrutinized me, though she released my head. "Those big eyes," she said, fluffing my short hair back into place. "What is your name? It's Sam, right? Oh my gosh." Her own peepers, framed with lashes so perfect that she could have been genetically engineered by the good folks of Maybelline, widened dramatically. "Samantha Neale."

"Dorringer." I stiffened.

"Oh right, I remember. You changed it, didn't you? Like, senior year?"

Neale had been my father's surname; after he'd upped and disappeared on my mom and me, I'd borne it like a badge of shame until the week I came of age. "Who are you?" I asked, trying to ground myself. At the moment, I felt as if I was having an out-of-body experience. My head was floaty. I couldn't remember why we'd come here. I wasn't even aware of the dog still in my arms.

"Ohmygosh, silly! I'm Jen! Jen Winfield!" Before I knew

what was happening, the woman reached up and rapped sharply on my forehead, twice. "Anyone in there?"

That brought it all back.

Okay, quick flashback to the most miserable time of my life. Picture me with uncombed black hair that hadn't seen a trim in months, smudged kohl around my eyes, lipstick the color of burnt persimmons. Imagine me in a wardrobe consisting of ripped jeans, flannel shirts worn open, and T-shirts from local indie bands no one had ever heard of (and that no one has heard of since). Yes, that would be Samantha Neale, circa age fifteen, scowling at everyone in the hallways, writing angsty poems she'd hope would get into the school's *Written Voice*, then writing scathing free verse with titles like "The *Written Voice* SUCKS!" when they were inevitably rejected.

Then picture this scared little creature, angry at her daddy and everyone around her, walking into the girls' room before lunch most days, hoping to have a quiet few moments to herself in one of the stalls—only to be confronted daily by gaggles of the pretty girls, the beach crowd, the ones with large allowances and friends, the clique that regularly trashed each other's houses when their parents would head to Catalina for a weekend. "Hi, Sam!" Jen Winfield would say back then, cascades of flaxen hair spilling down over her shoulders and onto the arms hugging a textbook she'd never cracked. When I'd disregard her and wash my hands, hoping against hope to repel any notice, she'd repeat, pointedly, "Hi, Samantha!" Finally, when I'd ignore her again, she'd march over, reach out, and rap my head sharply, twice. "*Anyone in there?*"

"No!" I said, jerking backward. I wasn't in the girls' room of Venice High School, basking in the smells of perfume and wood rot. It was a decade and a half later, and I was enjoying an impromptu reunion with one of the people I'd sworn, over and over again, that I'd never have to see after that happy moment I grabbed my diploma and tossed my mortarboard in the air. Why was life so darned unfair? "I mean, no! Not Jen Winfield! Gosh! I mean, gee whiz!" Why was I talking like June Cleaver?

"You look fantastic!" Jen was wringing her hands and jumping up and down like an excited ten-year-old. "You look so young! Weren't you only a year behind me? So you're like, thirty-two now?"

"Twenty-nine," I replied automatically. The world might have gone on without me for three years, but damn it, I stubbornly maintained I hadn't aged.

"Oh, aren't we all!" She giggled over what she thought was my little joke. Her eyes still scanned my face, though. "Have you had work done yet?" Before I could answer that question with a vigorous negatory, she continued babbling on. "Just a little Botox. Am I right?"

I should have been grateful for this break. I should have been jumping up and down and thanking the heavens above that we were still on the grounds, and that I'd found my in. Instead, all I wanted to do, when I looked into the vapid eyes of the girl who had been my nemesis fifteen years before—okay, one of my many, many nemeses—was to flee. Sometimes the past just isn't all that easy to confront, you know?

But I knew that I had two people nearby depending on me. Clearing my throat, I let loose with a smile that, while not exactly enthusiastic, at least wasn't unfriendly. "You know, Jen? Why don't you take your dog, here, and then we can have a good sit-down and catch up on old times? Whaddaya say?"

"Oh! How silly of me! Of course!" Her arms reached out. "Come to mama, Attila, darling baby. Sweet thing! Come to mama!" Gently she put her hands beneath the dog's front legs and lifted him into the air. "Did you love Sam, baby? Did she take good care of you? Did you just wuv Sammy-wammy?" Before I could protest, she thrust

Attila's face into mine. "Give Sammy a kiss and show her what you think of her, precious!"

Precious squirmed for a moment before finally lifting a leg up slightly, showing me exactly what she thought of me. Sadly, it wasn't with a kiss.

Chapter Seven

Of all the things in the room, it was a creased paperback that impressed me most. Not the circular mattress roughly the size of a small planetoid, laden with dozens of pillows upholstered in deep jade fabrics. Not the massive ceiling fan with its blades shaped to resemble elephant ears. Not the collection of vintage Oscars from the 1940s in an underlit display case next to the wardrobe, nor the carpet that was woven from some exotic and no doubt difficult-to-clean textile. Not the fact that I was changing clothes in what Jen had called "the larger of the pool houses." Because who the hell has more than one pool house? No, not even the weird and expensive toilet in the bathroom, with the strange little arm that had wanted to spritz and fluff my nethers dry. Though admittedly, that had been pretty darned impressive.

No, it had been the paperback copy of *The Da Vinci Code* lying forgotten at the back of a drawer (yes, I was snooping in someone else's bedside table—sue me) that had made my jaw drop, once I'd opened the cover and glimpsed the scrawl inside: *Jenny from the block . . . Think of me in London. Ben.*

"Do you *know* who probably *slept* here?" I called out to Cor in the bathroom, where he was changing. Rapidly I thumbed through the pages. For what, I didn't know. Stray Bennifer hairs, maybe? "This is an artifact. It's been here for five years!"

"How do you know it's been five years?" Cor's voice

reverberated on the imported stone surfaces of the cavern that was the larger pool house bathroom. He'd been in there longer than I had, changing.

Although he couldn't see, I jabbed my finger at the page in question. "Carbon-dating from before even the fabled era of another celebrity couple—Brangelina. Aren't you done yet? Why is it you spend more time in the bathroom than I do?"

As if in reply, I heard the toilet flush. It was rapidly followed by a masculine cry of outrage. Seconds later, Cor emerged, naked save for the pair of trunks barely covering his rear end. His hands still protecting his butt, he gawped at me. "That thing tried to attack me!"

"It's an electronic bidet," I reassured him. "Very big in Japan. Speaking of which . . ." Something other than the Dan Brown book had caught my eye. "You're looking very big in those trunks."

"What? Oh. Oh! You mean *big*?" His hands instinctively moved from his back to the front, cupping the contents of the skin-tight swimwear. "Are they too revealing?"

"Not from where I'm sitting!" Grinning, I shooed away his self-consciousness until finally he stood before me, hands at his sides, fidgeting with discomfort. The square-cut trunks were indeed brief, little more than a broad paintbrush stroke of black fabric across his midsection, laced up with a white cotton tie. The style flattered him; they drew attention to the muscular hardness of his thighs, the leanness of his waist, and the triangular blossoming of his upper chest and shoulders. He still regarded the swimwear dubiously. "Do you think someone else has been in these? It feels like wearing another man's underwear."

"Yeah, well. The things we do for our jobs." What I didn't mention was that I'd wondered the same thing about the one-piece number that Jen had produced for me from the wardrobe of the lesser pool house where Ginger was presumably changing. "These people are rich enough to keep spare swimsuits for impromptu pool parties *and* to have their own dry cleaning facility," I pointed out, since my ruined dress had been whisked away to the laundry five minutes before to have the piddle washed out. "I'm sure they wash the bathing suits between visitors."

Cor looked unconvinced, but at least he stopped adjusting his waistband and let his hands settle naturally on his hips. "Let me see yours."

"No!" I protested. I'd wrapped myself up in a towel the moment I'd put my borrowed suit on, and had kind of hoped I could stay muffled away from prying eyes.

"Let me see." It was less a request than a demand.

"It's not me," I said, standing up from the bed. Still, I hugged the towel's ends to my chest. "Seriously, it's really, really, *really* not me. It's more like. . . ." Impatient with my protests, he wiggled two fingers, indicating I should shuck both my inhibitions and my wrap. "I'm not going to get in the pool anyway. Maybe Jen has some jeans . . . *hey!*" I protested, as he reached out and yanked away the towel.

"Wow." His appreciative gaze danced over the stretchy fabric, taking in each of the multiple cut-outs above my hips and below my breasts.

"I look like Carmen Electra hosting some MTV spring break special."

"Who?" he asked, spinning me around to observe the skimpy swoop of spandex barely covering my backside. "Whoever she is, if she looks like you, I *like* her."

My eyes narrowed when he spun me back, gracefully whirling me into his arms in a move I'd only seen on *Dancing with the Stars*. I looked up at him, slightly out of breath. "Are we doing a tango?"

"You bet we are." I felt myself dipping backward as his face tilted and our mouths met. His lips parted mine gently. Although off balance, I let myself relax in his arms. He wasn't going to let me fall, I knew. "A sexy . . . sultry . . . passionate . . . tango." With every new word, he moved his lips up my neckline with a kiss, ending just behind and below my left ear. I shivered, and it wasn't from the insistent air-conditioning of the pool house. "I like to dance."

His fingertips moved beneath the triangular cutouts on either side of my ribcage, gliding against my skin. My back arched when his lips once more formed themselves around my own. "This really isn't the place," said some last remnant of my good sense.

"Oh, of course," he murmured. I felt myself being lifted, almost as limp as a child's ragdoll, and placed onto the circular mattress. The canopy of white gauze hanging above the bed blew around us when Cor put his knees on either side of my legs. "This is much better."

"We can't." My protest was weak, I knew. I was finding it hard to muster objections when his right hand was busily threading its way through the upper reaches of my swimsuit and out again, until he could stroke my neck.

"Oh, but we can. What do you wager that Brangelina and Bennifer did it here, too?"

"You know that's four people, right?" My question sounded more like a puff of air, wheezed from lungs too busy panting to support the words. "Cor," I breathed as he slipped the straps of my swimsuit from my shoulders.

"Ssshh." He leaned back, kneeling on the mattress. His index finger grazed my lips, silencing me. Slowly, carefully, he peeled my suit down, lifting me slightly from the bed to ease it down my torso, until the fabric hung limply around my hips. Only when I lay exposed before him, my skin tingling from the cool air the vent huffed on the both of us, did my shyness begin to vanish. I let him look at me, leaving my arms splayed over my shoulders, not trying to shield my nakedness. Letting him look at me was, at that moment, in the dim light of the pool house, more erotic than even the touch of his mouth and hands. "You're beautiful. And no, I'm not thinking of that Karma Electra woman."

"I didn't say you were." His long hair had fallen from

where he usually tucked it behind his ears, the loose strands dangling against his stark cheekbones as he stared down at me. Slowly, teasingly, he lifted his arms and grabbed the canopy rod overhead, hanging there languidly and stretching himself like a cat waking up from a warm nap. "You're the one who's beautiful," I whispered, this time letting my own eyes drink him in.

His blue eyes seemed almost to glow in the subdued light. I took in the shoulders etched with ink, the ropes of muscles that traveled down his biceps to his forearms. I marveled at the pectoral muscles that seemed more chiseled from stone than sculpted with flesh, the flat stomach, the blank area where a navel should have been. "You think?" he asked, grinning at me. His arms dropped. Cor let his thumbs hook under the waistband of his trunks. My lips were dry; I could only nod in reply while my tongue flicked out to moisten them. Our eyes locked once again, and slowly, he let his fingers tug at the white string holding them up. His eyebrows rose in silent question, and the corners of his mouth matched their curve.

"You're a bad man," I said. The air-conditioning was raising gooseflesh; I shivered slightly.

He nodded, breaking the quiet mood with a slightly goofy, mocking smile. "I guess I am." Then, with one fluid motion, the bow on the string flew apart, he bounded into a standing position, and his trunks fell down his long legs and onto the floor. I only saw a blur before he was on top of me again, his temperature hot against me. "But then, you like that," he whispered. Cor's hands slid along the sides of my breasts, warming my skin. His mouth busily pressed kisses where his fingers had traveled, pausing to envelop my left nipple. Involuntarily, my hips ground against him when I felt the edges of his teeth rake that tender spot. He responded by rolling me onto my side and pulling down the fabric tangled around my hips. I wiggled my legs to shimmy it down to my ankles, where I kicked it off one. I couldn't loosen it from the other, however much I tried to shake. With one of Cor's hands cupping the sweet spot between my thighs and the other frisking up and down my spine, all while his tongue played around and his lips busily devoured my nipple, frankly, I didn't care. I swept out with my arms, clearing the mattress of decorative throw cushions in a wide, broad half-circle, like the wings of a snow angel.

He shifted his weight so I was atop him now, straddling his abdomen. I reached behind me until I found first Cor's knee, then his thigh, and then the inches of hardened flesh bobbing eagerly between his legs. It stiffened and strained as I wrapped my hand around its thickness. When I squeezed gently, Cor let loose with moan of his own.

It was my turn to pay some attention to him. "You like that, do you?" I teased. Lightly, I ran my closed hand up and down his shaft, barely touching the red-hot skin. His jaw shot out at the sensation as I rounded the head, and his eyes half-closed. "I can tell."

Slowly I settled my weight back and gyrated my hips slowly and deliberately. "Not too fast," I said when he tried to lift me with his legs and slip inside. His hands reached out to grab me, but I wrapped my fingers around his wrists and pressed them down into the mattress. "Not fast."

A gust of air blew the thin fabric of the canopy outward. Cor turned his head and squinted. "We need to stop," he said.

"Not a chance," I mocked, grinding harder. "Not when you've got me all riled up like this."

"No, seriously," he said, pleading. "We have to stop."

He wasn't playing with me, this time; a serious note had changed his voice. I followed the direction of his gaze toward the outside door, which stood open. A breeze still blew the bed's draperies, bringing with it a humid warmth that was banishing the room's chill. Even broken by the awning immediately above the door, the daylight from outside was so startling that for a moment, it was too painful to look at.

Then my vision cleared, and I saw a figure standing there. It was Ginger, dressed in a one-piece swimsuit as cheesy as mine. Where was mine? Oh yes, down strangling my ankle, still. I froze. Then, as an afterthought, I covered my breasts with my arm.

Ginger had already averted her head, though. Actually, the tips of her fingers were touching her brow, shuttering off from sight anything she might have witnessed. "Your friend sent me in to see if everything was all right," she said, her voice both pained and vague. Then, plainly annoyed, she added, "We're *supposed* to be *working*."

This last comment was aimed clearly at Cor. She stared at him directly while she delivered the rebuke. I sat there, frozen, trying to pretend I was anywhere else. I didn't feel mortified, exactly—I mean, part of me felt that if one barges into someone's semi-private room without knocking, one gets what one deserves. But let's just say that all things being equal, I would rather have been caught playing a rollicking round of Yahtzee than the game in which Cor and I were engaged.

Cor didn't say anything. His hair hung limply over his face as he continued to look in Ginger's direction. It was the only limp thing on his body, though all my desire had flown out the door when Ginger had opened it. "So are you coming? Don't answer that," she added quickly, this time to me. Because what, she thought I'd be the type to pounce on those smutty puns? "Don't make me deal with this dreadful woman alone. Sorry, Samantha." She looked at me again, her lip curling. "I forgot she was your *friend*."

The canopy billowed again when the door slammed shut. Cor looked up at me once more, his hands falling to his side. He blew out a steady stream of air, as much to clear his face of the hair straggling across it as to indicate his discomfort. Traces of apology coloring his voice, he cleared his throat. "We'd better get dressed."

No question about it—I agreed. We made our poolside appearance three minutes later, me in my *MTV Cribs* costume, and Cor with his trunks back on and sporting a retro-style 1950s bowling shirt. Its hem hung roughly low enough to cover his crotch, but to conceal the fullness still lingering there, he also carried a couple of towels at waist level. "Oh my gosh! Don't you two look adorable!" I could hear Jen call from across the poolside area. Which was pretty considerable. What a view, too! Treetops spotted with roofs tumbled down in a mad rush to the ocean, and then the deep azure water continued for as far as the eye could see until it disappeared into the blanket of haze on the horizon's edge. All this grandeur lay just below the edge of the vast swimming pool, which had been fashioned to appear as if it cascaded into a sheer waterfall, pouring its bromined bounty onto the estate on the hillside below.

I barely had a moment to take it all in before Jen leaped up to drag us over to the comfortable little cabana she occupied at the pool's other end. "I knew that would look sweet on you," she commented to me, swinging both of our hands after she'd inserted herself between us. "You've really lost a lot of weight since high school!"

"Not really," I said drily, my mouth twitching when I noticed Cor looking over my figure. "Baggy was in, then."

"And you're married! To a real catch!"

"Yes, she is," Cor said, his smile mischievous. "And I really am."

"Oh, aren't you funny!" My high-school chum steered us both around the hot tub set into the ground, then past an elevated outdoor barbecue area with more counter space and shiny stainless-steel appliances than my mother's kitchen. "I can see what Sam sees in you!"

Even in her stilettos, Jen Winfield was still almost an entire head shorter than I. Over the platinum sheen of her hair, I narrowed my eyes at Cor to let him know that I certainly didn't want to see him in her. He winked, and then I heard his barely suppressed laughter. "We haven't even scratched the surface," he assured her.

"Oh, I'm sure!" Her hair swung as she turned her head to me. "And you! Look at you!" she said. "Samantha Neale!"

"Dorringer," I emphasized.

"All grown up! And pretty, for a change! And married!" I nodded, silently pleading guilty to at least two of the three charges. "And with children of her own."

"What?" I asked, surprised. "No. We don't have kids." Why was Cor shaking his head at me?

Jen's eyes went wide. "Hello!" she said, dropping Cor's hand and preparing her knuckles. I couldn't escape the rap on my forehead that followed, unfortunately. "Anyone home? Why else would you have a nanny?"

Oh. Crud. We did have an alleged nanny, I remembered, as I rubbed my already-sore brow. In fact, Typhoid Mary Poppins was lying back in a lounge chair with her legs drawn up and her arms crossed over her chest. Our little angry ball of hate turned her head at our approach. "Yeeeeees, why else?" I drawled, trying to think. "We have a nanny . . . because. . . ." I appealed to Cor for help.

"Because the waiting list was so long," he blurted out.

"Yes! Absolutely!" It made no sense whatsoever, but I ran with it. "Of course, it's impossible to get a good nanny these days *after* you're, you know. Pregnant. So all the *best* people are getting them beforehand."

"Really?" She blinked, taking it in. "That makes a lot of sense."

"Absolutely!" I said. The spot in the middle of my forehead still smarted. Had she scraped it with one of the rocks on her rings? Those things were monsters. Which brought me to the question I had for her. "But you know, Jen, you haven't told me a thing about you! What's been going on? What's happened since high school? Are you and Mr. Grant hitched, what's the scoop, what's the deal, go ahead and spill it all!"

I don't know. In high school, when one's social standing could be made with one nod of approval or destroyed by a fiery estrogen-fueled glare from the right girl, I'd never mastered the art of girlish confidences. My goth self had somehow missed all the slumber parties and mall marathons and after-school gabfests. My approximation of what I thought girl talk sounded like sounded too sing-songy, too pat, too rushed. Jen, however, didn't seem to notice at all. She eased herself around the bamboo bar beneath the cabana's shade, leaned down, and pulled a chilling blender container from a mini-fridge. It was filled with a slushy substance the exact color of sickly green that I'd always imagined viruses to be. "Oh, don't be silly. Mr. Grant and I aren't seeing each other!" she said, sounding cheerful. "He's my employer!"

"Ohhhh!" Cor and I said in unison, joining in her merry laughter. We sat down on the stools at the bar, making ourselves comfortable.

"Kiwi daiquiri?" Before I could make a horrified face, Jen began dividing the slush between three glasses. "Does your nanny want one, too?"

"We don't let her drink on the job," I said, my feigned mirth dying down as I realized that in the name of sociability, I was actually going to have to swallow the icy beverage she was pushing forward.

"They're non-alcoholic," she assured me. "Just wacky daiquiris. I use extra sugar and some rum flavoring!"

Cor had already picked up his and given it an experimental sniff. He parted his lips and downed a swig. "My," he finally said, mouth wrinkling. "It's sweet."

"Isn't it? I love them."

"So, um, what is it you do for Mr. Grant?" I ventured, taking in once again her casual attire. If she wasn't the man's wife or girlfriend, the only other possible profession that I could think up for her happened to be the world's oldest. "It certainly looks like you stay comfortable doing it. Or does he pay you to keep him in kiwi wacky daiquiris all day?"

"Silly!" She looked at me fondly, not at all taking offense.

Somehow, somewhere down the line, Jen had bought into that movie-set California lifestyle. The Beverly Hillbillies mansion, complete with ce-ment pond. The Malibu Barbie wardrobe. The Catalina tan. The don't-worry-be-happy smile. For a moment, I was ready to tender all the cash in my purse for a couple of the happy pills she seemed to be taking. She pulled out a martini shaker from beneath the bar, took off the cap, and poured in something from a bottle that looked and smelled like pineapple juice. "I guess you could say I'm in the relief business."

"Uh-huh." And there my mind was, back at the whole prostitution thing. My assumptions probably said more about me than they did her. "That's . . . um, what do you mean by relief, exactly?"

"Oh, you know." She added a little bit of lime, two spoonfuls of sugar, and a scoop of crushed ice to the shaker, fastened the cap back on, and with her right hand began jerking it back and forth in front of herself at waist level. My eyes almost popped out of their head at the unfortunate and crude movement. "Stress relief. Muscle relaxation." With a deft motion, she uncapped her fruit drink again and sloshed it into a margarita glass, then topped it off with a maraschino cherry. Because, you know, it wasn't already sweet enough. "They like it!"

"They?" I asked, somewhat in awe.

"The dogs." When I couldn't respond, baffled as I was, she giggled at my thickness. "Attila and Ghengis! Hello!" she said. I ducked, expecting her knuckles to come zooming at my forehead again, but this time she hadn't intended to rap on my skull. I tried to pass off my flinch as a reaction to an invisible fly. "I'm Marc's dog yoga therapist."

"Dog . . . yoga . . . therapist?" See? Even Cor, who despite a life sheltered from the worst of human inanities, had moved around California enough to have seen just about everything, had never expected to hear those three words in a sentence together. "Is that a real thing?"

"Well, of course!" Jen trotted around the bar, the points of her high heels shuffling on the floor, to join us on the stools. She sipped prettily from her drink through a pink straw. "Three times a day. It keeps them balanced and their *prana* flowing."

"And you get *paid* for it?"

I attempted to temper the raw disbelief in Cor's question with a little bit of wild enthusiasm. "Wow! That's fantastic! I bet their *prana* flows better than mine!" Jen seemed grateful for the praise. "And he lets you use the pool when you're not yoga-ing them? Yoga-izing?" I tried again.

"Well sure," she explained. "I live here. I love it!" My eyes might have glazed over for a moment here. I don't know—I was perfectly happy with my current life. I didn't lack for food or warmth or clothing. Something about the thought of lounging around an estate like Grant's all day, though, merely in return for rubbing his damned dogs' bellies three times a day, brought out my jealous side. How did people like Jen luck into jobs like that, when I'd been trying to scrape out a living as an insurance investigator in the armpit of Las Vegas? When I came to again, Jen was saying, "Oh, there's Marc now! Hi, Marc!"

Though her hand waggled wildly in the direction of a patio outside one of the house's longer stretches of acute angles and plate glass, the man walking around up the hill, cell phone pressed to his ear, didn't bother waving back. I could tell he was looking in our direction, but he didn't seem to be making any move to see what the dogs had dragged in. Had Grant's security guards informed him of the ruckus earlier? Was he calling the police on us? Doubtful—wouldn't they have been here by now? "That's Mr. Grant, huh?" I asked, trying to sound casual. He looked like any of the men you might see walking down Rodeo Drive or being driven from a studio lot: sport jacket, sunglasses, his head shaved bald to hide the male-pattern hair loss. It was definitely him, though. I recognized the stance and face from Rooster's photographs.

"Don't worry. He won't come down," Jen assured us. "He's always busy. He's a nice man. Really a nice man. So generous! You just don't know."

Cor's jaw had jutted out at the news that Grant wouldn't be coming down. For a moment, from the way he seemed to tense and half rise from the stool as he kept an eye on the man, I worried he might lunge up the garden path to accost him. There had to be something we could do to attract his attention. "I'm just happy you've found something that really suits you," I told Jen, trying to mean it. After all, I don't think she'd particularly excelled in her academics. What other career path could she take, other than door-knocker inspector or hostess at Hooters?

She cooed. "Aren't you darling? I'm so glad our paths crossed. We'll have to see a lot more of each other!"

"Yes!" I enthused. "I'd love to visit."

"I don't keep up with anyone from high school, you know. Veronica Smiley? Tiffany Somers?" She rattled off a few names from the A-list to which I'd never belonged along with tidbits of gossip she'd heard about them. I nodded and listened, but didn't really pay attention; I was too busy trying to think of some way that we could escape her and get to Grant. Or get him to come to us.

That's when it struck me. That Kinsman, Azimuth. He'd given me the key to the dilemma outside the estate gates. I'd been holding it all along. "Honey," I said brightly to Cor, interrupting Jen's flow of yearbook reminiscences. "This chit-chat must be awfully boring for you. Why don't you go for a swim?"

"No, thank you," said Cor, still alert as a springer spaniel eager to flush out some game.

"Honey," I repeated, gritting my teeth to put my voice on edge. "Go for a swim. Take off your shirt . . ." I put special emphasis on those four words, ". . . and dive into the pool."

He looked at me, not understanding. I sighed and made

an elaborate pantomime of drawing a circle around, and pointing at, my navel. At last his head turned toward the low diving board over the pool's edge closest to the house, and he began to understand. "Yes," he finally replied, very slowly. "I think I'll do that."

"It'll be nice and cool," I told him.

Jen watched—a little too closely, I thought—while Cor removed his shirt. "Your husband has so much ink!" she marveled, her mouth open wide when she first saw the expansive clan markings that hugged his shoulders and back like a second skin. "Is that tribal?"

"Yes, in a way," I said. Cor was walking along the side of the pool, padding quietly, his steps balanced and light. Azimuth had told me that it might be in our best interest to clue Grant in on his race. What better way to do it than put Cor's markings on full display?

"He is just so *hot*." I must have looked sharply in Jen's direction, because she corrected herself quickly. "They are. The tattoos. Bo, my boyfriend, has one on his back, but it's not like that."

I wasn't listening, though. I was too busy watching Grant. He'd been talking vigorously on his cell phone the entire time, occasionally jabbing his finger in the air to emphasize whatever point he was making. From time to time, he'd still cast glances in our direction. Cor reached the diving board, climbed its steps, and stood there, hands on his hips. He contemplated the water for a moment, pausing.

Just as I'd hoped, Marcus Grant looked down at the pool and saw him there. For a moment I thought he'd turn away, so engrossed was he in his conversation. The sight of Cor standing in the bright sunlight, the sinuous intricacies of his markings in plain view, caused the manager to stop in mid-word, the cell phone inches from his ear. While Cor stepped forward, leapt up, and made a perfect arc into the air, Grant followed as if connected by an invisible tether. He stumbled forward, remembered his call, barked a word into the receiver, then closed the phone and stuffed it into his jacket. By the time Cor hit the water and a splash of a thousand diamonds droplets closed over his lithe form, Grant was jogging down the path in our direction, his two dogs following on their shaggy little feet.

We'd gone casting for the big fish. Now we had him hooked.

Chapter Eight

"You," Grant shouted. Whether Cor could hear it or not, I wasn't sure. As he rose from the pool, water streamed from his hair, down his chest, and finally dripped in a fringe from the hems of his trunks. Cor ran his hands over his face and blew droplets from around his mouth and nostrils before seeming to notice the agent's approach. "You!" Grant repeated. As if echoing their master's bark, both Attila and Ghengis let loose with short yaps of their own, though their tails were wagging.

Cor, I was glad to see, played the hard-to-get approach. "How's it going, man?" he said, nodding cordially, while reaching for one of the towels he'd brought out earlier.

Grant's mouth opened, sputtering. Whether it was because Cor had turned his back to him, once again exposing for the agent's view his clan markings, or because Grant was clearly unused to being treated with such nonchalance, I didn't know. In the end, it didn't matter, because Jen slipped down from her stool and, while adjusting her leg warmers, trotted over and smiled brightly. "Marc, these are friends of mine."

"The boys said something about Greenpeace nutjobs." Up close, Marcus Grant looked older than he had in the photos. Though in good shape for a man in his mid-fifties and fashionably dressed in a sports jacket, pressed designer jeans, and tasseled loafers, he seemed much more jowly than at a distance. His skin, too, had that rough and porous quality acquired as one grows older. Unless, of course, one happens to be Kin, with skin still as tight as a drum five hundred years later.

"No, no, that was a misunderstanding, Marc." Any suspicions I might have had about Jen maintaining a sexual relationship with the agent were dissipating; he didn't seem to regard her as anything more than an employee, and despite the fact that she was still sipping away at her pineapple juice cocktail, she didn't seem to exude the kind of familiarity that I would have expected if they'd been, you know, boinking like bunnies. Besides, she'd mentioned something about a boyfriend, hadn't she? "They're not from Greenpeace. This is Sam. We went to high school together. She was several classes above me, of course." Ordinarily I would have protested that wicked little lie, but Jen's hand had reached out to hold mine during the introduction, and she prevented me from saying anything with a little squeeze. "But you said I was free to have guests. . . ."

He hadn't heard a word she'd said. "Fine. Fine. Yes. Sure. Whatever." The dogs seemed to adore Jen. They had wandered over to her and stood at her feet, panting. Grant gave them a quick look before turning back to Cor. "Where are you from?" he demanded.

"Don't be so rude, Marc! They're neighbors of ours. Where did you say you lived, anyway?" Jen asked me.

"Well. . . ."

"Actually, sir." Cor cleared his throat. He had been toweling off his wet hair during the exchange, and now that it was a damp and floppy mess, he tried to tame it with his fingers. When he stretched, his lack of a navel should have been apparent to anyone in his vicinity. "I was hoping you and I might have a talk. Privately."

The agent's eyes flickered to Cor's abdomen. For a moment Grant appeared torn between agreeing and having us carted out blindfolded and bound to be dumped headfirst in the raw sewage at the Hyperion Treatment Plant. At last, though, he said, "Yeah. Let's talk. Come on, kid." He nodded toward of the pool's far end and the larger of the pool houses.

"Stay here, hon," Cor said to me. Sitting put was the last thing I wanted to do, but his eyes told me that this conversation was best handled alone.

"Just us girls, then!" Jen, ever the pleasant hostess, navigated a reluctant me to the bank of reclining chairs where Ginger was still sulking. Oh, it was a pleasant sulk, to be sure, masquerading as simple relaxation in the sun, but a sulk it most definitely was. I wouldn't have been at all surprised if the chair I chose to sit upon had collapsed from structural sabotage. Jen wrinkled her nose. "I hope your husband isn't trying to sell a script or something. Marc *hates* that."

"No, he's not a screenwriter," I promised. "Or an actor."

"Oh good. He gets grumpy from that kind of thing, but usually Marc's a very nice guy," Jen said, stretching out her legs so she could remove legwarmers. "Very very nice. I mean, I divide my life into two parts. There's A.M. After Marc. And then there's B.M."

I winced slightly at the unfortunate acronym. "Before Marc?"

"Right! Let me tell you, A.M. is a lot better than B.M."

"Don't you find B.M. better in the A.M.?" Ginger asked, not even bothering to look at our hostess.

"No, I . . . wait. What?" Jen's brow furrowed. I cleared my throat, trying to think of some way to squelch Ginger's hostility. I mean, honestly. No reason for her to take out her annoyance at Cor and me on Jen. Jen, however, didn't seem to notice. "I think it's a fantastic idea to get a nanny ahead of time. I mean, wow. Where did they get you?" she asked Ginger.

The Peri studied her fingernails. "Oh, you know. I was pushing crystal meth on the street when they took me in."

"No, no, no," I said, horrified but trying to laugh.

" 'Guess you're better than nothing,' they told me. So, I thought, sure, why not. It's better than hooking."

Jen's wide eyes relaxed when I explained, "Ginger is a *huge* jokester. She's really from a very, very exclusive agency. In London."

"Wow. London. Nice. Well, what are you doing until Samantha and Cory have their baby?"

Ginger immediately replied, "Oh, you know. General dogsbody and whipping boy."

"What?" asked Jen, not getting it.

"It goes something like this." Ginger sat up and smiled at me as unpleasantly as she could. "They do whatever the hell they want, and I get to trot around and pick up the pieces."

"Such a jokester!" I laughed, resisting the urge to reach out and strike her. "I guess you could say that Ginger acts as Cory's personal assistant most of the time, until that special, blessed day." Ack. I sounded like some kind of demented Donna Reed. "She's highly *professional* and very *businesslike* and very *dependable*." I'd intended the three words I emphasized to stand in for the little slaps I wanted to land on her face. "We honestly couldn't do without her."

Ginger looked as if she wanted to mumble something, but she kept it to herself and managed a wan smile instead. None of it was intended for me, I could tell. Thankfully, our subtextual argument was zooming around over the no-fly zone that was Jen's little brain. She had crossed her legs and turned back to me. "You're not drinking your daiquiri!" she accused.

In penance, I thrust the straw in my mouth and tried to sip some down. It was a little like drinking a Slurpee with a corn syrup chaser. "Yummy," I managed without gagging.

"I don't mean to pry. Maybe I could get that agency name from you, though?" Over the brain freeze that was rapidly disabling my cognitive functions, I must have managed a look of polite expectancy, because Jen continued. "You see, I'm . . . well. Expecting."

"Jen!" The news was the perfect excuse to put down my wacky daiquiri. Sincerely, I exclaimed, "That's fantastic news."

The woman's hand instinctively went to her belly, which she caressed with a gentle and protective circle. Honestly, not once in the last forty minutes would I have at all guessed that my high-school friend was pregnant. Now that I looked, though, I could see that the curve of her stomach had been covered by the white shirt she'd been wearing. Maybe if I'd been paying more attention, we all would have spotted it sooner. "So that's why it's only wacky daiquiris these days. Do you really think it's wonderful?" she asked.

Something in the way she quirked her nose and in how she'd suddenly gone shy, made me realize she wasn't fishing for compliments. "Of course!" I said. "I'd love to have children of my own. I think it's fantastic. Why, is something wrong?"

"I'm not keeping it," she confided. The poor woman seemed sad to admit it; one of her hands unconsciously stroked the fullness beneath her blouse as she spoke. "Oh, I don't mean like *that*. I'm going to have the baby. But I'm, you know. Giving it up. I'm not ready for children of my own right now. We're not ready. But it's okay. It really is."

"Jen!" For someone claiming to be okay, Jen looked anything but. Her eyes were opened to their maximum wideness, and she'd sucked in her lips until they'd disappeared. Since I'd experienced many an impromptu crying fit myself, I knew all too well what was coming next. Right on cue, she held out both hands, fingers stretched wide, and began fanning her tear ducts before her eyes could glisten any more. "Honey!" I was surprised to find myself saying. "Are you okay?"

She nodded rapidly, sniffing. "I'm all right. Really. I'm all right. Just a little hormonal. I'm fine." Poor thing. She'd managed to purge the welling tears, but she still gulped deeply at the narrowly averted emotional crisis. "Don't worry about me. I always land on my feet, right? Right."

Jen appeared to be talking more to herself than to me.

Ginger had been watching most of the display almost clini-
cally, though I did notice that when the tears had started,
she had managed to sit up and pat Jen gently on the back.
An act, or genuine sympathy? I couldn't tell. "Of course
you do." I wished we could've avoided these confidences.
Jen gave off an almost needy scent now, as if she didn't have
anyone else to confide in. I didn't want to be that confi-
dante. Almost desperately, I looked to see what Cor was doing. He and Grant were still in plain view, though it was
impossible to tell what sort of conversation they were having. "Look how lucky you are!"

"I am," she said with a sniffle. "Really lucky. It's just that
my boyfriend isn't ready. He's older, you see."

"How long have you two been together?"

"A few months. I don't really see him that much. He's
never visited here. He's always busy." Ah. Jen had never really
gotten out of the bad-boyfriend habit she'd had in high
school, I was guessing. He probably wasn't anyone's boyfriend,
except in Jen's mind. "He says I'm too young to start a family.
He thinks I'm twenty-six. Oh, so does Marc," she warned me,
not noticing my double-take. "So don't spill the beans?"

This is how the clinging started. A little confidence here, a
little promise there. Next thing you know, we'd be Lamaze
partners. "Well . . ."

"I knew you wouldn't. But Bo—that's his name, Bo—
has been married before. I think he's had other children,
though he doesn't talk about it. It's just a feeling I have."

"Trust me," I assured her. "You don't want to have children with a man who doesn't take care of the ones he has."

"That makes sense, but men change as they grow older.
They settle. They have to think of their legacy, right? Bo
will change." She spoke in such a soft and glowing voice
that I felt it a pity to disillusion her. "And it's not like we're
living together or anything. Not yet. I met him right before
I lost my last job. . . ."

"Which was?" Ginger prompted. She'd seemed to have

had a little bit of a turnaround since my rebuke, and was now engaging in the conversation.

"It was an acting job. Do you ever watch channel 390?"

I shook my head, not even aware that cable channels went that high.

"Between the infomercials," Jen explained, "I hosted a little ten-minute game show called *Triviatastic!* I'd ask questions, and the person who called in got gift certificates redeemable for wonderful cash and prizes courtesy of Triviatastic.com."

"The first person who called in, you mean?"

"If there was more than one," she explained. Ouch. "That's kind of why the show got canceled and left me jobless. But I said to myself, 'Jen Winfield, things will turn around! You always land on your feet!' And then the very next day I got a tip about the ad looking for a surrogate mother."

"Oh," I said, somewhat surprised. "So the baby's not Bo's."

"Oh, no. Though he knows. He's fine with it. Just fine." Jen might have believed what she was saying, but I didn't. Typical story—one I'd grown up with myself, in fact. Woman falls in love with a guy, the guy's infatuated for a while, but then reality sets in and off he goes, leaving her in the dust. If Jen's relationship with Bo lasted past the swollen pregnancy feet, I'd personally pay for their twenty-fifth wedding anniversary blowout. "There was a *donor*," she said, speaking the last word in little more than a whisper. "Marc didn't tell me who. He just said . . ."

I was still busily watching the men conversing in the distance. Once I saw Cor glance over his shoulder in our direction, and shortly thereafter he pointed, but what he was saying I still couldn't fathom. "Hang on," I said, absently. "Marc didn't tell you?"

"Marc was the one advertising for the surrogate," she explained, babbling on. "More daiquiri? Yours is all melty."

I waved off her hand when it started in the direction of

my glass. She sucked down the dregs of her own drink, then hopped up and tripped prettily in the direction of the bar again. "I get so thirsty nowadays! Then I pee like a horse." She giggled at her confession. "But yeah, that's how I met Marc. It was after we talked and he picked me and I went through the *implantation*—" Again, she made the word sound dirty by whispering it. "—that he offered me the position here."

"The dog yoga therapist position," I murmured, not really paying attention. Ginger, too, seemed more fixated on what Cor was doing than what our hostess was babbling on about. "Well, that was nice of him."

"I thought so too!" I heard the slosh and tinkle of the drink shaker again. "I used to joke that it was so he could keep an eye on me. But he's been nice. So nice, Samantha." Jen had been one of those girls in school who had always attracted the biggest losers of the clique she ran with. She'd run through that hulk of a football player who'd been arrested for beating up a liquor store clerk, the triple-timer who'd been seeing girls from a nearby community college, and a schmoe I remember as the Cigarette Guy, who smoked behind the school, never spoke to her in public, and later turned out to be some kind of dope dealer to middle-school kids. It didn't take much to imagine her romantic trajectory continuing along the same dismal path after graduation, all the way to Bo. "He's paying for my doctor visits and things, of course, but he's also promised to send me to classes after the birth. Acting classes," she explained. Around the bar she came once more, toting another pineapple cocktail. "I've never had it so good."

Cor was pointing our way again. I saw Grant crane his neck and peer at Ginger and myself. He nodded, listening. "That's nice," I said. This was maddening! I hated not being in the know. Playing the good little missus and chatting with the girls while the boys were off making the important decisions was definitely not my style.

Jen was good at it, though. "At first I thought that I was surrogating for maybe one of his clients. Because you know why? He introduced me to Dana Claire and Patrick Mc-Connolly."

"Really!" The names meant nothing to Ginger, I could tell. However, they immediately captured my full attention. Dana Claire had been one of those ubiquitous faces on movie marquees for the past five years, starring in everything from that sci-fi thriller with Ewan McGregor, to the Academy Award–nominated western with Cate Blanchett and Clint Eastwood, to that Woody Allen movie that neither I nor anyone else I knew had seen. And Patrick McConnolly . . . I mean, what woman my age hadn't swooned over *Ghost of a Chance*, that weepy haunted house story with that cute girl from *Amélie* and that kid from *The Sixth Sense*? He was practically the go-to guy when it came to sweet romantic comedies or anything co-starring Sandra Bullock. As a celebrity couple, they were grade-A stuff.

"Mmm-hmm! They were so nice to me. Although, you know, she looks so much older in person than she does on screen. I guess it's all the makeup. Anyway, they took me out to dinner and asked all kinds of questions about my family. I had to tell them I didn't really *have* a family anymore, what with my dad passing and everything." I made the appropriate vague sympathetic noise as I went back to watching Cor. "I thought they wanted to know about my family history so they wouldn't have to worry about, you know, heart disease or insanity or anything." Well. Too bad on the latter count, I thought. "But then they said that the baby wasn't for them . . . which is a shame, because can you imagine carrying Patrick McConnolly's baby? Wouldn't it be gorgeous?"

"Right out of the chute," I agreed, then decided my metaphor was probably a bad one.

"I know!" said Jen, crossing her legs on the recliner opposite mine. "But no, they explained to me that the baby was for their friend, Mrs. Jones, who couldn't have babies of her own. And they were just *so nice.* . . . "

"Wait." If my voice sounded suddenly on edge, it was because my throat felt afflicted with paralysis. I'd barely been paying attention to anything Jen had said, resentful that Cor was getting to the real meat of the matter. But that name—Mrs. Jones—yanked all my focus back to her. "Mrs. Jones?"

Jen nodded. "She's been wanting a baby for a long time, they told me."

I felt as if my head were spinning. When I'd been abducted and held in a Peri construct by the mother and son leaders of the Order of the Crow, they had used that very name for themselves. Although the son had died trying to kill Cor, Agnes Jones had escaped without a trace. Until now, that is.

If it was the same woman, I reminded myself. After all, what name was more common than Jones? But something told me that all the pieces fit here. Movie stars wanting shelter in the Kinlands to preserve their youth and bankability. Jen's fertility getting her a nonsense job for Tinseltown's biggest talent manager. Mrs. Jones wanting a child.

Another child, that is. Six months before, she'd intended to hand over a little girl in order to claim a portion of the infernal regions for her own kingdom. A teind, they'd called the offering. I didn't want to alarm Jen, but the chances were very, very good that the baby she was carrying was similarly intended as a sacrifice . . . to Hell itself.

"Excuse me." My legs felt wobbly when I tried to stand.

"Are you okay? You look like you've seen a ghost!" Jen exclaimed.

When I thought to look at Ginger, I could tell she was just as shocked as I. "Something like that," I told her. "I've got to . . . I'll be right back."

What did I intend to do, once I reached Cor's side? I had to think about that one. Interrupting with, "Honey, can you take me home now? My friend from high school is carrying Satan's Lunchable in her belly!" might attract the wrong kind of attention, particularly if Grant was in on the plot. But what else could I do? I'd stumbled across important, scary stuff. I had to let him know.

It wasn't until I was within touching distance of Cor that I realized Marcus Grant had just answered his cell phone. "Yeah," he was saying. "Yeah, I hear you. But I don't give a shit. I said, I don't give a shit. Listen, I can't listen to that crap now. Tell . . . no, tell . . . no, you *tell* that motherfucking son of a bitch. . . ." He spied me, raised his eyebrows, and then turned around to finish the conversation with a breathtaking display of profanity that would have awed Tony Soprano himself.

"We have to talk," I murmured to Cor.

He reached out to take my hand. Our fingers intertwined, locking in a strong knot. "Not now," he said back in a low voice.

"But. . . ."

"Hah-hah-hah," chuckled Grant without any real mirth. He clapped shut the phone again. Beads of perspiration had broken out across his forehead. He dragged a pocket square from his jacket, mopped them away, and stuffed it back again. "Sorry about the language. Motherf . . . I mean, bloody producers. Wot ho?"

The last question was directed at me. So . . . he was a pirate, now? I didn't get it. I smiled, though, to let him know that the profanity was no problem. Hey, if I used it occasionally, why shouldn't he?

Then, without warning, he loomed closer—close enough that our noses almost touched. The only reason I didn't lurch back was Cor's steady grip on my hand. "Remarkable," he said, peering at my face. Though the citrusy scent of his aftershave wasn't unpleasant, I really was not used to anyone examining my skin at such a microscopic level. Plus the stench of the Cuban cigar in his jacket pocket was tickling my nostrils.

"I told you," Cor replied. He sounded confident and sure of himself.

"Absolutely remarkable."

"What is?" I wanted to know.

For a moment, Grant stood back out of my personal space—but it was only long enough to let out a hearty laugh. "What is? she says. Good one. Good one," he told me, before zooming in again. He tipped up my chin, then lightly slapped its underside with the backs of his fingers. "Damned fine skin tone. Shit, there goes my mouth again. *Fuck!*"

"No, really, it's okay," I assured him, before his self-punishments escalated to more pyrotechnic obscenities. "Don't sweat it!"

"Huh. Not a trace of an accent," he said, cocking his head and looking at Cor. Cor merely dropped my hand, crossed his arms, and shrugged. "Good. Good. Helps to blend in. Yeah," he continued, reaching into his jacket pocket again. His index and middle finger drew out a business card that he uncurled in Cor's direction. "Deal. We need to talk more. Call me after the weekend. And you," he said with a wink at me, "nice. Very nice. Enjoy your visit. Make sure to try out the pool, all right? And yeah, don't let Jen yap at you too much. She's a good kid, but . . ." He threw his hands in the air. "Blah blah blah blah blah."

Before I knew what was happening, Grant gave us both a wave and danced up to the house a changed man. He'd come down the hill tense and suspicious, but he returned to the house with a spring in his step. "What in the hell was that all about?" I demanded.

Cor put his arm around my shoulders. "When I tell you, will you promise not to yell?"

"Tell me," I said, wary.

"Promise?"

"Fine. Whatever. I promise. Tell me."

While we walked back to the cabana, he leaned down and whispered a few simple words in my ear.

If I may be technical, my reply came out as more of a screech than an actual yell. "*You told him what?*"

Chapter Nine

"I told him that Samantha had been born a long time ago," Cor explained to his second-in-command.

"Tell her when," I snapped, glowering from the corner of my little living room.

Ginger raised her eyebrows in expectation. Cor wet his lips, swallowed hard, and bit the bullet. "I believe that 1792 was the year I chose."

"1792!" So miffed was I that I couldn't contain myself to the sofa any longer. I leapt up and began pacing back and forth. "1792! In seventeen hundred and ninety-two, Samantha sailed the ocean blue."

"I believe that was Columbus, in fourteen—"

"I know it was Columbus!" If my face could have been any redder, the cause would have had to involve a blast furnace and a packet of chili powder down the neck of my blouse. "Tell her the rest," I said, making a sweeping motion so that Cor could get to the good stuff. "Go on."

In the same way I'd earlier slipped on my jeans and a light top, both he and Ginger had already changed back into everyday outfits. Ginger, in her camouflage fatigues and olive green tank top, motioned to Cor to continue. Cor, his charcoal shirt open mid-chest with the tails hanging out, stuffed his hands deep into the pockets of his black slacks. "Grant was grilling me about who I was and how I'd gotten into the compound.

He knew I was Kin from . . ." His finger traced a line over his shoulders. "Luckily, he couldn't read the markings." Ginger nodded. "I had to think of something. I told him that you and I were independent agents and we had intelligence that he was looking for members of our Kin who could provide shelter to several of his clients. Then I suggested that we could do it much more cheaply in the future."

"And he bought that?" Ginger asked.

"He knows more than I thought he would. He knew about the four portals to Resht in Venice—he said that if I was on the up and up, I'd be able to tell him their names and locations."

"Did you?" For a moment I thought I heard a note of panic in Ginger's voice.

"The names, yes. I was general with the locations. It was enough to satisfy him. I tried to get information on who was taking his money, but he wasn't talking. He wanted more proof that we were legitimate. So I told him that . . ." Here Cor grew a little nervous as he judged my likely reaction again. "That Sam was one of our paying customers. A countess."

"A countess." He'd been right to be apprehensive. I was a shaken can of warm soda waiting to explode. "A goddamned countess. Born in 1792."

"You're always telling me to take chances! He thought you looked good for your age."

"Funny one, Mr. Funny . . . Fairy . . . Hilarious Guy."

Ginger shook her head, thinking it over. "Who in his right mind could mistake Samantha for a countess?"

"Thank you!" I crowed, triumphant that someone else saw the logical flaw in Cor's flim-flammery. Then, I paused, suspicious. "Wait, what?"

"What if he had started asking her questions on the spot?" Ginger wanted to know. "What if he had asked her to perform one of her childhood country dances?" Again I nodded, fierce at being justified in my resentment. "What if, ancestors forbid, he had asked her to display a countess's good manners?"

Again, I wasn't so certain I liked the way Ginger was thinking. "Exactly! The dance part, anyway."

Cor's expression was calm. The amused quirk to his eyes almost infuriated me. "He didn't. And if he had, Samantha is perfectly capable of improvising. As she's shown under some extremely difficult circumstances in the past," he reminded Ginger. It was true that I had. Being reminded of it under present, more irritating circumstances didn't soothe me, though. "And you." Cor faced me, arms crossed, his neck angled so he could look me straight in the eyes. "Why are you so upset?"

"This whole thing seems so . . . so un-thought-out!" I said, letting all my emotions spill. "It's just crazy! Reckless!"

Cor clapped a hand over his mouth, as if he wanted to say something but physically had to stop himself. At last he answered, "So what was invoking the wrath of Greenpeace to get us past the gates?"

"That was different."

"Furthermore, what about telling your friend that Ginger was our nanny? How is that different? I don't see her squawking about it."

"Leave me out of this one," Ginger begged, holding up her hands.

"Squawking!" Before I'd been fairly vexed, but somehow that word fanned the flames high enough to make me genuinely angry. "Oh, is that what I do? Squawking? Who's the person who found out that Jen is handing over her baby to the Order of the Crow?"

"You don't know that for sure," Ginger pointed out.

"I'm pretty damned certain!"

Cor struggled to remain calm. "Samantha. . . ."

I whirled on him. "Furthermore, I don't like people who address me using the word *furthermore*!"

"*She's like a spoiled mortal child,*" Ginger interjected in her native tongue. Like I needed her two cents. "*Everything has to be her way. And she's bossy.*"

"That is not at all true! I am not bossy!"

"Oh, so you're *not* the one who's always on top?"

All argument came to a screeching halt. Flames reddened my face as I remembered the compromising position she'd caught us in that afternoon. I could feel them creeping higher and higher, licking my hairline. "You know," I stammered out, "you wouldn't have been subjected to such a *horrible* sight if you'd been minding your own *beeswax.*"

"I don't know what bees have to do with anything." Ginger stood up from the sofa where she'd been sitting, crossed her arms, and advanced, addressing Cor. "My point is, if you had been paying attention to your mission instead of your pizzle . . ."

"Ginger." Cor bristled, clearly disturbed by her words. "Samantha is no ordinary mortal. She's particular and driven, and the fact you're the very same is what prevents you two from getting on. I love her."

I should have been bowled over. It was the first time he'd spoken those three words aloud to anyone else. A public declaration of devotion should have made me swoon into his arms, right? It's a pity I'm such a stubborn wench. "Oh, don't feel obligated to love anyone who's *particular* and *driven* and *bossy,*" I snapped. Almost immediately I regretted it, but my heart was pumping too quickly for my ire to cool. "I'd hate to make you do that."

Ginger ignored me. "Copulating with a mortal at such a time! There is more of your father's blood in you than you . . ."

"Enough! Both of you!" I'd never known Cor to be moved to anger lightly; even in the darkest of moments, he could be counted on to remain calm and level-headed. Now, however, his face was as dark and gloomy as the storms his ravens left in their wake when they flew in formation.

But Ginger couldn't leave it alone. "Your great-dame. . . ."

"Not a word more, Jinjurnaturnia. Not one word more!" Even I shrunk back a little at the thunderclap of his voice. His tone worked, however. Ginger closed her mouth, though it still seemed as if she had plenty more to say.

I surely did. "What's your grandmother got to do with this? Or your great-dame, or whatever you want to call her?" Cor's nostrils flared, though his expression remained unchanged. Ginger, on the other hand, sucked in her lips and looked at the ceiling. "I totally get why she'd bring up your father. I mean, you're carrying on an affair with some trampy little human girl, right?"

Cor shook his head. "Samantha. Stop it."

"But your grandmother? What, is she some evil kind of nose-to-the-grindstone type? Every time one of you guys has brought her up in conversation, you've made her sound like a real bitch who can't stand the thought of Cor having a little fun. What's she going to do, step out of the Kinlands and beat me with her walker? Oh, wait, I forgot. She probably looks all of what, twenty?"

"My great-dame has nothing to do with this conversation." I'd seen Cor angry. I'd seen him passionate and tender, and tolerant and amused. Never before, however, had I seen him irritated. Especially with me. I felt a little frightened, recognizing that at that moment, it almost seemed as if he wanted me to go away. "Nothing."

"But I know nothing about her." I heard an echo from earlier in the afternoon: Azimuth asking, *Does he tell you everything?* Obviously not, and realizing it just made me angrier. "Why is it I know nothing about your family? Is it because you think I'm unlikely ever to meet them? I'm not the kind of gal you take home to dear old Mom? Even Rooster knows more about your dame and great-dame than I do!"

"Why are you pushing this?" Cor asked, tilting his head. The irritation had left his voice. In fact, he sounded a little sad. He might have been getting back on a more even keel, but I still had miles to go. Before I could say anything, Ginger threw her hands in the air. "Why don't you just tell her?"

"Jinjurnaturnia." The icy coldness of Cor's voice made us both jump. It was the bark of a commander to his subordinate. "A private word. If you please." He nodded in the direction of the kitchen.

"Oh, don't bother," I sighed, stomping across the living room. I'd kicked off my shoes earlier, upstairs. Now I stuffed my feet into a pair of slip-on flats I kept by the door leading into my mother's backyard. "I'll go. You two play secret agents all you'd like."

"Don't leave," Cor said.

If I'd been a smarter woman, I would have listened to the regret in his voice. Oh, I heard it, all right, but in my anger I chose instead to turn my back on him, grab the doorknob, and stalk into the daylight. I'm also sad to say that I let the door slam behind me.

Ginger had been right. I'd known all along that I was acting like a spoiled brat, throwing a tantrum because . . . why, exactly? I didn't know. The only thing I was certain of was that I'd hated every excruciating moment of arguing with Cor.

With slow, shuffling steps, I trod up my mom's back porch. I suppose I could've gone on a credit-card rampage to shop out my frustrations, but retail therapy wasn't really my style. Nor was bingeing on ice cream, though I was reserving the right to give that route a go later if needed. Apparently, in these situations, I was the kind of girl who just needed a good, long hug from my mother. "Mom?" I called out into the stillness of her house, after I'd knocked and popped open the kitchen door.

My mother's kitchen smelled of cinnamon. It was an illusion produced by a scented candle on the nearby counter, of course, since the closest my mother had come to baking in recent years was dumping a pack of Archway cookies on her good china. One of her many cats paused from washing its face as I closed the door behind me. It blinked, narrowed its eyes at me, then went back to rubbing its paw over its nose. "Mom?"

Maybe she was teaching? I'd never managed to keep straight her class schedule at Oxy. Another cat entered the kitchen at the sound of my voice, a long-haired calico that looked like a black-and-orange skunk. It rubbed around my feet and made a little chirruping noise when I bent over to stroke it.

I was about to give up and leave when I heard voices in the living room. I pushed through the swinging door and stopped. "Oh," I said, seeing my mother sitting on her loveseat. She had company in the form of Landemann, Cor's sometime bodyguard and, judging from the fact he had taken over half of the dresser upstairs, my mother's boyfriend.

Thankfully, they weren't *in flagrante delicto*. In fact, they were sitting quite decorously next to each other, inside knees touching, as they held each other's hands. "Oh," said Mom, sounding surprisingly vague, even for herself. Almost immediately, she dropped Landemann's hand and let her own rest upon the lap of her flowered dress. "Samantha, dear. I didn't hear you come in."

"Don't let me stop you crazy kids from your necking," I said. "I'll get going." Then I noticed that Landemann, for once, wasn't wearing his usual sunglasses. I'd imagined that by this point the Ray Bans were actually part of his face; apparently not. Without them, his head seemed rounder than usual. His eyes were small and pink, and it looked as if he'd been . . . but no. Surely the redness around them was my imagination.

As if he realized I was staring at him with unfettered curiosity, the bodyguard groped for the missing eyewear that lay on the coffee table. "No, it's all right," said my mother, picking up the frames for him. She unfolded the temples and lifted them to Landemann's nose. Together they settled the lenses in their accustomed place. After letting out a brief sigh, she turned back to me and said, "Samantha, Mr. Landemann has just proposed."

They were the last words I'd expected my mother to say. "Marriage?" I gawped, for a few seconds forgetting my own woes and letting surprise overwhelm me. "You mean, proposed as in down-on-one-knee, please-say-you-will goodness? Oh my gosh." I blinked rapidly, then lowered myself onto the recliner opposite. The Ragdoll cat sleeping on it had something to say about that, but once she was shooed away and I was sitting, I spoke again. "That's fantastic!"

Hearing good news had temporarily lifted me from my funk. I was doomed to return to it, though, when my mother spoke again. "Thank you, dear," she said. "I've refused him." Landemann's head hung down. He raised it again to look her in the eye. "Darling, I can't. You know I can't." Without saying a word, Landemann reached for my mother's hands. She allowed him to collect them between his own, a tight ball surrounded by his own meaty paws. "Don't make this any more difficult than it already is," she said. The tiniest hint of a sob colored her voice.

I froze in my seat. Hearing that she'd turned him down had been embarrassing enough. Now I had to witness an intimate scene to which only the two of them should have been privy. I didn't know whether to blend in with the surroundings or flee. At long last, after a show in which the two stared at each other dumbly and I tried not to wince with discomfort at the awkwardness of it all, he stood, turned, shook his head at her, and stormed into the kitchen. A moment later, we heard the back door open and shut. He was gone.

"Oh dear," said Mom, her lower lip trembling. She held up a hand to cover it. "He doesn't understand."

"Mom, *I* don't understand!" In a flash I closed the space between us until I occupied the spot just vacated by the heavyset bodyguard. Mom was crying now. Not noisily. Not even enough to warrant a Kleenex. But this was the woman who had, after having her heart broken by my dad, perfected the art of never appearing affected by anything. Even when I'd vanished for three years against my will and she'd given up on me for dead, I'd gotten a bright smile and a brisk hug on my return. Seeing her tear up was a major disaster. "I thought you liked him!"

"Oh, I do." She sniffed prettily.

"Do you love him?" I asked, trying to lean in to catch her eye. She nodded. "Then what's the matter?"

"It's your father," my mother said, so softly that I could barely hear her.

"What does that rat bastard have to do with anything? Oh, Mom, you're not like, hanging on to some hope that Jerry Neale is out there somewhere, thinking of you and hoping you'll take him back?" She let out a little laugh at that, relieving my fears instantly. "So what's the problem? If Landemann loves you and you love him, marry him! Oh my God, marry him now! At least you *can*!"

"Before we both keel over from advanced old age, you mean." She sounded a little bit better now. She sniffed again, sat upright, looked around for something, and in lieu of a tissue, delicately dabbed at her nostrils with the back of her index finger. With her thumb she wiped away the tears at the corners of her eyes. "I know what you mean."

No, she didn't. She didn't know about Cor, though, and I wasn't going to break his secret. "Not at all," I said. "No, not at all." Stroking her hair, I explained. "But why in the world would you want to break the heart of a man. . . ." A human man, I wanted to say. "A *good* man? Especially because of that buttwipe who spawned me?"

"Don't talk about your father that way, Samantha." My mother had used that stock response whenever I dared bad-mouth him in front of her. "I won't hear it."

"Then what?" Now I was a little impatient with her. Why in the world was she denying herself this shot at happiness?

"We're still married," she blurted out. I sat back, blinking. I'd honestly never considered that possibility. "When your father left, we were still married. We still are, as far as I know."

"But . . . !" It seemed the flimsiest of excuses. Yet if that was the only thing standing between the pair, it had to be fixed and fixed quickly. "Fine! Track him down and get a divorce."

"I don't know where he is!" she cried. "I've never known! He's not on my Christmas card list!"

"There have to be laws." I threw my hands in the air, exasperated. It had been twenty years, and she hadn't done a thing about it? "Desertion laws. Expiration dates. I'm sure the marriage can be invalidated or annulled or whatever they do, if he hasn't been around in that long. My God, Mom. Even if Landemann was out of the picture, you need to do it for your own protection. What if you won the lottery tomorrow and he tried to sneaky-snake his way in here to claim half your fortune? What if he tried to sell your house out from under you?"

"The house is in my name."

"And a good thing!" I was outraged now on her behalf. "But you're a woman all by herself! Not totally all by herself," I hastened to add, in case that sounded depressing. The last thing Mom needed was more depression. "I mean, you have me. And Cor, of course. And you have Landemann, who's devoted to you."

"He always talks very fondly of you," Mom confessed with a smile. "I had hoped you'd accept him as a father."

I didn't want to consider that one too closely. After all, Landemann was technically Cor's half-brother, the offspring of Cor's sire and one of his human mistresses. If he married my mother and became my stepfather, and Cor was his brother . . . well, it was a little too incestuous to linger on. Perhaps it was better to take the Peri approach to half-bloods and not regard Landemann as any kin to Cor at all. Personally, I was more amazed at the disclosure that Landemann actually talked. In the six months I'd known him, I'd only heard him speak once. "That's sweet," I agreed. "But we have to do something."

"Can you . . . ?"

"Of course I can help!"

"You're an investigator," my mother said, looking hopeful. "You could track him down, couldn't you?"

Very likely I could. I had the skills and the resources and some of the old connections still. "I'll see that it's done," I hedged. "Honestly, Mom, I don't know if I can do it myself. When I think about that man and what he did to you. . . ."

"I know." At long last, Mom leaned over and gave me the hug that I'd come for. Until that moment, though, I'd forgotten that I needed it. "I know, baby. It's good of you to care."

"Of course I care. Don't be silly." I squeezed back. We Dorringer girls didn't go in for these displays of emotion all that often with each other, so I meant to make the most of this one. "Let me take you out to dinner. Something indulgent. With cheese. Pizza? Do you want to ask Landemann?"

Mom had brightened at the mention of dinner, but her shoulders slumped slightly at my last question. "I don't think he wants to be with me right now," she admitted. "Why don't you get Cory and we can go to that little Italian place near the beach?"

"Cor and I aren't all that thrilled with each other right now, either," I said.

Mom made a sympathetic face and cupped her hand on my cheek. We studied each other for a moment, and then, as if we'd planned it, stood up and simultaneously announced, "Girls' night out."

"My purse is in the house," I mourned, unwilling to go back there quite yet.

"My treat," she said with decision. "Italian food. Extra pepperoni. And there will be margaritas."

It was an offer I couldn't refuse.

Chapter Ten

"Oh my God, Mom!" I exclaimed, grabbing her elbow. She was weaving all over the sidewalk, barely able to keep herself upright. Or maybe, I realized with a little bit of a shock when my chin nearly collided with the top of her head, we were both a little on the unsteady side. "*Naked?*"

"It was only the seventies, dear. Not ancient Room." She began to erupt with little giggles. "I said ancient Room! I meant to say Rome!"

We were both lurching our way up the front steps to her house, victims of the restaurant's Coliseum Margaritas. In our defense, we'd only had two apiece. It was true they had been roughly the size of a fishbowl and made with massive amounts of Grand Marnier, and it was also true that the restaurant refused to serve more than one round per hour, but still. Only two. I hadn't been so intoxicated since an all-girls bachelorette road trip to Tijuana when I was twenty-four. And at least on that trip I hadn't banged my shins on the Mini Cooper and tumbled on the hood in the parking lot while a family of six stared and kept their distance. I was still limping a little from the accident.

"Ancient Room!" I howled. We clutched at each other as we staggered up the stairs. For some reason, our codependency seemed only to make us both laugh more and more, until finally we were on the porch with our heads hanging at roughly belly level, our shoulders rocking with mirth. "Sssssshhh," I told her, holding a finger up to my lips.

"Oh, sorry!" She mimicked me, trying to line up her index finger with the middle of her mouth. Eventually she was successful, but it took several attempts and using her other hand to steady it. "What am I supposed to be doing?" she asked, trying to stop the gigglefest.

"Keys," I told her.

"Oh, right. Keys!" For a moment we both stood there in the night's scant light, listing back and forth like ships at dock, while she dug around in her purse. "These aren't keys," she said, pulling out a pair of replica Columbian fertility idols.

"No, they aren't," I agreed, letting out a bark of laughter that was immediately cut off by a hiccup. "Sssssshhh!" I reminded her.

"Sssssshhh!" she whispered back. She set the little stone idols on the porch railing, then produced a pack of sugar-free gum, a miniature flashlight, several linty caramels, and a collection of photographic slides bound together by a rubber band. Finally she produced the keys, dropped them, and then scooped them up on the third try. "What are we being quiet for?" she asked.

I snorted. "I don't know." Our resulting giggles were quiet, though. To me, it seemed a pity to break up the low, constant buzz of the distant streets or the quiet of the canals with our slightly drunken tittering. Okay, our extremely drunken tittering.

Mom had managed to sort out the correct key by this point; she used both hands to guide it into the lock. "Oh, Samantha, dear. That was fun. We should spend more time together."

"Absolutely!" I enthused. I'd never had such a good evening with my mother before. It was as if with both of us miserable, we'd felt perfectly free to let loose. The free fried ravioli appetizers might have helped, too. "Girls' night out. Every Friday. Put it on your calendar."

"Oh, I don't think I could handle a Coliseum Margarita every Friday!" She sighed so suddenly and so heavily that I could tell the giddiness was beginning to fade. "You'll come in for a while, won't you? I don't think I could stand to be alone in this state."

"Are you going to be sick?"

She shook her head and pushed her shoulder against the door. When it heaved inward, light from the living room streamed out in a narrow shaft. The floorboards of her bungalow had never looked so inviting. "I don't *think* so," she said, after a moment. "That moment has passed. Although." She considered once again. "Through sickness you recognize the value of health. Through evil, the value of good. Through hunger, satisfaction. Through exertion, the value of rest!"

"So is that a yes? Because it's better to puke in the canal than it is on your rug."

"No. That," she said, waving her finger unsteadily, "is Heraclitus. The weeping philosopher, they called him. He wrote of loss, of flux."

"Okay," I told her, scooping up the little idols, the candies, her keys, and stuffing them back into her purse, which I tucked underneath my arm. I let her put her arm around my shoulder as we pushed open the door. "Let's get you some coffee, you old alkie."

Without warning, Mom suddenly let loose with a series of sleek and sensual foreign syllables. I never understood a word of my mom's Greek, but whenever she spoke it, she made the dead language come alive—more like a Romance tongue than the gobbledygook of its strange alphabet. "That means . . ."

"*We both step and do not step in the same rivers.*" It was Cor's voice that finished the translation. He stood beneath the archway between my mother's living and dining rooms, chin in his hand, half turned, as if the door's opening had caught him in the middle of reflection.

"Lovely!" Mom smiled up at him. "I didn't know you studied the tongue, Cory."

"A smattering, Mrs. Neale," he said in his most charming manner.

"Samantha never would. But you have poetry," she said, shuffling inside. "Poetry. In your soul. *We both step and do not step in the same rivers.* That's what life's all about. Love, too. Tell her, Cory."

"I think your daughter knows, Mrs. Neale," he said, watching me. In fact, since we'd burst through the door in our drunken state, he'd only had eyes for me. I was almost afraid to meet them with my own, fearful of—what? That I'd see something final there? If so, I was mistaken, because the moment we connected, the emptiness I'd walked away with that afternoon began to fill up. I felt like a dry well, beginning to be replenished with waters from deep underground. "She's not without her own poetry."

"Well, I'm glad you think so. Where's my purse? There it is," she said, delicately taking it when I held it out. She took two steps into the house and then stopped cold. "Oh."

Cor wasn't alone. Landemann was sitting on the sofa in the very spot where I'd found him earlier in the day. He wore his sunglasses, of course. It wouldn't do to be without them at ten-thirty in the evening. His arms were crossed over a checked, short-sleeved shirt, and he'd changed into a pair of white pants and even whiter socks and shoes. It looked as if he expected to head out to a round of night golf, in fact. At my mother's surprised reaction to his presence, he turned his head.

"What's *he* doing here?" she asked.

"I'm not having him sulk up our place," Cor said, grumbling humorously.

"Well, he's not welcome here!"

"Now, Mom," I chided. "He's angry with you. Not the other way around."

"No?" She blinked several times. "But he and I argued, didn't we?"

"If you can't remember," I said, steering her in Landemann's direction, "then you can't hold a grudge. Them's the rules."

Like a petulant child, she shuffled across the rug reluctantly, pausing to pet each of the three cats occupying space along the way. "I know there was something," she said, suspicious of everyone. "I just can't—oh!" Her jaw suddenly dropped into a cavernous yawn. "Oh, my!" She blinked rapidly. "I must be more tired than I thought."

Cor crossed the room and took my mom's other arm. I saw him raise his eyebrows at Landemann. What followed was obviously a struggle for the man. His wounded pride obviously still smarted at having his proposal rejected, but it was apparent that he still wanted to do the right thing. For long seconds, his backside hovered over the seat of his chair, up and down, up and down. Cor cleared his throat and cocked his head in silent communication with his half-kin. Though the bodyguard was my elder by many years and had celebrated a few more birthdays than my mother, Cor was still the big brother in this particular relationship, and his unspoken advice carried weight. At long last, Landemann hefted himself from the chair, walked over to take my mother's hands, and began to lead her to the sofa.

Cor clapped him on the back as we both let go. "Talk to her," he advised in a whisper. Then, at a normal volume, he said, "Good night, Mrs. Neale."

"Good night, Mr. Rivers," she said, seemingly befuddled. "I mean, Mr. Donais."

I didn't resist when Cor put his hand between my shoulder blades and guided me in the direction of the kitchen. When I looked over my shoulder, Mom was already sprawling on the sofa with Landemann beside her, his hands gently patting hers. She'd be okay. That I knew instinctively. I didn't say a word until we were in the backyard. In the dark canyon between the house and our garage apartment where the street lights and porch lights didn't penetrate, his hand moved down to my waist. "So you must have heard," I asked, to break the silence between us before it could grow uncomfortable. "About the proposal, I mean."

"I did. For several hours he talked about it." Was I the only one Landemann didn't talk to? Because it sounded as if whenever I stepped out of a room, he suddenly became awfully loquacious. "He's never proposed to anyone before, you know."

"It's complicated for my mother!"

"I'm not asking you to apologize for her," he said softly. I had sounded defensive, I realized. While I tried to let go of some of the tension gripping my shoulders, he stopped outside the garage door. "I have too much to apologize for, myself."

"No," I said immediately. "Let me. Honestly. I was unfair, accusing you of going over the top when I'd already run the Gauntlet of Crazy and come out the winner. You know?"

My apology was as clumsy as my feet, drunkenly trying to navigate familiar ground that had seemed so smooth only that afternoon. He didn't seem to notice. "I don't like fighting with you." The way he emphasized every word warmed my heart.

"I don't either," I blurted out. "I hate it. It makes me miserable. And it was totally stupid."

He was standing closer now, facing me, both hands resting upon the curves above my hips. "I didn't know if you were coming back."

Part of me was gratified that he had worried. The better, more caring half hated that I'd made him worry. "See? It's idiotic. Why do people do that to each other? Do the Kin fight like humans?"

His chest rumbled against mine, amused. "You *have* seen Jinjurnaturnia and me in the same room before, right?" I felt a little mollified. It wasn't just the taint of my humanity dragging us down, then. Woozily I followed as he pushed open our doorway. "I hoped you'd come home so I could make it up to you."

"You don't have to make up anything to—woah!" My stomach gave a mighty lurch as the world turned upside down. For a moment I thought it was the tequila doing a number on my head, but it wasn't. Cor had swept me off my feet, quite literally. I was cradled in his arms, while he navigated the length of my body through the door and over the threshold. "Okay, for the record," I gasped, stomach roiling, "this kind of thing is really bad on a stomach that's having its lining eaten away by alcohol, lime juice, and marinara sauce." Another rush of motion, and I found my feet unsteadily meeting the ground, though he still supported me. "Oh jeez. Thank you. Wait." I blinked, not recognizing the place. "What have you done?"

What he'd done, apparently, was to raid all the dollar stores in Venice for every tea light in stock. In neat, even rows they ran across any available surface—around the perimeter of the tiny table where we ate our meals, across the front of the table that served as our entertainment center, on the top of the flat-screen, atop the bookcase. In a few of the empty spots around the sparsely furnished room he had lined them along the floor, close to the wall. On each of the stair treads they burned as well, those perfectly spaced tiny lights that lent the room a golden, almost antique glow. In the room's center, where the coffee table usually rested, were all the throw pillows we had in our tiny domicile, arranged in a rectangle. The sight of it all almost took my breath away.

The heat certainly did. I'd never thought that a few dozen tea lights could produce that much warmth. In my woozy state, it seemed to slap me like a hot brick to the face. "Just a minute," Cor said, noticing my reaction. He knelt down so that my bottom gently met the futon. Once I was steady enough to support myself, he was off to tilt open the window on the stairwell. A dozen diffuse shadows of him

flickered across the walls as he ranged the length of the living room to open the window at its other end. The tiny
lights sputtered for a moment as the cool night air made a
cross-breeze that almost immediately brought gooseflesh to
my skin. "Better?" he asked.

"Much," I agreed. The candles were back to burning at
full strength now, although two on the table beneath the
window had blown out. A shy smile crossed my lips as he
began pacing his way back to me with an almost feline
walk. "So, is this the way you make up fights with all your
girlfriends? Because if it is . . ."

"Are you more concerned that I've had other fights or
other girlfriends?" he asked. It was a reasonable question, but
in my off-kilter state I couldn't really figure out an answer.
"Besides, who said that I've started to make up yet?"

"Hmmm?" I'd forgotten about the fight at that point,
honestly. I was more than content to bask in his unwavering
gaze as he began lowering himself to my eye level. He
wrapped his hands around mine. My own had never felt so
small before. "Oh, my," I breathed. He was in front of me on
one knee. The shock of a sudden slice of the cooler night air
cutting through the room momentarily brought me to my
senses. Was he about to . . . ? Surely not. The likelihood of an
ordinary proposal was one of those issues I'd driven from my
head as out of the realm of possibility. But it certainly looked
like . . .

"You're very special to me," he said, murmuring softly. He
brought my hands to his lips and kissed my knuckles. "When
you walked out this afternoon . . ." He shook his head. "I
couldn't stand the idea that you wouldn't come back."

"You didn't not believe I wouldn't not return," I said,
feeling more off-balance than any amount of alcohol might
account for. Apparently it showed with my speech. "Wait a
minute. Too many double negatives. You didn't really
think . . ."

"I know what you meant. Come here." He pulled me

down onto the floor, in the center where the pillows made a comfortable little pit. I noticed for the first time that he had laid down one of the blankets in their midst, making a comfortable nest for the two of us. "Relax."

Now that the shock of the previous moment had passed, mentally I shook off the notion that he'd ever intended to do anything so formal—so *human*—as to propose. Silly, really. What we had was beyond that. Still, part of me knew that it would have been nice. Beyond nice. Yet when was the last time I felt so cared for? I couldn't remember. All I knew was that no one else in my life had ever done anything of this sort for me. A big goofy grin crossed my face, partly at my own amusement at myself, but mostly from the attention he was lavishing. "Okay," I whispered, once my head was on a pillow. "I'm relaxed."

Cor propped his head on a hand as he lay on his side next to me. His left hand drifted to my shoulder, stroking my arm to the elbow. Then it moved to my stomach, rubbing through the cotton of my blouse before gliding under and traveling over the flesh beneath. My smile grew wider as his knuckles grazed the underside of my ribcage and his palm rubbed my hip. His fingers turned south, slipping beneath the denim waistband of my jeans. "You like that?" he asked when I shifted my weight.

"I just like it when you touch me." It seemed almost a shame to speak in more than a whisper. Somehow the lights had transformed our tiny carriage house-turned-residence into a larger space, a temple's worth of high, vaulted ceilings held up with massive marble columns, like a place of worship. My words even seemed to echo a little when I spoke. "So, I guess make-up sex is on the agenda?"

He shook his head, his eyes never leaving mine. "Not in the least." Even as he denied it, though, his left hand deftly moved up my blouse, unbuttoning it from the bottom. When my top lay open, his palm lightly planed against my stomach and side, encouraging me to lean forward so it could scoop up my spine. His fingers began to toy with my bra, nimbly working at the catch.

Not too nimbly, because after a moment of fumbling, I sat up. "Let me," I said, removing my top and tossing it aside. So long as it wasn't in reach of a licking flame, I didn't care where it landed. I undid the bra and drew my arms through the straps, feeling the relief of my skin coming free of its bindings. We were both sitting up now, face to face. He took my face between his hands, pulling it up to meet his in a kiss. "It seems like the agenda to me," I said, having to clear my throat of the desire clogging it. "Not that I mind."

When I moved in for another kiss, he pushed me away. Well, not pushed. His hands were already on my shoulders; they simply prevented me from closing the distance between us. "Nuh-uh," he said. I ignored him and pushed forward again. His eyes opened wide. "I said, no."

"Oh, and who made you boss, mister?" I said in a low, playful voice.

He wasn't kidding, though. Slowly, steadily, the pressure on my shoulders increased until I found myself lying back down once more. "Tonight, I do," was his reply.

"Bossy." His hands began tugging at my waistband, unbuttoning and then unzipping my jeans. That part he had down to a science. I conspired in his scheme to undress me by lifting my hips so he could shimmy the denim down my legs. I wasn't entirely surprised, when lying back down on the blanket, to find that his pinky fingers had caught at my panties and lowered them as well. Once the tangle of fabric had cleared my ankles, he tossed the clothes onto the futon.

"If you have a problem with my bossiness, take it up with my supervisor," he said, then paused for a beat. "Oh wait. That would be me, wouldn't it? Fancy that."

"Funny," I said, giggling despite myself. He was still clothed, but when I reached up to unbutton his silky black shirt, he batted my hand away. A second time I attempted it, only to meet with another rebuff. "Stop!"

"This evening isn't about sex," he told me, one hand still protective of his buttons while the other reached out to run through my hair.

I couldn't resist the sensation of his touch on my scalp, leaving behind tingling trails where my hair passed between his fingers. My eyes closed involuntarily. "What's it about, then?"

"I would be loath to take advantage of a woman in your state."

"My state!" I tried to protest. It was useless, though. I was indeed in enough of a state that it was much more comfortable simply to lie there, eyes shut, and listen to him breathe.

"It wouldn't be gallant." I snorted a little bit at that one. It was true, though. Though half the time he seemed absolutely unable to predict what I might do, and the other half it almost felt as if he was doggedly tagging behind, trying to catch me, he'd never been anything but respectful. "Taking advantage of a lady in her cups."

Okay, my eyes wouldn't stay closed for that one. "In her cups?" I had to ask, whuffing with amusement. "Oh, Lord Smedley Codpiece! Little did I know when my little heels pit-pattered down the staircase to my first Assembly that my honor would be besmirched so handily while I was in my cups! Do not take my maidenhood, lest I be shamed before the *ton*!"

He swatted away another attempt of mine to undo his shirt. "And you were worried about not being able to pretend you were nobility."

Somewhere in the alcohol-muddled morass that was my brain, a thousand objections began to bubble. Before they came to a boil, though, I instantly damped the fire beneath them. "I cannot possibly pretend to be a countess based on a brief, two-month mania for the novels of Georgette Heyer that was the direct result of Arthur Friedman breaking my heart at the tender age of thirteen," I said, quite loquaciously for someone who'd been complaining at the restaurant that the tequila had made her tongue numb not two hours before.

"Arthur Friedman, eh?" I didn't resist when Cor rolled me over, exposing my back to the draft coming in through the window. I shivered slightly. "What did the scoundrel do?"

"He went out with Lisa . . . ah!" The slightest of touches from his fingertips made me gasp. With the greatest of delicacy, he moved them from the nape of my neck down my spine. "He made out with Lisa O'Connor at the mall."

"Was he your boyfriend?" I shook my head, unable to think of anything but the minute point of contact between us, and how it was sliding down my smooth skin. "Were you in love with him?"

"As in love . . . ohmygod . . . as a thirteen-year-old can be with a boy she'd never talked to but . . . oh my . . . sat behind in pre-algebra. Don't stop," I begged when the tiny touch vanished, right above the cleft of my buttocks.

"I'm not," he promised, softly amused. I gasped when, without announcement, the curve of his fingertip made contact with my shoulder. It was as much of a shock as being slapped with an unexpected raindrop on the coldest and driest of winter days; I shivered and drew in my arms, protecting the sides of my breasts. Where his finger traced, it left gooseflesh in its wake. "Do you like it?"

"Oh, yes." How could I not? I felt as if great waves were coursing across my body, tides of pleasure ebbing and flowing in the direction of his slow and deliberate strokes. "I love . . . I love . . ."

"You love being touched. I know." I could hear in his voice an enjoyment at my speechlessness. I was sure it was something of a novelty for him.

"Yes," I managed to say. It was the last word I could gasp out for some time. Without warning, he added his thumb to the index finger that was reducing me to a quivering jelly. Together they swept down the length of my body, one moving in a straight line from my shoulder blade to the base of my spine, the other making a sinuous path under my arm, across the sides of my breasts I was trying to protect, beneath my ribs, and onto the most sensitive areas of my waist. I squirmed, almost unable to bear it, and kicked my feet a little when he repeated the motion on my other side. "This isn't right," I croaked out when, once again, he broke off the trail at the top of my shaking behind. "Let me."

He pulled away when I tried reaching for his pants. "Down, girl."

"I'm being so selfish!"

"Deal." For someone who still used phrases like *in her cups*, he sometimes produced some remarkably curt idioms when needed.

"But you're still clothed. And I'm all naked."

Batting my doe eyes at him and pouting prettily didn't convince him to join me in a state of undress, either. As punishment, he used three fingers this time, all of them swirling in circles around my left buttock. When my shoulders clenched and I cried out, all the digits of his free hand stroked my neck.

Punishment, I say. In a sense, that was almost what it felt like, to be deprived of the ability to tell where he'd touch me next. Without telegraphing his next move, suddenly one stroke would disappear. It might land on my shoulder, my neck, the small of my back, or the place where it had left off. It might reappear instantly, or take what seemed like unending moments before it began again. Maybe Ginger had been right. Perhaps I was a control freak, and the simple not-knowing of this particular experience was what drove me crazy.

At the same time, though, the not-knowing felt so good. Every touch between his skin and mine tingled so wildly that my foggy mind wondered if there might not be actual electricity between us—a spark created by the difference in our races, spread into a current by the contact between him and me. None of my previous lovers had made me gasp as he did. His hands began to play over the lower half of my body.

Cor and I had made love many times over the months, but the sensations he was awakening in me with his fingertips were unlike anything I'd experienced with him before. I wanted to cry, they were so beautiful. All this pleasure was intended for me alone. I wanted to relax and enjoy it. Yet at the same time, I wanted to be as aware as possible of every pleasurable sensation, so that when the night passed I might remember it.

For several minutes, his eyes closed, he continued to play my body like a skilled musician would play the cello. He drew his fingers back and forth across my spine until they made me respond with deep, sweet music. Although every sensation was very much in the now, for a few moments they seemed almost remote, as if I'd stepped away from my body in a trance. I laughed to myself at the distinct perception that I was watching him, watching me.

I must have fallen asleep or begun to doze, because as I looked around me, the entire room seemed almost to blossom with green. It was as if I'd been given a Chia Apartment for Christmas, and only now, after weeks of watering, had it started to sprout. "Are you doing something magical?" I managed to murmur, while my delighted and sleepy eyes took in the wonder of a light layer of plant growth invading the garage.

"Oft I have been so told," he replied. "Lo, these magical fingers of mine, how they have brought pleasure to innumerable. . . ."

"Ass." The sensation of walking outside my body vanished as I started to giggle; once more I was purely within my own naked body. "I meant, are you doing some kind of fairy magic in here? Everything looked green." Cor made a small, curious noise. I opened my eyes again and found the strange arboreal effect vanishing as I watched. Apparently I really had been dreaming. "Never mind."

"Did I send you to another world?" he joked. "I *am* good." He raked his blunt nails down my back lightly, making trails of sheer pleasure. "What in the world," I managed to pant out, "did I do to deserve this *wonderful* treatment?"

"Sssshh," he advised.

"No, seriously," I said, withdrawing my face from the pillows so that I could prop myself up on my arms. It didn't interfere whatsoever with his ministrations on the backs of my thighs. "It's like *The Sound of Music.*" Over my shoulder I could see his eyebrows rise. "You know, when Julie Andrews sings that song to Captain Von Trapp about how . . . ohmygod . . . somewhere in her youth or childhood, she must have done something . . . crap!"

"Something crap?"

"No, something *good* is what she sang. I can't imagine Julie Andrews . . . oooooooo. Yes. There." Both of his hands traced small figure-eights across identical spots on the backs of my legs. "I think you're giving me a kneegasm."

He chuckled at that, then said, "I was worried you were talking about the part of the movie where the Von Trapps were hiding from the Nazis. What?" He responded to my surprised grunt with a shrug. "Nikki watched it during one of her human culture appreciation binges. I liked it."

"You liked *The Sound of Music*?" I asked, incredulous.

"It was the recipient of five Academy Awards." He sounded suspiciously defensive to me. I rolled over onto my side to face him. "What? Nikki told me."

"Your sister told you that?" I said, keeping my voice flat. "Or is it that maybe you know because *The Sound of Music* is your favorite movie?"

"The story of the Von Trapp family has a theme of mankind triumphing over adversity, and . . ."

"Oh, I see," I mocked. "It's your favorite movie because of the inspiring theme. Interesting."

"And its music is catchy."

"Wow," I said, relaxing to the little waves of touch upon my legs. "Here I would have thought that your favorite movie, if you admitted watching human entertainments, might have been something along the lines of *Raging Bull* or *Apocalypse Now* or maybe even something from the early *oeuvre* of Winona Ryder, but here I find out that you have a secret preference. . . ."

"I never said it was a secret!"

"A secret, dark, hidden preference for the later works of Rodgers and Hammerstein, and very likely an equal fondness for raindrops on roses and whiskers on kittens." Abruptly the lovely sensations on the side and backs of my right leg ceased. When I looked at him, he had withdrawn his hands and held them into the air. "I went too far, right?" He nodded. "Sorry." I lay back down on my belly, letting my hair fall over my arms and shoulders. "There's nothing *wrong* with whiskers on kittens. And I've always been an absolute fan of brown paper packages wrapped up in string. Although when I think of brown paper packages, I think of liquor. Or porn."

"You," he said, changing from his kneeling position to one in which he had both legs tucked beneath himself, "have a remarkable knack for knowing how to spoil a mood."

"It's my prerogative," I announced, grinning at him. "And it's your burden to put up with me."

"If that's the only burden I ever had, it would be the lightest I've ever carried." He brushed a tress of hair from my face.

"Wow," I said. The sincerity of his compliment had ignited one of those slow-burning blushes that seemed to spread from between my shoulders up my neck and around my face, tickling me from the inside out. "Mr. Corydonais, you really bowl me over."

"As do you, sweetheart." His hair fell to either side of his face as he leaned over to give me a quick kiss. "Now. Are you going to shut up so I can work on your front?"

I did as he commanded, hands stretched luxuriously over my head as I sank back into the pillows with a happy smile. A pleasurable tingle from his index finger began at my elbow and traveled in the direction of my armpit, causing me to shiver ticklishly. "Why do I mess things up?" I asked after a few moments, into the stillness. "I mean, we have it so good. And then I do something stupid to mess it all up. Even though I *know* it's stupid and that it's going to cause trouble."

"Sometimes I wish you would trust me more," he said. "Don't take that the wrong way."

"You don't think I trust you?" He worried me.

"I think sometimes your need to question everything— it's your nature, I'm not criticizing—prevents you from accepting things on faith."

"You don't think I trust you?"

"Let's forget the argument," he suggested. Now two fingers began running crazily down my front, passing quickly over the sensitive spot beneath my arm and circling my breast in ever-decreasing circles until they traced the outline of my nipple. "Can you do that for me?"

"Yes. You're right, and I know it. I need to trust more." How could I say otherwise when I was under the spell of that touch? Like some kitten desperate for attention, I would have done anything just to keep his hands stroking me. "I won't mention it again." I was rewarded by a flurry of touches cascading across my skin, causing me to writhe with delicious euphoria. It wasn't until my head cleared again that I asked sleepily, "But, Cor. Honestly. Your grandmother. . . ."

"My great-dame Tania is very old Kin," he replied, his voice low. It sounded as if he were telling me a bedtime story. "You know that as a race, we accept our elders' word as command."

"But why does Ginger . . . ?"

"Jinjurnaturnia knows that my great-dame's opinion is very important to me. That's all there is, Samantha." Both of his hands were lightly stroking my breasts now, then my ribs, and finally down to my belly, dancing over an area that could barely stand the sensations. I tried not to swat him away, though.

"Tania," I said, repeating it. "That's a nice name. What's your mother called?"

Cor waited for a moment before answering. "Mabelle. Now. Are you happy?" Oh, I was absolutely happy at that moment. Blissful, in fact. It must have shown in my face, because Cor shifted position once more until he was positioned between my feet. "Then let's change the subject."

"To what?" He slowly parted my legs and inserted his body between them. Soon I felt his fingertips exploring areas that proved more sensitive to his caress than even my back had been. "Yesssss," I moaned. "I like this subject very much!" So much, in fact, that we conducted the rest of the conversation in absolute and blissful silence.

Chapter Eleven

"Ohmygosh." I tried to mask my horror as I watched Jen Whitfield spear a still-steaming lump of fried chicken breast and then add to her fork a chunk of waffle. She rolled the unlikely pair in the maple syrup oozing all over her plate, then stuffed it in her mouth. While she chewed, she made kitten-like mews of pleasure. "Thish ish sho delicshoush. Aren't you going to eat yoursh?"

I couldn't watch. I cannot stand for syrup to touch breakfast meats, much less carnivorous delights intended for dinner. There, I've admitted it. I'm a breakfast food segregationist. Let them stay separate, but equal. There's nothing inherently wrong with syrup. I like it on the pancakes or the French toast or the crunchy waffles. I like it very much indeed. Yet what did that chicken do to deserve being covered with something so sticky and sweet? All it wanted was to be delivered to the table with its savory, seasoned goodness intact.

At Roscoe's Chicken and Waffles, though, I seemed to be very much in the minority. The hefty waitress who had deposited the lunchtime plates in front of us beamed at Jen's obvious appetite. "Glad you like it, honey!" she crooned, flipping her braids. Jen nodded and smiled through a full mouth. Then the woman turned to me with heavy lids and pursed lips. "Something wrong with yours?"

"No, not at all." I flashed her a smile. As if sensing its falseness, her eyebrows shot up. She put her hands on her hips. "It's delicious," I assured her. Aware that I was under intense scrutiny, I hastily cut a slice from the thigh lying atop my waffle, shoved it in my mouth, and chewed. "Mmmmm!" It was greasy, and so hot that I nearly burned the roof of my mouth, but at least I hadn't lied. It was delicious. That didn't mean I wanted Mrs. Butterworth to put her sticky little fingers all over it.

Once the waitress had left us alone, I returned to sitting on my hands and watching Jen chew her way through her meal in much the same manner that the *Cloverfield* monster ate Manhattan. I also attempted to get back to one of the topics I'd been pussyfooting around all morning. "Sooooo," I said, smiling at her as brightly and sincerely as I had the waitress. "I hope Mr. Grant—Marcus—wasn't too upset about Cory and I dropping by the other day."

"Oh no!" Jen dabbed daintily at her mouth with her napkin before taking a big swig from the Arnold Palmer she'd ordered. "He's not like that. In fact, he's the one who told me I should ask you out today."

"Did he?" I had to admit, I was surprised when Jen had called and suggested a day out. I'd agreed immediately, of course, but I'd been a little shocked nonetheless that the initiative had come from the Grant camp without any effort at all on our part to weasel ourselves back in. "That's sweet!"

"Oh, he really is a nice, nice man. It is so nice to meet a nice man who's really, really just nice, you know?" I nodded, listening. "You're like that. I mean, most of my old friends thought that I was getting into trouble with this job. *Oh, no, there goes Jen with another bummer of a guy*, they said. *He's going to turn out to be a perv or something. Just watch.* But no. He's just been so generous and given me so many opportunities!" Her maw opened wide for another giant bite.

I occupied myself with trying to cut off another piece of the cholesterol-laden thigh so that I wouldn't have to watch her chomping. "He did seem very ni . . . amiable," I quickly amended. She smiled brightly at me through bulging chipmunk cheeks. "I think it's great, the things he's done for you."

"I knew you got that!" She took another slurp of the disgusting iced tea and lemonade concoction. Seriously, I had to wonder how in the world, with all that sugar she sucked down, she managed to keep her figure. Perhaps it was a pregnancy thing? "I think a lot of my old friends are just jealous. Cassie Arturo? You remember her?" I had a flashback to a pretty girl with dark skin whose eyes would roll whenever she talked about school, teachers, boys, her parents, or anything that bored her. "She works for Universal now."

"The studio?" I said, momentarily impressed.

"The theme park. Bo took me and she was ushering people into the Shrek ride and we talked a little bit. Do you know what she told me? That I was selling out. And we used to be so close! We even shared a limousine for senior prom! Finally I had to tell her that I didn't have to take that kind of talk from someone wearing a baseball cap with green horns, thank you very much." I shook my head to indicate my shock at that cautionary little tale. "But you're different. You've got substance. I always told people that in high school."

"You did?"

If she noticed my skepticism, she didn't let on. "Oh yeah! Totally! I always told people that you were going to do something important some day, like write a book or be president."

"Well. Thank you." It was easier to focus on the plate in front of me than on my own conflicting feelings. I hadn't liked Jen at all during high school. I didn't really like her now. Strike that for a rephrase: Jen had a certain childlike need for someone to depend on that made her difficult to turn away, but I couldn't exactly say that she and I would ever be BFF. At the same time, I felt like a definite SOB for pretending to be her friend merely to extract information.

Unless, of course, she was totally in on it. Maybe she was

the one leading *me* on, hoping I'd trip up and reveal something about *our* plans that she could use to her advantage. Hmmm. It was difficult to envision Jen as the brain trust of anyone's secret mission, but for the sake of Cor and the Storm Ravens, I was going to have to stay on guard. It was a thought that kept me sober and watchful through the rest of my chicken and the quarter-waffle I managed to down while I observed Jen eat and prattle on about long-lost high school days.

It wasn't until she'd thoroughly masticated the last of her lunch that she tossed down her napkin, squirmed in her seat like a girl at her own birthday party, and squinted her eyes with happiness. "Where next?"

I had to blink. In the two hours before lunch, we'd already visited a scented candle store, a place that sold Jelly Belly candies, an organic pet food establishment (so she could pick up some treats for the "sweet puppies," who were probably having a nice yoga-less day at home terrorizing wildlife and ripping up Grant's leather furniture), and a guitar shop on Sunset Boulevard, just because the "windows were so pretty." Which would have been fine, save for the fact that she was wearing tight jeans and a pink knit top Bedazzled with the legend MAJOR JENERAL in sparkly rhinestones, while I'd gone to the trouble to dress like some kind of upscale Mulholland zombie housewife. If you've never received wide-eyed, agog stares from white guys in dreadlocks before, try walking into a grungy Hollywood head shop specializing in rolling papers, bongs, and domestic incense dressed up like you're bringing the green bean casserole to the Bel Air Presbyterian Church annual choir jamboree, just because your friend said she'd heard they had some "neat posters." Trust me, you'll get noticed. "Where would you like to go?" I asked cautiously.

"Well." She had a mischievous glint in her eyes. There wasn't a Hello Kitty outlet store in Hollywood, was there? "You didn't really have your heart set on going, like, clothes shopping on Rodeo, did you? Because that's so *boring*," she added, before I could explain that I'd dressed in my ultra-conservative dress and flats precisely because I'd expected just that sort of agenda. "It's the kind of thing I have to do with Marc's friends *all the time* and I hate it. With you I totally can be myself and do the stuff that's really, really important!"

I smiled wanly. How could anyone resist such honeyed words? Still, I was a little bit worried to find out what might be really, really important in the world of Jen Winfield. Pokemon stickers? Tupperware? God only knew. I was a little relieved, then, to find ourselves only walking from Roscoe's to West Sunset Boulevard and taking a brisk stroll west until we reached an ivory-colored building I'd been in before. It bore a huge mural on the side, a pseudo-psychedelic array of one-eyed flying cherubs dancing and playing musical instruments over the pyramid from the back of a dollar bill, while on the ground below a giant music turntable spun a disc among a thousand frothy bubbles. *Amoeba Music,* the sign read. *The Supreme Source for Your Musical Inspiration.*

"This place is my absolute favorite in the whole world," Jen said as she pushed us inside the doors. From the excited hush in her voice, one might have thought we'd entered a church on a day when she had some particularly juicy secrets to confess. "If I'm feeling blue, I like coming and looking through the used CDs or listening at the stations. They're always so friendly here!" She waved at one of the staff members behind the banks of registers, a poker-faced girl with black hair whose expression didn't change in the least. We might have been gnats, as far as she seemed concerned. "She rang me up last time," Jen continued. "Isn't this fun?"

"Oh, I like CD buying as much as anyone," I agreed, tagging along behind as Jen immediately zoomed in the direction of a bin of just-in used discs.

"They have videos, too," she said, nodding at the second floor. "I always save those for last!"

"I'm surprised you just don't have someone go out and

buy them for you," I said, only half-jocular. Though Jen denied it, to me it sounded as if Grant kept her on an awfully tight leash. "I mean, Marc's probably got the resources, right? And I'm sure he pays you enough."

"Oh yes! Want to know what I make?" She named a figure.

For the first time in my life, I performed a spit-take. An actual, turn-the-head, look-back-and-spew-saliva-from-my-mouth spit-take. (Well, a little dribble, maybe.) "I guess that's good," I said, trying to sound casual. She hadn't named a salary. She'd named a freakin' lottery winning ticket. For doggie yoga!

"Marc's been really good to me," she repeated for the hundredth time that day. It was her mantra.

"Tell me more about this Mrs. Jones," I prompted, joining her at the CD racks. While she was actively reading the titles, however, I was merely flipping. "You know. The one you're doing the surrogacy for."

"Oh, I haven't met her. Do I like Christina Aguilera?" she asked aloud. Apparently she did, because she hooked the CD holder onto her arm and kept shopping.

"Did Dana Claire and Patrick McConnolly say much about her?" In case I sounded too curious, I added, "I know they wouldn't let you give your baby to just anyone."

"Oh, no," she agreed with wide eyes. "She's an old friend. They said she was a little bit, you know. Menopausal." She whispered the last word. "Poor thing."

"Well, aging happens to the best of us," I joked. It wasn't easy. I didn't like talking about the Joneses, or the time I'd spent trapped in the Kin construct.

"Marc says there are ways around it." Jen moved on to another rack, flipping through the oversized CD holders so quickly that as they landed against each other, it sounded like tap dancing. "I don't know how, though. I'd hate to be one of those Guinness Book women who's pregnant at sixty-five. It doesn't seem very fair to the baby, you know? By the time they get out of college, you'd be what, like eighty?" She shook her head. "That would suck."

It struck me that her interpretation of Marc's words and mine were very different. Maybe it was very possible that she didn't have a clue of what Grant was attempting to do with his more marketable stars. "You mean, surgery? Hormone replacement?"

"Oh, I don't think Marc approves of surgery for his big clients. Boobs, sure. He told me after the baby I could get my boobs done if I wanted." She paused in her search for bargain discs to thrust out her chest and consider her ample cleavage. Two youths on the opposite side of our rack stopped their conversation to stare with appreciation. The shorter and more pierced of them went slack-jawed, then removed his baseball cap to rub a hand over his cropped hair. "I don't know. Do I need new boobs? What do you think?"

I thought that anyone who had to whisper the word *menopause* should probably refrain from saying *boobs* so loudly and often, but instead I said merely, "No. Your boo . . . breasts are fine."

The taller of the two youths, who sported a piercing in the middle of his lower lip and a unibrow, laughed. "I'll say."

Out of female solidarity I glared at him and steered Jen down the aisle. She hadn't seemed to notice the boy's comment, or if she had, she seemed to accept it as her due. "Ignore them."

"I think you're right," she said, still staring down at herself. "I mean, I know my boobs aren't *perfect*, but they're mine, right? And if I want to have my own babies in the future . . ."

"With Bo?" Remembering too late his seeming reluctance to have anything to do with children, I regretted having said anything.

Jen didn't respond. Instead, she seemed to ignore me altogether. "Excuse me!" she called to a clerk passing by.

The guy she'd hailed was one of those short, skinny alternative types who'd chosen to project his personality through a pair of thick, old-fashioned horn-rimmed glasses that all but obscured his blue eyes, a day's growth of facial stubble, and a pink-tinted fauxhawk. "Can I help you?" he said, friendly.

"Yes," said Jen, smiling at him. "I was wondering if you had any used Justin Timberlake come in this . . ."

"Sorry. Be right back." Suddenly the clerk grew curt. The clipboard he'd been hugging dropped to his side as he spotted something or someone in the distance. He marched off without a word.

Jen's mouth quirked into a pout. She obviously was unused to people being the slightest bit brusque with her. "Weird," I suggested. "He must've seen a shoplifter."

She gravitated to my explanation with a grateful nod. "Yes, with Bo," she said, as if we had been on the previous topic all along.

"When's the last time you saw Bo?" I asked out of idle curiosity.

"A month, maybe?" Ah. Thought so. That's a barely boyfriend, not a love match. "And Bo has never said he didn't like my boobs. So why change them?"

"Atta girl," I commented, looking over my shoulder to see where the trendy clerk had gotten to. Almost immediately I froze, losing whatever Jen was saying.

Standing just within the front doors of Amoeba Music was a tall, platinum-haired man dressed in a tight-fitting Gold's Gym T-shirt and a painted-on pair of jeans. Even by the already elevated standards of West Sunset Boulevard, Azimuth stood out in a crowd. Yet how could he ever blend in with the startlingly blond mane that hung perfectly straight down his back and the sides of his head? He was looking for someone. Me, obviously. I was being stalked again, and it pissed me off a little. Just as I was about to duck, though, and pretend to, I don't know, look for imaginary dropped change on the floor, Azimuth's head turned. He spied the clerk with the pink highlights, smiled broadly, and began walking in his direction. The clerk, meanwhile, had already been making a beeline for him. They both turned slightly. The moment they intersected near the bulletin board where local bands were advertising their gigs, the clerk began talking animatedly to the Peri; they obviously knew each other.

I barely heard what Jen was saying in the background, but I nodded and agreed. "Mmm-hmmm." My response was merely to keep her talking. All my attention was focused on Azimuth, waiting for that moment when he'd oh-so-casually turn his head in my direction and give me that smug, knowing look that I'd come to expect from him. The clerk was occupying his attention, though. I'd lost the impulse to hide from sight by then. Now I planned to cross my arms, wait, and give him the glare of his life to let him know I was on to his little appearing-and-disappearing game. What's more, I wanted him to know I didn't like it. Who did he think he was, Angel keeping an eye on Buffy from afar? Was his shape-shifter form some kind of bloodhound?

"So anyway, Marc said he was talking to your husband about opening some kind of really exclusive, like, spa, for his clients, and I was like, why, because there aren't enough spas already? No offense," Jen said, her touch on my hand bringing me back to reality.

"Oh, none taken."

"So is that what he does, Cory? Run spas?"

"Well." If that's what Marcus Grant had told my friend, I'd best play along. "Something like that."

"Because I would l-o-v-e love a hot rock massage. And maybe one of those seaweed facials. If you can get a discount," she quickly added. "I'm not asking for any freebies! But you know, being the wife of the owner and everything. . . ."

"I'll see what I can do," I promised, wondering if I could get Cor and his expense account to cover a gift certificate to some *primo* Beverly Hills spa to keep her from bugging me. While I watched, the clerk jerked his pink fauxhawk in the direction of the back of the store, where a massive library of used vinyl spread like fungus from the walls to the bins in front. I cocked my head and waited for Azimuth to turn his head and give me a knowing smile, or a wink, or some indication that he was aware of my presence. Still, nothing.

"That would be *fabulous*," Jen was still saying. "Maybe we could both go get facials before the party next weekend?"

"Party?" I found myself asking, dragged back to the here and now. "What party?"

"Oh. My. Gosh." Jen closed her eyes and clapped her hands over them. Then she closed her hand into a fist and rapped her knuckles, hard, on her own forehead. "Anyone home? I totally forgot."

"Forgot what?" I spared Azimuth my attention while he wound his way through the aisle of media.

"The party. The cocktail party. You and Cory are supposed to come. You *have* to come." Her voice had changed. It wasn't the happy prattling of a baby any longer. It was the desperate wheedle of a freshman who'd forgotten her book report and was begging an extended deadline from her teacher. "Marc wanted to introduce you and Cory to some of his clients. He'll k-i-l-l me if he finds out I forgot to ask."

A party for us, eh? All right. I'd bite. We both wanted to find out what Grant knew about the Order of the Crow. A Hollywood cocktail gathering among the glitterati would be just the ticket. Would it be tacky to bring my *Ghost of a Chance* DVD to have autographed by Patrick McConnolly? Very likely, especially if I was supposed to be a countess. I was going to have to be collected and cool about this one. "Oh sure, we'll be there!" I promised, sounding genuinely enthusiastic.

"Oh. Whew!" Somehow I could have guessed that Jen was going to go through an elaborate cartoon pantomime of wiping pretend sweat from her forehead and clutching the rhinestones over her heart. Watching her do it, though, endeared her to me a little. In a way she was just a cute little thing—like a performing Affenpinscher, only one that didn't constantly nip me or wet my blouse. "It's not a huge group. I can tell Marc to set it up, now that I know you guys are free. Oh, you can bring your nanny if you want. Does she know anything about Lamaze classes?" She touched my arm. "Do you?"

Crap. I'd known it was going to come to this. "Do you mind if I let you browse for a minute?" I asked her, gently detaching myself. "I see a friend over there, and I wanted to say hello." She craned her neck to look in the direction I was pointing. "You don't know him, do you?" I asked, suspicious.

"Which one? Him? With the hair? No, I don't know him. But wait. I've seen him before." Oh, she had, had she? If Jen recognized his face, it was because he'd been hanging around the Grant estate. It would only confirm my suspicion that Azimuth had to be mixed up with the Order of the Crow affair somehow. My hopes for an über-conspiracy were dashed, though, when she waved her hands in front of her mouth and whispered, "He's in the movies, isn't he? Or is he from that TV show? You know. The one with the talking car."

"Um, nope. I'll be right back!" I told her, leaving her in the ABBA-Beatles aisle.

Azimuth had his back to me when I approached. I half-expected him to whirl around and make some snappy remark in order to prove he sported eyes in the back of his head, but no. He merely kept talking to the clerk, his arms crossed. I stared at the Gold's Gym logo on the back of his T-shirt for what seemed an inordinate amount of time, one hand leaning against a record bin fronted by a beat-up Ella Fitzgerald LP. Finally I cleared my throat.

Nothing. I might as well have been invisible.

I coughed, raised my eyebrows, and waited.

He didn't look around.

"What in the heck does a girl have to do to get a little attention in this joint?" I griped.

Finally Azimuth turned. His face was impassive when he saw me, but quickly he replaced the blankness with a smooth, angular smile. He reminded me of a pleased cat that had dragged a small animal into the house to set at its master's feet. The gelled-up clerk spoke first, however. "Marcie standing over in New Wave Classics can help you. I'm a little busy."

"Samantha." Azimuth exposed his teeth in a leonine smile. "What are you doing here?"

"Oh, right," I said, snorting.

The blond demigod turned to survey the immediate surroundings. Most of the store's customers were browsing either the CDs at the store's other end, or the video section upstairs, so we were fairly isolated in our vinyl paradise. "Are you stalking me, perchance?"

"Don't give me that baloney."

I would have launched into chiding him more forthrightly, but our bickering had pushed the clerk's nervousness over the edge. "Yes, *sir*," he said in a too-loud voice. He ran his hands backwards through his highlights, then wiped them on the seat of his sagging jeans. "I'll be glad to take that *return of yours* now." His eyes were fixated on a leather wallet that Azimuth was fondling with both hands.

Azimuth ignored him and continued staring in my direction. "I wouldn't give you baloney if you weren't following me."

"Following *you*? You're following *me*!" His eyebrows shot into the air. "Oh, deny that you came in here to lay down another of your spooky warnings."

"All right." The Peri had turned to face me fully, now. He inclined his head. "I did not come in here to give you a warning, spooky or otherwise." I sputtered, still not trusting him. "Believe it or not, Samantha," he said gently, "the world does not revolve around you."

"I never thought it did, thanks. Then why are you here?"

With his right hand, Azimuth held up the small portfolio he'd been carrying. "I'm making a business delivery."

Softly, the clerk murmured to Azimuth, "Do you know this *Eirethin*?" For a second, I let my glance flicker to him. I should have seen it before—no matter how grunged-down he'd made himself, no matter how thick the spectacles, he still couldn't obscure the deep blue of his eyes. The fact that he'd just used his native tongue to describe me as an outsider nailed it. He was Kin, and very likely dropping out of the Kinlands and taking a place in our own.

I made a grab for the wallet. The clerk protested and lunged when it ended up in my greedy clutches, but my hands were much quicker than his. "Let's see. A driver's license for . . . Nathan Birkmann, resident, West Hollywood, California." I glanced from the license photo to the clerk, who had jutted out his jaw as I put him under scrutiny. "Born in 1988?"

"Ronald Reagan was president," the would-be Nathan said, stubborn and prim.

"Ah-hah. Who was vice-president?" When he said nothing, I nodded. "Thought so. Birth certificate for Nathan Geoffrey Birkmann, born in Madison, Wisconsin. Oh, I see. A newcomer to L.A."

"The winters are cold in Madison," Nathan said, on cue. Azimuth, amused for reasons of his own, shared with me a conspiratorial smile that I didn't return.

"Passport for Nathan Birkmann. Apparently you visited Mexico when you were eighteen?"

His response was immediate. "Spring break."

"Drink a lot?"

He cocked his head. "It was spring break. What do you think?"

"I think," I said, flipping through the other documents, which included registration, car insurance, a college transcript, and a Social Security card, all excellent facsimiles, "that someone is pretty much set here for a new life as a human." I stuffed the documents back in their case and zipped it up before handing it back.

"Is she enforcement?" Nathan wanted to know. Azimuth handed over the documents to him without a word. "Because it's not illegal, you know."

"The forged birth certificate and license aren't illegal?" I asked, eyebrows raised. Azimuth shrugged a little, still wearing that implacable smile.

"The dropping-out part," Nathan said. "I can leave the Kinlands if I want."

I'd put him on the defensive. I felt a little bit sorry for rifling through his personal papers, fake or not. I'd only done it to mollify my suspicions that Azimuth had been telling me the truth. "Why are you doing it?" I was curious, though it was none of my business. "Just between us. So I understand."

The Kin now known as Nathan looked at Azimuth for assistance, but the elder Peri remained impassive. His eyes danced between us as if he were enjoying my interrogation. "I . . . I don't know," he admitted. "I just like it out here better. I like the music and the food. Especially the music." He reached for the clipboard he'd set atop the jazz LPs and hugged it to himself. "I know it's a big decision. I couldn't go on living that way, though. Nothing ever changed. Everything changes out here."

"What's your calling?" I asked. Toward the end of their adolescence, every one of the Kin discovered their calling, the shape of natural creature into which they could shift at will.

The boy seemed surprised I knew about that. "A . . . a pigeon," he said.

"And your allegiance?"

"The Order of the Silver Wing," said the boy. His voice was soft. I could sense he felt uncomfortable talking about it.

"It's an administrative order," said Azimuth, speaking up for the first time. "Couriers, message bearers."

"Human IT, too." Nathan looked at both of us. "That's what I've studied for the last twenty years."

"It's a relatively esteemed order," Azimuth explained. "They work for the circle of the Copper Crown."

"The Copper Crown?"

Azimuth shot me the most curious of looks at my question. Even Nathan seemed a little bit incredulous. "Who is she?"

"She," said Azimuth, unconsciously flexing his pectorals so that they rippled beneath his shirt, "is a friend."

"She," said the she in question, "wants to speak to you. Alone."

"Fine." Nathan was tired of me, anyway, I could tell as he sidled by without a glance. "I'm going back to work."

I waited until he'd gone before speaking again. "Why the car and everything, then?" Azimuth shook his head, not following. "Listen, I live with someone who sprouts wings at every opportunity. If he can fly somewhere, he flies. The only time he and his buddies tuck themselves into that ratty van of theirs is when they have equipment that can't be carried in their scratchy little claws. So why is Nathan there looking to own a car when he could just wing his way to work every morning?"

The look that Azimuth bestowed upon me was of pure, unadulterated pity, uncorrupted by scorn. "Samantha," he said. "When one of the Kin drops out of the Kinlands, they drop out for good."

"But that doesn't mean they can't shift."

He nodded. "That's exactly what it means. The ability to follow one's calling depends upon the drawing on the energies of the Kinlands. Dropouts have to cut all ties in order to become part of this world. All ties, including shifting."

I thought about that for a moment, turned and tried to find Nathan in the daytime crowd milling around Amoeba's floor. At last I located him, somewhere in the Rap section. He seemed to be answering a question for a guy in braids. After a second, he flipped through a row of CDs and pulled one out to hand to his customer. The man nodded and thanked him. Nathan waved him off with a smile. He'd never fly again, I realized. The kid was possibly as old or older than Cor's little sister, Nikki. He'd lived for centuries among the Kin, and decades with the ability to shift at will into his pigeon form and wing his way into the sky. He was giving that all up of his own volition. And for what? Some weird kind of faith that things would be better out here, facing the same fates as the rest of my own race—uncertainty, doubt, and death? I just didn't understand.

I had a lump in my throat for the boy when I turned back to Azimuth. His eyes were narrowed slightly, as if he was trying to figure me out as well. "Stop," I told him. "It's just a little sad."

"You were convincing, though. I'll grant you that."

"Convincing about what?"

Peri or not, I recognized the expression he gave me, the *oh, don't give me that!* tilt of the head, the slight roll to his eyes. He crossed his arms in a way that made his biceps pop and his forearms seem to double in size, a bit like a platinum-blond Popeye. "The Copper Crown. Pretending not to know what it was."

"I don't. What is it?"

"The circle of the Copper Crown?"

I bit my lip. "Repeating it over and over isn't going to make me know what it is."

"Corydonais hasn't told you?" I shook my head, indicating impatience. His eyes widened. "Seriously?"

"Yes, seriously." I wasn't at all amused. "What is it?

"It's not my place." He bowed and attempted to retreat from me, as if he really intended to browse the jazz LPs.

"Azimuth, by God, I swear I'll rip that weave off your head if you don't tell me."

"All right!" he said, reaching up to pat his mane. "You obviously know there's a royal court among our people. The Copper Crown is one of the few artifacts from the founding of Resht—the original Resht in its glory, not the diminished city of now. She who wears the Copper Crown is the matriarch of all the Kin."

"The queen?" I asked, feeling as if I was being given a crash course in Peri history. I began storing away the facts in that portion of my brain where I kept all the Kin folklore I'd learned until now. One of these days I could write a freakin' book. "Like, you know. *The Faerie Queen*."

"Edmund Spenser? There's a surprise."

"Coming from me, you mean? I had enough college to read excerpts in English Lit 201, thanks. Besides, a picture of Queen Elizabeth dressed as the Faerie Queen decorated the front of my textbook."

He tilted his head once more to grant me the point. "Gloriana, he called the Queen. Our first matriarch was known as—" He pronounced a multi-syllabic word that sounded vaguely like Gloriana, though different enough that an English-speaking poet would be tempted to Anglicize it. "When someone refers to the circle of the Copper Crown, they might mean the matriarch, her family, and courtiers of influence. Or they might mean the ruler, Titania, herself."

"Titania," I repeated, imitating his emphasis on the second syllable. He made the word sound very clipped, very British. "Pretty. Like in, um, that play. *A Midsummer Night's Dream*."

"Titania," he agreed. Again he gave me a curious look that seemed to probe deep. "And Corydonais has told you nothing of this?"

"Why should he?"

At my question, Azimuth held up his hands. He seemed to be dissociating himself from the answer. "Ah. Well. It's certainly been a pleasure to see you again, Samantha Dorringer," he said, managing to give the impression that if he hadn't been dressed in super-tight workout gear, he'd be donning a cape right then and reaching for his riding crop. "Let's try to meet again soon. Yes?"

"No, seriously, why should he?" I asked, before he could turn to go. My brain was riffling through the information that he'd just presented me more rapidly than Jen had flicked through the plastic CD cases. "I know that the Order of the Storm Ravens must work for the Copper Crown, but . . . oh, holy hells."

I'd figured it out. I'd fucking figured it out, and the sudden and total *rightness* of my conclusion rang out in my soul like the striking of a major chord—though that chord had sour overtones that left me jangling to the bone.

"Titania," I said, then left off the first syllable. "Tania. Cor's great-dame is the goddamned Fairy Queen."

"I thought he would have told you." Azimuth's words were slightly reproachful, and mostly apologetic. "You told me you didn't keep secrets."

"It wasn't a secret. It was . . ." I shook my head, stunned. I didn't know what it was. Worse, I didn't even want to think about why he hadn't told me himself.

"Hi." Jen's voice, both soft and enthusiastic broke through my reverie. I hadn't even noticed her standing there. What had she heard? How long had she been eavesdropping? "I really really really didn't mean to interrupt. I'm a friend of Sam's?" she explained, when I was still too shell-shocked to say anything.

"Charmed." Azimuth bestowed a smile upon her and bowed deeply. "Any friend of Samantha's . . ."

"Oh, aren't you something." I still couldn't speak. I'd staggered back against the bins and leaned there as if I'd had the wind knocked out of me. "I just wanted to tell you . . . if you don't mind, that is . . ." Azimuth gestured with a hand for Jen to continue. She looked giddy and guilty at the same time, jumping up and down with schoolgirl excitement as she spoke. "I just *loved* you in those movies!"

"The movies?" Jen had stumped him with that one, I could tell, even in my abstraction.

"But oh my gosh. You are so *mean* to Harry Potter! Well, that's all I wanted to say. I know you must get mobbed all the time." She turned to me. "Are you ready? I want to check out and then I'm thinking Pinkberry for dessert!"

As she dragged me away, arm in arm and uncomplaining, I didn't even have the satisfaction of telling Azimuth that I wasn't the only one who thought he looked like Draco Malfoy's dear old dad. It wouldn't have begun to pay him back for the bombshell he'd dropped on me, anyway.

Chapter Twelve

Six months ago I'd trotted into my mother's house with a cheerful hello, after a three-year absence in which I'd been presumed dead and had all my worldly possessions packed in boxes and moved into her garage. At the time, I'd wondered exactly how it was she could have given me a cheerful hug and gone back about her business as if I'd only made a five-minute trip to the Dunkin' Donuts in downtown Venice. What kind of effort had it taken to choke down all that emotion and rage, and how had she ever survived?

Well, it was my turn to find out. One of the things I discovered over the course of the following few days was that I was very much my mother's daughter. Instead of yelling or screaming or arranging any kinds of confrontations, I simply swallowed what I knew, let it burn in the pit of my stomach, and kept on with the day-to-day routine. If I were the kind of woman who was competent and organized, rather than competent and chaotic, and if I had kept my daily planner full for the four days that followed, it might have begun a little like this:

8 a.m.: *Wake early and exfoliate to rinse off crusty layer of sublimated fury.*

8:30 a.m.: *Endure breakfast of stale shredded wheat in Mom's kitchen instead of delicious breakfast in my own in order to escape having to endure alone time with the lying son-of-a-bitch . . . no,*

> *pardon me, the lying grandson-of-a-flippin'-*
> *QUEEN sharing my bed.*

9 a.m.:   *Plunge myself into work with my personal trainer*
            in order to take my mind off my own troubles.

Noon: *Break for lunch so I can feast on something*
            other than my own spleen.

Deceitful? Yes. Dishonest? Definitely. Was it worthy of all that I owed Cor, after everything we'd shared since we met? Not at all. I knew that bottling it all up and pretending nothing had happened was the spectacularly wrong thing to do, but if we all did the exact right thing at the exact right time, we wouldn't need Dr. Phil hanging around dispensing advice, would we?

My personal trainer gave me a slap on the wrist. Not metaphorically. I mean he actually reached out and whapped me. When I say my *personal trainer*, I didn't mean to imply that I'd hired someone to get myself into shape. No, after I'd thrown my little fit at Cor's improvisations, the week before, he'd called in an expert—someone to give me a crash course in what a centuries-old countess might be expected to know. The expert's name was Beecham—though I suspected he probably would prefer it spelled *Beauchamp*—and for one of the Kin, he was a mouthy son-of-a-gun. "Daydream on your own time," he commanded, then snapped his fingers to get my brain back into the present.

"I'm not daydreaming." I sighed, drew myself out of my tight ball of concentration and woe, and steeled myself for the hours ahead. This party was big. I couldn't afford to mess it up. "I'm just nervous."

From the front seat of the peach-colored convertible, Cor gave me a quick glance in the rear-view mirror. "You look beautiful," he said, his eyes smiling. "You'll be fine."

There I was, made up to the nines and wearing a dress by a designer whose name I couldn't even spell, much less pronounce, on my way to my first (and possibly last) Hollywood party. It's the kind of thing that most girls who grow up in L.A. dream about. Was I enjoying it, though? Not thanks to the hefty chunk of resentment clogging my chest like post-double-cheese-pizza phlegm. "Thanks," I said, my own glance sliding away before it could betray how I really felt. "I'll just be myself, all right?"

In the backseat beside me, Beecham jumped. "Oh by all my ancestors, don't do *that*."

"Gee, thanks," I growled.

"Oh my. Did that sound condescending? Hmmph. Well." Beecham gazed without concern from the window.

"All right. Here's a situation." Once again we were navigating down the streets of Bel Air in the 300L with Cor at the wheel. This time, however, I wasn't really noticing the manicured shrubberies or the immaculate sidewalks. The sense of doom I kept feeling in the very pit of my being wasn't going to be eased away by gazing at five-star landscaping or gold sundials. "You're talking to Dana Claire."

Beecham interrupted Cor with an enthusiastic, "Who, by the way, *Extra* announced today is in the running for the lead in the remake of the Jane Fonda camp classic, *Barbarella*!" When Ginger turned around from the front seat to stare at him, he shrugged. "I just thought it could be a conversation point. Pardon me for caring."

"You're talking to Dana Claire," Cor repeated, turning onto the street that would eventually end in a cul-de-sac at Marcus Grant's. "About *Barbarosa*." Beecham let out an unamused *whuff* from his nostrils. "And she says, 'Countess Samantha, tell us about your youth. Did you dance the sarabande with your husband on your wedding day?' What do you say?"

"Okay." Beecham leaned forward so that his seatbelt strained against his chest. "First of all? There are so many levels of wrong with that question. The sarabande? Is so 1583. And addressing someone as 'Countess'?"

"I'll be fine, boys," I said, to put an end to their back-and-forth.

"I'm just making sure." Again, in the mirror Cor gave me one of those smiles that was supposed to win me over. "I want you to feel comfortable."

"Beecham and I have been going over every detail of my backstory for the last four days." I looked at my watch, unable to tell if we were fashionably late for the four o'clock party, or whether we were just late-late. "I think I've got it down pat."

"And what are you going to say if someone asks why you went to high school with Jen?" Ginger wanted to know.

"I'm going to tell them that I was relocating to California and that I was doing research on the customs and patois of American youth."

Beecham added quickly, "Like Drew Barrymore in *Never Been Kissed.*"

Patois was a word I'd never used before Beecham. "It's still a stupid reason," I told him.

"But if you play the Barrymore card, it will dazzle and distract them." I raised my eyebrows, dubious. "The Barrymore card dazzles and distracts even the most unbedazzleable of souls," he assured me.

I hoped so. From what hints he'd let drop here and there, Beecham seemed to have a fascinating background. I knew that he'd been an official ambassador from the Kin to courts of both England and pre-Revolutionary France, which was what made him the perfect choice to give me the background necessary for this subterfuge. I hadn't even been aware that there had been periods of history in which the two races were officially in contact, but according to Beecham, in some distant centuries it had been fairly common. Not well-known, necessarily, but apparently he'd been in demand. These days, with the Kin laying low, the only court gossip he absorbed was from the dizzy heights of Tinseltown royalty.

Cor, however, was still concerned. "Okay," he said. "Let's say that someone comes up and asks you. . . ."

I cut him short. "Do you think I'm not capable of carrying this off?"

"No, not at all."

Aware that I sounded brusque, I added, "Because if you don't trust me to do it . . ."

"Samantha . . ."

". . . You should probably turn the car around right now."

Ginger shifted uncomfortably in her seat, smoothing her skirt and plucking imaginary lint from around its hem. Beecham cleared his throat, pulled down his jaw, and mouthed a single word: *drama*. "Why wouldn't I trust you to do your job?" Cor asked, genuinely baffled.

"Never mind." There I was, acting badly again, and I couldn't help myself. Why was it so much easier to grump and harrumph than to be honest with him? Partly it was because others were present, of course, but primarily I just couldn't stand having to face this particular issue when wishing it would simply go away seemed so much easier.

"What?" He was so absorbed in our conversation that he nearly rear-ended the Hummer parked at the security checkpoint outside Grant's gates. Luckily, at the last minute he jammed on the brakes and avoided concussing the pristine peach exterior of our ride. I could only begin to imagine the expense.

"Nothing!" I tried to make my response sound as bland and free of reproach as possible.

"If something's bothering you . . ."

The gates opened and the Hummer zoomed through. "Pull up," I told him, to get his attention off of me and anywhere else. With a sign, he tapped on the accelerator and nosed forward, but from the corner of my eye I could tell he was still shooting worried looks my way.

The acknowledgment Cor received over the intercom this time was much briefer and more welcome than the hassle we'd gone through on our last visit. Within moments we once more were wending our way through the grounds on the driveway and parking in the guest area next to the lime-green Hummer. The lot was over half-full already and looked like the showroom of a European luxury car importer, or maybe the prize shelf of a boy who put all his time and energy into making shiny model cars. Along with the big toys like the H3, we parked among an enormous Escalade with extra chrome trim on every corner, a Maserati, a couple of Mercedes-Benzes, and a Rolls Royce Phantom so shiny and pristine that it almost seemed never to have been touched by grubby human paws. Even the unflappable Ginger seemed impressed by the display of conspicuous consumption on parade. Or just maybe she'd been driving around the battered, older-model Storm Ravens van long enough that she'd gained a sudden appreciation for vehicles that boasted luxuries like intact upholstery and working brakes.

Our party was greeted by Jen, who came flying down from the house with a ruby-colored drink in her hand. If there were some kind of special Olympics event for cocktail-schlepping, she'd be a gold-medal finalist. Not a drop of the liquid spilled on her white blouse, despite the fact that she was coming at us down a fairly steep slope in high heels. Apparently the extra weight she was carrying with the baby hadn't yet convinced her to switch to flats. "Hi! Hi hi hi!" she yelled, ever the gracious hostess. "Oh, you can't believe how I've been waiting for today!"

Cor extended his arm. I didn't stop him from gathering my hand into the crook of his elbow. We were supposed to be a happy couple, after all. "As have we," he told her, bowing slightly.

"Aren't you continental!" she gushed. I couldn't tell whether she was talking about his black suit, tailored to accent his trim waistline and with which he was wearing an open-necked shirt of royal purple, or his manners. She turned to smile at Ginger in her dress recycled from the other morning, and then at Beecham, who had managed to out-dapper Cor in a chamois-colored shirt, brown suede slacks, and a sports jacket of the deepest emerald. "And you're . . . ?"

"Our nanny's date," Cor said at the same time as Ginger stammered out, "My plus-one."

"Charmed," Beecham announced. His posture was perfect as he reached out, took Jen's fluttering free hand in his, and drew it to his lips. On the back of her knuckles he planted a kiss. "You must be Miss Winfield. I've heard so much, and all of it extremely naughty." While Jen dissolved in a frisson of delighted giggles, Beecham continued pouring on the charm. "Don't you look delicious. If you were a sundae, I'd eat you up!"

Still tittering and giggling uncontrollably, Jen leaned over and whispered, "The gays always love me!" Then to Beecham she said, "You are going to fit *right in*! But guys, I wanted to get to you before anyone else, because there's some *very bad* stuff going down."

Cor and Ginger and I exchanged glances, suddenly all attention. It was up to me, in the role of best school chum, to ask the obvious question. "Something very bad like what? Is someone here who shouldn't be?"

"Huh?" Jen peered at me, then shook her head. "No, we have security for things like that, silly. Hello!" Automatically I reared back before she could plant a rap on my forehead. Given that her hand hadn't moved in my direction, I ended up looking pretty silly, but I tried to pass it off as if I'd been waving away a bug.

"Did someone get arrested?" Cor asked.

Ginger cocked her head. "Is someone dead?"

Beecham cupped his hand in front of his mouth. "Are we out of *amuses-bouche*?"

"What? Are you guys crazy or something? You sound like you're on *CSI*." She looked at Beecham. "*CSI: Project Runway*, maybe. No, it's worse than that. It's Patrick." When a fellow in a business suit climbed out of the Escalade, still talking on his cell phone as he headed up to the house, she dropped the volume and mouthed the last word. We all leaned in to listen, wondering what could be so terrible that she had to whisper. "You know about him?"

Well, we knew that he was selling my friend's womb for a hotel room next to the fountain of youth, and that didn't really recommend him any too highly to me. We all shook our heads. "Patrick McConnolly? What about him?" I asked.

"He's kind of a germanphobe," she explained.

"He dislikes Wagner and schnitzel?" I asked, wondering why she'd made a point of explaining his prejudices. We hadn't arrived in a Volkswagen.

"No, he's afraid of *germs*." She still spoke so softly that we had to filter her words over the music playing up at the house. "Like, totally freaked out by them."

"I read a rumor about that on TMZ!" Beecham said, excited to the point of prancing.

"So you have to follow some rules. Don't offer to get him a drink. Don't try to shake his hands. Don't hold out your hands like you're thinking about shaking his hands." She ticked off finger after finger as she spoke. "Don't try to hug him. Don't offer to get him a drink. Did I say that one already? Don't touch him on the shoulder." She ran out of fingers. "If he likes you, he might want to do an elbow bump with you. Like this." Jen raised up her hand with the fist curled, then held out her elbow so that she could knock it into mine. "But only do it twice, and use your right elbow only. When it comes to Dana, she'll shake hands, but when you're talking to her, don't bring up Harvey Graves."

"Her first husband," Beecham said, nodding and absorbing it all. "Technically her second husband, if you don't count the annulment she got from her high school sweetheart when she was seventeen. So they *say*."

"Maybe you shouldn't bring him up, either." Jen bit her lip. "Probably not. Oh, and there aren't any in the *hors d'oeuvres*, but never eat pork products in front of them."

"Oh my God," I murmured. Then to Jen, I added, "Is all this for real?"

She gave me a solemn nod. "I wanted to make sure you knew about the germs because one of the Lakers tried to high-five Patrick a while ago and it kind of got ugly. He was in the bathroom for twenty-five minutes and went through an entire stack of towels. And then we ran out of alcohol for him." When Beecham opened his mouth to ask a question, she anticipated it. "Rubbing alcohol." He nodded sagely, understanding. "But now that he's clean again, he's really a nice guy!"

"Wow," I finally said, clearing my throat. "Sounds like it!"

She smiled at me brightly, as if happy that I understood, and told us to follow her up to the house. It took a lot of effort, though, to gather enough air to clear my head. I felt so nervous—and thanks to Jen's latest round of warnings, so frightened of doing anything wrong—that I seemed to have lost the ability to expand my lungs to full capacity. Cor must have sensed my unease, because he patted the hand he already carried in the crook of his arm. I should have responded with a squeeze, or at least had the decency to acknowledge his kindly gesture. By the time the pat filtered through all my confusion and feelings, however, and once it had percolated and stewed in my resentment until I'd digested it and realized there was a correct response I wasn't returning, long moments had passed and we'd almost reached the house. Even if I'd thanked him for his silent support as an empty gesture, it would have seemed oddly late in coming. Simpler, probably, to let it pass.

The doors through which we entered the house weren't the official front entryway, I could tell; that would have been at the end of the other branch of the driveway, in the older and more traditional part of the estate. The space just beyond our entrance, though piss-elegant in its smooth black surfaces and cream-colored textiles, was too casual to be a formal living room. Some howling emo male artist wailed away over invisible speakers in the background. Despite the fact it was still seventy degrees outside, gas flames burned in the fireplace. Their light danced on the polished black wood floor that extended to a darker room just beyond. "Everybody's mostly around the pool," Jen said. "Isn't this exciting?"

"Yuh-huh!" I said, still scanning the room. All of us were. I could see Ginger and Cor both swiveling their heads and taking in every detail that might be important in the future. They had decades of experience in hunting out transgressions involving the Kin in our world. Me? Not so much. Despite my years of working in insurance fraud, I felt more like a casual spectator gawking at the sheer expense of it all while being led through the back half of the house. Like Beecham, who was obviously toting up the cost of every stick of designer furniture and square inch of imported beech until the dollar signs registered in his eyes. "Real silk damask," he whispered to me, fingering a pillow as we passed.

Several of the catering staff occupied the huge kitchen, bustling around as they prepared trays of canapés. Two industrial-grade stoves occupied the far end of the room, both covered by an enormous hood overlaid in a mosaic of unpolished marble. The cabinets had been carved with vines and grape clusters from old wood, wormholes and all, while the floor here was the same highly polished dark surface as the other rooms in this wing of the house. The overall impression was that we'd wandered into an old world monastery—that just happened to have the latest in dark steel appliances and twin Sub-Zero refrigerators. "Drink?" Jen ran to the closer of the coolers, opened the door, and pulled out one of her patented blender containers full of slush. This particular mix was snail green. "There's a full bar down at the pool, but I've been making my special alcohol-free cocktails up here. This is, um, watermelon-wheatgrass."

"Down by the pool, you say?" Beecham had turned nearly

as green as the slushie, but Ginger caught his arm and glared when he tried to make a beeline from the room.

"I think we'll probably have real drinks, so you don't have to make more," I told her, trying to remain diplomatic.

"Okay! Why don't we just go down . . . Oh, Marc!"

I followed the track of Jen's broad beam. Grant had stepped from the patio outside into the kitchen, wine glass in one hand. "Why, hello, friends!" His eyes were as hard and dark as the floors of his house. I didn't like the way they glittered as he looked us over. "I'm so glad you could make it."

Cor stuck out his hand. "Wouldn't have missed it for the world," he said in his strongest voice.

"Good. And Samantha, baby!" Grant turned his attention to me. Now that I was experiencing those obsidian eyes dancing over every inch of my body, I regretted my jealousy over being left out of the conversation the last time we'd been here. I would have done almost anything at that point to get away from his direct regard. "Samantha, Samantha," he breathed. Before I knew what was happening, he took my right hand by the outermost finger joints, lifted up my arm, and twirled me slightly in place. "Don't you look fantastic. A true classic. A well-preserved classic, eh?"

I gulped at his wink, which seemed to imply all kinds of conspiracy. "You're very kind," I managed to stammer out.

He pinched my fingers for a moment longer while Jen, in the background, poured out more of her slush. "Very nice," he said, finally letting go. Even with my freedom, I still felt like a small bird encircled by a hungry snake. "And I see you've brought quite the entourage."

There was no mistaking his intent. He knew that Ginger and Beecham were of the Kin as well. Cor, trying to make amends, started issuing a polite apology. "We thought the invitation included . . ."

"Is there a problem?" I asked, not caring if a touch of irritation showed. I was, after all, supposed to be a countess, and one who had wrangled her way to near-immortality.

He seemed to respect my question and the arrogance it implied. "Not at all," he said. "The more the merrier, in fact." Grant rubbed his hands together. They were stubby and pale as lard. "Why don't we move the party down to the pool area?" he suggested. "There are lots of people looking forward to meeting you both."

The patio split off into two walkways, one down to the property's back edge and the poolside, and another leading in the direction of what had to be a garage, though it had more doors than any suburban garage I'd ever seen. Both of the paths had been paved with blocks of the same reddish granite as the area where we'd parked; the outlines of stars surrounding gold-lettered names had been similarly set into the stone. Growths of low-lying plants with fan-shaped leaves brushed our ankles as we followed Grant down to the party. From above, I could see a chef in a white hat working the grill in the massive outdoor kitchen; the scents of spiced kababs wafted to my nostrils on the light breeze.

A few members of the waitstaff moved unobtrusively around the pool's edge, but my eyes glided over them and to the clusters of guests they visited. It wasn't at all difficult to pick out the familiar faces among the two dozen there. I recognized one young woman as the photogenic tennis player who had gone so far at Wimbledon only the summer before. One of the men slouched against the large pool house doorway looked familiar. It took me a few steps before I remembered he was that guy who started out as the computer analyst in the fast-paced TV thriller series, then almost immediately left it for a movie career that never seemed to get into gear. Without having to think too much, I recognized a middle-aged woman who'd been a hot commodity in the mid-nineties when she'd been in an ensemble comedy, a television journalist, and a long-haired young woman who I thought was one of those sensitive singer-songwriter types.

Grant hadn't been kidding about the guests being happy to see us, either. When our party began trooping down the

hillside, trailing the bald-headed agent, all eyes turned to in-
spect us. I didn't think that Grant had been crass or stupid
enough to make a mass announcement in advance about
who we were or what he thought we could do for them, but
his clients definitely took notice when we descended. The
slouching actor straightened up and stared at the four of us
over the top of his stiff drink; the singer-songwriter and the
tennis player both paused in their conversation to give me
the once-over. There were two people in particular, however, whose attention seemed to rivet upon us. I noticed
them right off and tried not to gawk, but it was pretty impossible not to. With Dana Claire and Patrick McConnolly
staring at you, expectant and almost pale with anticipation,
how could anyone look elsewhere? I wasn't the only one
feeling giddy from being noticed, either. From behind me,
very softly, I heard Beecham breathe in a soft, "Oh my!"
followed quickly with, "Aren't they *short*!"

Cor put his hand on the small of my back. I couldn't stand
it, though. I knew he meant it kindly, but even if I'd been in
the best of moods toward him, I would still have broken away
from his touch. It made me itchy and irritable—more so
knowing that we were both under scrutiny. I shot him a
quick smile and turned to wait for Jen to catch up with our
group. Anything to postpone actually having to hit the
ground and begin the mingling. "Are you okay?" I called out
to her. She was walking strangely. So strangely, in fact, that I
was a little worried for her. "Are you having cramps?"

"Oh no," she called out. A bright smile crossed her lips as
she took a careful step down one of the stairs. "I just walk to
the side." That was what was so strange about her gait, I realized. Instead of merely clomping down the path like the rest
of us, Jen had been walking on the very edge of the granite
pavers, avoiding their middles and at the same time trying to
keep her heels out of the spongy garden ground. She must
have seen me blinking, because immediately she explained, "I
don't like putting my feet on the stars."

"Why? Because it feels like walking on graves?"

She shook her head. "I know it's crazy, but it's the same thing on the Hollywood Walk of Fame. Like, only in Hollywood do they go to the trouble to lay the stars down at people's feet. And what do we do? Step all over them." Her nose wrinkled. "Sorry. I know. Crazy, right?"

"Don't apologize. It's not crazy." On impulse, I reached out and grabbed her hand at that moment. Jen might have been an airhead and a candidate for gestational diabetes, but her confession had earned from me a moment of genuine affection. It buoyed me just enough to catch up with Marcus Grant and the Kin. "Where's Bo?" I murmured to her, looking around for the kind of older gentleman I expected her to have landed—gray-haired, distinguished, and with a bulging wallet.

"Probably in my place, watching television," she said, letting go of my hand. "He doesn't like crowds."

I wasn't prepared for what followed. Barely had my feet hit the brick at the bottom of the steps than Grant had clapped together his hands to gather everyone's attention. "Everybody," he announced. "I hope you'll join me in welcoming two new friends of mine. I'm sure in no time they'll be friends of yours as well." The speech sounded rehearsed, but none of the other guests seemed to care. While I tried to keep my cool and not flush with embarrassment at having Patrick McConnolly inspecting me at fairly close range, the assembly began to smile at each other and nod appreciatively over their wineglasses. "So please join me in welcoming Mr. Cory Donais and the lady Samantha."

A few of the guests began to pat their hands together, but the sound was immediately drowned out by an immense crash on the far side of the pool. I saw a flash of black-and-white as one of the waitstaff, a woman with her hair pulled back in a severe ponytail, dove after the tray of wine glasses she had dropped. I winced at the speed with which she disappeared behind a table—it couldn't have been safe, with all that broken glass. But scarcely had everyone gotten over the shock of the commotion when some of her coworkers began running toward her with towels and a dust pan. Just as quickly as it had happened, though, the incident was forgotten as people's manners overtook their shock, and I found myself once again basking in unwanted attention and light applause.

"Isn't that funny?" Jen leaned in and let me have a blast of her watermelon-scented breath. "He forgot your last name."

So at least she was out of the loop. I felt better knowing that. I didn't have much of a chance to reply, though, because two big, enormous celebrities had abandoned the couple they'd been talking to and were heading in our direction. And by "big" and "enormous," I really mean "eentsy" and "weentsy." Because as Beecham had callously pointed out higher on the steps, they really were tiny little people. Patrick McConnolly was almost an entire head shorter than I—he couldn't have been more than five-foot-six—and Dana Claire was a good three inches shorter than he. They were little Munchkin people, mini-celebrities whom I could have put in my glove compartment, taken home, and kept on my bedside table for luck.

"The lady Samantha." Patrick McConnolly approached me, staggering forward with a posture of exaggerated masculinity—hands on his waist, hips jutting out, nodding as if we'd met before. "The famous lady Samantha."

I saw Cor give me a look of concern from several feet away. I nodded to let him know I was all right. "Jen," I said, trying not to sound nervous, "you know, I think I'll take you up on that offer of one of your watermelon-wheatgrass specials."

"Oh!" she said. "All right!"

Yes, I was making the pregnant woman trot up the sides of the pavers back to the house in her heels. Call me a sadist if you must, but I wanted to get her as far away as possible from these two. I already knew they were toxic . . . or at least desperate, and in my experience, desperation drove people to do some pretty shady things. "Mr. McConnolly," I said pleasantly, once she'd trotted off. All the instructions Jen had given us earlier flew out of my head. I remembered I wasn't supposed to shake hands. But what if he interpreted one of my random motions to mean I was going to lunge at him with a germy paw outspread? I was afraid to move a muscle.

"Just call me Patrick." He managed to get all his teeth exposed in one leer. Up close, he was as handsome as he appeared on the screen. Just a lot smaller. My wee little pocket celebs.

"And Dana." Dana Claire's hair was four shades lighter than I remembered from her last movie, but it was still the same face that had launched a thousand CGI ships in *Heartbreaker of Troy*. I'd never imagined her smelling of cigarettes, though. That was a twist. She held out her hand, making me hesitate. Safe or not? I couldn't remember. At long last, and hoping I wouldn't send Patrick running to the bathroom shrieking from my cooties, I tentatively let her pump my hand up and down. "Don't you look *marvelous*."

While we'd been making introductions, Cor had allowed himself to be led off by Grant, who had an arm around his back while they strolled and talked, with Ginger following. He looked over his shoulder at me to make certain I was all right. Beecham, in the meantime, had sidled over. That was fine; he was there as my backup, in case I became stumped by some Georgian teaser. Before I knew what he was doing, he took a swipe at my skirt, wiping some kind of schmutz from the back and fluffing it out a bit. "This is Beecham," I said, feeling some kind of explanation was necessarily. "He's my . . . er, stylist."

"You're one of them," said Patrick, looking him square in the eye.

"One of the Fair Ones," Dana marveled. She reached out

and let two of her fingers touch the back of Beecham's hand. "You're real." Beecham and I exchanged astonished looks before she burst into laughter. "You must think I'm crazy."

"Not at all." Beecham looked pleased to have been touched by one of the *Us Weekly* crowd. He nodded at Patrick. "*He's* the one I think is crazy." Then, because we were all staring at him with utter horror for having said such a thing, he let out a cackle. "Crazy to let you out of the house, you're so gorgeous!"

Dana, who was wearing a lightweight dress that came dangerously close to being little more than a camisole, put a hand to her nearly naked chest. "Aren't you charming!" she exclaimed.

Even Patrick, whose eyes had been bulging with outrage at the near slight, had recovered and was letting loose with a loud and manly laugh. It was while he had his head reared back and his mouth wide open that I noticed his hair didn't move in the slightest. It seemed almost as plastic as his teeth. "Beecham, eh?" His hands remained firmly plunged into the depths of his pockets as he leaned forward, butted Beecham with his shoulder, turned his head and said, "I bet you were one of the Fair Ones who got her out?"

"Marc told us about you," Dana said to me in an exaggerated whisper. "Under the greatest confidence, of course."

"How you're not of this century, shall we say." Patrick leaned in again.

"Yes," I said automatically, rearing back in case Patrick and I made accidental contact. "I was born on October second in the year of our Lord 1792 in the county of Kent. At the tender age of fourteen . . ."

"I don't think Mr. McConnolly . . . *Patrick* . . . needs to know the boring details right now, my lady." Beecham gave me a quick pinch to bring me out of the trance of my rehearsed history.

"Oh!" I gulped. They were both watching me with some

kind of expectation. "So. Why is it you call him a Fair One?"

"Because that's what they prefer to be called. Isn't it?" Dana seemed confused for a moment.

She appealed to her husband, who nodded. "We have been told that it is the form of address they prefer." When I looked at Beecham, it seemed like news to him. "Fair Ones, or Blessed Ones. What do you call them?"

"Servants," I said, a note of finality in my voice. I let out a little bark of laughter to lighten the impact of that sentence, but by that point, Beecham had already bowed in my direction. I was beginning to like playing the countess. She was ballsy and decisive where I wasn't. She didn't mind being a little bit arrogant. Samantha might be too wimpy to lay it all out on the table, but the countess? She didn't care. I flagged down one of the waitstaff, grabbed a flute of wine from his tray, and took a deep drink.

"So I see." Patrick's eyes had lit up at that one word. What I knew about celebrities—what I really knew, as opposed to what had been fed to me by the paparazzi and infotainment magazines—could fit on the head of a pin, but I had guessed at two things: that they were so used to projecting multiple personas that they might not notice, or care, that I was acting with mine, and that they might appreciate someone who had stepped on a lot of people to get where they were.

"If that's what a Fair One servant looks like . . ." Claire had turned her attention to Cor, his palm splayed out as he leaned against a tree at the patio's edge. "I wouldn't mind at all."

"Down, girl," Patrick breathed through gritted teeth that he'd formed to resemble a smile.

The stare I bestowed upon her at that point was cold, but it was more my own than anything coming from my fictional countess. Cor might have made me angry that week, but I was still in love with his lying face. "That one," I announced, any trace of good humor absent, "is mine." Over her ineffectual protests that she hadn't meant anything, I continued, "But there is a reason they call them the Fair Ones. Dispose of this, would you?" I asked, handing off my empty wine glass to Beecham.

The power couple watched him bow slightly, then turn to deposit the flute on a nearby table. I noticed that the Wimbledon champ had moved slightly closer to our group and had almost breached the outer barrier that socially kept her from breaking in. Patrick nodded at his wife, who grabbed my arm and began walking me away. Beecham had to take quick little steps to catch up. "The thing is," Patrick said, walking beside me with his hand clenched behind his back, presumably to keep them from touching anything, "you look absolutely sensational."

"Incredible," Dana assured me, clinging to my arm like I imagined a limpet would, if I only knew what a limpet was.

"Stunning, in fact." I knew that they spoke not really of my looks, which weren't really all that, but of my alleged state of well-preservedness. I didn't let the compliments go to my head. Instead, I gave them both a satisfied smile that I hoped conveyed the message of, *Yes, I know.* "I mean, I don't know my math, but you've got to be what? A hundred and fifty? A hundred and seventy-five?"

"Mr. McConnolly—Patrick—I was born in 1792. That would put me closer to two hundred and twenty, actually." I snapped my fingers and pointed at a passing tray of prosciutto-wrapped white asparagus spears. Beecham, after shooting me an annoyed look, stopped to gather a few for me.

"Well, if you don't mind me saying so, my lady," he said, drawing himself upright as our group glided to a stop at the pool's far end, "you don't look any older than thirty-two."

"Twenty-*nine*," I automatically snapped.

I must have sounded as brittle as the last traces of shattered glass the catering staff were still busy sweeping up nearby. The ponytailed woman I'd seen dive for the ground earlier appeared to be unharmed. At our approach, the several black-and-white uniformed staff finished their task and, probably warned about Patrick's quirks, moved back several feet. "Amazing. Just amazing. And you don't find the land of the Fair Ones . . . boring?"

"Not since we had cable installed." I laughed lightly to let them know they could enjoy my little joke as well. Beecham rolled his eyes behind their backs. "*Restful* is the term I would use." Not that I'd gotten a single night's rest since I'd gotten mixed up with the Kin. The last relaxing time I'd enjoyed had been—well, the night Cor had lavished me with touch and made me hallucinate forests. I'd never felt closer to him than that night, and now I felt a distance between us. Admittedly, he was only a swimming pool away, but somehow it felt like the Atlantic.

"And not to be crass," said Patrick, tipping me off that he was about to be just that. "How much?"

When I blinked, Dana interpreted my surprise as affront. "He didn't mean to pry," she assured me. "It's just that we were curious, is all."

"Naturally." I tried to buy a little time by nibbling on an asparagus canapé. "To enter the land of the Fair Ones, it cost me a king's ransom." I finished off the spear and swallowed, then brushed off my hands and smiled. "Luckily, the king paid up." We all shared a delicious little laugh over my bon mot, though I don't think either of the stars quite understood it. Once our amusement had died down a little, I asked a question of my own. "It was my impression, from Marc naturally, that you'd already . . . made arrangements?"

The pair exchanged glances, as if checking with each other before divulging anything. "We have," said Dana. "But . . ."

"It's like this, if I can be frank." When Patrick lowered his voice so that the waitstaff nearby couldn't overhear, both Beecham and I leaned in. "We had. Made arrangements, that is."

"And your questions weren't answered then?"

"Well." Dana looked to Patrick for permission to continue. He nodded. "Our Fair One had an *unusual* request."

"A baby." Patrick nodded back at the direction of the house. When I glanced around, I saw Jen walking down the pavers again, this time carrying two glasses.

"A surrogate mother."

Were these two developing an actual conscience? I had to know. "And you don't feel right about that?"

Patrick laughed and gave his wife what I guessed was an affectionate and sanitary dab with his elbow. "Don't get me wrong. I don't give a damn. But Dana. . . ."

She shook her head, silencing him. "Don't." I almost felt sorry for her.

"What? We're not getting any younger, hon." He shook his head at me. "It's just that we've got months and months more to wait, and neither of us have seen our Fair One in a dog's age."

"And we thought that you and your Fair Ones might be able to get us in faster if we simply paid." The thimbleful of sympathy I'd begun to collect for Dana quickly disappeared. Her eyes were hard and glinting now. "And that way, I could keep the baby for myself." Patrick nodded and rubbed his elbows in a circular motion on Dana's shoulder. "Angelina does it."

"Here we go!" Jen was nearby and closing in fast. "I don't remember which one is mine and which is yours, though. Probably this one's yours," she said, handing me one of the dark green concoctions. "It's less melted."

While I accepted the margarita glass and tried not to spill its contents, the star couple smiled at Jen. "How are you doing, sweetheart?" Patrick asked.

"You look fantastic," said Dana, letting her light hair bounce as she nodded vigorously. "Glowing."

"Oh thanks, you guys!" Jen winked at me. "See, what did I tell you? They're so nice, aren't they?"

"So nice," I said, feeling a little unsettled. "Beecham. Do you mind . . . ?" Concerned, he moved forward to take my arm.

"Are you okay?" Dana wanted to know. Jen grabbed my other arm as if I were about to faint.

"No, I'm fine, really. It's just . . . the chlorine smell."

Dana wrinkled her nose as if someone had planted a cow patty at her feet. "Oh, I know. Awful."

"Maybe if I could have a moment?" I suggested to them. I just needed to clear my head of all the ugliness.

Both of them murmured sympathies. Dana patted me on the back. Patrick even went so far as to give me an elbow to the ribs. "We'll be right over there. Just let me know, if you get a chance to . . ." He looked at Beecham with meaning. "Talk."

"Absolutely," I assured him. I waited until they'd gone before I spoke again. "It's just so *ugly*," I told Beecham.

"You're doing spectacularly," he assured me. "Just keep it up. They're not even asking for details. All that training gone to waste!"

I knew he was keeping his words vague because Jen was still standing there, drinking her slush through a straw and listening to every word we said without any comprehension at all. I hated to send her on another wild-goose chase, but I needed some privacy so that I could talk to Cor or at least Ginger about what the star couple had just told me. "Jen, I know you were just up at the house," I began to say, "but . . ."

I got no further with my request. Now that Patrick and Dana had retired to admire each other over a shared kebab, one of the catering staff approached. It was the woman with the jet-black hair pulled back into a ponytail, and she carried a broom and a dustpan set at the end of a pole. For a moment I thought she was going to offer to take away the extra canapé I'd been carrying for five minutes. She stared me straight in the face and asked, "Samantha Dorringer?"

"Yes?" It took me a moment to notice that Beecham had

stepped back from the woman. Only then did it occur to me: how did this woman know my name?

But by then it was too late. The dark-featured stranger with the deep sapphire eyes had opened her mouth to let out a scream that seemed to slice through my consciousness. I know that I clapped my hands to either side of my head at the sound of it, my ears deafened to the clatter of her broom and dustpan hitting the ground. With a bound, she leapt into the air and took to the sky on black wings, her scream transformed into the raucous cry of a crow. Something sharp brushed my forehead, forcing me to close my eyes and stagger back.

I'd seen the expression on her face before her metamorphosis, though. She had been possessed with sheer and utter hatred. The realization left me quaking in my heels.

Chapter Thirteen

"What in hell!"

Marcus Grant's outraged shout made me whirl in place. I still couldn't open my eyes. When I tried, it stung. "Sweetie," I heard Beecham say. A hand gripped my shoulder, keeping me in place. "You're bleeding. Stay still."

"Bleeding?" I asked. My voice sounded as if it were coming from a distance. "Why am I bleeding?"

"What *was* that?" Jen's voice was distinct enough. She sounded distant as well, and in shock.

"Honey, can you get some ice? Clean ice? Your friend is hurt," Beecham said, trying to rouse her into action. "And a towel or something."

"Yeah. Okay," she replied. "But what *was* that thing?"

"Oh my God, that bird *attacked* you." That was Dana Claire, from not too far away.

"How badly is she hurt?" Grant was at closer range now. "Let me see."

"I've got her." Beecham shifted me around, probably to keep me out of Grant's clutches.

Difficult as it was in the rising tide of panicked voices, I tried to make myself heard. "I'm okay," I assured everyone. "I'm fine. Don't crowd."

"Samantha?" It was Cor's voice. For the moment, every slight I'd imagined against him flew out the window. My hand reached out blindly, searching for him. I felt his fingers thread through mine. "What happened?"

His concern brought me back to the earth. Beecham had found a cloth somewhere and wiped away the blood trickling down my brow. I blinked a few times and found I could open my eyes again. "Crow," I gasped out, once I saw Cor's beautiful face. "Order of the Crow. One of Mrs. Jones's agents. She knew who I was."

"Pardon me." Ginger, purse awkwardly dangling from her wrist, pushed her way through the crowd, like a fish struggling upstream. I knew she was trying to find someplace isolated where she could shift.

"Are you sure?" Cor was asking.

"Yes. Just . . . find her! She's got to be heading back to Mrs. Jones." He knew as well as I that the entire delicate balance of this subterfuge could come crashing down around us with just one word from the mysterious Agnes Jones. Of course, if the Ravens managed to locate and take her before she got back to Grant, we wouldn't have to keep up this charade at all.

"Don't leave her alone," Cor said to Beecham. "Don't you dare leave her."

"Where would I go?" the Peri asked, plaintive as he examined my cleaned wound. "It's only a scratch. Go do your thing."

"Go!" I urged Cor, before the trail got too cold. He nodded, giving me one last look of concern, and then dashed off, like Clark Kent in search of a phone booth. A few moments later, I saw two ravens shoot from behind the pool house into the air. They circled the compound, crying loudly to each other, until one of them spotted something on the horizon. It was a good thing I didn't blink, or else I would have missed the pair encircling each other rapidly as they propelled themselves away from the compound. In response to their wake, the trees shifted, their branches seeming to whisper uneasily to each other of the storm to come.

"How bad is it?" Marcus Grant had leaned over. Both his hands rested on his thighs as he tried to peer at my forehead. "Do we need to call a goddamned paramedic?"

"Sam?" said Jen.

"It's not deep," Beecham assured him. "She doesn't need a paramedic." I didn't know what Peri magic Beecham had been working with his fingers, but the horizontal stripe of pain where the crow had scratched me with its talons had all but vanished. I felt a slight sting on my skin when I reached up to touch the scrape. Beecham slapped my fingers away.

"Sammy?" Jen bounced on her toes.

"Did you provoke it?" Grant asked. "Did anyone see? Did she provoke the bird? Because if you're thinking about suing, and you provoked the bird . . ."

"Jesus, Marc." The last person I expected to be sticking up for me, when it came to the question of bird-baiting, would have been Patrick McConnolly, but there he was, shaking a naked hand in his agent's direction. Maybe I could Netflix *Ghost of a Chance* without shame, now. "Why in the hell would she provoke a bird? Do you know how many parasites they carry?" He and Grant started to argue, leaving the rest of the crowd to drift back to their drinks now that the excitement was over.

"*Sam!*" At the sound of Jen's shrilling, I turned. "I have to talk to you," she said in a normal voice.

"Can't it wait?" I pleaded as Beecham gave one final dab to my forehead. "I kind of just got Tippi Hedrened here."

"Hello!" she almost screeched in her old high-school voice. I swore by all that was holy and not, if she rapped me on my still-sore forehead, I was gonna deck the wench. She wasn't so inconsiderate, though. Instead, she leaned in close and opened her eyes so wide that I thought they might pop out of their sockets. She took a deep breath and spoke as quickly as possible. "Fine. So no one else saw what I saw, or else they don't want to say in case someone else thinks they're crazy, but I don't care and besides, I am totally freaking out and I know you saw it too so if you don't agree with me and say that you saw one of the help turn into a big bird and fly in your face before she disappeared I am going to start screaming and I'm not sure I'll be able to stop." Finally she ran out of air.

"Jen." Beecham had overheard her speech as well, but when we looked around, it was obvious no one else had. Grant and Patrick were still arguing away, while Dana Claire stood by herself beneath the cabana overhang, her arms shaking as she lit a cigarette. As far as the rest of the guests, save for the occasional nervous smiles people continued to cast my way, one might have thought that absolutely nothing had happened. "First of all, calm down."

"Did you see it? Did you see a lady turn into a bird?" she demanded.

We were getting perilously close to the screaming part, I could tell. Beecham and I exchanged a quick glance. He nodded. "Yes," I said. "A lady turned into a bird."

"I'm thinking she wasn't much of a lady, with a temper like that," Beecham sniffed.

"Jen, I'm going to need you to trust me on this one, okay?" I grabbed my friend's hands and shook them. "Look at me," I demanded, when her eyes drifted to my forehead.

"Your cut is almost gone."

"Jen, honey, you're going to have to trust me about this, all right?" I felt as if I was talking to a child. "Something very freaky just happened, yes. It wasn't your eyes or your mind playing tricks on you. But for right now, I'm going to have to ask you to trust me and not ask any questions just yet. Do you hear me?" She nodded, eyes still wide and her mouth shaped in a little o. "Cor is going to find that bird-woman, and she's not going to bother you or anyone else again. All right?"

"Is it like *The X-Files?*"

There was such a note of hope in her voice that I thought there couldn't be anything but good in helping her sort out the weirdness by comparing it to a television program. "Yes. It's like *The X-Files*."

"That show used to scare the pooper-doo out of me!" she whimpered, burying her face in her hands.

"It's like a totally unscary version of *The X-Files* and absolutely doesn't have any alien abductions or liver-eating killers in it," I hastily amended. "So can you be Scully for me? Brave, unflappable Scully?"

Thankfully, she pulled herself together and nodded. The tears that had been pooling at the edges of her hysteria receded; she sniffed and took a deep breath. "I can do that. I always kind of liked her hair color."

"Atta girl!" I said. "Don't say anything about it to Dana or Patrick, and definitely, definitely don't say anything about it to Marc. I know he's been very good to you and everything, but this is important. Okay?" She nodded. "You trust me? We're friends, right?"

"I trust you."

Good. At least we had that established. Maybe I should have thrown an extra warning about Marc into the mix, but we were probably already tightrope-walking the edge of reason with the crow-ladies, here. Besides, the agent was striding back over, considerably calmer. "You know, Samantha . . . Lady Samantha . . . I probably shouldn't have lost my temper a minute ago. Heat of the moment and all that. You've got no reason to sue, right? Right. I mean, look at you. It doesn't even look like you got much of a scrape, huh? Right?" I raised my hand to my face again and brought it away covered with mere flecks of dried blood. He took a stiff drink from the glass in his hand. "That's a sign of good living, right there. That's a sign of good, *clean* living. The kind of life I want for my talent. At any price. Am I right?"

"Jesus, Marc." Patrick McConnolly finished up his glass of red wine and immediately wrapped his napkin around the stem of another so he could pick it up and swill it down. "Try to have a little more subtlety."

They wanted to eat me up, all of them. That was the way they were looking at me, anyway: starved, as if I had the one meal that would satisfy their hunger for the rest of their lives. Or as if I *was* that one meal. The would-bes and the has-beens and the definitely-ares alike, all of them so anxious to prolong their lives. Desperate. The waves of need were so overwhelming that for a moment it was tough for me to think of what to say to reassure them all, particularly when I was the one who needed heartening. It was my lover who was out there risking life and wing to chase a mortal enemy. "Maybe I could freshen up," I suggested, to keep everything light and prevent Jen from getting any more upset.

Although she was considerably calmer, Jen still clutched onto her margarita glass like she would have a lifebuoy after a shipwreck. "You can use my apartment," she suggested. "I kind of need to sit down anyway."

"Great idea. Great idea. You ladies go make yourself pretty." Grant laid his stubby hands on both our shoulders and began to steer us toward the smaller pool house. Beecham solemnly trudged behind, obviously considering himself one of the girls. "Come back, and I'll introduce you to some other folk. All right? All right." With that settled, he turned back to his gathering, determined to make it work. "Josh! How the hell are ya!"

I was just grateful to get away for a few moments, so I wouldn't have to maintain a party face while worrying about Cor. And Ginger too, of course. Oh, they'd been on countless missions before and managed to emerge unscathed without the benefit of my hand-wringing. That didn't stop me from fretting. Besides, I hadn't been in Jen's apartment yet and was kind of interested to see what kind living space she'd snagged for renting out her womb.

My notion that seeing the smaller pool house might temporarily distract me from wondering about Cor was right on the money. "Holy crap," were my first words on entering the place. "Small" pool house, my Aunt Fanny. The thing was freakin' huge. It was like that British show *Doctor Who*, where the guy traveled around in a tiny police box that opened up and turned out to be way bigger on the inside than without. It was pretty much a one-room apartment with different corners devoted to the bed and a living room space and a kitchenette, all decorated with oversized comfy furniture of the sort that IKEA wished it could be. Although I spied a carton of Whoppers and an open bag of Red Vines on the coffee table, I couldn't tell that Jen had adulterated the tasteful interior decorating with her own, well, execrable tastes.

"The bathroom's right in there," she said, leading the way across the deep and fluffy rug that had crawled like an oversized cat into the room's center and laid down for a nap. She entered before us and flipped on a light. "Sam?" she asked, before leaving me to it. "When *do* I get to ask questions?"

I couldn't help myself. She deserved it. I reached out and gave the woman a hug. "Soon," I promised in her ear. "Just trust me, okay? We won't be a minute." She nodded and gave me a quick squeeze back, then wandered over to the wet bar near the front door, where she scooped up a handful of pillow mints and began to go to town. I jerked my head at Beecham, telling him to get into the room with me. Once he'd squeezed beyond the mirrored sink and planted his back against a wall hanging that seemed to consist mostly of hot-glued Pacific beach shells, I shut the door behind us. "She is seriously going to freak out on us."

"Something's going to have to be done about her," Beecham agreed. "You might have been Hitchcocked by the bird, but she's going to go all Janet Leigh in *Psycho* before too long."

"What will they do?"

He shrugged. "I'm not one of your Storm Ravens, sweetheart," he said. "Ask them."

"Don't you represent the court? The Copper Crown?" I asked, using its proper name.

"I've been in the service of the Crown for centuries," he agreed. "But the domain of the Storm Ravens and that of the Copper Crown's ambassadors rarely intersect." He'd abandoned his light tone for one that carried more gravity. I knew he was speaking of a subject close to his heart and his life's work. "Besides, our parties are better. Not as good as this one. Well, we don't usually have ours ruined by enemies of the queen, but we don't get the A-list celebs, either. So maybe it's a tossup."

I'd been examining myself in the mirror while he'd been talking. Beecham had managed to take care of most of the blood, for which I was thankful, and none of it had gotten onto my dress, which was a further blessing. Again, I didn't know what he'd done to my wound, but already it was healing and appeared to be little more than a slightly throbbing pinkness intersecting the middle of my brow. By the morning, it probably would vanish altogether. "I'm sorry they dragged you into this," I said to him. "I didn't need any of that background you spent so much time researching. All they needed to see was my Noxzema complexion and they were willing to buy whatever snake oil I was selling."

"Are you kidding?" he said, pushing me out of the way so he could have mirror space. "I'll be dining out on this story for years. I should be hanging out with you guys more often."

"At your own peril," I said. I was done primping, and my head was clear once more. "Jen?" I called as I opened the bathroom door. "Let's have a little talk now, before we go back outside." I didn't receive an answer. "Jen?"

After a second I realized my friend was sitting on the living room sofa. I hadn't noticed her, however, because she was sitting so quietly and motionlessly that she seemed almost to be one with the furniture. A woman stepped out of the shadows, her slim figure draped from top to bottom in black fabric. The woman pulled away the loose cowl covering her head, and a familiar face emerged from the depths of darkness.

"Why, Samantha," she said in a voice as frozen as the deep blue core of a glacier. "What a pleasure."

"Mrs. Jones," I breathed. Every hair on my body seemed to be standing on end. Something about the woman radiated danger.

"Holy Rula Lenska," I heard from behind me. "What is that?"

"Keep away from her," I warned Beecham. I extended my arms behind me to shield him. Together, our backs to the wall, we began inching along the room's perimeter. "Nice outfit," I snarled at the woman. I'd never seen the Peri I knew as Agnes Jones without some kind of costume. She was as much an actor as anyone at Marcus Grant's party; the first time we'd met inside of the construct in which I'd been imprisoned, she'd assumed the guise of my mother-in-law, prim and proper and reeking of old money. The next time we'd met, she'd been the lady of the manor, very British and stiff-upper-lipped. "I just hope you and the Grim Reaper never walk the red carpet together."

"Embarrassing!" whispered Beecham in agreement. His voice trembled, though. I could tell he wasn't used to the adrenaline rush that came with this kind of danger. "Jen, are you okay, hon?" he called out.

"She can't really hear us," I explained to him. "Something Mrs. Jones here does freezes the will and the mind. Like a spider paralyzes its prey before binding it in its web, isn't it, Mother Jones?" The leader of the Order of the Crow inclined her head. "She used to do it to me during my visits to her house, so she and her son could carry on conversations in front of me that I wouldn't remember." At the mention of her son, the Peri's lips twisted into a cruel parody of a smile. His loss had hurt her more than I'd realized. "How is your son, anyway? Oh, that's right. My condolences."

With every foot of the room's exterior that we inched across, Mrs. Jones had turned her body to face us a little more. "It was you who killed him, wasn't it?"

"Nope." We were near the door, now. "It was an unfortunate accident. And by 'unfortunate,' I mean 'couldn't have been happier.'" My remark elicited a hiss of displeasure that contorted her face.

It wasn't that Mrs. Jones wasn't a handsome woman. Like all the Kin I'd met so far, she had been gifted in the looks department. Yet years, if not centuries, of rage and hate had left her eyes cold and her lips thin and angry. At the moment, all that rage was focused directly on me. "What are you planning to do, Samantha?" she asked, nodding at my hand as it reached for the knob. "Run away to your precious Corydonais? Or is he on a wild goose chase, perhaps?"

I hated her knowing tone. When she took a step forward, I opened the door. "Get out of here," I ordered Beecham.

"You've got to be kidding me," he replied.

"Get out."

"No! Corydonais will have my head!"

"Beecham." I didn't dare turn my head from the hooded Peri, not when she could strike at any moment. "You are going to head outside and contact the Storm Ravens. You are going to let them know that an enemy of the Copper Crown is here."

"An enemy? I should have thought *the* enemy more appropriate, my dear."

I ignored the woman's taunt. "So go now."

"Your lover will have my head on a plate if I left you."

"I'll have your nuts on that plate if you stay."

There was a note of desperation in Beecham's voice as he pleaded with me. "I'm not very fast!"

"I know Cor said you had some kind of bird form. *Get going!*"

"All right. But . . ." I didn't get to hear the last of that sentence. Probably sensing my growing impatience, Beecham got moving. I heard the sound of a weight hitting the ground and felt something light and feathery brushing against my ankles. When I dropped eye contact with Mrs. Jones to see what had happened, I was treated to the sight of a fat peacock, its body shining with teals and greens, trotting out the front door. It let out an irritated squawk at me before disappearing around the corner.

Well, then. Maybe I wasn't going to get help as quickly as I hoped. "I'll just stand around and wait for them to arrive, shall I?" asked Mrs. Jones. "What a fine, sharp mind you have, Samantha. I can see why Corydonais has you as a toy."

"Sticks and stones, bitch. Where's your posse of little baby reapers?"

"You're more frightened than you would have me believe," she smirked.

"Damn right I am." There was no shame in admitting it. "If it weren't for my friend on the couch there, I would've been out the door with the peacock." I was convinced that if she'd truly intended to do something awful to me, she would have done it by that point, people present or not. "I'm sticking around. So, you know, you can injure me cruelly with your—oh wait, all you have is insults. What's the matter, leave your construct at home, or did you finally realize that I'm going to break every single one of them you lob at me?"

"It thinks it's a clever monkey," she hissed.

Feeling emboldened, I took a couple of steps forward. "I know what you're doing with Jen."

"Do you? What, then, am I doing?"

"You need another child to sacrifice. A *teind*. A wiggling rent check so you can rent a little chunk of Hell to call your own kingdom. Or queendom. Or matriarchdom or whatever the hell your kind calls it." Jen was glassy-eyed still. It would only take a touch or a gentle shake to rouse her from the mental fugue into which she'd fallen, but I was loath to do it too quickly. She'd already been frightened enough by the sight of Mrs. Jones' follower turning into a crow. What would she do when she saw the figure of Death standing in her own living room?

"Of course I want my own realm for the faithful. Something lasting and permanent, as the race of Peri deserve." Mrs. Jones didn't seem at all taken aback by my accusations. "Titania is too soft as a queen. She would have the Kinlands wither away and die, rather than make the tiniest sacrifice to save them."

"A tiny human sacrifice, you mean. One you'll have to make to the Devil every seven years to keep that so-called permanent kingdom of yours. But you're not going to get this baby. You're not going to get any more children. Not as long as I'm strong enough to do anything about it. I don't care if I'm a feeble eighty years old, Mother Jones. Every seven years I'll get up out of my damned nursing home and beat you with my walker if I have to." She narrowed her eyes until they were mere slits, measuring my words. "So get out now." She didn't shift a muscle. Not so much as an inch of her robes moved. "Jen's not going with you. And she's definitely not giving up her child. I'll see to that."

I'd thought my threats might have done some good, but the Peri merely tilted her head sideways, like a curious bird. "I think the child's father might have something to say about that, don't you?" It was the last thing I'd ever expected her to say, and it probably showed. "Or did you not think about the father?"

"Why would he matter?" I didn't get it, nor did I get the particular sense of pleasure she seemed to be getting out of the question. "Why would the sperm donor care?"

"That," she said, pointing to her nose, "is the question, isn't it?"

Outside I heard the sound of wind, once again sweeping down the hillside through the trees. A strong draft moved the open door inward by an inch, and on the patio I heard the noise of glasses clinking. "She went to a clinic to have it done,"

I said, repeating what Jen had told me over our lunch. "You think that the father's, what, going to show up out of nowhere and insist that the baby be handed over to you? Does he have influence over Dana and Patrick? That's no good. Because when I finish telling her exactly what you are and what you've done, she's going to be keeping herself and her loins out of your clutches." From the Kinswoman's self-satisfied moue, I could tell I wasn't even close. "Who is the father?"

"A friend of mine." The stirring breezes had already made me shiver. Her smile, however, chilled me to the bone. "A close friend, you might say."

"One of your flunkies? One of those mini-reapers who floats around in boats with you up the river Styx?" She shook her head. I wasn't even warm with my guesses. "Don't tell me you had your son make a deposit before he died, all so you could carry on the line of little Joneses? That's creepy! Not to mention Oedipal."

Still not right. The fact that my guesses were landing so wide of the truth was driving me nuts. "This would be where you and I diverge, Samantha," she said.

At the sound of my name, Jen began to stir. In a sleepy, far-away voice, she whispered, "Sam?"

"Ssshh, little one." Before I could respond, Mother Jones reached out and touched Jen on the shoulder, silencing her once again. "You see, for all his connections and importance, Corydonais thinks small. Why wouldn't he? He chases after the small-time hoodlums of our worlds. Whereas I, on the other hand . . . what's the quaint mortal phrase? I think outside the box."

Far in the distance I heard a rumble in the skies, low and almost gentle. Thunder. The Storm Ravens were on the way. "What do you mean?" I had to stall her, to keep her talking until the troops could arrive. "What have you done that's so clever?"

"My line of thinking comes directly from the real estate market. That is, why rent when you can own?" She let me chew on that one for a moment. "The business with *teinds* is so tedious. Every seven years, picking another innocent sacrifice. It's tiresome, preparing them for the rite—all that cleansing and. . . ." She pretended to shiver. "Mental intim- idation."

"Yeah, I'm sure you never get a kick out of it," I drawled.

"It's a drain on energies and resources that could better be focused elsewhere. Especially now that I'm a woman alone in the world."

"Pity," I said, without any sympathy whatsoever.

"So I thought to myself, now, why should I have to renew my lease when I could come to a more secure arrangement with the landlord?" Across her features grew an expression that I couldn't help fearing. It was of confidence, of arrogance—of unadulterated pride. "And what better way to secure myself a large and comfortable share of Hell's lands than to provide their master with what he most desires . . . a son and heir of his own?"

I shook my head, fascinated against my will. It was un- thinkable. "You didn't."

"Oh, but I did. The spawn blooming in that girl's womb springs from the seed of Abaddon." I didn't recognize the name, but it certainly didn't sound good. "He is the corrup- tor of all things, the whisperer in the night, the angel of the abyss." Her hands reached up to pull her hood over her head. "And he is glorious!"

As if on cue, the door blew all the way inward, slamming so hard against the wall behind it that it shuddered and rocked on its hinges. A flare of light from outside briefly lit every- thing in the room, the flash giving every object a hard, knife- like edge. Beneath her hood, Mrs. Jones's face was the only thing that remained unlit—it was a visage of darkness in a room that had been flooded with brilliance.

"Jen," I said, my voice panicked. Thunder answered the lightning's call, no mere rumble this time, but an angry roar. The storm was nearly on us, and just beyond the doorway I heard the sounds of dismayed cries and clattering china from party guests as rain began to patter on the concrete and water. The wind that had blown the door open was now whipping through the room, flipping open the pages of Jen's magazines and scattering the subscription cards within, tangling her curtains into the plants and furniture, and knocking over the margarita glass of melted slush. "Come on, Jen. We've got to get out of here."

"What?" As I feared, she came to from her trance, took one look at the chaos around her, and began to panic. "Sam?" she asked, her voice rising both in pitch and volume. "Freaky things are happening again."

Jen startled as lightning flashed through the windows, this time so close by that the accompanying thunder boomed at the exact moment it struck. For a split second, the hooded figure of Mrs. Jones loomed ominously, her arms slowly spreading, looking as if she might swoop down and devour Jen entirely. I tried hauling my friend's substantial weight over the top of the sofa by the armpits, but in her frightened condition she was dead weight. Just as it seemed it would fall on the both of us, the figure animating the draped cloth vanished, leaving the robe to drift to the ground for a moment, until the strong winds caught it and flung it against the wall. "Come on!" I yelled in Jen's ear, over the noise of the rain.

Glass shattered into the room as one of the poolside windows broke inward. Jen screamed, then scrambled back into my arms. Desperately she clutched at me as the room began to fill with birds. The dark, sleek bodies of ravens whirled around us in a vortex, their wings beating furiously as they sought their prey. I hushed my weeping friend, pulling her toward me. "It's okay," I assured her over the noise and furor of the birds' angry cries. "Trust me. We're safe now."

From outside I could still hear the sounds of panic as the partygoers tried to flee from the bad weather. The air had changed, smelling both sour and charged with ozone at the same time. Though several ravens still flew wildly around the room, the majority zoomed out the door and broken window, calling wildly to each other. Cor was somewhere in there, but I didn't know how to pick him out.

For the moment, though, the only thing that mattered was keeping ourselves safe. "Let's go!" I yelled, sheltering Jen's head with my arm and leading her to the door. The heavens had opened while we'd been inside. The skies, so dark they were nearly black, poured down a cold rain that seemed almost to fall in sheets. Only the catering staff remained in the vicinity, vainly trying to rescue food and bottles of expensive alcohol from the torrential downpour. "Watch out," I warned Jen, as we both nearly tripped over an umbrella that had fallen over with its table.

Another wave of birds flew by in formation directly in front of us, causing Jen to shriek again. "I can't!" she yelled at me. The air crackled with electricity; a jagged finger of lightning cut the sky in half. As the thunder bellowed, Jen broke away from my clutches and began to run back to the pool house.

Before I could react, a figure ran by me, white hair flying in its wake. "Don't let her go!" it called out. "It's a trap!"

"Azimuth?" The lightning strike had blinded me for a moment, making me think I was seeing things. What in the hell was he doing here? He hadn't been among the guests earlier. Yet there he was, racing after the terrified Jen and grabbing her around the waist before she could re-enter the house.

"It's a trap!" he yelled again, tugging at Jen with all his might. His eyes, wild and wide, appealed to me for help. "Can't you smell it?"

I'd immediately joined him in dragging away Jen, who had turned into a wildcat, yelling and screeching as she tried to get back to the safest place she knew. I shook my head, realizing I did smell something—the rotten scent of methane. "Jen, sweetie," I begged. "You trusted me earlier. Trust me now, okay? There's a gas leak. We've got to get away."

"Clear out!" Azimuth yelled. His voice was strong enough

to be heard over the thunder and rain, carrying to the out-door cooking area where some of the catering staff were seeking shelter. "Get out! Get to the house!" The staff stared at him, startled. As he kept yelling, though, they began to move, first drifting, then walking, then finally trotting away from the pool area and up to the house. Azimuth's hair was plastered to his head and chest; his clothing was drenched through. That didn't stop him from urging us onward until we were stumbling up the hillside across the red granite steps.

Jen's weary feet stepped hard upon the stairs; she looked as if she might fall over. "Keep going, sweetie," I urged her. "Keep going."

"But why—?"

"Just trust me, please!"

The first sound that carried to our ears was of glass exploding outward, tinkling and jangling with a high-pitched protest. The explosion followed, less like the thunder that echoed across the horizon after and more like a mighty, weary belch that accompanied a bright orange blossom of fire. The blaze poured forth like liquid under some alien gravity, issuing up into the sky and licking at the rain clouds. I could feel the heat from where we had landed on the ground, uncomfortable against my legs and arms and neck. Then the fireball vanished, leaving behind only smoke and a dark smell.

"Cor!" I scrambled to my feet. Jen was all right; confused and upset, but intact. Every cell in my body was focused at that moment on Cor. I had no idea if he or the other Ravens had been in the pool house when it had exploded. The storm was receding now. The rain had almost stopped. "Cor!" I yelled again and again, wandering down the hillside.

I felt Azimuth catch at my arm with his big hands. Where he made contact stung; the heat from the explosion had left my skin sensitive and slightly raw. "It's not safe," he warned me.

"I don't care!" I tried to pull away, but he was much

stronger. I found myself restrained by both of Azimuth's hands as he pulled me against him. Our two wet bodies met, back to front. "Corydonais!" I cried, my throat raw and ragged. I felt as if I'd swallowed a mouthful of glass.

From the confusion of wings, a single bird separated itself and swooped down. My eyes caught the iridescent sheen of its dark, feathered body before it began to transform itself. From the haze and confusion of light Cor rose. He was shirtless and barefoot, his lank hair dripping, his body glistening with rain. I gasped to see his body peppered with spots of red; a bloody cut, long but not deep, arched from the area where his navel should have been to just above his left nipple. "Oh, my baby!" I whispered, trying to reach for him. "Are you all right?"

Cor stared at the man restraining me, his head moving up and down as he inspected my captor before looking me dead in the eyes. Then finally he spoke. "Who the devil is your friend?"

Chapter Fourteen

"What absolutely flabbergasts me is that she would be so stupid as to allow this kind of liaison to happen." Ginger managed to make the word *liaison* sound particularly dirty, as if it needed to be rinsed and sanitized, *Silkwood*-style, by the giant hoses with the power nozzles. "She doesn't know who he is. *We* don't know who he is. There's no way to tell if he is who he says. He's totally off anyone's radar."

Beecham had been very calm during Ginger's impassioned speech. He'd kept his legs crossed at the knee and his hands folded, waiting for a chance to break into the monologue that had been going on for more than five minutes. "Well, I for one am glad he was there." He seemed surprised when both Cor and Ginger swiveled their heads in his direction, almost as if they'd forgotten he was sitting in my living room with me as they paced the floor together. "What?" he asked. "They would have walked right back into that deathtrap if he hadn't warned them. That means nothing to you?"

"Why is he even still here?" Ginger asked Cor, ignoring him.

"Look, missy." Grim as this evening had been, I still had to cover my mouth with a hand so that Ginger wouldn't catch me smirking. Beecham narrowed his eyes and continued. "If it weren't for me winging my way to the rescue, you wouldn't have had your comrades backing you two up.

And you certainly wouldn't have known that Samantha was in danger."

"If it weren't for me posting guards at the perimeter in advance," Ginger reminded him, "you would have had to run your fat, flightless hindquarters all the way down Sunset Boulevard and the 405 instead of the, what, entire two hundred yards that you *maybe* had to waddle."

"I take extreme exception with your insinuations of excess avoirdupois." Beecham lifted his narrow face and looked down his nose. "And I most certainly am not flightless. I fly. Not far. Or for very long. But I fly."

"Again, why is he here?" Ginger queried her superior.

"Apparently not to be debriefed, or deboxered, or whatever it is your operation chooses to call it. In that case, perhaps I ought to be on my way." Beecham stood and stretched his long frame. His beautiful outfit was a little the worse for wear. Apparently suede is one of those fabrics that doesn't appreciate a good drenching. "I should probably file my report. To the Crown," he said, the words laden with meaning.

"Sit down." Cor's command was the first word he'd spoken in the several minutes since we'd gotten back home.

"I am here as a courtesy, Master Corydonais." Beecham's manner was stiff and dignified; I could catch a glimpse of the seventeenth-century courtier behind the gossip-hound. "I have no official affiliation with the Storm Ravens. Members of the Plumed Circle are not required to abide by your orders. In fact, we share no common allegiance other than our ultimate responsibility to your great—"

"I'm asking you to sit down not as your superior," Cor interrupted, cutting off whatever Beecham might have been about to say. My eyes narrowed; I knew damned well what had been about to fall from his lips—the one secret that everyone except for me was supposed to know. "I'm asking you because . . . by all that's holy in Resht, Beecham. How long have we known each other?"

His dignity still trembling, Beecham lowered himself next

to me again. "Since you were a boy." How much older was he than Cor? If they'd been human, I would have guessed Beecham to be no older than his mid-thirties, and perhaps only three or four years older than Cor. I didn't want to try to figure out the math of it. My brain hurt enough already, plus I was still in shock. That was my excuse, anyway, and I planned to stick to it.

"And in that entire time, have I ever once treated you with disrespect?" Beecham inclined his head, his long nose pointing down to the floor, admitting the truth of the question. "Then bear with me. Bear with *us*. Please. Jinjurnaturnia?"

"Sorry," she said automatically. I knew her well enough by this point that, to her credit, I could tell she meant the apology. "I'm very sorry."

"It's not you," I explained to Beecham with much matter-of-factitude. "It's me that she's mad at. Rather than take it out on me directly, though, she attacks other people."

"Why would she do that?"

"It's one of those passive-aggressive Storm Raven things." I shrugged. "I've given up understanding it. Though if you ask me, I think it's probably because of a deep-seated hostility stemming from the fact that the Kinsman she's followed unconditionally for years is crossing a line she's unwilling to contemplate. And it scares her." While I'd spoken, Ginger had seethed silently across the room from me. If arm-crossing and scowling were classified as an Olympic sport, our little Flo-Jo would be bringing home the gold. Beecham seemed distinctly uncomfortable with my candor, but he nodded. "Am I right?" I asked Ginger.

"Oh, so we're speaking our minds now, are we?" Ginger stepped forward and stood across from me, pelvis to face. "How about this one, then? How would you feel," she said to Beecham, who reared back slightly from the proximity to her lower half, "if you had been conducting investigations for over one hundred and fifty years—one hun-dred and fif-ty years," she stressed, over-enunciating every word. "I started shortly after California started scraping itself out of the Spanish *dust* and only three years after the township of Los Angeles was established. My first assignment was chasing down refugees from Resht trying to make quick money off the pioneers trekking their way here."

"No one is questioning your qualifications," Cor told her, stone-faced.

"And then out of nowhere—absolutely nowhere—some little upstart with five years' experience as an 'insurance investigator' . . . one-two-three-four-*five* . . . and the stupidest little automobile that I've ever seen marches in and grabs control of an operation that I had always assumed was running flawlessly."

"Oh, you did *not* just diss my Mini Cooper!" I gasped, outraged.

"Perhaps in your report to the Crown you could give them a little bit of advanced warning that soon the clan may be changing its name to the Order of the Samantha Ravens."

My voice trembled with barely suppressed rage as I spoke again. "See?" I asked Beecham. "She can't bring herself to address me directly. It's called keep-ing it re-al," I told Ginger, articulating every blessed syllable in the same maddening way she had. "It's called talk-ing di-rect-ly to your sub-ject. Maybe it's something they didn't do back in days of yore. What is yore, exactly? I've never known." Beecham shrugged.

"You are so infuriating." Now she was addressing me. "None of this has anything to do with whatever . . . *physical acts* you and Corydonais might be performing on each other when you're alone. I don't care about that. Yes, Corydonais and I, we. . . ." For lack of words, Ginger's hands flailed in the air. "Once. *Once*. I'm sure he's told you that neither of us enjoyed it much."

"He said you were a biter." I don't know what devilish impulse prompted me to blurt that out, but I did take a perverse pleasure in watching her jaw drop. She looked to Cor for confirmation. He closed his eyes and shook his head. "Well, he heavily implied it," I informed Beecham.

"I fear we're treading too heavily into the off-limits government-classified research zone known as Area TMI," he announced.

"This is exactly the kind of thing I'm talking about. She's always . . ." Suddenly aware that she was talking about me in the third person again, Ginger changed stances and faced me. "This operation has always worked on a logical and consistent plan of attack. You, on the other hand, are always stumbling into things rear-side outward."

"I think you'll find the phrase is *ass-backwards*," I replied. One could practically see the frost curling from my mouth.

"Thank you. You walk in, blunder around, and then you're surprised when disaster rains down on your head. This Azimuth person is a rogue. Are you really surprised that he's causing nothing but trouble?"

"He saved our lives!"

"*We* saved your lives. *You* never get anything done."

"Except rescue children intended as *teinds*, and oh yes, I seem to recall you thanking me after I'd liberated Cor from execution."

"Which he wouldn't have been in danger of except for you," Ginger said, stabbing a finger at me.

"Which I wouldn't have been involved in at all if I hadn't been kidnapped by *your* people."

"We should have left her in that construct." The red-headed Peri threw her hands into the air and turned to Cor. "I told you that from the start."

Beecham studied his nails and appeared to be considering how best to disappear into the upholstery. Cor had been standing quietly by during our girl fight, teeth dug into the ball of his thumb as he listened, probably waiting to step in only when one of us went to bitch-slap the other. He shook his head now, though. "We don't leave people in distress because they're a different race, Jinjurnaturnia. I don't want to hear that coming from your mouth again." Any sense of triumph I felt was short-lived, however, because Cor then turned to me and announced, "She's right, you know."

"What?" I couldn't believe it. I'd been the one in danger that afternoon. The last thing I needed was Cor, allegedly the one person in the world who'd agree with me unconditionally, siding with the enemy.

"Not the fault finding or the finger pointing. Not the part about how you never get anything done. And definitely not the part where she said we never should have helped you in the first place." Like a dog eager to get back in good graces with the pack leader, Ginger hung her head and looked at the floor. "But she was right about this Azimuth person. He's a rogue operator that we know absolutely nothing about."

"You seem to be forgetting the fact, over and over again, that he was the one who warned Jen and I away from the house," I said through gritted teeth. "Mrs. Jones had set up a booby trap. And he was the one there to alert us." Jen was, at that moment, supposed to be taking a warm bath over at my mother's. I'd reassured her several times that I'd check up on her, so I couldn't prolong this conversation very much longer.

"You're implying . . . ?" He left the question dangling.

"That you were too busy doing what you needed to do. And that he came in damned handy." I was perfectly capable of returning the hard stares he was sending my way. "I'm not saying you were neglectful. I can take care of myself. But he saved our lives, and you should be thanking him instead of treating him like a criminal."

"You know what he trades in?"

"Yes, I know. Documents. Passports. Driver's licenses. Birth certificates. I've seen them up close and personal."

Cor's eyebrows shot up at that news. "And that doesn't concern you at all?"

"Are they illegal?"

"They're counterfeit documents."

"Yes," I said, feeling the heat begin to build right under my rib cage. I disliked being talked to as if I were a child. "But how are any of the Kin coming from Resht and dropping out of the Kinlands going to get a legal human birth certificate? Do his actions fall under your jurisdiction as a Storm Raven?" With a shrug that seemed to take forever, he admitted that they did not. "Then I don't see what the problem is."

"His kind encourage people to leave Resht," Cor said, still using that condescending voice. "He makes it easy for them."

I clenched my fists and tried to keep my tone even. "It sounds to me like you'd prefer to see your own people not integrating into human society. You really want it to be tough for them? You want them to drop out and starve and suffer just because you don't agree with their choice? Hey, maybe I'm just the girl who grew up in the big melting pot of Venice, but to me that sounds pretty elitist."

"Please don't put words in my mouth."

"I'm just saying." I knew this was one of the turning points of an argument in which I could either step back and cool down before it escalated, or plow ahead and fan the flames. My conscience knew which path I should be taking, but in the heat of the moment, the other road seemed so much more attractive. Still, I tried to resist its pull. "Forged documents might not be technically legal on the human side, but these Kin don't have any other choice. And they're not illegal in your world, so . . ."

"Exactly," said Cor. "Your friend, Azimuth, works in a gray area that no one can oversee."

"You don't know what else he's doing," Ginger butted in. "Those documents might be the tip of the iceberg."

"He's not—"

Cor interrupted me. "Anyone who works in those gray areas is naturally going to attract a criminal element. You must have seen it yourself when you were working in Las Vegas. Insurance fraud. . . ."

"Insurance fraud is a crime, not a gray area." I wouldn't let him get away with a lousy analogy. "You don't like him because you don't like him."

"I don't like him because there's too much we don't know." Cor's retort made it plain that he was cross with me. "I don't like that he persuaded you to keep your mouth shut about him for so long. Keeping him a secret—by everything that's holy, Samantha. You must have known I wouldn't like that."

"Oh." Although I'd been content to occupy my perch on the sofa's edge until then, his speech propelled me to my feet. Damn the higher, cooler path. If he wanted to walk us straight into the flames, I'd meet him there. "So you don't approve of keeping secrets, then?"

"No! Of course not! What's gotten into you?"

I stood across from him now in the room's center. Dusk had been falling when finally we'd gotten back home, but we'd been arguing too much to remember to turn on the living room lights. It was almost dark now, and he was little more to me than a dark outline in the gloom. "Absolutely nothing," I lied. "I'm just a little surprised how high and mighty you are on the matter of secrets, considering." For a second he looked as if he was going to ask me exactly what I was talking about. Then he shut his mouth. "That's right. You know exactly what I'm talking about."

"I haven't kept anything important secret from you."

"So it's not *important*, then, for me to know that your great-dame is, oh, I don't know, queen of your flipping world." There. The secret was out in the open. Like a landed fish I'd flung it, heavy and helpless, into our midst, and left it flopping and gasping for air. "It's not important for me to know that you're, what, a prince?"

He wouldn't look at me. Cor's head was turned and his eyes shuttered. "Samantha."

"Or is it me? Maybe I'm just not important enough for you to tell?" I hadn't intended it, but my throat began to close during my last sentence. I cleared it so I wouldn't sound so weak. "Because if that's it, fine. But don't you ever—*ever*—dare to give me a lecture about keeping secrets when I had to find this out from a total stranger." Before he could say anything, I added, "I know Ginger knew all about it. All the Storm Ravens did, right? Did you forbid them to say anything? Is that what he did to you?" I asked Beecham. "You had to know. Did he tell you on the pain of his displeasure never to mention to his human play-toy that he had family in high places?"

"I think it's time," said Beecham, rising slowly, "for me to find a roost for the evening. Good night, all." Once he was on his feet, he leaned over and turned on the lamp beside the sofa. From the guarded appearance of Beecham's normally expressive face, I could tell I'd hit close to the mark.

"Jinjurnaturnia." Ginger startled guiltily at the room's other end, as if she was being reprimanded for a crime she hadn't committed. "If you could give us some privacy." After a moment's hesitation, she nodded, shrugged, and walked out the front door. Beecham followed seconds later. The door shut behind him, leaving us alone. "So."

"Yeah, so." Maybe I should have felt remorse about airing our dirty laundry in front of his colleagues, but I didn't. He'd involved them in this conspiracy, after all.

"How angry are you?"

"Very." Why not be frank? He'd asked. "How in the world could you think I wouldn't want to know? And it's not even the secret itself. Why in the world would you think I'd care? What horrible scenarios have you cooked up in your head? That I'm going to insist on going to court balls in my pumpkin carriage? That I'm going to ensnare you into some kind of interracial marriage so I can claim my half of your fortune in the California divorce courts?"

He seemed pained. "No."

"Then what?" I demanded. Now that we were alone, I'd abandoned any pretense of trying to sound cool and collected. "What, exactly?"

"How long have you known?"

"Why does it matter? I had to find it out from the very person you and your little Mussolini Jr. have been bad-mouthing. The one person you don't want me to trust, Mr. Gray Market, Mr. Beach Blanket Bingo, is the only person who's been telling me the truth. How ironic!"

"You don't understand." Cor shook his head and tried to reach for me, but I jerked away. "I was trying to protect you."

"You're not making sense!" I yelled. "Protect me from what?"

"From exactly this kind of thing!" His hands clenched into fists. "From people who would try to use it against you! There are hundreds of Kin who would swarm you so they could curry favor with the Crown. Or attack you to get at my family. I can't avoid who I am."

"And everyone knows who you are. Except me." My words tasted bitter on my tongue. "If you wanted to protect me from it, you should have told me. Forewarned is fore-armed!"

He lifted his hands to his head, then pressed the palms against his temple. "I didn't think it would come to this."

"You didn't think at all!" Tears were beginning to spring to my eyes. "You left me wide open for the very thing you *claim* you were trying to protect me against! You're freakin' lucky that Azimuth didn't have an ulterior motive and that he let the information drop accidentally." When Cor's eyes narrowed, not believing me, I felt like giving him a good shove right in the middle of his chest. "I had to *drag* it out of him, if you really want to know. And how do you think it made me feel?"

I wanted to sit down again. I backed up until I was able to lower myself to the sofa. Without hesitating, Cor came to sit beside me. "I honestly never intended . . . it was for your own good."

"Let *me* decide what's for my own good," I urged him. "Am I really that helpless, in your eyes? You couldn't tell me you were a prince?"

"I'm not a prince."

"Your grandmother is a queen."

"It's not as easy as that," he said.

"Then tell me!"

I recognized the shrillness in my voice as the hysteria that rises right before I start shrieking and become an emotional madwoman. He must have, too, because while he made shushing noises, he reached out for my hands. I let him take them, though they felt like soggy cardboard between his warm fingers. "All right," he said, trying to keep me calm. "We don't officially use the title of *queen*. Well, some of us do. I don't." He sensed that he was making things worse, because he started running his fingers through his hair in frustration. "That's a human honorific. My great-dame is our race's matriarch. That's what she's supposed to be called. But over the centuries, human words have crept in. It's the same as when we were called *fairies* for so long, even though we don't recognize that as our official . . . do you hate me?"

"I don't know," I said. His long-winded explanation had at least averted the frenzy I'd been working myself into. "No, I don't hate you, but I'm just so . . ." I couldn't come up with the right word. Deflated. Tired. Weary of how stupid this issue was and how tiresome the argument was, and of how I couldn't seem to let it go. I shrugged.

"I'm not a prince," he assured me. "I'm not in any line of succession."

"A king's daughters might not have any hope of inheriting the throne, but they're still princesses," I reminded him. "Are you going to tell me that no one treats you differently because of your blood? Honestly and truly?" He sucked in his lips, bit them, then at long last shook his head. "I didn't think so."

His voice was choked with emotion as he stared into my eyes, willing me to believe him. "I didn't want you to think of me any differently."

"Because you're a prince? Not a prince. Because of your lineage?" I didn't care how it looked. I sniffed and wiped my drippy nose on the back of my hand. "Oh, sweetheart. I wouldn't think of you any differently because of that."

"You wouldn't?" Though he was centuries older than I, for the first time since I'd known him, Cor looked more like a little boy with his eyes full of hope.

"Never."

"Then everything's all right?"

I'd always thought of Corydonais as my invulnerable warrior, the one person in any world who could be counted on never to be caught defenseless. Even when I'd had to rescue him, he'd never seemed as vulnerable as he did at this moment. I knew that our happiness hung in the balance. Yet I had to tell the truth. "I don't know," I told him, withdrawing my hands from his lap.

"But . . ."

"I said I wouldn't think of you any differently because of your blood," I reminded him. "But I do think of you differently because of the things you left unsaid." He looked up at me as I stood. "For now, I don't know what to do about that. I don't know. Maybe we weren't meant to work."

"Samantha."

"Don't," I asked him. My throat was closing again as I crossed the room. "Just . . . not now."

"Please. Don't go like this."

"I need some kind of sign that we're supposed to last," I told him.

"Don't you have faith?" He did. I could tell by the light in his eyes, though I feared it was slowly dimming.

I swallowed, hard. I knew the tears would be visible on

my face, but I didn't care. There was no avoiding them now. "I've got to go check on Jen. I don't know what to tell her about today."

"Tell her the truth," he suggested. "Tell her that for her own safety, the Kin will have to quarantine her."

"That's such an ugly word. *Quarantine.*"

"Then just tell her we'll take her somewhere safe until she has the baby. Let me come with you. I'll explain." My face pained, I waved off that suggestion. Already this conversation had been prolonged for too long. "Samantha, please. Let me."

"Don't," I warned him when he shot to his feet. "Let me do this on my own. Please."

For a moment I thought—or maybe hoped—that he'd lunge after me and hold me in his arms. Instead, he stuffed his hands into his pockets and bowed his head. In a low, choked voice, he asked, "What's going to happen to us? Why are we so . . . out of synch, right now?"

"We both step and do not step in the same rivers," I reminded him. Then, as I backed out of the room, I whispered, "Good night."

Once the door had shut, I leaned against its wood and shuddered. The cool night air chilled the moisture, leaving long tracks down my cheeks. Leaving had been the most painful decision I'd ever made in my life. I could only pray to whatever powers were out there that something would happen to prove my decision wrong.

Chapter Fifteen

"Samantha. Dear. We need to have a little talk." My mother primly sat on the front seat of the Storm Raven van, purse in her lap and her hands daintily crossed over its clasp. She perched with pinched buttocks on the edge of the passenger seat, her back refusing to touch the leatherette or the duct tape covering the hefty split down its middle. In fact, the way she let her feet dangle through the open van door so that they almost touched the celebrity star-studded surface of Marcus Grant's guest parking lot, it appeared as if she was one loud noise away from leaping out and vaulting into the greenery to run away like a frightened deer. She was very much the lady, that following afternoon. Having heard that we'd be driving Jen to the estate of a Hollywood agent, she'd done herself up in her Oxy professor tweedy best.

I, on the other hand, had sooty smudges all over my face from the boxes I'd been carrying. My sweatshirt smelled like smoke. And once we'd managed to collect the last of Jen's things and get her somewhere safe, I'd very likely have to consign my jeans to the Dumpster. "Can it wait?" I asked, wiping sweat away from my forehead.

"I'd prefer not to have it in earshot of your friend." Mom nodded in Jen's direction. To say that I'd been working a little bit harder than she was an understatement. Compare: I resembled someone who'd been slaving in a coal mine all day. In her sparkly personalized knit top emblazoned with the legend JENERALLY UNDERESTIMATED, Jen looked like a bunny flown in from the Playboy Mansion to wander around the post-bomb rubble of Hiroshima as a goodwill ambassador. Mom and I watched as Jen knelt down, turned over a crispy magazine lying by the poolside using only the tips of two fingernails, paused to read the remnants of an article, then stood back up again before moving on to the next relic of her past.

"All right. Shoot."

"Well. Do you remember when you were seven? And along the canals you found the mangiest old cat? Honestly, I've never seen one in such terrible condition. It had mats in its fur and a scratch on its face and oh, the stench!"

"Fred," I said, remembering.

"Which was a highly unusual name for a girl cat, by the way." She lifted up her hands and waved them as if she could still smell the ammonia stink of its urine. "And you would insist on bringing it into the house."

"And then it fought with the other cats, hid under your mother's antique sewing machine, vomited, and I got sick at the sight of it. After you cleaned everything up, out went Fred."

"Actually," she said, "it was your father who cleaned up the sick. I can't abide it. And your father took the cat to a shelter and also put several posters around the neighborhood. But that's not my point." She cleared her throat.

Grateful as I was for a break from the last two hours of looking over the pool house for anything salvageable, I already knew where this conversation was going, and I wasn't looking forward to having it. "I bring home too many strays," I said flatly.

"It's not that I'm complaining, mind you. I don't want to give the impression that I'm not completely happy to have your guests stay in my house." Poor Mom. She looked as if she'd been dreading this discussion and was thankful it had come as no surprise to me. "I don't mean you. You'll always have a place in my home if you want it, of course. And Cory. Well. He's part of the family, now. Oh, and I don't mean Nikki, of course. She was a sweet girl, always helping out with the kitties."

"Just Jen," I said, bringing us around to the point.

"It's not as if I dislike the poor girl. She's very pleasant. And the way she talks about you! You'd think you were her personal savior." I ducked my head at that, a little embarrassed.

"She's temporarily homeless," I explained, not for the first time. "It's only for a couple of days, until Cor's friends get a place ready for her. She needs pro . . . help." I'd been about to say *protection*, but that might have required more explanation than I could give. "If it's money, I'm sure I could . . ."

"Stop it." I shut my mouth. Disobeying my mother might have been my hobby of choice in my teens, but I'd learned to outgrow it. "The only reason I bring it up is because this morning, when I woke up with you in my bed with me, and your friend in the guest room, and Mr. Landemann on the sofa, it just felt so *crowded*. It's silly, I know. But I don't have the biggest of houses, and lately I've been feeling as if I had a hundred people living with me." What my poor mother didn't realize was that with the dozens of Storm Ravens roosting in bird form atop her cottage and the neighboring houses, she actually did have nearly that many people occupying her land. "Don't mind me," she begged. "It's been a strange few months. Why, this morning I looked out the bedroom window onto the porch roof and do you know what I thought I saw? A peacock! I don't know what the neighborhood association would do if they thought I had a peacock!"

"Um, yeah." I cleared my throat. Marcus Grant and his two hellhounds were coming down the walkway. It had been my goal over the last few hours to keep him from reaching the ratty Storm Ravens van and my mother, lest she actually introduce herself as such. Although it looked like he was headed for Jen with a cardboard box, I kept my eye out for a sudden change in direction. "Listen. I'm sorry if you feel put out. But Cor and I had an argument. . . ."

"Dear." Unexpectedly, my mother reached out and cupped my chin with her hand, not seeming to mind that it was filthy. "I wouldn't have it any other way. You have a good heart. I'm very proud of who you've become." I swallowed, feeling suddenly gawky and awkward and extremely young again. It wasn't often that my mother bestowed such high praise; even in her department she was known as one of the toughest graders, highly begrudging of an A. "I won't complain any more."

"I'd hug you, but—" I gestured to the griminess of my general self, and she nodded with understanding. "You complain any time you want. Okay?"

"All right. Now that you mention it," she said, taking me at my word. "You're not getting any younger, and somehow you avoided inheriting the child-bearing hips the women have on my side of the family, so you might want to consider . . ."

"Except not about that," I said, curt as could be.

"I'm not saying you have to get married to Cory first!" I rolled my eyes at my mom as I walked in the direction of the house. "Out-of-wedlock children are fully accepted by society these days!"

As if Cor would want to have a child with me, after what had happened the night before. Sighing, I shoved that thought aside. The mental pain still throbbed, but after a mostly sleepless night and a few good hours of poking around a burned-out shell, I'd learned to ignore it. Or at least not to think about it quite as obsessively. When I reached the point near the pool where Grant and Jen were talking, she brightened visibly. "Guess what?"

"Monkey butt?" I asked, then shook my head when they both stared at me. "Never mind. Third-grade thing. Or so I've heard. What?"

"Marc's found a box of personal things of mine from when I moved in." She knelt down on the ground, laughing when Attilla and Ghengis leapt up on their hind legs to lick her face. "I didn't know where to put this stuff when I moved into the pool house, so it got put into storage and I forgot about it. But it's some old photographs, and like, my yearbooks, and some CDs." She looked up with a bright, sunny face. "So I didn't lose everything after all!"

I couldn't help feeling a little warmed by her optimism. I'd have been curled into a fetal position and bawling, had I been in her shoes. "Fantastic!"

"And your friend is coming down with a suitcase of clothing that should last you for at least a few days." To me, he added, "My third wife. Never did get rid of her outfits."

I had an uneasy feeling that I didn't want to know where his third wife went to or why she hadn't taken her clothes. The other restless feeling in the pit of my stomach came from the mention of Azimuth, who we'd found waiting outside of the estate like a hitchhiker. It was as if he'd known we were coming. "Again, I'm really sorry about the . . . gas leak and subsequent explosion caused by an usually violent storm cell." That had been the phrase the fire department had been quoted as using in the paper that morning, and damned if I wasn't sticking to it. "I just hope it didn't cut your party short."

"Oh, who cares about the party? Do I? I don't." He put his arm around Jen and began shaking her. "All I care about is my baby girl here. Are you okay, kiddo? I worry about my Jenny."

At that point I was slightly worried about what was to come. After her soak last night, Jen and I had shared a sit-down and a quiet talk about what had happened. I'd ended up giving her a highly edited version of events. How in the world, after all, do you tell a friend that she's carrying Rosemary's Baby? All she'd really needed to know was that the woman named Mrs. Jones was not her friend, and that Dana

Claire and Patrick McConnolly had only been affectionate with Jen for selfish reasons, and that the baby she was carrying was very . . . I think *special* was what I ended up using . . . and what she needed to know for the night was that she couldn't be anywhere safer than my mother's house, where Cor and I could look after her. All that was a tough bushel of nuts to swallow, to be sure, but she'd accepted the information at face value, although once I'd finished, she had one question. "What about Marc?" she'd asked. "Does that mean he's not really my friend, either?"

Frankly, I'd been surprised she'd managed to figure it out on her own, but apparently she'd worked out that not everyone had the good fortune to fall into the money pit with no family or education or qualifications whatsoever. My response had been guarded, but I couldn't conceal my concern. Now, with Marcus Grant in such close proximity, Jen managed a facsimile of a smile. It might have been left over from the unadulterated delight of finding a few of her personal possessions intact and undamaged other than the jewelry and odd pairs of shoes we'd managed to pick from the rubble. "I'm okee-dokee," she said, her spirits and acting abilities rallying.

"You know, I've got no problems putting you up at the main house, girly-girl. The insurance for this deathtrap should be coming through pretty quickly. I know people. We can get the pool house back in ship-shape order and even better in, what, a month? Six weeks? No reason for our little Jen here to intrude on your personal life."

"It's no problem," I assured him. Azimuth emerged from the house carrying two suitcases Grant had given him. Vuitton, by the looks of it. At least Jen would be heading off to her new home with a few valuable consolation prizes. He began walking down the star-studded pathway, the heavy bags causing his muscles to bulge from his square-cut tank top. I averted my eyes from the sight. "We just want her to be happy."

"Don't you think you'd be happier with me, Jen?" When Grant put his arm around her, trying to buddy-buddy his way back into her heart, Jen knelt next to the carton that represented what was left of her most valuable personal possessions. She rubbed her hands over the dogs' heads, letting them snuffle her affectionately. "You know Patrick's got that premiere coming up for that knights of the round table flick. He told me he wanted you there."

"Oh, I wouldn't miss it! I'm totally stoked!" Attagirl, Jen, I thought to myself. I'd been worried about my friend's ability to walk the tightrope between getting herself clean away from the agent and not tipping off her intentions. Who could distrust her blandly sweet exterior, however? She might have unwittingly been carrying the spawn of Abaddon, but she was innocence personified.

The agent bestowed on her an affectionate, almost paternal smile. "That's my girl," he said, the fondness in his voice not seeming at all feigned. "A temporary change of address shouldn't keep you from being part of the family. Am I right? I'm right. Give me a kiss, sweetheart." He proffered his cheek. Obediently, Jen stood on tiptoe and pressed her lips against the man's hanging jowl. I shuddered. It might have been my imagination, but I thought I saw her recoil slightly as well. It might have been his aftershave. "Nice. Papa likes."

"I'm just going to go put my stuff in the van." Jen shot me a smile that seemed almost to be an apology for the act she'd just put on. She turned to Marc and gave him another of an entirely different quality: high on both ends, broad, and to my eyes, totally false. "Don't worry. Once I get settled in, the dogs and me will get back on a regular yoga schedule. Won't we, guys? Roll over!" Obediently, Attila obeyed the spinning motion Jen made with her hands. "Play dead!" I thought she might lie down on the ground again, but Attila flopped onto his back. Ghengis, however, merely panted and wagged his tail.

"They love you, baby girl!" gushed Marc.

Jen waved as she walked away. She seemed genuinely sorry to be leaving those mangy mutts behind. When Marc bent down to prevent them from following her, they actually whimpered. "I'll be back," she promised them. "I'll be back!"

We watched her trot off, carrying the box toward the van in the distance. "Sweet girl," Grant said, nodding and smiling. "Sweet, sweet girl." I was about to agree with him, but that was when he turned on me and let the fangs show. "Unlike you." Before I could blink, he added, "So what's your plan, you double-dealing bitch?"

Chapter Sixteen

"I beg your pardon?" Grant's sudden about-face had caught me completely off guard.

Although the mogul still spoke in that buddy-buddy, intimate tone he'd been employing with Jen, his eyes were cold when he looked me up and down. "You heard me, sister. You're going to snatch her off to fairyland or whatever, right?" From his pocket he pulled a cigar, which he began rolling between his thumb and first two fingers. "And don't pull that aristocratic shit with me. I know you're no countess." I started to shrink back, because I had indeed started to puff myself up like the countess would. "I bought it for a little while. You and that fairy friend of yours might have had me going before yesterday. Dana Claire was even gonna hire you as an advisor for this bio-flick she's doing about Jane Austen rescuing aristocrats from the guillotine or some kind of crap. But I sure as hell know the truth now."

"I don't know what you could be talking about." The countess might have receded, but I still managed to convey some of her icy hauteur.

"Bullshit." Although he hadn't yet lit the cigar, he stuck it in his mouth and began to rummage around in his jacket pockets. Although I tried to meet his frank stare with unwavering eyes, my brain was still calculating escape options. Azimuth was less than twenty yards from us; I doubted Grant would try anything with a witness so close. I wore sneakers, and the agent wasn't in the best of shape, so I suspected I could outrun him if I had to. His goons, though, might prove to be a problem. After thoroughly wetting the smoke's rounded end, he brandished it at me like he wanted to poke out my eyes. "You know what that little bitch is carrying, too."

Immediately I saw there was no use in pretending. If he was on to me, it had to be because Mrs. Jones had filled him in. "That means you do, too," I said, happy for once to use my own little human, contrary voice in front of him. "And you can still live with yourself."

"What's to live with?" he asked. The platinum lighter he'd produced from his pockets flipped back and burst into flame. "I knew from the get-go. She was my pick." He huffed and puffed the tobacco until it began to light.

"And you let it happen?" I asked, ire and bile rising in equal proportion. "You actually stood back and let them impregnate a girl with the most vile, inhuman . . ."

Azimuth was within hearing distance now. "Got everything in here," he said to Grant. Then, seeing the anger on my face, he added, "Everything okay?"

"Fine," both Grant and I replied at the same time. We shot each other looks of hatred as we did it.

"Well. All right. I'll see you at the van. Lady Samantha," he added, using the title I'd briefed him on earlier. I nodded, silently willing him not to drop out of sight, just in case.

"Lady Samantha." Marc's cheeks blew out like a fish as he inhaled the acrid smoke of his cigar. "You must get a kick from that, huh? Yeah, I picked Jen. Sweet young stupid piece of trash. No family. Perfect, right? And yeah, I let them knock her up. Hell, I provided the clinic, the nurses, the doctors to do the job. The only thing I didn't provide for the whole shebang was the junk they shot in her. But they didn't need me for that. You think?"

"You're insane." At that moment, I didn't care how

important he was in his industry. I didn't even care that he could have pressed some panic button and brought a dozen weapon-bearing heavies down on my head. The only thing keeping me from lunging at him was knowing that I had to get my mom and Jen out of the estate intact. "You'd do all that—get a girl pregnant with the devil's child—for what? More of this?" I waved my hand around what I could see of the estate . . . the pool with its hillside vista, the garages, the extensive house, the tennis courts in the distance. "You don't have *enough*?"

"You don't get it." His eyes narrowed. I ducked and waved my hands when he blew a stream of foul smoke directly into my face. "This doesn't matter. My clients do. I do for my clients, and this is what I get in return. Yeah, it might seem a lot to a nobody like you, but not one of my clients is gonna tell you that I don't do for them. To the bitter end, you hear? To the bitter end." By now, Grant had given up on trying to sound friendly. Though his volume was low, the hatred had been dialed all the way up to eleven. "And if I've got clients who want to preserve their looks for as long as they can and a crazy old dame who'll get them into the, whaddayacallit, Kinlands, I figure I'll do whatever it takes to get it done. Knocking up some little nobody with some demon's junk so the old broad can get her hands on a baby? I think of it as a public service. People love Patrick and Dana. People hand over their money to see them on the screen, because both those kids have got a knack for taking people out of their skins for a while and making them feel good. When's the last time you did something like that, sweetheart?"

I shook my head, too enraged to answer.

"Yeah, I thought so. You come back and talk to me when you're a public institution, and then we'll see what you have to say about this whole eternal life business. If I can get an extra ten, fifteen years out of these kids in their prime, that's what I'll do before I store them away for a while. Then in another fifty years, Hollywood will get a couple of fresh new stars. Remember Patrick McConnolly?, people are gonna say. Whatever happened to him? Who cares, this new guy is even better. Same for Dana Claire—that kind of beauty never goes out of style. And if it does, it's not like she hasn't had enough work done already, right?"

"Oh my God," I spat out.

"So yeah, if I have to get a blond bobblehead nobody knocked up, I do it. Sure, maybe he's the devil. All couples got problems though, right?"

He cackled with glee at his own little joke while I stared on in horror. When the laughter became a deep, painful-sounding bronchial cough, I started walking away. Then, changing my mind, I turned. "What are you going to do?" I asked him. "Are you and your goons going to stop us from leaving?" Because if that were the case . . . well, I didn't have a plan for that, yet. But I'd think of one.

"Nah." He waved his hands. "Get the fuck out of my sight. Hide her where you want. I'll find her. Or if not me, your friend will. She's the one you should be worried about." Apparently I wasn't allowed to be the first to walk away. He turned, cigar in his mouth, and started strolling in the direction of the pool. "Oh yeah," he added, swiveling around. "I'll be collecting her sooner, rather than later. Shouldn't let the dogs go too long without their yoga, right?" Again, he laughed. The sound grated on my ears. "Catch ya on the flip side, sister."

It took me a moment to gather wits enough to stumble back to the van. By then, I felt light-headed and unsteady, almost as if I were just getting over a severe bug that had laid me out for days. Hearing my mother's voice again made me feel a little more grounded; the preceding moments had been positively unreal. "Isn't that nice," she was saying to Jen, who was standing outside the passenger side door with an open book in her arms.

"And *this* was my best friend, Melanie Black, only after

high school she got married right away and changed her name to Melanie Gray, which we all thought was hysterical," Jen was saying. Suddenly feeling overheated, I whipped off my sweatshirt, adjusted the tank top I wore underneath, and threw the grimy outerwear into the rear of the van. "We thought her third husband was going to be named White, but she was totally rude about the fact that no one got her gifts for her second wedding, so we never found out if it took."

"My goodness, what a *thorough* explanation you have for all your friends." My mother widened her eyes and appealed to me silently for aid.

"Did I show you Sam's photo?" Jen began flipping through the pages, her mouth moving as she worked her way through the alphabet. "I mean, you've probably seen it and all, but remember when her hair was black and she wore all that eye makeup and the dark lipstick?"

"Jen, get in the car," I barked, before we could take a nostalgic walk down Goth lane. "We've got to get out of here."

"Just one sec. . . ."

"Now." I barely hesitated from adding, *while we still can*. That thought was definitely on my mind, however. Marcus Grant might have claimed he had no intentions of preventing us from leaving the estate, but I didn't trust him any further than I could throw him. Which, with my little strength, was not very far.

"Well all right," she said, closing the book and obediently ducking through the side door into the van. Azimuth, from his seat in the back, leaned forward and yanked the sliding door to a shut position. When I'd nicked the keys from Ginger that morning, I'd managed to clean out some of the grunge and the clutter from the van's back, but the vehicle was too well-used ever to pass for clean. Even now, it smelled of damp and soot and the sweet smell of stale coffee. Apparently a lot of the Storm Ravens had developed a serious Starbucks addiction during their time in Venice.

Strapping herself in, Jen continued babbling. "But it's not like I was making fun of you or anything. We all had our bad fashion years. I mean, I used to like Candies. Do you remember that ad they had? With Jenny McCarthy? On the toilet?"

"So glad I came!" My mother's enthusiasm was less bubbling than grumpy.

"'Could I just come along to see what it looks like? Just a peek?'" I reminded her in a low growl, imitating the voice she'd used to wheedle herself into this expedition. "'I won't bother a soul. I can help move boxes.'"

She gave me an exasperated sigh, yanked the seatbelt into position, then pulled her door closed. "Now that we're settled," she said, her voice all puppies and warm hugs again, "why don't you find that photograph of Samantha, dear, so we can all enjoy it?" I shot her a hateful look before putting the van into gear and backing out of the lot.

As I said, I'd worried about getting out of the compound safely. Would we round the drive and find the gates down and surrounded by the sports jacket brigade? Apparently that wasn't in the works for us. The gate shuddered open, lifting in the same slow and deliberate way as it always had. The only one of Grant's thugs that I could see was the fellow who waved us out with a cheerful smile and a two-fingered salute from his brow. No devouring monsters reared to stop the Mystery Machine when we rolled over the sewer gratings. And most important, we weren't descended upon by hundreds of ravenous crows intent upon our destruction.

Despite all these things, it wasn't until we'd left Bel Air and were once more safely on busy Sunset Boulevard that the tension from my shoulders began to dissipate. Sunset is just too mundane and ordinary a street to harbor traces of the supernatural, apparently. I must have been clutching the steering wheel like crazy, because once we reached the first stoplight and I pried my fingers from it, they stung as the circulation started to return. We'd had a close call there. But once we got back to Mom's house, Ginger and Cor would have returned from their hasty trip to Resht to make arrangements for a place to harbor Jen for a few months. I hoped she could do without her high-def flat screen.

In the rearview mirror, I could see Azimuth staring at me from the very back of the van. "What?" I asked over my shoulder. Both my mother and Jen turned to see why I was talking to him. He simply shook his head.

"Are we going to lunch?" my mother wanted to know. "I think there's a deli in the area that's supposed to be good."

"Chicken and waffles?" Jen asked hopefully, causing Mom to turn around in her seat, appalled.

Although I was partly gratified to discover that I wasn't the only one who found Jen's idea of lunch off-putting, I had to squash the food talk before it got out of hand. "We're going to Jen's boyfriend's place," I reminded everyone. What I didn't say was that it was so Jen could say a proper goodbye to him, so that the infamous Bo wouldn't be tempted to call the police and report Jen as a missing person. I wasn't really sure that even Jen had realized the actual purpose of the visit; she seemed to be nurturing a belief that she'd be able to give Bo a jingle on the phone any old time she wanted. Of course, I hadn't told her that telephone lines didn't reach to where she'd be going.

"Oh really?" Smiling, my mother turned around and peered behind her seat. "Where is that?"

It took a moment for both Jen and me to realize that she wasn't addressing Jen, but Azimuth. "Mom," I told her, sparing only a glance as I coasted from the left lane into the right. I couldn't quite remember how far it was before Sunset hit Santa Monica Boulevard. "He's not her boyfriend."

"Oh! Really!" Never was my mother more interested in someone than when she could plumb the depths of their love lives.

"My boyfriend's name is Bo," Jen said, looking over her shoulder at Azimuth with a big, obvious, *Fabio hair? As if*.

"Oh, a Southern boy?"

"I don't know," Jen said, biting her lip as if she had never considered it before. "I don't think he's from L.A., though."

"What does he do, dear?"

"Science?" she said, not really seeming to know. That was news to me, though. I'd mentally pegged him as a failed actor or career waiter.

My mother, not getting the dish she wanted, changed tacks. "Well, whose boyfriend are you, Mr. Azimuth?"

"Mom." In the rearview mirror I tried to shoot an apology at the Peri. He simply gave me the same impenetrable expression he had before. "What?" I asked him again. He shook his head. We'd managed to get away from the Grant estate intact, and now everyone was acting weird. "He's a friend," I told my mother.

"Your friend?"

"Yes, my friend," I said, glad that the van's motor was most likely obscuring the details of our conversation.

"Well." We pulled up behind a car at another stoplight. I spared a moment to raise my eyebrows at my mother. There'd been a certain degree of implied censure in that one word. It surprised me. "Does this have anything to do with why you were sleeping in my . . ."

"Mom!"

"Fine." Her voice was short and sharp, and it wasn't merely because we weren't going to that deli. Mom always had been testy when she wasn't fed at bi-hourly intervals. "I won't say a word."

"Good," I told her.

"I won't say a word about how a good relationship is a very delicate thing and how a single misperception can alter it for the worse." I hoped that if I didn't say anything, she'd shut up. No such luck. "I also won't say a word about how it seems to me that you and Cory are well-suited for each other."

"Yes," I said, stomping on the accelerator, sadly aware of the fact that all the speed in the world wasn't going to leave her behind. "It would be nice if you didn't say a word about that."

"I also won't say a word about. . . ."

"That would be helpful, Mom. Speaking of good relationships, how's Mr. Landemann?"

"Well!" My mother faced fully forward once more, lips pressed together. "If you're going to be like that." She began to rummage through her bag, until at last she pulled out several of the chewy peppermints she'd filched from the restaurant where we'd enjoyed Girls' Night Out. For several minutes, the only sounds in the car were of heavy sighing, Jen flipping the pages of our old yearbook, and the crinkle of candy wrapper paper.

When Jen had told me that Bo lived in an apartment in West Hollywood, mentally I had assumed he'd be in one of the city's pleasant new constructions, or at least one of the nicely refurbished buildings that were attracting the higher-income professionals filling the town. You know. A nice courtyard. Protected parking. A security buzzer. That kind of thing. But no, Bo lived in what was barely a step above a transient hotel—one of those anonymous old structures between Santa Monica Boulevard and Melrose that had been so far overlooked for redevelopment. Inexpensive, I'm sure it was. Roach-free? I doubted it.

Jen, though, yanked back the sliding door and leapt out of the van with an eager air when, after circling the block and those surrounding a good three times, I finally found a parking space around the corner. Azimuth's long white hair swung in a well-conditioned rope as he joined her on the pavement. "Come up and at least meet Bo," she begged.

I sighed a little, shrugged, and unbuckled. "You coming?" I asked my mother.

It wasn't hard to figure out, from the way that she refused to look at me, that she was still a little miffed about our previous disagreement. "I think I'll stay here for a while," she announced, rolling down her window three inches, then back up one. I guessed that she was more wary of the scrappy-looking kid walking down the street with a guitar on his back than the open-shirted gay couple casting Azimuth appreciative glances as they passed.

"Fine." I wasn't going to cajole her into being sociable. "I'll leave the keys so you can listen to the radio. If you change your mind or feel unsafe you know where to find me." Deep in the heart of a junkie palace. She was probably better off in the van, truthfully. I heard her snap shut my lock after I slammed my door.

The three of us pushed through the front entrance with its broken latch and past the collection of mailboxes that had fallen from its perch and lay propped up against the wall. Jen saw my expression as I scanned a bulletin board tilting precariously just next to the staircase. It seemed to be covered with nothing but ads for rehab centers and wig makers. "It's not that bad," she assured me. "Besides, Bo's out of town so much that he's hardly ever here."

"I'm sure."

The stairs creaked ominously with every step up. In case they suddenly gave way, I was careful not to stay more than two risers close to either Jen in front of me or Azimuth behind. At least the wig-making ads were explained when, after the second landing, we found ourselves having to squeeze along the wall so that two drag queens in full glamazon regalia, both taller than even Azimuth, could inch by. Other than the occasional muffled voice or sound of a television as we'd pass through the hallways winding to the roof, there wasn't much evidence of life.

Finally, on the building's fourth floor, just as I was getting winded, Jen stopped outside one of the doors. It was distinguishable from the others only by its unique pattern of flaking brown paint chips and a missing digit square in its middle. "I hope he's home," Jen said, right before rapping. "I left him a message earlier."

A voice rumbled from the inside and her face alit. Jen twisted the knob and let herself in. I felt a hand on my wrist. "Let them have a couple of minutes," Azimuth suggested. He was right; it made sense. I let him pull me away from the door and onto the wall where we leaned. I could hear Jen's voice trilling through the cracked door as she greeted Bo. She sounded genuinely happy to see him.

It wasn't until a moment later that I realized Azimuth hadn't let go. I looked at him, and then down at where his hand wrapped around my wrist. Feeling oddly self-conscious, I pulled it away. Or tried, at least. Because before I really fully understood what was happening, Azimuth met my opposing force and pulled me to him, moving his grip to my upper arms. His breath, soft and without scent, was warm on my face as he leaned down to kiss me.

"Whoa!" My shoulders rebounded against the plaster when I yanked myself backward and away from his lips. "What the hell was that?"

He didn't answer.

"Was I giving off signals? Because the only thing that's gotten me through the past twenty-four hours is an unshakable confidence in my own innocence, and if it turns out that I have been shaking a tail feather in your direction, I'm just going to . . ."

"You haven't given off a signal." When I searched his eyes for the truth, his expression remained grave and unmoving. "I'm so sorry. I shouldn't have done that."

"No, you definitely shouldn't." He was only inches away. If he tried it again, I'd have to fall flat on my back and scrabble away like a centipede.

"I want to apologize."

For a few moments, neither of us stirred a muscle. "Oh, thank God," I finally breathed, relaxing. I'd genuinely been worried that there had been some latent physical attraction that everyone but me had picked up on. Then, energized and angry, I lashed out again, batting at him with my hands to push him off while I tried with my legs to regain a standing position. "Then what did you have to go and do that for? I know I'm not that attractive. I've seen your Kin women. They're uniformly gorgeous."

He leaned against the central stairwell's banister, biceps rippling and shoulders filling out his tank top, looking for all the world like an Abercrombie and Fitch model still wearing the goods fifteen years after his heyday, but still wearing them well. "I told you," he replied, his voice small. "I was apologizing."

"That's how you apologize?" I shook my head, then realized I was overlooking the obvious question. "What are you apologizing for?" He shook his head. I thought about it a minute from my side of the narrow hallway, and then began putting pieces together haphazardly. That was my job, after all. "You were acting weird in the car. Something's on your mind, and it's not puppy love for me." His expression was as unreadable as ever. "Did you do something? What have you done? Azimuth—" I looked around the hallway. The only things that could have heard me were the vermin in the walls, but I lowered my voice anyway. "Are you in trouble? Cor said that Kinsfolk who deal . . . well, in the black market . . . often are involved in, well, other. . . ." I didn't know how to say what I meant without offense. "Have you done something wrong? Something you want to tell me about? Something I can help clear up?" He still wasn't answering, though I suspected I was getting closer to the heart of it. "I can talk to Cor. You've helped me. You've helped him. If it wasn't for you, he might have been in that pool house when it went up."

"Samantha." I'd been babbling with such intensity that I'd missed the moment when he'd launched himself from the banister and closed the space between us. This time, however, he didn't kiss me; instead, he reached out and ran his fingers through my hair. "Listen carefully, because we haven't much time. The DeRengiers were family in Cornwall, originally French. An isolated fragment of the Kinlands had a failing portal on the DeRengier lands. The clan there was like a large group of people trapped on an iceberg in warm waters, pulling back from the edges, never sure of when it would vanish beneath them." I couldn't move. When he'd mentioned my family name, I felt as if I'd received a minor electrical shock. "Some of them emerged through the portal before it disappeared in the fifteenth century. The rest were lost. Those who made it through interbred with the DeRengier family."

"Why are you telling me this?" I asked, stammering. "How long have you known?"

He put a finger on my lips to shush me. It smelled like vanilla. Or, I realized after it receded, like hair product. "For many years the DeRengiers were regarded as oddities. Witches, even. Like the Kin they had absorbed, they grew reclusive and fewer. Most eventually left Cornwall and dispersed to the winds. That is who you are. I've known since before I ever saw you."

I blinked several times when his tale came to an abrupt end. "Are you apologizing for not telling me earlier?"

"I'm apologizing for what's going to happen soon," he said. His wooden expression softened. He almost seemed to be pitying me. "Forgive me if you can, and try to understand."

"What's going to happen?"

Before he could answer, Jen's voice rang loud and clear from inside her boyfriend's apartment. "Sam? Aren't you coming in?" With a creak, the door swung in and her cheerful, round face appeared. Her eyebrows quirked with curiosity. "What're you doing?" Before I could answer, she opened the door wide. "Don't be shy! Come on in!" In a confidential whisper, she added, "It's okay. I told him that I had to go to London with Marc and the dogs for a couple of months."

"Good one." My congratulations sounded empty, primarily because my head was still spinning from the revelations of a moment before. When I turned to Azimuth, he was all politeness and smiling eyes, preparing to meet the nice mortal. I didn't know why he'd told me that information right then, or for what in the hell he was apologizing, but if he'd been trying to throw me off balance, he'd done a primo job.

"Bo?" Jen called out. The boyfriend wasn't in the living area, which was a marvel of stark simplicity. The walls were white—far cleaner than the dingy paint clinging to the stairwell hall outside. A wooden sofa of no particular distinction occupied the longest wall of the fairly small room; a woven rug of red and green covered the splintery floor. And in the corner opposite the door stood a waist-high wooden bookcase, handmade and lovingly crafted and stained. It was full of volumes, but not of the trashy airport bookstore novels one might expect in a building like this. The spines of the books were leather, by and large, and quite old. A patina of decades had worn their titles unreadable. "Hon?" Jen called through a doorway that led to a dark and outdated kitchen. "Come meet my friend Sam."

"Yeah, sure," said a masculine voice from the rooms beyond. Those two syllables riveted me in place, though my mind didn't yet know why. Though my feet were fixed to the floor, instinct screamed at me to get moving. Something terrible was going to happen, it told me, jabbing forks in my spine. I had to get moving.

Yet I couldn't. I felt as if I'd been frozen in ice. I was facing the kitchen door full on when Bo stepped out, a plastic mug of milk in his hand, his shirttails hanging over his jeans. He was of average height, dark-haired, with black, shaggy eyebrows. They framed a pair of deep blue eyes that regarded me with mild curiosity—and Azimuth with a slight, immediate wariness. Even among the competitive good looks of Hollywood, anyone would have found Bo handsome, in a rumpled sort of way. He couldn't have been any more than thirty-six or thirty-seven.

But then, he had been thirty-six or thirty-seven the last time I remembered seeing him, twenty years before. When I was twelve years old, he'd taken me to Catalina Island, bought me ice cream, and smiled at me with those eyes, and I hadn't had a damned clue of the misery that was to come only days later when he walked out on us.

"Hi there," said Jerry Neale. As in, Jerry Neale, my father.

Chapter Seventeen

The mythical gorgon is reputed to have turned her victims to stone with one look of her flashing eyes. My father wasn't having a gorgon's snaky bad hair day, mind you, but a single glimpse of the one face in the world I'd never thought I'd see again rendered my poor flesh into marble. I don't even think I breathed. How in hell could this be happening? I would have been less traumatized by the sight of my grandmother rising from her grave.

Apparently my father had held out his hand when Jen introduced me. It hung in midair for a moment until he realized I was staring at him like a lunatic. "Okay then," he murmured, his eyes sliding sideways in Jen's direction. "Nice to meet you, Sam." He spoke to me as if I were slightly hard of hearing, or foreign.

It seemed as if I stood there for an eternity. Maybe I did. Maybe time stopped for me as it apparently had for him, flowing around the two of us like a river, letting us part its center as it rushed past. Dimly, in the back of my consciousness, I heard Azimuth's voice. "Jen, let's head out to the car for a minute."

"Why?" she asked.

I didn't hear his answer, nor did I actually witness them leave. All I knew was that I'd been left alone in a sparsely furnished room with the man I least wanted to see in the world. What he must have thought of me, standing there motionless and unable to speak, I didn't know. I didn't really care. Putting that man at ease was the last worry on my mind.

"Is there something I can get you?" he asked. His voice was the same. His face was the same. Though the thatch of hair atop his head was shorter than it had been twenty years before, it was still as black and thick as I remembered. "Water? I might have some guava juice."

Still I said nothing.

He thrust his hands into his pockets, then withdrew them just as quickly so he could lay them on his hips. "Um, are you okay?" Plainly he thought he was dealing with a madwoman. It might not have been too far from the truth.

Still, I had to find out for sure. Though it felt as if I was breaking myself from a crust of stone several inches thick, slowly I moved my mouth until I felt it making sounds. "Bo?" My voice sounded husky and cracked. "That's your name? Bo?"

"Ye-es," he drawled. Very discreetly he eyeballed his watch, then looked out the door, obviously hoping that Jen would return and relieve him of the responsibility of babysitting her lunatic friend. "How about that guava juice? Hmm?"

He was making a polite excuse to get out of the room and away from me, I could tell. Before he could go, though, I had one more question to ask. "It's not Jerry?"

He stopped in the doorway to the tiny kitchen and turned, his hand resting on the lintel. "Jerry?" he repeated. "Jen called me Jerry? Bo was always her nickname for me, for some reason." Right as I was starting to believe, though, that maybe my moment of insanity was simply that, he added, "My name's Jeroboam. Talk about old-fashioned. Right?"

"Crap." Why couldn't he have denied it? If he had, I could have pretended that I was wrong and I might have walked away with my heart intact. Instead, I was having to face the truth. "You're one of them, aren't you," I said before I could stop myself. "Don't even bother to deny it, you god-damned . . . *bastard!*" He recoiled when I started marching toward him. "You've got the eyes. You've got that long face. Do you have clan markings? Huh?"

When my hands started scrabbling for the neck of his shirt, to yank it down and see what was between his shoulders, he ducked, then backed away. "You're cracked, lady!" he yelled. "Back off!"

Only now did I notice the tears running down my cheeks. "I hate you," I sobbed.

"Yeah, well, you're not making that great a first impression either." His brow tense and hostile, he held up his hands in front of his chest in case I decided to dash at him again. "That other fellow with you was of the Kin too, wasn't he?" he asked, curiosity getting the better of him. "He's not looking for me, is he?"

"No one's looking for you," I announced, finally letting emotion get the better of me. "Because you're too busy not wanting to be *found*, ass!" Without a word more, I whirled and stomped away, out of the room and into the dismal hallway, around the bend and down the steps. I didn't care that any one of my heavy steps might have sent the splintery staircase crashing to the ground below and carrying me with it. That might have been a fate preferable to what I was going through at that moment. It felt as if my brain were on fire and nothing in the world could put out the flames. That was my father, my brain kept repeating, over and over and over again. That had been my father up in that room. The man my mother had wept her heart out over during my teen years—the man I'd wished dead countless times and whose name I'd gone to such lengths to expunge from my own.

When I reached the bottom landing, I realized something else, too. I was half Peri. I was one of those racial oddities, like Landemann, or any of the by-blows Cor's own sire had spawned through the centuries. Did I feel any different? No. I still was mad as hell, which surely had to be a human quality. Oh good lord. I was a half-breed. Like old-school Cher, only without the feathered headdress. Apparently my brain still had the same propensity for drama as before, too. But no. I was more than a half-breed, if what Azimuth had told me was true and I had distant generations of Peri blood in my veins from the DeRengiers. Did my mom have a clue?

Azimuth had known about the Dorringers, and he'd known about my father. He'd known more about my family and my ancestry than either me or my mom, and yet he'd let me walk into that room to confront something no child should ever have to face. Wait, I was being dramatic again. I was no child. And how had he known I'd react so strongly? He might have just as easily assumed I'd leap into my father's arms and pepper him with kisses. Then again, Azimuth hadn't congratulated me. He'd apologized. That meant something.

My heart was still thudding like a jackhammer when I pushed my way through the door and out of the stinking hallway back onto the street. The air was cooler there, or at least it circulated more freely. I found myself able to think again. Jen obviously didn't know that the guy she'd been seeing and presumably sleeping with . . . oh, ick. I hadn't considered the ramifications of that little bit of information. For some odd reason, it seemed to hit closer to home than anything else.

The drag queens we'd passed on the stairs, eons ago, were standing near a post box on the curb, purses hanging conspicuously from their wrists as they gossiped with animated gestures. I looked around, remembering only after great effort that I'd left the van around the corner. On what felt like lifeless stumps, I trotted in that direction and stopped. The van wasn't where I thought it would be. I was so certain it had been only four or five cars down on the cramped road running south to Melrose! I put my hands on my hips and surveyed the area, my pulse quickening.

As quickly as I could, I ran back around the corner, past Jeroboam's apartment building and the two tall drag queens, then down the sidewalk of the parallel street. No van. My chest tightened; I felt a catch in my throat as I scrambled back down the same block for a third time to look down the original street more carefully. I'd had that same panicky feeling before when I'd misplaced my bag or my keys, but the van was considerably bigger than my damned keys, and I'd never had a bag big enough to carry my mom. Maybe I was panicking over nothing, though; it was entirely possible that I'd been so disoriented by discovering my father that the shock had shoved from my head the real location of the Storm Ravens' van. How many times had I gone shopping at the mall and lost my Mini Cooper? Not that many, damn it. Okay, perhaps there was a more logical explanation. Maybe my mom had gotten nervous and decided to drive around the block. She didn't know how to drive a stick-shift, I remembered. Apparently it was very much time to panic.

On legs that felt increasingly like overstretched rubber bands, I flew around the block adjoining Jeroboam's. This rapidly was turning into one of those nightmares in which every step felt like fighting through quicksand. Next I'd find that I'd completely lost the power of speech. The van wasn't anywhere to be seen. It wasn't two streets down, or on the street behind my father's, or down either of the two perpendicular streets to the west. By the time I reached the apartment building again, I was panting like a dog. My tank top was soaked through, and my hair had fallen out of the bands holding it. I was exhausted, and the prospect of running another gauntlet made me want to flop down on the pavement and die. The only thing I could think to do was approach the drag queens, no matter how much they intimidated me.

The pair appeared to be waiting for a ride. At first they

pretended not to notice when I approached. When I huffed and puffed my way to their sides, resting my hands on my knees because I was so exhausted, however, they both turned wary faces in my direction. "Hi," I said, in what sounded like an unusually high-pitched and nervous voice. "I know I've got to look like a mess."

"Mmm-hmm. A hot mess," said the more masculine of the two, a guy with an enormous nose and eyes lined with what had to have been a Sharpie marker.

"A hot tranny mess," said the pleasingly plump black drag queen with the curled blond wig.

"Nice. Thanks." I tried to catch my breath and came up with a lungful of air that felt like I'd inhaled knives. "I don't know if you saw me running by just now."

"Four times?" said the blonde, moving a little closer to her friend and away from me, as if afraid I might drip perspiration on the hem of her red dress. "Didn't see a thing."

"Do you remember passing me in the apartment building?" I asked, pointing at the rathole where my father lived. "A few minutes ago? I was with a guy? Long, white, white hair? Kind of muscly?"

The pair exchanged a look. "Sweetheart," said the one with the nose and the pink dress with black fringe. "Neither one of us pays attention to other girls' husbands."

"Or boyfriends," said Blondie. "Therein lies t-r-o-u-bull, trouble."

I'd caught enough breath to stand upright again. "He's not my husband. Or boyfriend."

"In that case, honey, I certainly did see him booking his way out of here with Miss Olivia Newton-John." I blinked. It took a moment to realize the black drag queen was talking about Jen.

"And I would not call him kind of muscly," said the other, lifting his bag to shoulder height and twiddling it between his enormous man-fingers. "I would say he had muscles for *days*."

"Yes." I could see we were going to have problems keeping this conversation on track. "Which way did they go?" Both pointed long red nails in the direction I'd originally thought, to the east and around the corner. "You didn't see them after that?"

"I'll see him in my dreams later," said the blonde, dabbing at her friend's arm with her hands. They both burst into laughter.

Maybe I was asking the wrong question. "How about this?" My voice grew thinner and thinner by the second as my stress level shot up. Soon I'd be having a stroke from the blood pressure. "Did you see a van drive by?" When Fringie gestured to the road with its usual amount of midday traffic, I hastened to make myself even clearer. "A really old, beat-up van. Kind of the color of an old filing cabinet. And with some of that awful fake wood paneling on the side, like on old station wagons." I didn't know how Azimuth would even have started the van, but—oh. I had a sudden and vivid memory of leaving the keys in the ignition, for my mother to listen to the radio.

"Oh, that beat-up old thing." The blonde was growing tired of me, I could tell. She looked at her nails and then peered hopefully out at the street for their ride.

"You mean the van, or the woman riding in it?" joked the other.

"Who was the woman?" I asked. "Did she have kind of a round face? Gray-brown hair? Big eyes?"

The black drag queen shrugged. "I didn't pay a bit of attention to her after she yelled at us."

"Yelled?" I sounded like I was yelling myself.

"Mmm-hmm. The woman saw us in the window, pressed her face up against it and started yelling."

"She even beat at the glass."

"Sure did," drawled the blonde. "And I was all, 'No you *didn't*. This is *our* neighborhood. You take your saggity ass back to the Valley and leave me *be*.'"

Yelling. Beating at the window. The new emotions flooding in to replace my panic at losing the van were worse than the original. Anything else, and I'd drown. "Thanks," I said, my voice sounding a million miles away.

"Honey, if you find that muscle bunny of yours, you tell him to come back and ask for Hershae Chocolaté, you hear?" called the chubbier of the two to my back. "I'll take care of him for you."

"I'll take damned good care of him myself," I growled as I dashed off to the sounds of their staccato laughter.

It had to be done. Two minutes later, with legs that were even more rubbery than before, I found myself banging at the door on the fourth floor with the missing number. From within I heard the sounds of metal scratching against metal as he unfastened lock after lock. When he pulled open the door, the chain holding it swung just below the familiar face that peered out at me. "No," he said, shutting the door again.

"Open up," I barked at him.

"No. You need help, lady."

"That's why I'm here. Open up or I have two drag queen friends outside that I will summon to snatch you bald," I warned him. The door remained shut. I needed to try a different tack. "It's Jen. She's in trouble. And unless you open up . . ."

The door popped back open, though the chain remained swinging on the latch. "What did you do to her?"

"I didn't do *anything* to her, you moron. Open the goddamned door!"

Jeroboam hesitated, then shut the door. Right when I thought I might have to beat it down myself, I heard the chain rattle as the door opened again. I didn't need an invitation. I shoved my way in and began looking around the apartment, totally uninvited. "Here's the deal," I told him as I scanned the living room. "Azimuth has taken Jen. And Mom. Not that *you* care about her. I don't know why he did it, and I don't know where he's taking them, but the drag queens saw Mom yelling and beating on the window, so I'm guessing it wasn't to the deli."

My father studied me, stroking his chin. "Do you have some medication that you haven't taken?" I hadn't seen what I wanted anywhere in the living room. When I stepped into the kitchen, however, with its array of midcentury linoleum and sagging cabinetry, I saw the telephone I sought hanging on the wall. It was ancient, and I hadn't used a phone with a rotary dial since my childhood, but so long as the line out worked, I didn't care. "Don't you have a cell phone? I thought everyone had a cell phone these days."

"It's in the van," I growled as I wrenched my index finger through the necessary digits. "With my sweatshirt."

"Of course." He nodded sagely and backed off. "In the van with the Azimuth and your mother." I glared at him while the phone rang. Why wasn't Cor picking up? When he tried to say something else, I shushed him. The cell phone I made Cor carry with him when he was in his human form rang and rang, never picking up and never going to voicemail.

I hung up, feeling angry at the world. I was mad at Azimuth for—well, I didn't know what he was doing, but it was either something diabolical at worst or inconvenient at the least, and I feared for the worst. I was mad at Jeroboam for standing there like a big witless idiot, staring at me like I was off my rocker. And most of all, I was mad at Cor for not being there when I needed him most. "Of course he's not there," I muttered to myself. "I basically walked out on him. Why should he be there for me?" Oh, Cor. How stupid I was.

"You know . . . what was your name? Pam?" I lolled my head sideways and gave my father the insolent stare I'd never gotten to bestow upon him during my long adolescence. "Pam, let's go sit down in the living room. Then I'll call for someone to help you, okay?"

"Pam? Seriously? Pam? You don't have a damned clue

about who I am, do you?" I folded my arms and leaned against the chrome of his countertop.

He attempted to soothe me. "You're Jen's friend."

"My name's not *Pam*," I spat. "It's *Sam*. As in *Samantha*. As in your daughter, *Samantha Neale*. I go by Dorringer now, by the way."

I had always thought that when someone was described as having turned pale from shock, it was a slight exaggeration. Yet when I dropped that little bomb, my father's face turned blue-white, as if all the blood in his body had suddenly drained away. He sagged. Suddenly he appeared tired and old, as if my news had returned to him all the years that he'd cheated from time.

"But oh wait. I forgot. Your kind don't have daughters. You just *spawn* with humans, isn't that right? The seed you plant in my race just springs up as weeds, right? The kind you just step over and move past?"

"Oh, by all my ancestors." My father muffled his words with a hand in front of his mouth. "Samantha? You weren't supposed to find me. You were never supposed to . . ."

"Yes, well, don't worry. I haven't come with my hands out for a chunk of the family fortune. I've got no claim on you whatsoever, *Dad*. In fact, I'd rather not be talking to you right now, except for the fact that Azimuth, that guy you recognized as Kin? He appears to have kidnapped your girlfriend. And my mother."

"Barbara?" he whispered.

I was so angry that I propelled myself from the counter so that we were face-to-face, seeing each other for what we both really were. "Don't say her name," I snarled. "You don't have the right to say her name to me." I'd crossed the line from civilized to feral. When had I become capable of such savagery? More than anything that had happened in the previous half hour, it left me shaking.

"I'm sorry," he said, mouthing the words more than pronouncing them.

"Landemann." I snapped my fingers in my father's face.

He still stared at me with frightened eyes, as if worried he was caught in some kind of hostage situation. Feeling once more hopeful, I crossed the kitchen, picked up the receiver, and dialed my mother's home number. "What's a landed man?"

Landemann picked up on the second ring. How could I tell it was him? Because of the grunt. Without pausing to identify myself, I filled him in on where I was and a basic outline of what had happened. When I heard the stiff intake of his breath after I'd informed him that Azimuth had spirited Mom away to heaven knew where, I felt oddly optimistic. If, after all the yo-yoing she'd put him through, he could still fret about her (albeit in the stoic, silent Landemann way), maybe there was hope for me and for Cor. Best to put those thoughts away for the moment. Already there were too many crises on the table for me to deal with one more.

Once I hung up, I found Jeroboam clutching the refrigerator for support. Some of his color had returned, but he was still very much the marionette, hanging from limp strings. "*You're supposed to be twelve or thirteen*," he said in his native tongue, still regarding me with wonder.

The sentence fell like tinkling bells onto my ears. I translated the words with no effort. "I understand your language, you know. You're the one who doesn't get older," I reminded him with no small degree of hostility. "I'm the mayfly that hatches and dies in one of your days. Remember how that works?"

"Samantha." On impulse, he took a step forward, his hand raised.

"Don't." I was having none of it, and my body language sent him scuttling back to the fridge. "This isn't some Very Special Episode of your favorite sitcom. You can't fix things with a hug, and I'm never going to fall into your arms and call you Daddy. Got it?"

He nodded, keeping his distance. It still hurt to be in the

same room as him, but at least the panic of my current situation had reduced this particular inconvenient confrontation to the level of an annoyance, rather than a major trauma. "Who did you phone just now?"

"Landemann. Mom's fiancé." I delivered the news with no little degree of satisfaction at first, but then had to bite it back. "Or he would be, if she wasn't still married to you."

He blinked rapidly at that information. "I thought that by now Barbara would have had the marriage dissolved. It's been . . . how long?"

"Apparently, it's one of the little inconveniences you neglected to clear up when you deserted us." Of all the things that angered me about this Jeroboam fellow, the worst was how vague he was about the details. I wanted him to remember, damn it. "One of these days you'll be doing the same to Jen. Is that your M.O.?" I asked, stomping past him into the living room so I could sit on the sofa. My legs were still wobbly. "You'll get the urge to wander and you'll tell her you've found some other woman who's caught your fancy?"

From the defensive way he reacted once he'd followed me in, I could tell I'd struck a nerve. "Jen and I are barely seeing each other. She's pretty, definitely, and nice in her own way. But she's no—" However he'd intended to complete that sentence would have to remain a mystery, because he closed his mouth. At least he'd confirmed what I'd always suspected about his relationship with my friend. Cold as it might have seemed, I was glad it wasn't any more involved. Jen deserved a much better guy than this schmuck. "We've never been . . . to tell you the truth, I was relieved when she told me this afternoon she was going to London."

"I'm sure," I said, not bothering to hide my scorn.

We were at an impasse. He couldn't find anything to placate me, and there was nothing I wanted to hear. For a few long minutes I sat on one end of the sofa with my arms and legs crossed, wishing I could be anywhere else. If I knew anything about Cor, though, it was that he'd want me to sit tight at the address I'd given Landemann so he could send someone to get me, rather than to hare off on my own and make myself unfindable on the streets of L.A. Instead of talking, I looked around the room again. Its starkness was almost monklike. The last time I'd seen such extreme asceticism had been with the particularly poor work-study students at school. Save for the books in the opposite corner, there was scarcely anything personal about the apartment.

I was trying to make out the lettering on the spines when finally Jeroboam spoke again. "I never told your mother I was leaving her for another woman."

"Yes you did," I retorted, unable to hide my contempt.

He shook his head. "Did she tell you that's what I said?"

"Yes." When he raised his eyebrows, I shrugged. "No. I don't know. I thought she did." I'd no actual memory of my mother saying any such thing to me. It might have been a scenario I'd come up with myself, which once floated, Mom simply had never denied.

"What I told her was things were complicated and that I'd have to leave."

"Well, whoop-de-doo, haven't you earned the honesty-while-breaking-up-a-happy-home award." Did he really think he could talk his way out of twenty years of built-up resentment? It simply wasn't going to happen.

"You didn't used to be so hostile."

"I didn't used to be fatherless," I reminded him. "Things change, right? I'm surprised you remember anything about me, considering how easy it was for you to leave."

He perched on the far arm of the sofa and rested his feet on the wooden coffee table. "You make a lot of assumptions."

I shrugged, recognizing the truth of his accusation, though I was trying not to care too much about it.

Another long silence fell before he spoke again. "How do you even know about us?" he finally asked. "The Kin. It's inconceivable that you should have found out."

I stared at him levelly for a few moments before answering.

My father's curiosity made me resent him; it was much too late to pretend to care about picking up the frayed threads of my life. At the same time, I recognized the impulse. After all, hadn't my curiosity led me to be an insurance investigator? "All right. You want to know? Here it is. Do you know what a construct is?"

He nodded. "A bound-energy architectonical construct? Of course. I was on the philosophical team that contributed to the original research that led to their implementation in the fifteenth century."

"Oh, so you're an expert on them, hmmm?" The news did not endear him to me. "Well, thanks to your team of philosophers, *Dad*, I was trapped in one of those constructs. When I escaped, I discovered three years had gone by, that I was all but presumed dead, and that I'd lost my job, my apartment, my possessions. Everything except my family. Well, half my family, anyway."

I couldn't tell what was affecting him more—my sob story, or the notion that he'd contributed to one of the most miserable times of my life. "Oh, Samantha. Who did that to you?"

"The Order of the Crow."

He shook his head. "There's no such thing. That's a mythical clan. Something the Kin scare their children with."

"Isn't it pretty to think so? I can tell you for a fact that the order exists."

"And you escaped from one of their constructs? On your own?"

He seemed so flabbergasted at the idea that it was with no small degree of pride that I informed him, "I escaped from *two* of their constructs on my own. I'm a dab hand at them by now."

I didn't feel like telling him anything more, particularly about my involvement with the Storm Ravens. I didn't know Jeroboam from Adam. All I had was his word that he was a Peri philosopher, which I'd gathered was their lingo for a scientist. For all I knew, he could have been some kind of black market operator like Azimuth. Or a cohort. He might be delaying me here now so that his accomplice could make a clean getaway. No, I couldn't dwell on scenarios like those; that way led to madness. Besides, I'd made my way to him. He hadn't kept me here.

Jeroboam didn't say anything after that for quite some time. He seemed to be studying me askance, apparently afraid that facing me head-on might frighten me away. I admit that I was doing the same. If a Resht council of philosophers had done a pie chart of my brain at the moment, it would have seen that while the lion's share of activity was devoted to rat-in-cage panic over having lost Mom and Jen, a goodly slice would have been engaged in active rancor against Jeroboam. Then there would have been the unexpected piece of the pie, the part that was curious about him. How could I not be? Even in his absence, I'd invested so much energy in vilifying his name. Now that he was here, in all his underwhelming presence, I couldn't help but bubble over with questions.

Thinner than any other portion of the pie, though, would have been the last piece. What did it mean, that I was half Peri? More importantly, why did knowing it somehow make me feel even more isolated than before?

From the other end of the sofa, my father left out a soft whuff of laughter. "I'm remembering things. When you were six," he said, staring at the coffee table, "you had a doll named Kimmy. And you used to be afraid of a mirror hanging in your room, the one with pegs hanging from the bottom. When the lights were out, you thought it looked like a giant bird trying to get you." He studied his hands for a minute, then let his glance flicker in my direction. "There was one Christmas when you had read all the Little House books, so your mother got you Lincoln Logs and a pair of moccasins. And oh, my, you were in heaven."

I shifted on the sofa, crossing one leg over the other and trying without result to wipe grime from my sloppy tank top. He'd managed to make me feel awkward. "It was Tammy. The doll."

"No, it was Kimmy. I'm pretty certain of that. You used to have these little overalls, denim, that had a pink kitty-cat patch your mother got me to iron onto them. Barbara never liked ironing."

"Don't bring her into this," I warned him. He raised his hands, surrendering. "A few happy memories of days gone by aren't going to soften me up, if that's what you're hoping. Because do you know what?" I had to press my lips together for a moment, so that the emotions about to tumble out might settle down. When I felt a little calmer, I continued. "I don't have any good memories of you. You might have gotten me water at night, helped me unwrap Christmas presents, or blown my nose or wiped my butt, but it's not there. None of it." I pointed to my head. "Gone, every single nice thing you might have done when I was a kid and I assumed you were going to be there forever. All the ugly thoughts I had after you left burned the happy parts from my brain, D—" I'd almost called him *dad*. The fact that the word had risen so instinctively frightened me a little.

"I. . . ." He seemed to be grappling for something to say. "I'm sorry." I sat there, trying to remain unmoved. "I know it's not enough."

I nodded. Those two words weren't going to erase years of absolute hatred.

"Sometimes, though, things happen for which one just can't plan."

My battle to choke down the lump from my throat and the tears in my eyes was rapidly failing. "You knew," I said, aware that I sounded as emotional as I felt. "You knew you were going to have to leave one day, and you did. You had all that time to plan your exit."

"You're one hundred percent right, but I wasn't talking

about the leaving." My father's voice was soft. He stood and boldly moved next to me before sitting again. "I meant the moment that I met your mother, at an Occidental College new faculty reception. That," he said softly, "I never planned for."

I couldn't find anything to say to that. My chest felt heavy. When I inhaled, it almost seemed as if my lungs had turned to liquid. When he put his hand on my shoulder, tears began tracking down the left side of my face on the half away from him. I didn't shrug off his touch. I didn't welcome it, but it didn't bother me as much as I thought it might. "Just don't mess up her life," I whispered, resting my forehead on my hand, and my elbow on my knee. "It's taken her this long to find someone else. Don't screw it up again."

A loud, violent bang on the door interrupted the thorny moment. It sounded like the hand of God himself, trying to batter his way in. The door shuddered on its hinges as it burst inward. The chain that had been hanging limply from its back rattled and struck the wall with such force that it chipped the paint. "Thank the heavens. There you are," said Cor, lowering the leg he'd used to kick his way in. His eyes were only on me as he crossed the room in several quick strides. He stopped, though, once he realized that I wasn't alone.

Jeroboam's hand fell from my back as I stood. He seemed as shocked by Cor's impressive entrance as I had been, and staggered to his feet as well. "My door . . ." he said, wincing at the sight of the broken latch.

"Samantha, my dear? Why is it," Cor asked, a touch of humor softening his eyes, "that whenever I find you lately, you're in the arms of another Kinsman?"

Chapter Eighteen

I didn't bother to reply. There hadn't been any ill intent behind the remark. To my ears, it sounded like the sweetest of apologies. "Oh, Cor," I said, lunging at him and burying my face in his chest. He smelled of the outdoors. Obviously he'd flown here as fast as he could. "Sweetheart." I didn't imagine he could grip me so tightly. It was as if he was afraid I might vanish from within his arms. "I didn't know you'd come yourself."

"Did you really imagine I'd send anyone else?"

"I don't know." I was clinging to him with such intensity that it was a wonder either of us could breathe. "I hoped you'd come—I wanted you to come, but—I don't know."

"Sssshh." His lips pressed against my ear as he gave me comfort. I felt the strong line of his jaw rub against the skin of my head. Then his chest rumbled as he spoke again. "Your mom and Jen are gone?"

"I think Azimuth . . . you were right. He's up to something, and I didn't see it. I'm so sorry. He took them and it's all my fault."

"Don't. You couldn't have known."

"You told me! You and Ginger both!"

"Ginger and I are accustomed to suspecting everyone we encounter." His hand rubbed my back. "You're a different person altogether. Don't ever change to be like us." I sighed, still feeling awful at how I'd gotten us into this situation.

Cor had turned his attention to other matters, however. "Hello. You are?"

"I'm—"

"Oh." In my moment of happiness I'd forgotten that he might appreciate an explanation. Dabbing at my eyes with my pinky, I sniffed, separated myself, and waved a hand at Jeroboam. "Cor. Remember how you told me there were only two ways I could possibly understand your native tongue, and one of them a parent being one of the Kin?"

"Your mother's not, though." Cor leaned back from me and shook his head. "She's definitely not."

"She's not," I agreed, then nodded at Jeroboam, who was rubbing the lower half of his face in a bemused fashion. "He is."

"That I could tell. But he is . . . ?"

"Jen's boyfriend. And my . . ." I took a deep breath. I could say the words. "My father."

He didn't seem to believe me. "Jerry Neale?"

"That's one of the names I used. I'm Jeroboam, of the Philosopher's Circle."

Cor released me almost immediately, then stepped around to examine the two of us next to each other. Several times he shook his head. "Having one of the Kin as your sire would explain much." He stalked his way around Jeroboam, studying him up and down in almost exactly the same way that Jeroboam was inspecting him. Finally he crossed his arms and glared. "You have a lot to answer for."

The gravity in his voice made me smile. Capable as I like to think myself, apparently I still thrill a little when the man I love stands up to those who've wronged me. "I know," said Jeroboam, accepting the criticism without flinching.

"In the name of the fall, do you know how reckless you've been with this human's family?" Cor crossed his arms and puffed out his chest. "By all rights I should . . . deck you!" I beamed at him with approval not necessarily for the sentiment, sweet as it was, but for having absorbed the idiom.

"Whatever you think, I am this girl's family," said Jeroboam, not standing down. "My decision to leave wasn't made lightly."

"Then how do you account for it, sir?" For a moment, I thought Cor was going to make good on his threat to strike my father, but he only shifted his weight, invading Jeroboam's personal space by a few inches more. He still looked like a prize boxer on edge, gauging his opponent for the first opening. "Because from where I stand, you left a lot of wreckage behind."

"I don't know where your clan allegiance lies, *sir,*" said my father, mocking Cor's formality. Though he was a head shorter than Cor, and had none of Cor's lean musculature, Jeroboam nonetheless moved in a little closer himself, matching Cor's puffed chest with thrust-back shoulders. "But I am sworn to the Philosopher's Circle to protect the Kinlands themselves. I had a duty." To me, he added, "I hadn't appeared to age in any of the fifteen years I was married to your mother. People were beginning to notice."

"Then you should have been honest from the beginning," was Cor's decree. As true as the words were, to my ears they sounded harsh. To Jeroboam's, too, from the appearance of it. He flinched, and for the first time stepped down. His mouth remained pressed shut as he refused to offer any more evidence in his defense.

"Corydonais," I said, reaching out and, with a touch on his arm, dissuading him from any further verbal violence. "Much as I love watching Peri pissing matches, this one's not getting me to my mother any more quickly."

"Or to Jen."

When Cor quirked his eyebrows at Jeroboam's remark, I explained again, "This is Jen's infamous Bo. Her boyfriend."

"We weren't really . . . it was never a formal arrangement. . . ." His stammers were cut short by a quick look from Cor. "But I don't want her hurt."

Cor shook his head. After a moment, he sat down on the

sofa and pulled me by the hand down beside him. "There are too many overlaps here. Too many intersecting circles."

"It's Azimuth. It's like I said. I was wrong to have trusted him at all. It's insane that I did at all, what with all that lurky-lurky business he did, jumping out at the wrong time. I don't know why I let it go on. He tried to . . ." I'd been about to tell Cor about Azimuth's attempt to kiss me, but at the last minute I thought it better to let the incident fade from memory. I still didn't know where our relationship lay. "He tried to tell me he knew about my father, before we met. He apologized for bringing me here."

"He apologized?" Cor shook his head. "That doesn't make sense."

Jeroboam had been thinking while we held our little powwow. "Corydonais?" He repeated the name as if he were hearing it for the first time. Awe tinged his words. "As in Corydonais of Mabelle, of the branch of the queen? Or are you merely named for him?"

Before answering, Cor looked at me with steady, tense eyes. He'd gone to such lengths to conceal from me his ancestry, and here it was being thrown in my face. It was a good thing I'd found out sooner than now. Of course, if things were different, I wouldn't have been sitting there. What a stupid thing, to let something so silly as his parentage come between us. After all, had he ever said a word against my mother, even when she gave him silly underwear for Christmas? I held his hands tightly. "People recognize you everywhere. You're totally like a rock star, aren't you?" I asked, a hint of a smile twisting at the corners of my lips.

He let out a breath of relief, understanding that it wasn't really an issue any longer. "Except without the parking privileges," he admitted.

I nodded. "Or the really good seats at the best restaurants. You've got groupies, though."

"Do I?" He grinned.

"Yuh-huh." I let the smile blossom as I squeezed his hand. "One groupie, at least."

"That's all I need. Yes, I'm that Corydonais," Cor admitted. "How long have you and Jen . . . ?"

"I don't know. Maybe nine months." He shuffled away from me, hands plunged deep into his pockets, still seeming amazed to be in Cor's presence. "We met at a bar. She thought I was funny. I brought her home for a night. She kind of ended up staying for six weeks. I haven't really had any relationships since Barb—since your mother," he said, still not looking in my direction. "And if I were to, it wouldn't be with Jen. She's a sweet girl, but kind of . . ."

"When did Jen move to Grant's place?" I asked. I didn't really want to hear any more. The more relationships he'd had, in fact, the better I might feel about having painted him mentally all these years as a lusty satyr straight from a Hieronymus Bosch triptych.

"Like I said, after about six weeks. She'd lost a job she had. Some silly . . ."

"*Triviatastic!*" I supplied.

"Right. That was it. It wasn't even trivia. It was more like . . . pop culture detritus. Anyway, one of her friends called. It was kind of a strange thing, because whoever it was that called, told her about how someone was looking for a . . . I can't remember what it's called."

"Surrogate mother."

Jeroboam nodded. "That's it. I didn't know the phrase. We don't have such things in the Kinlands." When I looked over to Cor, he was nodding in agreement. "And that was it. She packed her bags and was gone. I saw her maybe once a month after that. She still called me her boyfriend?"

"All the time." Cor and I both said the words in unison, looked at each other, and smirked a little. "Why was that phone call a strange thing?" Cor asked.

"Because she never found out which one of her friends

was calling," Jeroboam explained. "The call was disconnected or something. You know these cellular phones your people use." Apparently he reminded Cor of something, because the lanky Peri leaned back in the sofa and reached into his pants pocket to pull out the mobile phone I'd given him a few months back. He flipped open the lid and began to scrutinize the display. "You've seen my telephone," my father said, addressing me. "I don't have that thing . . . caller ID. No answering machine."

"Why do you live so spartanly?" I asked.

"The Circle doesn't have as much funding as, say, the Storm Ravens. No offense intended." Cor inclined his head at Jeroboam's apology. "I've chosen frugality so I can continue my research on this side."

"What do you do out here?" I didn't know why I was asking all of these questions. Perhaps having Cor around emboldened me. At least I could sound as if we were trying to pursue this little mystery, instead of asking out of personal interest.

"Trying to save the Kinlands." He rested his back against the door jamb as he spoke. "If you know about our people, you likely know that the Kinlands have been eroding over the centuries."

"Since your people stopped giving *teinds* to Hell, yes."

"Approximately six hundred years ago, the Circle of Philosophers invented the energies you call constructs," he explained, obviously trying to simplify the science behind it as if I were a student in an introductory seminar. "Self-contained spheres with finite limits. Almost like worlds unto themselves, never diminishing, never expanding. That was the kind of energy we had to harness to keep the perimeter of the various remaining Kinlands from deteriorating. We were successful in locating many of the remaining isolated realms where Kin still dwelled, and stabilizing them."

"But those constructs can be destroyed. I've done it twice."

He nodded. "The energies around the perimeter of Resht and the other Kinlands are less volatile than a small construct, but yes, absolutely. That's a danger still, though it's not discussed or publicized much outside the Circle. There are ways—in theory—we believe that even Resht itself could be dissolved from within. Like a soap bubble."

"The Crown is aware." Cor had finished reading whatever was on his cell phone display, and had begun to punch out a few numbers. "I got your message," he said to someone on the other end. Ginger, if I was guessing correctly. "Tell me," he said, in response to something she said on the other end. "Who's there?" He listened for a while longer, than closed the phone. "Azimuth."

My pulse quickened. "He's been seen?"

"He was behind that phone call, somehow. The one to Jen. Do you have papers?" Cor asked Jeroboam, standing on his feet and tucking away the cell phone. "Forged human documents?"

The question obviously flustered my father. "Well, of course . . . diplomas, references."

"Driver's license?" I asked.

He shook his head. "I believe in public transportation."

Good lord, he was like my mother. "But passports, that kind of thing?"

He nodded. "The Circle assured me that it was all aboveboard. . . ."

"Who sold them to you?"

"I . . . I . . ." Our battery of questions had so flummoxed Jeroboam that he didn't know how to answer. "The Circle has always arranged for their manufacture and provided them to me. I haven't bought them from anyone. Not personally."

"I'm willing to bet that if I put some investigators on that trail, we'd find out that the person who supplied them was—"

"Azimuth," I said. "If he's had his fingers in a lot of pies over time, he could have found out that Jeroboam had sired me."

"You'll think I'm paranoid again, but I think this whole setup was a strike at me," Cor said, his expression thoughtful. "When he found out that you and I—"

"Yes," I said, my mind racing alongside his. "I see it. When he made the connection between me and a past customer, he realized he could capitalize on it. He would have known that Marcus Grant was looking to rent out a womb to Abaddon."

"What?" From his slouching position against the door, Jeroboam suddenly lurched upright. Apparently he hadn't heard that bit, yet.

"Particularly if he was working with the Order of the Crow. He wouldn't even have to have met Grant face to face. He could have lured Jen into it with a faked phone call," Cor said, too busy with our train of thought to explain or reassure my alarmed father. "If she hadn't bitten, he wouldn't have lost anything or been exposed."

"But she did," I theorized. "So he had an in with both us and Grant."

"Making a profit by landing you right back into the lap of Mrs. Jones."

"And taking a cut of the unholy union of Jen and Satan, I'm guessing." It made sense to me.

"By all that's holy." Jeroboam's mild baritone broke through our excited chatter. "This is insanity." We both stared at him. He turned to address me. "Is this what your life is like, Samantha? Mythical death cults and Abaddon? You should be . . . !"

"What?" I wanted to know. If I sounded slightly belligerent, I was entitled. "What should I be doing?"

"Living your life! Working! Watching television! Going out with girlfriends and reading and going to graduate school! Getting married and having a family!" He seemed exasperated with me. "All the wonderful, human options

that you're supposed to have. Not the stuff of nightmare."
He glared at Cor, as if he were the source of all my problems. "I never would have wanted this for you. Surely you don't have to."

Chinks were beginning to appear in my armor, I could tell. Jeroboam might not ever work his way past the layers of stone that I'd constructed against him over the years, but even I could hear in his voice the distress of a parent worried about his child. I'd heard it from my mom often enough. "You're wrong. I do it because I do have to," I told him, shrugging. "Who else will?" The information made him sag. I pitied him.

"Speaking of which. We need to get on the move." Cor tapped the phone in his pants. "That call was from Ginger. She says one of our sweeps reported an unauthorized portal opening in quadrant three-seventeen. Santa Monica Pier," he translated, for us non-Raven types. Then, turning to me, he added, "The van was abandoned in the parking lot."

I was already on my feet. "Let's go."

"Problem." Cor interrupted my mad dash out the front door. "You can't fly."

I halted. I hadn't considered that little fact. "Eleven miles in L.A. traffic. It'll take me twenty-five minutes to get there by cab. That's assuming no stops along Santa Monica Boulevard." Cor didn't have to tell me that time was of the essence. We'd wasted enough already. I could sense his yearning to spring into action, and I knew what sacrifice I'd have to make. "Just . . . go without me. It's okay. Go without me."

"Are you sure?"

As honestly as I could, I told him how I was feeling. "Yes. I want to be part of it, but this is bigger than my ego. Go."

Cor leaned down, took my head between his hands, and pressed his lips against mine until they tingled with pleasure. "I love you."

"I love you too," I murmured.

"I love you more than you imagine. Twenty-four hours is

the slightest fraction of my life, but not being able to say it for that long . . ." He pressed his brow against mine and shook his head.

"Do your thing," I urged him. "Don't worry about me."

So engrossed in each other had we been that we'd nearly completely forgotten about my father, standing across the room watching. "I don't mean to interrupt," he said, clearing his throat. "But if you wanted to stay together, have either of you considered taking a shortcut through the Kinlands?"

Chapter Nineteen

I believe I summed up my reaction succinctly: "Do what? Huh?"

"Not the Kinlands themselves, exactly." Jeroboam's comments were directed more to Cor than me. "The OZ. I don't know if you have the capability to create a bubble.

"Oz?" I turned to Cor, my eyes narrowed in suspicion. "Is there a wizard there?"

"Outer Zone," he explained. "Coincidence. We *think*."

"Actually," said my father, in the exact same didactic manner my mother used whenever she picked up on an anachronism in a gladiator movie that I was appreciating solely for the glistening male torsos, "the abbreviation comes from the Latin *zona*, but the O is from *obscurare*, or *making dark*." More and more I was beginning to understand the past attraction between those two. "Oh." He had finally noticed our impatient fidgeting. "Sorry. It's a barren place that occupies the adjacencies between the human world and ours. It's not a world, per se. Nobody lives there."

"Refugees often do," Cor said. "Though not for long, if we have anything to say about it."

I felt as if I were getting a crash course in physics, with the promise of an exam just around the corner. "Adjacencies?"

"There are spots in your world where the Kinlands are still adjacent to ours," explained my father. If he'd been my mom, he would have been pulling charts out of the umbrella stand and hauling out a dry erase board to draw an illustration. Thank God his apartment was so spartan. "With Resht, it's parts of greater Los Angeles. Pacific Palisade to Studio City to Redondo Beach, with Venice at the center."

"Right now, adjacent to here, is the outer zone of Resht." Now that there was a chance he didn't have to fly at his highest speeds to Santa Monica, Cor seemed a little less on edge. He still spoke quickly, laying it out for me. "We could move a lot faster in the OZ than through this space. It takes a portal to cross over, though. Either a natural portal like the one in Venice, or one of the few that's been opened, legally or not."

"Illegal," I said, "like the one in Santa Monica?"

He nodded. "There aren't any portals in West Hollywood."

Apparently I was the only sane one in the room. "Right now, guys, the only thing adjacent to here is a kitchen that would send Martha Stewart running for bleach and a scrub brush."

No one was paying any attention to me, however. The boys were too busy discussing their Peri toys. "Is there someone in your order who can open a bubble?" Jeroboam asked.

"What's a bubble?" I wanted to know.

Cor shook his head, not seeming to hear me. "I don't believe so."

"If there was, they could bubble into the Outer Zone, then reach here relatively quickly, bubble you back. . . ."

With a shake of his head, Cor crossed his arms. "If any of the Ravens has that particular talent, I've never heard of it." He sighed. "It would be helpful at times."

"Oh."

"What's a bubble?" I asked again.

"You're the expert on these energies," Cor pointed out to Jeroboam. "Aren't you capable of doing it?" My father slowly shook his head, obviously wishing he could. "Is there some-one else from the Philosopher's Circle who might be able?"

"Of course." Cor's face relaxed at Jeroboam's news. "But they're in Resht, and the Circle's private portal is on the USC campus."

"Damnation!" Cor's voice thundered across the room, past the splintered door, and echoed out in the hallway. There were probably roaches on the ground floor cowering at the sound of that roar. "Don't you have some kind of . . . technological . . ."

When I saw him struggling with his words, I leaped in to help. "Space gun portal–opening–type thingie?"

Jeroboam stared at me, then at Cor, and shook his head. "One of your Ravens has to have the talent. It's not com-mon, but not particularly rare either. A latent ability could have been activated if one of them worked very much with any of the architectonical energies." Cor was about to ex-plode with frustration, I realized. We both knew that he could have been well on his way by now if we hadn't trav-eled down this particular dead end. I was about to suggest once more that Cor just fly on without me, when my father added one more thing. "If one of them had entered and ex-ited several bound-energy constructs, for example, he might have absorbed enough of the wave patterns to . . ." He halted, then turned his head to stare at me. "Or she."

"What?" Cor's gaze rested squarely upon me as well. Like a ping-pong ball being batted between crack Chinese experts, my head bounced between them until I protested. "Nuh-uh."

"She told me she'd successfully escaped from two hostile constructs," Jeroboam remarked.

"Of course she was successful," Cor told him, studying me. I swelled with slight pride for a moment until his next remark. "If she hadn't been, she wouldn't be standing here."

"Hate to admit it, guys, but I am not your gal." I resisted the urge to back away from them. They looked like hungry cats who'd just spied a mouse, sized triple-X. "I'm just your run-of-the-mill, ordinary, average earth chick with no special talents whatsoever beyond the ability to uncart her groceries at the supermarket check-out so that they're bagged by container type. What?" I asked, feeling uneasy. "Some people think that's a talent."

"She is half-Kin."

I glared at Cor when he said that. "You told me that half-Kin are entirely human!" That assurance had been the only thing keeping me sane during the last hour. "You can't take it back now!"

Jeroboam shook his head. "No, it wouldn't work." I began to relax as he explained. I didn't need that kind of pressure. "Ancestral philosophers—you'd call them geneticists, Samantha—would say that my line alone wouldn't produce even the most benign of latent effects. The genes would have to be passed from her mother. Who, as we both know, is far from . . ."

"Normal," Cor finished, his face grim.

With the utmost diplomacy, Jeroboam bowed a little at the waist. "I was going to say *of the Kin*."

"Oh, crap." I now officially knew what a sinking feeling felt like. While they'd been talking, my feet suddenly seemed to be engulfed by the worn wooden floor beneath them, submerging themselves into the layers of metal and concrete and plaster and slowly dragging my legs with them. At my expostulation, they both turned and looked at me again. "Once again, I ask you: what's a bubble?"

Cor's eyebrows rose. A spark of hope animated his countenance as my father spoke. He, too, seemed less defeatist than a moment before. "Picture yourself chewing a stick of . . . what is it . . . chicle?"

"Gum? Chewing gum?"

"Yes, exactly. When you stretch it to blow a bubble, the gum is like the barrier between two worlds. The outside, human world. . . ."

"And the fascinating, bacteria-teeming wild kingdom of my mouth. Yes, I get it," I said, impatient and frankly, more than a little frightened.

Dear old Dad hadn't quite gotten used to me, I could tell. He blinked a few times at my abruptness before proceeding. Though he only looked to be in his mid-to-late thirties, he had a professorial, ruffled way of speaking that made me want to knock him around a little to speed things up. "Picture the gum expanding in a bubble outward and capturing something on its exterior, then being inhaled back into the mouth in a reverse bubble, as it were. What happens to the object adhering to the exterior?"

"I get it, Mr. Wizard. It gets sucked inside. Great. Fine." Cor seemed as if he had a dozen questions he wanted to ask me at that moment. Namely, why had my tune changed so suddenly, and why was I so interested? "But what would one of these bubbles *look* like?"

"Samantha." Cor couldn't contain himself any longer. Just as I could have predicted, he said, "Why are you asking?"

"Well." The slogging feeling that had been weighing down the lower half of my body grew twice as heavy, threatening to drag me down through four floors into the bedrock of Los Angeles. "You remember the other night?" He shook his head. Yes, I knew there had been a lot of other nights recently. "The one where we . . ." I flushed a little, and suddenly couldn't look at my father. "Were on the floor? With the candles?" To Jeroboam's credit, he had the decency to suck in his lips and turn his head, which is the closest I guess he could come to leaving the room.

The squint that Cor gave me indicated that he wasn't following. "Of course."

"Remember when I asked you if you'd done something? I asked if you were doing some kind of magic, then you said something conceited, and I said . . ."

Now he remembered. "You said the room had looked

green for a moment." I nodded. "But how in the world? Your mother's not . . ."

"Don't ask." The last thing I wanted to bring up at that moment was how I knew the blood on my mother's side wasn't pure human. I wouldn't have even connected my strange, out-of-body experience with the bubble theory or whatever Jeroboam wanted to call it, if it hadn't been for the information Azimuth had given me shortly before he'd disappeared. Odd, that. Why had he helped me, and so intensely yet, knowing all the while he was about to attempt a kidnapping? "Let's just say I'm the muttliest mutt this side of the dog pound. So what do I have to do?" I asked Jeroboam. "Let's get this bubble started. The quicker the better, because when it doesn't work, you'll have to wing it to Santa Monica."

I didn't know whether the deafness that my father had been feigning during the nooky-talk had risen out of embarrassment, or whether it was a puritanical pose adopted solely for my benefit. None of the Peri I'd encountered had seemed particularly prudish about sex. He seemed relieved, however, to be back on more of a scientific ground. Or perhaps I should say, spiritual ground, because the first thing out of his mouth were the words, "You'll have to go into a trance."

I blinked. Then I turned to Cor. "There's a window over there. Get flying."

"Sweetheart." Even though the situation was grim, I'd made him laugh a little. He put his hands on my shoulder, smiling at me with his eyes. "It's not difficult. No one's asking you to levitate. All you need to do is relax and breathe. Like yoga."

"I don't do yoga!" I yelled. "I'm too high-strung for yoga!"

"Try." Cor's hands slid from my shoulders down my arms to take my hands. He led me over to the sofa and sat me down. "Just relax. Try to think about nothing. If you have to think of something, try images of important things to you that will calm you down."

"All right." The words coming from my mouth sounded incredibly small and timid. Nonetheless, I waved my hands in front of my face to cool it. Then I closed my eyes and began to think of nothing.

And everything. All I could picture, really, were images I'd rather not see. When I tried to make my mind a blank, my mother's face popped up, prim and displeased as I left her in the stinking van after our last argument. I saw Jen poring over her yearbooks, one hand resting unconsciously on the bump swelling her midsection. She was replaced by the sight of Landemann, sharing my mother's sofa with three of her cats. This wasn't blank! I tried again, wiping from my head all the faces of those I felt guilty about.

Almost immediately, up popped Mrs. Jones as I'd first known her in the time I'd spent in that blasted construct: dressed in black and white, smart and elegant, with her hair pulled back into a bun, ladylike and deadly. I saw her son, too, intent on clipping Cor's wings for good. A wild shudder forced my eyes to open.

"I can't." Though I knew I was disappointing the two men, I had to be honest. "I'm not one of those special people who can do things!"

Across the living room, Jeroboam shook his head. "Perhaps she can't."

"Sssshhh." Cor's gentle reproach was meant for both Jeroboam and me. He looked into my eyes, and one of his hands cupped my cheek. "Samantha. You are a woman who does things every day. Impossible things. Six of them. Before breakfast." When I shook my head, feeling puny against his generous praise, he stilled me. "If anyone can do this, it would be you."

"I'm not special that way," I protested, more weakly than the last time. "I'm not a part of your crazy world."

"Sweetheart." He leaned in to embrace me, nestling my

head in the curve of his neck. Through his skin I could hear the rush of his blood. "If my world is crazy, it's because you're part of it."

I snorted wetly. "Gee, thanks."

"I'm proud of that," he assured me, his fingers brushing hair from my face. "Because I wouldn't want a world without you."

I let him hold me for a moment more—but only a moment. I knew time was fleeing from us. "Fine," I said, snuffling. "I'll give it another go. But I don't know how to put myself in a trance."

"Let me." Cor separated himself, then put his hands on my shoulder, applying enough pressure to rotate me in place. "Just close your eyes and relax."

When I looked over at my father, he had once more pressed his mouth and jaw into a curled hand. His thumb rested squarely between his top and bottom teeth; he rubbed the nail on the underside of his incisors, plainly worried. About me, I supposed. "All right," I agreed, trying to relax. "One more try."

"Pull up your feet," Cor urged. With a silent apology in the direction of Jeroboam, I obediently planted my dirty sneakers onto the sofa cushion and let Cor push me forward until my crossed arms rested on my bent knees. My brow touched my forearms as I felt the sensations of Cor's hands running up my neck and through my hair. "Try to breathe. Regularly. Evenly."

"All right."

"And don't talk," he ordered. I shivered as he touched me once again. The smooth roundness of his fingernails left trails of raw sensation as they traveled up the side of my neck from my shoulder, trailing to a vanishing point below my ear. "Just think about what you're feeling."

I was beyond identifying what I felt. Too much emotion from too many shocks had short-circuited my nerves. At that point, they were so ragged that they couldn't sense anything refined; only the biggest, broadest strokes, like the sharp cut of anxiety and the red, slowly pulsating throbs caused by guilt. Cor's fingers, though, were nice, the way they were sweeping along the nape of my neck, then down my shoulders. Maybe those were the feelings he'd wanted me to mind, come to think. I didn't mind concentrating on those.

My muscles trembled at the simple pleasures he was arousing with his fingertips. They brushed over my shoulders, my neck, then tickled their way along my jawline. Without warning, one dipped below the strap of my tank top, following the hemline until it reached my spine, where it took a turn north and disappeared into my hair. I wanted to tell him that it was all very nice, this impromptu session of making my skin tingly, but it wasn't getting us very far, or fast. My head was feeling less crowded, yes. Every touch seemed to erase the black shadows that had been making it difficult for me to think. All I wanted to do was sit there, curled up like a cat, and luxuriate in that touch. But was I drawing out a bubble? No.

"I'm sorry guys," I said, shaking my head. "This isn't working."

As if from a distance, so far away that it sounded like a whisper, I could hear my father's voice saying, "There she goes."

"Oh, my." Cor's voice was equally faint.

"Don't lose contact with her. You obviously work best as a team."

"I've never seen anything like . . ." Cor's words trailed to nothing.

Something in my head told me that I should have been frightened, yet I felt perfectly calm when I opened my eyes. My father was still on the opposite wall, rubbing his face with his hand as he watched. Cor still sat behind me. When I looked over my shoulder in his direction, his lips were moving, but no sounds were coming out. "Honey?" I asked, jerking around to face him. "I can't hear you."

That's when the strange thing happened. Although I moved to face my lover, I stayed perfectly still. That is, it seemed as if I split, leaving behind one of me. I was looking at the top of my own head, resting my hands on my knees. Cor still stroked the back of my neck, his hands not leaving my skin. When I stood, I seemed almost to be as light as a feather. For a moment, I thought I'd continue to rise and rise like a balloon until I bounced across the ceiling. "*Okay*," I said aloud. "*This is very weird.*"

I was speaking in the tongue of the Kin. Every word sounded unexpectedly lovely, chiming with the bell-like overtones I'd always associated with the speech of the Peri. I tried again. "*La la la la la*," I babbled, until I realized that nonsense syllables were nonsense syllables in any language. "*How much wood could a woodchuck chuck if a woodchuck could chuck wood?*" Even that tongue-twister sounded languid and poetic. "*Hey, Cor. Listen.*"

I tried to reach out and tap him on the shoulder, but Cor wasn't there anymore. Neither was I. The other I, that is, who had been sitting on the couch. Our outlines still remained, but they'd been blurred over with green and reduced to their most vague and general forms. On one of my trips to the East Coast a few years ago, I remember stretches of highway where an ornamental vine gone wild—kudzu, that was the name—had grown over and consumed road signs, junked cars, and entire empty buildings alike, reducing them to life-sized out-lines covered with green carpet. Something similar seemed to be happening to Jeroboam's apartment. With every passing second, moss seemed to be overtaking the surfaces, from the walls and ceiling to my father's very skin. My nostrils tingled in the same way as when I passed a sunny yard where the grass had just been cut; everything around me smelled like the out-doors. I could sense the fresh, sweet nectar of flowers, but also a dark, earthy undertone of a scent that reminded me of de-caying autumn leaves. Only I—the I that hadn't been covered over moments before—remained untouched.

And yet I wasn't frightened. I knew perhaps I should be, but somehow this place didn't call for fear. All the turmoil I'd felt only moments before had vanished, quelled in the utter hush. It wasn't that I was suddenly deaf; when I'd spoken, I'd heard my voice perfectly clearly. In my box of green, the quiet was unbroken by the sound of other beings, or of wildlife. It reminded me of waking early in the morning as a kid, before anyone else had risen to eat their breakfast or start their cars, and the world seemed to be mine and mine alone. Giddy at the idea, I pushed through the hanging vines where my father's broken door had hung and stepped outside.

I was alone; that much I could tell. A forest had sprung up where before had stood the dingy hallway and the stairwell that could barely accommodate two people standing side by side. Trees shot to the sky, branching out at impossible heights nearly invisible to my eye. Their bark, pale gray in color, curled with such delicacy around the slender trunks that it looked as if it might crumble to powder if I dared touch it. Silvery illumination filtered down through the treetops, sending shafts of light through what looked like the most insubstantial of mists. The scents of the outdoors were even more pungent than they had been in my little room of green. When I inhaled, long and slow and evenly, as Cor had urged me to do, the entire life cycle seemed to fill my lungs, from the sprouting of new growth to its blossoming, to its decomposition and return into the rich earth underfoot. The only sounds were of my shuffling through the leaves.

I trod lightly. To me, the surroundings seemed ancient, and holy.

I don't remember how long I walked in that forest. It felt like an eternity, though my legs didn't tire. If anything, they felt stronger for being in this world, as if after all the exertion that had turned them to rubber, they were absorbing energy from the place and invigorating my body once again. I don't even remember exactly how I knew where I was going, but I did. Some inner force seemed to be pushing me forward, not letting me tarry long enough to enjoy the languorous spirals the leaves took as they slowly descended from treetop to ground, or to observe the complicated patterns in which vines hung between the trunks. I had a destination. Of that I was certain. I simply didn't know exactly where it might be.

Time passed, yet I didn't have any clear indication of how much distance the sun had traveled. I wasn't even certain there was a sun at all, so diffuse was the light that spread all around me. Still prodded onward by invisible urges, I trekked forward with sure feet on the soft and uneven ground. Not once did I stumble—if I had, I would have fallen face-first onto the downy cushion of leaves that had been accumulating underfoot for months, if not years.

It wasn't until the leaves began to grow more sparse underfoot that I realized I actually was getting somewhere. Through the slim trunks ahead I could see a vast shape looming, a dark mass of wood more mighty than any I'd seen in this world or my own. It was wider and deeper than any giant redwood, with branches thicker than the thousands of trees surrounding it, each laden with enormous evergreen needles. It was onto a bed of fallen needles, a rich orange-red in color, that I stepped as I drew near. I hastened my step. I'd arrived.

There were people near the tree, occupying a spot beneath where the lowest of the giant tree's branches stretched out to mark its perimeter. Women, specifically—three of them, each with long, thick hair that they had restrained into braids as thick as rope. The first was fair, beautiful, and blond, with three long braids that fell over her shoulders and onto her lap. The woman next to her, a plump redhead with pigtail braids hanging from either side of her head, sported an enormous mole above her upper lip. The last woman had only a single plait of woven hair that disappeared down her back. Her skin was the dark brown shade of the earth itself. Yet the oddest thing about the three women was not their seemingly impromptu gathering at the foot of the tree, nor their stripped-down mode of dress that seemed to consist of halters and long draped skirts, nor the fact that they were sitting around a round table that looked like it had been purchased at the nearest IKEA. No, it was the fact that they were all on Apple laptops and all busily tapped away at their keyboards.

"Hello," I said, drawing to a stop a few feet away from them. I no longer seemed to be speaking the language of the Kin. I waved my hand.

Only the last of the women looked up from her keyboard, but her face failed to register any expression other than a stony impassiveness. "Hail, Samantha." The fact that she knew my name surprised me, but failed to alarm. The woman's dark skin glowed in the light of her laptop screen as she turned her head to the others. "Samantha Dorringer," she told them. "Check your list."

"Got it," said the first, the blonde. She looked me over briefly, tossed back her braids so that they flew back over her shoulders, then peered around her laptop to get a good look at me. "Oh. That's her?"

The redhead opened her lips and blew a large bubble with gum that she quickly sucked back in. I could have sworn by the scent that it was grape flavored. Snapping and popping the gum at the back of her mouth, she gave me the once-over as well. "You always say that. It's like you expect them to have horns or something." While the dark-skinned woman had spoken in a deep and cultured voice and the blonde in lighter tones, the redhead's accent was pure, unadulterated Boston. *Hawwwwns*, was how she'd pronounced it. I wondered if I could get her to ask me to *paaaak* the *caaaa*.

"I don't expect her to have horns, silly." The blonde smiled at me in apology. "It's just that they never look like I expect. You know. Heroic. Big." She curled her arm and poked at her biceps. "Muscly."

"It says she's an insurance investigator, not an American Gladiator." The dark-skinned woman appeared to be reading something on her screen. She studied me, then returned to the page she'd been browsing. Out of curiosity, I tried to edge around to see what she was reading. With a cold glare, she angled the laptop away from me. Then she tilted her head, crossed her arms, and raised her eyebrows.

"Sorry," I said, backing away again. "So who are you?"

"She's Ursula," said the redhead, pointing to the blonde on her right. Ursula looked around her laptop again and gave me a friendly wave. "She's Scold." The dark-skinned woman continued to stare at me without expression. "And I'm Dainty." Scold snorted at that. Apparently it was an old joke between them. Dainty looked down at the ample cleavage bursting from the halter holding it up, and then at her wide, but attractive, hourglass figure. "Shut up," she said, almost automatically.

"Nice to meet you all." I had their full attention now; even Scold had stopped tapping at her keypad. I repeated my question. "So who are you?"

"Honey, we're the three wired sisters," Ursula informed me with a dimpled smile.

"You mean the three weird sisters?"

Scold put both hands down on the table and tilted her head again. "Do I look weird to you?"

"No, not at all," I said hastily, taking another step away. "Wired sisters it is."

"You are *not* supposed to be here," Scold continued. "Why is she here?" When she looked at the others, they all seemed to shrug. "We do our best work remotely," she informed me. "Fate works best from a distance."

Dainty stuck her finger between her teeth, wrapped her

gum around it, gave a yank, and let the elastic mess spring back into her mouth. "I don't think she did it deliberately." Ursula shook her head, apparently in my defense. "Good timing, though."

"What do you mean, good timing?" I asked. My pulse should have quickened, but it didn't; I was as calm as I had been walking through the forest. "Does it have something to do with Mrs. Jones? Is that why I'm here? To learn my fate?"

The three sisters turned their faces to each other, silently conferring. "We do not normally comment on unsolicited inquiries into one's personal destiny," Scold said.

"Oh come *on*. I've got to be here for some reason. You said yourself that it's unusual I'm here."

Scold looked at Dainty for guidance. Dainty merely shrugged, blew another bubble, and then looked at Ursula. "I say we tell her," urged the blonde. "Just a hint."

"Fine. A *hint*." Scold peered at her computer screen, reading the information there.

"If it's about Mrs. Jones . . ." I started to say.

Dainty shook her head. "You don't want to hear about your fate instead?"

I blinked rapidly. "She's not my fate?"

Scold didn't look up from her information retrieval. "You're missing the forest for the trees."

"We thought you'd want to hear your real prophecy," said Ursula.

"I do! A real prophecy would be swell. Fantastic, even. In the purest sense of the word. Not that you're a fantasy of mine or anything. I don't think." Aware that they were all regarding my prattling with astonishment, I zipped it. "Done now."

"Regular or rhyming?" Scold wanted to know.

Ursula seemed to be the friendliest of the three. I looked to her for a little advice. "Which do you recommend?"

"Regular," said all three in a chorus, without hesitation.

Ursula gave me a little smile of apology. "Rhyming's easier these days with the online rhyming dictionaries, but still."

"Much more prone to misunderstanding," agreed Dainty.

"Regular it is, then!" I tried to sound jaunty as I said it. "Lay it on me."

Scold raised her eyebrows, then rose from her chair. "Ladies? Shall we?"

Sleeping or not, I certainly felt as if I'd been trapped in some kind of dream when the three sisters joined hands and leapt into the air. Twenty feet up they bounded in one swift motion. Then over the table they began to fall in slow motion, gently sinking to earth with their robes flapping around them, graceful as a trio of dandelion seeds drifting on a breezeless day. "A world will die at your hand," Ursula called out, her free hand cutting a fluid path through the air.

"Another will be saved." Her fingers held firmly by her sisters, Dainty seemed to be falling faster than the others. Her feet stretched out toward my face.

"One will be born." Of all three, Scold's voice was the firmest, sounding like a trumpet on the last day. A thrill went through my very blood at the sound of it.

"When?" I asked, turning my head as the sisters continued their descent. Scold shook her head, while Ursula turned away her face. Was she crying? "When is this going to happen? What do I have to do?"

Only Dainty continued to look at me. Her feet touched the earth, mere feet away from my own. Her sisters fell beside her, the tips of their toes making soft contact with the bed of needles.

"Do I have to do this alone?" I asked, suddenly desperate to know. The lovely calm sensation I'd enjoyed until now was beginning to fade. In the light of prophecy, sheer panic had begun to return. "Tell me I won't be alone. Please!"

Dainty's jaw worked. For a moment I thought she was going to reassure me, but she was only chewing her gum.

From the middle of her lips puffed a translucent globe. So strong was the grape flavoring that it completely obscured the spicy scent of the giant pine. Bigger and bigger it grew, expanding outward, until with a deft motion she raised her index finger and plunged in her bright red nail.

The bubble popped.

The next thing I knew, I was on my knees, somewhere hard. Concrete. Hot concrete. "Sam?" The word was dim at first, faint and almost inaudible. Then more loudly it came. "Sam?"

"Cor?" My head was spinning with that awful, dizzying sensation I sometimes got when I rose too quickly from a sitting position. "Ow," I said, clutching it. "Did you see them?"

The noises beginning to rush in were almost overwhelming after the silence of that great forest. I could hear the chatter of people talking, of cars, of music, of seagulls loudly crying for scraps. Then I felt hands on both my arms, gently lifting me to a standing position. "Sweetheart." My face was against Cor's chest. That much I could tell. "You didn't say a word all the way."

"All the way what?"

"Through the OZ." That was my father talking. I hadn't expected him to come. I was too busy dealing with the ringing in my ears to spare much energy toward being irritated. "We had to drag you."

"What time is it?" I asked, cracking open my eyelids. They felt crusty, like after a particularly hard sleep. "How long has it been?"

"About three minutes since you went into your trance. I knew you could do it." The pride in Cor's voice gladdened my heart. I could see him now, though the sun brought tears to my eyes.

"And we're where?" Once I'd wiped my face, I tried peering around me. We were standing to the side of a blue and white archway leading over a four-lane road. *Santa*

Monica Yacht Harbor, it read in art deco lettering. *Sport Fishing & Boating. Cafes.* When I focused on the distance, past a parking lot and long stretches of concrete, I could see a roller coaster and a Ferris wheel. Pacific Park. We'd ended up where we needed to be. "Oh," I breathed, astonished. "But did you see them?"

"See who?" Cor asked. Now that I could see his face, I noticed how tired he appeared. Tiny lines widened his eyes, and his face was a little paler than it had been in Jeroboam's apartment. He beamed at me, though, obviously happy to have me back. "We didn't see anyone."

"You didn't see three women?" I looked from Cor to my father. They both shook their heads. "The wired sisters?"

"You mean weird sisters?"

"That's what *I* said!" I crowed. Cor still shook his head, though. "Okay. Maybe that part was a dream." It certainly hadn't felt like one, though. And even in the harsh California afternoon sunshine, the memory of it wasn't fading.

Across the bridge I heard the slap of footsteps racing toward us. Ginger, of course, in her camo pants and tight-fitting top, followed by several of the Storm Ravens in less conspicuous beach attire. "We've located the general area of the portal," she announced without any greeting. She looked Jeroboam up and down, apparently recognized him as one of her own, and then dismissed him from her thoughts. "We spotted the Azimuth fellow entering the park, but lost him."

"We think through the portal, sir," chimed in one of the other Ravens, a lean woman I recognized from regular yard duty.

"And my mother?" I asked. "And Jen?"

She shook her head, not happy to have to deliver the bad news. "There's someone you should talk to, though," she told Cor.

"Who?" he asked.

She made a loopy motion around her ear. "You'll see." Without a word more, she made a motion to her Ravens and began jogging back across the bridge.

Cor and I looked at each other. It didn't sound good. Grabbing hands, we started to follow.

Chapter Twenty

"Hellfire and damnation will soon be raining down upon us, hallelujah! It was a demon, I tell ya!" I'd never seen quite so many terrible tattoos on a single person before. The Mickey Mouse facsimile on the woman's shoulder was particularly inept, recognizable only by the trademark big ears—the face looked like a squashed submarine sandwich and the body like an oozing blue sore. In fact, it and all her other amateur ink appeared to have been done on the cheap with a Bic ballpoint and a hot safety pin. "A demon!"

"You've said that. Why don't you calm down and tell me some details," I suggested. Emmy Jo Graves and I were sitting on a metal park bench together. I tried to muster up enough patience not to shake the woman. "Maybe if we had some space," I added with a meaningful look at the crowd around me. Not only were Ginger and Cor pressing in close, but several of the Storm Ravens and a few gawking passers-by watched as well. Save for recognizing a few familiar faces, I found it almost impossible to tell the difference between the civilians and the lower ranks of the Ravens.

Cor remained in place. Jeroboam immediately backed away. Frankly, I didn't know why he was still with us. "Come on, everybody. Clear off," said Ginger, immediately dispersing the crowd. Once we had some sunlight restored,

I leaned forward and tried talking to the woman Ginger had isolated for us.

She had passed the hysterical stage long before Cor and I arrived on the scene, and was now repeating her tale with an obvious relish. "So you were on the Pacific Wheel," I prompted, nodding at the big solar-powered Ferris wheel ride nearby.

"Yeah," she said, rocking back and forth. "I already told this to the guards." She pointed at a park security officer who stood not too far away with his hand on his walkie-talkie, watching her with narrowed eyes. "They didn't be-lieve me."

"We're not with them," I said, trying to get her attention back.

"Called me a crackhead."

"Well. That was just rude." Given Emmy Jo's wild wiry hair, the tattoos, and the scrawny and slightly malnourished appearance, I couldn't say that it was too surprising a guess, but for the moment I wanted to stay on her good side. "So what happened? Can you tell me?" I asked with a smile.

"It's like I told them," she said, grudging at first, but rap-idly following up. "I wanted to get out of the house and have some fun today. So I got myself a ride wristband *that I paid for!*" She yelled the last words in the direction of the se-curity guard, brandishing the band dangling from her right arm. There must have been some little altercation about that. "And then I got on the wheel over there."

I waited until the cars from the West Coaster swooped by with a roar overhead before asking my next question. "And what happened?"

"I was riding up, just like normal, and then all of a sud-den this *head* appeared. Out of nowheres!" She gestured with her hands for emphasis. "Just this *head!* And he had, like, fiery eyes. And this really long hair, white as his fangs. So I knew it was Satan."

"Fangs?" The white hair made sense, but the fangs must have been her own embellishment. Behind Emmy Jo's back, I mouthed a single word at Cor: *Azimuth.*

He nodded, then asked, "It was a him? A male?"

"Well yeah. Ain't no such thing as a girl demon. And I said, Jesus Christ, protect me! Get thee back, demon! Then he breathed fire at me and disappeared. They have to do that, you know, once you threaten them with the Lord God almighty."

"Just a head?" She nodded at my question. "No legs, no hands? A disembodied head?"

"I told you, it didn't have no disembody."

"Where did you see it?" Cor turned on the charm and leaned over so he might be more at face level with Emmy Jo. I noticed that she allowed herself quite a lingering inspection of his chest through the open top half of his shirt. "How high was it? Just off the ground? Halfway?"

Emmy Jo responded to him like a cat in heat hearing a man's deep voice. Her back arched forward, thrusting out the pancakes she had for breasts underneath her tight T-shirt and denim jacket. "All the way," she purred, then clarified. "At the very top."

"Thanks, hon," he said with a wink. Cor reached out to give her a pat on the shoulder while I reminded myself not to let him touch me with that hand until he'd washed. "You've been a big help."

"That's not what *he* said." Emmy Jo glared at the poor security guard again. Nursing righteous outrage, she jabbed a finger at him. "He said I should be locked up. *He* said I was making up lies to get attention."

Ginger leaned in and murmured to Cor, "They closed the wheel down for twenty minutes before you got here."

Overhearing, Emmy Jo reacted with even more indignation. "Now it's open again, exposing helpless children to perdition." She was on her feet, waving a fist at the security guard, whose hand immediately began hovering above his holster. "Hellfire and damnation will soon be raining down

upon us!" That was where we'd gotten on this crazy ride.
Now that the security guard was approaching with forcible
expulsion obviously on his mind, we decided to scatter.

Five minutes later the four of us found ourselves queued
up for the Pacific Wheel, bands fastened around our wrists.
"Lucky me," I said as the line slowly and surely dwindled in
the direction of the loading platform. "Two portals in one
day. Maybe I'll pass out and hallucinate again."

"I'll be there," said Cor, squeezing my hand. I supposed to
anyone else at the park that day, we looked like an ordinary
couple waiting on a ride. Somehow I liked that notion.

"Technically, the OZ you experienced wasn't a portal."
All that Jeroboam needed to make himself even more of a
science nerd, in his professor's khakis and plaid shirt, was a
pocket protector. "The energies of a bubble are much less
stable. Portals tend to be established at points where the adjacencies are much narrower, and therefore the transition
from one state to another is less disorienting."

"Who are you, again?" Ginger asked, staring at him.

I sighed and bit the bullet. "Ginger, this man is my sire.
My father. Whatever."

She looked at me, then him, and sniggered. "You mean,
your *boo-hoo my daddy ran out on me so no one can ever be mean
to me or I'll pout and whine because I was so depriiiived* father?"
My expression soured at the little melodrama she'd acted
out in that sentence. She noticed. "Seriously?"

"The information is confidential," Cor reminded her, his
face grave.

"Which means that if you so much as breathe one word
of it to my mom, I will personally see to it that you come to
some dire and evil end," I growled.

I hadn't considered what might happen if Mom found
out that the man she still thought of as Jerry Neale was still
in Los Angeles. Worse, that he looked the exact same as the
day he'd walked out on her. It would crush her—absolutely
reduce her to smithereens. Now it was imperative to me

that she never found out. I had to protect her. "Get out of line. You can't follow us in," I told my father. "Mom cannot see you."

He started to make weak protests. Cor, however, started to nod. "Samantha's right."

"It's been nice, you've been helpful, great to meet you." I took a deep breath and said what had to follow. "But good-bye."

Odd, how pronouncing that one word, *goodbye*, made me feel. I hadn't ever had the opportunity before to say it to him. Rather than get into any psychodrama about it—particularly with Ginger standing there, lapping it all up—I squashed any conflicting emotions I might have about him, hardened my heart, and prepared myself never to see him again. I fully expected him simply to turn tail and run. Apparently, however, I'd underestimated him. "No."

"It would be unfair of you to show up unannounced after all this time," Cor said, sounding displeased. "Especially looking like that."

"Don't judge me. I cannot alter the laws of nature, nor can I age more quickly to suit my mate." I had to admit, I hadn't seen many people stand up to Cor with such vigor. The four or five people ahead of us in the line were beginning to turn around and look at us. I reached out, touching my father's arm to quiet him. He responded by reducing his volume to a hiss. "You of all men should know, Corydonais! What are you going to do in ten years—twenty—when people see you with my daughter and mistake you for her son? She's . . . what, thirty-two now?"

"Good God! When will you people learn that I'm twenty-nine!" I growled.

Cor put his arm around my waist and pulled me close. "I will remain with your daughter for as long as she can stand the sight of me." Ginger turned her head and moved forward in the line.

"Oh, Cor." If I'd actually been an eighteenth-century

countess, I might have swooned onto a fainting couch. Instead I clutched him back, my heart pounding at the declaration. Though simple, it had moved me more than I could say.

Jeroboam didn't seem to know what to say. "It's different for you."

Cor's eyes grew cold. "Because I told her the truth from the start."

"You had no choice," I reminded him, as gently as possible. "Be fair. I figured something was strange when we spent our first date chasing hellboars from the Blighted Plains of Nefarion up and down the Las Vegas strip."

"Romantic, isn't it?" Ginger drawled, urging us forward. Only two people stood between us and the wheel.

My father shuddered. "I'm sorry," he said, crossing his arms and moving up in line. "I refuse to stand by while you drag Samantha into these kinds of dangerous affairs. It's obvious that she's bull-headed and stubborn and won't listen to reason, but she does it for the right reasons. So I can't stand in her way. That doesn't preclude me from coming to keep an eye on her, though."

"Oh, Dad," I groaned, until I realized that I sounded exactly like a teenager who'd just been told to be home by midnight or she'd be grounded for life. That recognition brought me up short. I unbent a little. "Fine. Your call. But stay out of the way if anything happens."

Cor didn't seem to welcome him as readily as I had. "I'm the leader of this rescue mission. Don't interfere."

"And for the love of all that's holy, do *not* let Mom see you," I begged.

"Fine." He held up his hands, begging us not to bark any more orders at him. "I'll do what you ask. I'll hide in the back. I'll shift so your mother doesn't have a heart attack. Anything you say."

We had stepped onto the loading platform at this point. The bored young fellow loading the cars asked Cor how many we had in our party. He raised four fingers while the next covered gondola swung down. I stepped in first, and then Ginger. Cor and my father followed. The car swung from side to side as the ride operator closed its gate, and then we were aloft.

I didn't even have a chance to enjoy the view of the Pacific before Cor started to bark out orders. "Jinjurnaturnia, keep an eye on our position. I don't know how wide the portal is, but we won't have much time to leap through once we're there. Sam and I first, and you two follow. If you have to, wait for the second revolution before using the portal."

"The Ravens are ready to enter as well on your command," Ginger assured him.

"How?" I asked. The car swung to a stop as the ride operator below let out one more couple. "Did you buy them all ride bracelets?"

"*They* can fly." Ginger intended her dry reply as a reminder that they would have been through the portal already, save for me. We lurched forward again, circling the hub at a steady rate.

I chose to ignore the implication that I was holding everyone back. "Why hasn't anyone on the ride vanished into the portal when they reached the top?"

Jeroboam wrinkled his nose. "Good question, but portals aren't like the Bermuda Triangle. Entering one is an act of will."

Against my will, I found myself interested. "Um, does that mean you know what the Bermuda Triangle is?"

Before he could answer, I felt Cor's hand snake around my waist. "Get ready," he told me, his legs tensing. When I looked out, we were a considerable distance from the ground, rounding the upper half of the wheel's arc. There wasn't much room to maneuver with the four of us in the gondola, but he reached out and grasped the steel pipe running from ceiling to floor, his head turning and moving as if he was watching something I couldn't see.

"What? What am I supposed to do?" I asked. I would've taken an answer from anyone, but they were all too busy. Doing what, I couldn't tell. Six months I'd been with Cor, and I didn't have anywhere near a comprehensive list of what the Peri could do that I couldn't.

We were rounding the peak, now; as our angle flattened to match the ocean horizon to my left, the gondola jerked on its pivot. It was then that I had a terrifying thought. What if the portal, or whatever, was *outside* the car? Was I going to have to jump? Because the very thought of it was making my stomach churn. "It's slightly outside the car. Right there," Cor announced, pointing. Ginger, following his gesture, nodded. When I looked at the point where he stared, though, all I saw was an empty space somewhere between our gondola and the one already beginning its descent in front of us. Empty space, that is, under which stretched nothing but tons of structural steel and a wide expanse of concrete. "Hang on to me," he warned.

"W-w-wait!" My mouth hardly worked. He was angling himself toward the outside door, as if ready to burst through it and jump. Which would be all very well for him, since he could shift in midair and wing his way to safety. I had a vision of me, however, plummeting like a soft sack of blood and bones. "I don't see it!"

"We're going to jump," said Cor, his mouth against the hair over my ear. "Trust me, okay?"

"I can't do this!"

"You've got to have faith in me." Hadn't I been saying the same thing over and over again to Jen, the last couple of days? "Do you have faith in me?"

I had to choose, right then. Right there. We couldn't wait the length of another entire rotation. Did I trust him? Yes, absolutely. Did I believe in that portal, hanging in midair, although I couldn't spy it? Someone with better authority than I could see it. I decided to take the leap. "Yes," I found myself stammering. "I trust you."

Was I even audible? I couldn't tell. Adrenaline coursed throughout my body. Without any fanfare, the gondola reached its peak. All time seemed to pause. I couldn't hear any of the music or babble of the crowds below—only the thick, sludgy course of my blood through my veins with every thunderous heartbeat. "Here we go!" Cor cried.

My heart seemed to flip as he charged forward. Both of his arms, firmly wrapped around my waist, dragged me along with him. I clamped shut my eyes. Yes, I might have screamed a little, though I preferred to think of it as the sort of loud yelping to which one is entitled when facing an uncertain leap into the great beyond.

The tips of my sneakers scudded across the gondola's metal floor as we lunged. I could have sworn that the next sensation I'd feel would be the gondola's gate crashing against my thighs, accompanied by the thud of my skull hitting the cab's roof, but instead I merely felt a gentle brushing sensation that began at the top of my head and followed the contours of my body, ending at my ankles. It felt almost exactly as if I'd passed through an opening in a pair of dense velvet curtains trimmed with tassels. Then I found my feet connecting with something hard that threw us both off balance. I somersaulted down a steep incline until, with a mighty thump, my shoulder slammed against a rough and irregular plane of stone.

When Cor landed on top of me, the impact seemed to squeeze all the air from my lungs and put stars in my eyes. Thank goodness, though, that there had been ground immediately on the portal's other side—solid rock, by the way it had banged up my knees and hips. When the sparks started to fade from my vision and I could see again, I rolled out from under Cor and tried to sit up. Dust was everywhere; I waved a hand to clear it from my face.

The only light in that place came from the portal we'd just entered. When I blinked the debris from my eyes and looked back at the downward ramp we'd just tumbled, it appeared very much as if someone had draped a pair of thick curtains over an arch-shaped opening that led to nowhere. Instead of fabric, however, the draperies appeared to be woven from darkness of differing shades, some pitch-black, others less opaque. Through the translucent areas, a deep blue gloom filtered into our cramped enclosure. Still, it was enough light for me to see the outline of Cor beside me, righting himself. "Sorry about the landing," he whispered, coughing on the dust. "I should have come alone."

It appeared we were in some kind of cavern that spiraled downward into blackness. I couldn't see a thing past the veiled pool of light spilling beyond the portal's entrance. "We'd better get out of the way before the others land on top of us," I said in a soft voice. "Where are we? Is this part of the Kinlands?"

For some reason, as if we'd discussed it, it seemed better to speak in whispers in this strange grotto in the middle of nowhere. "None that I've seen," he replied. I heard him rise, then complain with a subtle, "Ow!" From above me, I heard him say, "Don't try to get up too quickly. There's only about five, five and a half feet of headroom in here."

I heeded his advice and crouched in place, feeling the rock surface ahead of me to make certain I wasn't shuffling off the edge of a precipice. "The ground is pretty smooth. Even, for the most part. Nothing icky. No debris." Or insects. Or snakes, I hoped and prayed. "I just wish we could see."

"Hold on." I heard Cor murmur a few words in his own language that I didn't recognize. To my ears, it sounded like a prayer or incantation. Above me where he stood, a small flicker ignited in the darkness, spreading and blooming like a flower. When it had unfolded completely, it glowed as warmly as a firefly, though it was more the size of a large berry and radiated enough light to let us see several feet ahead. The yellow glow lit Cor's face from beneath. When he smiled down at me, he looked like one of those Baroque

Dutch paintings of a saint, bathed and blessed by the light of a single candle. "When our kind fell to earth, we were instructed to be a light that shineth in a dark place," he said, embarrassed by my astonishment. "So there you have it."

"All righty," I agreed, awestruck. "Let's go."

We'd managed to travel several feet around the first bend in the tunnel when behind us we heard the flutter of feathers and wings. We tensed and froze, but almost immediately it was followed by the sound of my father saying, "Ow!"

"Well, don't stand up all the way, then," said Ginger, reasonably. When Cor shushed both of them, they collected themselves and joined us. Soon two other small blossoms of light joined his, so that a pool of gentle light surrounded us. "Where are we?" Ginger asked.

"Is it one of your outer zones?" I appealed to Jeroboam, since he seemed to know more than anyone else.

"It's an outer zone," he said from his crouched-over position. He kept his hands cupped together as he held his little flame up to the ceiling, and then moved it to examine the walls. "But not one of ours. If I had to guess . . ."

"Let's move, crew," Cor prodded, taking the lead.

Ginger could almost stand up straight in the chamber, while Cor and Jeroboam moved forward with their necks and backs arched over. I was the only one who proceeded on all fours, like some kind of frog. Somehow it seemed safer. "If you had to guess, what?" I asked, peering up at Jeroboam.

He was still studying the walls as we descended, standing a little straighter as the ceiling became a few inches higher. "This rock is highly compressed, but this corridor is quite smooth. I would guess that it has been eaten away by a high-temperature substance. If I had to venture an educated theory, I would say that long ago it served as a volcanic vent for . . ."

"Hell." Cor stopped ahead of us. The light between his fingers disappeared as he held out a hand, halting us from proceeding any further.

"I was going to say Hell-adjacent. But yes. It would be . . . oh, my." Jeroboam's steps, too, drew to a stop.

"What?" I asked from my knuckle-dragging position. When no one answered, I noticed that they were all standing totally upright beneath a much higher ceiling, staring over the natural ledge of rock where the path had ended. None of them were cupping their hands any longer, yet there was light enough to see their faces. "What?" I asked again, stretching my muscles and joining them. Then I turned to look at the vista below.

Our tunnel had emptied out into a vast cavern, oblong and almost egg-shaped. Although there was a crude incline leading downward around the cavern's perimeter—almost a rudimentary set of steps—our view of the cavern's floor some fifty feet below was obstructed by the outcropping immediately before us of sharp, almost sword-like stones projecting out into the void. Obstructed, but not obscured, for when I pressed my way among the three Peri and peered between two of the blade-like edges, I could see the floor below.

And smell it. Although I hadn't noticed any particular odor other than dust in the tunnel, now that we were in the larger room, I caught a whiff of something so awful that it made my toes curl—the rotten egg scent of sulfur, mixed with a charred, black smell of something else I couldn't identify at first. Only after it recalled to my memory a disastrous Thanksgiving dinner I'd tried to cook by myself my first year in Las Vegas, I realized it was the smell of burning bone. Adding to the bouquet was a healthy dose of decomposing garbage. I tried to resist the urge to gag.

That urge immediately vanished, however, once I saw Jen below. In the middle of the cavern, my friend was lying on a chunk of stone carved to resemble a table. She wasn't chained down, like some hapless victim of a cheesy horror movie, or tied with ropes like Gulliver among the Lilliputians; instead she was curled up in a fetal position on her side.

With her figure so tiny against the expanse of stone, it was almost worse than the alternatives. "Is she alive?" I whispered. Ginger shushed me.

I wouldn't have been heard below, even if I'd spoken aloud. The table sat on a peninsula of rock surrounded by a viscous black mass. Its bubbles released loud hisses of steam every time they broke. In the light of the torches set around the table's perimeter, its surface was almost shiny. "Is that tar?" I asked, pointing through the layers of rock. I was remembering a school field trip to the La Brea tar pits that I'd had to hold my nose through. Its faint scent was nothing compared to the absolute stench of this place, though.

"This is Hell," Cor said once more.

Chapter Twenty-one

"Hell-adjacent," murmured Jeroboam. He, too, was looking at Jen with a face wracked with worry. They might not have been lovers in the truest sense of the word, but it was obvious that he cared about her safety. "I've got to . . ."

"No," I warned him.

Ginger grabbed on to his waistband before he could run to the perilous path down. "This is no place for heroes," she told him. "Or philosophers."

"Peace." Cor held out a hand to quiet us all. I turned back to peer between the stones again to see what he saw.

Behind the table, a silhouette rippled along the uneven wall, lit from a vent similar to the one we'd just traversed. It was of a moving figure carrying a long pole, at the top of which was the distinctive outline of a sickled blade. I shivered, knowing where I'd seen that very weapon before. "Mrs. Jones."

"Blessed ancestors," murmured Jeroboam, the moment the leader of the Order of the Crow stepped onto the path leading to the stone table. Her face was invisible beneath the ritual cowl she wore, but I knew it was her.

She yanked at a length of rope she had been grasping in her free hand, pulling at something far behind that refused to follow. After another vicious tug, I understood why. Mrs. Jones had a pair of prisoners at the end of the rope, one of whom was my mother. Her hands were bound. At some point in the afternoon she'd lost the tweedy jacket she'd donned especially for her Bel Air outing; the oversized bow on her blouse had come undone and hung loosely down her front. Several of her buttons had either popped off or been loosened as well, so that she displayed an ample amount of cleavage. "Your behavior," Mom was yelling at the top of her voice, "is absolutely unconscionable. I insist—nay, demand—that you let me and my young friend go immediately, madam!"

"She looks exactly the same." In the excitement of seeing my mother still alive and feisty, I'd forgotten that Jeroboam was still there. I wanted to question not the awe in his whisper when he saw my mother for the first time in twenty years, but his memory. When he'd left, my mother had a smooth and unwrinkled complexion and a head of dark blond hair. The slightly plump middle-aged woman loudly making her complaint down below had neither. "Exactly the same," he murmured again.

Mom wasn't alone, however. Another prisoner straggled along behind her, tied to the same rope. His progress was infinitely slower, however, because not only had his hands been bound, but his feet as well. When Mrs. Jones yanked at their binds and attempted to wrench them both along, he lurched forward and stumbled into my mother. "And you, sir," she said with as much dignity as she could muster, despite being trussed like a turkey, "reek like a tobacco warehouse."

"I'm the goddamned victim here, lady!" protested Marcus Grant. Without his shades and cell phone and tailored suit jacket, I scarcely recognized the man. His chrome dome was covered with soot. "We had a *deal*," he yelled at the hooded figure. "Just because I decided to explore other options is no reason for you to turn on me! I held to my side of the bargain. I got the kid knocked up!"

"Aren't you a charmer," said my mother in the same tone she used to reserve for my high-school boyfriends she most disliked.

"I brought her here to you today! Arranged for it, anyway! You're supposed to give my prize couple their spot at Rancho Fountain of Youth, chickadee. You can't just welch on a deal like that. Not with Marcus Grant."

Cor motioned to us, indicating that we follow him onto the ramp that led down and around the sprawling room. The flickering lights of the torches illuminated only a few feet into the shifting morass of tar. If we were careful, we could begin working our way down without being seen. I hoped, anyway.

"Oh, *you're* the victim," said my mother. She sounded harried. I knew she had to be freaked out beyond belief, and under great stress she had a tendency to become highly verbose. It was a propensity that had served her well through many years of confrontations with university administration, obnoxious store managers, and the faculty at my high school on parent-teacher conference days. "*Excuse* me. I was under the impression that *I* was the one who, along with my young friend, was *abducted* and brought here under *gunpoint* for heaven knows *what* nefarious purposes by a man who appeared to be *your* hired mercenary."

"Azimuth," Cor and I whispered at the same time. Further down the ramp, Ginger stumbled, then regained her balance without making any disturbance. Suddenly I was happy for the loud fuss my mother was making.

"*You*, however, appeared to be here of your own free will, waiting for us."

"I wasn't waiting for you, you old hag. I was waiting for him to bring me Jen. I don't even know who the hell you are. And you call this free will?" Grant hoisted up his wrists and displayed the ropes binding him. "Huh? You tied these ropes too damn tight."

"Again," said my mother, her temper flaring. "I remind you. I was ordered to tie you at gunpoint."

"You didn't have to do the feet! Jesus Christ, woman, why the feet?"

Mom stopped in her trek across the narrow ridge of rock that led to the table in the middle of the tar pit. "I considered that part of my bonus."

Mrs. Jones, having reached her destination at the cavern's center, leaned her scythe against the block of stone where Jen lay. Was my friend unconscious? I couldn't tell. It was probably better if she were. Fed up with the bickering couple, Mrs. Jones grabbed the rope connecting them and jerked with all her might. "Silence!" she thundered in a voice that echoed throughout the dome of rock. All four of us on the wall froze as if we'd been highlighted with a megawatt klieg light. I felt Cor tremble. I knew it wasn't from fear, but from the inability to do anything without risking us all. I felt the same way. "By the sacrifices of my foremothers! Why are you still speaking?"

"I don't know where *you* come from," said my mother. The last pull had sent her sprawling to the ground, but already she was rallying and trying to push herself back up. Unfortunately, with her hands tied, she only succeeded in falling back on her bottom. "But the United States of America is founded on the philosophy of democracy and freedom of speech, which had its origins in the ancient world as far back as . . ."

"Your effrontery I understand." Mrs. Jones threw back her hood, revealing her face for the first time. I don't know if Mom had seen it before, but the sight of those steely eyes and the grim jaw made her close her mouth and take a step backwards. As the figure of the Grim Reaper, Mrs. Jones had been formidable. When she revealed in the light of the torches the human-looking face behind the darkness, she somehow managed to become more sinister. "You are the one who spawned that Samantha Dorringer creature."

"And proud of it!" My mother had lost her purse somewhere in the abduction, but ankles and knees clenched in a ladylike fashion, she clutched her hands together below her bosom as if she still carried it.

"Rethink that." The Kinswoman turned her attention to the agent. "But you should know better. You know what I am capable of."

"What I know is you're capable of gypping the crap out of me!" If Marcus Grant had been carrying one of his cigars, I knew that right then he'd be stabbing it at her face. As it was, he had to make do with a belligerent tone. "You know how much I laid out on that girl? You think it's easy keeping a kid that age in shoes and clothes and DVDs and whatnot? Not to mention the outlay on my two stars . . . getting the press releases written about their early retirement, buying some fake secret getaway home in the Islands to throw off the press . . . shit, lady, you don't know."

"Nor do I care. Keep your mouths shut! And stand clear." Her hand still firmly on the rope, she turned her back to her captives, spread her arms over the table so that the long sleeves cast a shadow over Jen's form, and began murmuring something too low to hear.

I touched Cor's arm. "Why hasn't she killed them?" Not that I wanted her to, heaven knew. I just didn't understand why, when she'd had the opportunity to smite her hostages before we got there, she hadn't taken it.

"She wants something," he said back in the lowest possible voice.

Suddenly I understood. "She wants us."

Cor nodded. "That had occurred to me."

This entire situation almost made sense now. At any point in his flight, Azimuth could have done a much better job of covering his tracks. He could have left the van anywhere but the main parking lot for the Santa Monica Pier. He could have closed the portal he'd somehow opened at the top of the Pacific Wheel. What had been bothering me most of all, though, was a simple question: why had Azimuth bothered to scare Emmy Jo Graves by sticking his head out of the portal? I hadn't believed in the fiery eyes or fangs, but he'd obviously made enough of a scene to send her into hysterics. Why?

Because he knew we'd hear about it and follow him. We were walking into some kind of trap, with Jen and my mom as bait. Cor realized it, and now so did I. I suspected Ginger did as well. Heaven only knew what my poor father thought, in over his head as he was. If that were the case, though, where was the welcoming committee of Mrs. Jones' followers? Where were the Boars of the Hunt, the demons, the nets falling from the ceiling? None of it had happened yet. From what I could see, there weren't any indications that it was coming. If this were a trap, it was the most ineptly planned, trap-free trap ever conceived. Cor tugged at my hand. We were on the move again.

Her incantation complete, Mrs. Jones lowered her hands. The shadows that had covered Jen's face receded, leaving her pale and unconscious in the firelight. I caught my breath. She was still alive, wasn't she? Yes, she was. When Mrs. Jones moved her left hand in a sweeping motion over Jen's motionless form, it brushed some of her blond hair from the side of her face, causing Jen to stir sleepily. Maybe she'd been drugged—or, with any luck, Mrs. Jones had merely incapacitated her with one of her tranquilizing suggestions. Satisfied with what she saw before her, the Kinswoman reached back with her free hand and pulled her hood forward until it covered her face. Involuntarily, I shivered.

Mom had been fairly silent from her position on the floor, but when Mrs. Jones once again reached for her scythe, she spoke. "What are you planning to do to her?" I'd never heard Mom's voice so strained and frightened. I could only imagine how helpless she felt. When Mrs. Jones did not deign to reply, Mom raised her voice and tried again. "What, may I ask, are you intending to do to that poor, helpless creature?"

The head beneath the hood turned. "You may not ask." With her right fingers and thumb still entwined in the rope, Mrs. Jones grasped the scythe by the hilt. Its wooden shaft and enormous metal blade had to have weighed more than my own biceps could have contemplated, yet she hefted it as easily as if it had been fashioned from Styrofoam. "In the name of Morgana, of Melusina!" she intoned, calling to some force that none of us could see, but which all of us knew was watching. "By the rights invoked in the Oath of Blood!"

"Cor." I squeezed his arm. Something terrible was about to happen, and it had to be stopped.

He had already reached the same conclusion. He made a quick and complicated series of gestures to Ginger, who immediately sprang forward on both toes and vanished into the gloom overhead. I only caught one glimpse of her sleek black figure before she disappeared into the shadows; it seemed as if she were flying back up the ramp and around to the cavern's far side. Cor, in the meantime, pulled Jeroboam back and thrust him next to me, indicating that we should stay together, before continuing further down the ramp.

Mrs. Jones had raised the scythe high into the air. It seemed more like a wicked extension of her own arms than anything Kin-made. The blade, sharp and cruel, sparkled in the torchlight, brighter and more lethal than anything fashioned of mere steel. Its tip pointed down, aimed directly at its victim. "To thee I sacrifice this, the Bride of Abaddon, and the consecrated bounty that she carries within. Grant me in return that which I most desire."

I saw her shoulders tense, ready to let the scythe fall from its own weight. If Cor was going to do something, he had better damned well do it now.

It was my mother, though, who leapt into action. "That innocent girl is *pregnant*," she yelled. At the same time, she seemed to realize that the tether connecting her to Mrs. Jones could be tugged with equal vigor in two directions. With all the force she could muster, she yanked her bound hands down and back, causing Mrs. Jones to stagger away from the table. The scythe dropped, but fell in a direction behind her shoulders. For a long, terrible moment that seemed to last for a lifetime, I thought that it was going to descend upon my mother instead.

"Barbara!" Jeroboam's voice rang out, loud and clear, across the cavern. Farther down the ramp, I heard Cor say something, but it was too late; my father had already transformed, taking wing across the cavern at a blazing speed. That he had a bird form was no surprise to me—it ran in the family, I supposed. But I was slightly astonished to see that he had transformed into an owl. A horned owl, with two tufts of feathers where his ears should have been. He zoomed unerringly toward Mrs. Jones, letting out a surprisingly savage cry just as the scythe hit the ground, mere feet away from where my mother had scuttled. Its hilt began to sink into the tar.

Mrs. Jones, at the sound of an unexpected voice, had out of instinct cupped her hands together. A light blazed in their center, stronger and wilder than the ones Cor and Ginger had summoned. With a toss of her arm, she threw it in my direction so that it arced across the space between us, exploding in a flare mere yards away and framing me in that brief klieg light's worth of illumination I'd worried about earlier. After the flare faded, I was in darkness yet again. "Oh, look. It's Samantha," Mrs. Jones called. She sounded—well, surprised. I hadn't expected that. I scurried along the ramp, scrambling to find a safer spot. "Have you come to join my little par—?"

Before she could finish her question, Jeroboam reached his target. Legs outstretched, he connected with Mrs. Jones' skull, knocking off her hood and raking his talons hard enough to take a chunk from her ear. She screeched with outrage. When she reeled away from her avian attacker, a crimson gush began to pour down the side of her face. I was astonished; I didn't think there was that much blood in her. "Oh, no!" she crowed, acting almost as if the wound didn't affect her at all. "There will be none of that!"

From her hands flew more flashes of the very same light,

scooped from some unknown energies and tossed as readily as snowballs. The first smashed into the wall where I had stood only a moment prior, exploding with a flash of smoke. Another soared high into the air, briefly illuminating Ginger's path above. The third Mrs. Jones tossed directly at the owl returning for a second swoop at her head. It connected, sending Jeroboam spinning in a crazy downward spiral toward the rock.

I yelled out, then turned my head so I wouldn't have to see his inevitable collision. I'd betrayed my position again, but I didn't care. "Stop!" I cried out, running down. "Just stop! I surrender! I'm coming!" I prayed that Cor would have the presence of mind to take wing before I reached him on the ramp. He must have, because I didn't pass him at all. I felt safer with him out there, somewhere in the darkness, watching.

"Samantha?" My mother's voice sounded uncertain. She may not have seen me during that brief flash of light, but she certainly recognized my voice. "Is that you?"

"I'm here, Mom," I called out. By then I had made my way down the ramp and along the back perimeter of the cavern. With my hands up to show that I wasn't armed, I made my way carefully along the rocks until I was standing at the end of the bridge leading to the table. "It's okay. I'm here."

"Are you mixed up in all this nonsense?" That was the good old tart Mom that I loved. Beyond her, lying motionless on a pallet of rock, one twitching wing hanging down at a perilous angle, lay the body of an owl. I had to turn my head away, too pained to contemplate it.

"She's in it up to her fuckin' *neck*," Grant announced. He'd been quiet, cowering to himself during the light show, but now that I was near, he apparently felt emboldened again. I chose to ignore him.

"I've got nothing," I told Mrs. Jones, waving my hands. Step by step, I made my way over to my mother. "No weapons. I'm just collecting my mother. As you've found out, she's kind of a handful."

"Well!" My mother tried to pretend outrage.

It was tempting to try to grab for the scythe. The handle lay only feet away, barely sinking into the tar. Mrs. Jones, however, studied me with eyes that seemed almost to spark with electricity. Another of the glowing balls of light was forming between her hands. One wrong move, and I knew I'd end up scorched. "I'm going to untie her," I said, kneeling down. The binds around my mother's wrists weren't complicated, but they were sturdy.

"And what good is that going to do?" she asked.

"About as much good as she's going to do you," I announced. "She's served her purpose, right? She brought me here." Mrs. Jones cocked her head, not seeming to understand. Had I not comprehended Azimuth's plan correctly? Was my mother not part of the trap? Was there a trap at all? "Never mind," I said, struggling with the knot. Finally, the end of the rope gave way. My mother's hands, loosened slightly, assisted me in smoothing away the rest of the knots. "She's not valuable." Seeing that my mother was about to protest, I added with a set jaw, "To you."

Once free, my mother clung to me. "I am so glad I am no longer part of your family, Samantha." Mrs. Jones's tone was arctic. Though her ear continued to bleed from her wound, she didn't make any attempt to stanch the flow. "Tiresome, all of you." I squeezed my mother's hand so that she wouldn't say anything cheeky. I needed a diversion. I needed Cor or Ginger to swoop in and get Mrs. Jones' attention off me temporarily, so I could get my mother to safety. I needed to do *something*, and my ill-thought-out plan wasn't good enough.

"To be honest, I can't say I've been all that impressed with your little clan either." I squeezed my mother's hands. "And what's all this business with the human sacrifice? First you want the baby, then you don't want the baby, circle of blood, sacrifice, blah, blah. Don't you have a plan? Or are you just winging it?"

I hadn't intended my last two words to act as any kind of cue, honestly. The moment I said them, though, the two ravens dove in from either side of the cavern, converging on their target with one objective: to bring her to the ground. The ball of light that Mrs. Jones had been playing with flew from her fingertips and into the air, seeming to follow the flight of the larger of the two birds. I cried out in fear when it nearly clipped his wing. Cor switched direction in mid-flight, however, so that the projectile crashed into flames on the ceiling. Another ball of light flew toward Ginger. I turned my head again. I couldn't simply sit there and watch the ravens be destroyed.

"Mom," I said in a low voice, shaking her hands so that she would look not at the fiery bullets being flung around the cavern, but at me. "I need you to listen to me. I have to concentrate." She shook her head, not understanding. "Hang on to me," I warned her. "Hang tight. Don't let go, no matter what happens."

"What are you going to do?" she asked, obviously frightened.

I shook my head. Nothing, if it went badly. Even if the germ of the idea I'd had could work, the cavern was too loud for me to think, much less relax. Mrs. Jones was sending out too many flashes of light for me to concentrate; the explosions were coming much more rapidly than before. Mrs. Jones turned in my direction, but she wasn't focusing on me. "I see you!" she taunted the two ravens. In her hands grew two blue globes, their surfaces brimming with energies that even to my untrained eye looked ominous. Black spikes pulsed around them, making a deep electrical tone with every pass. "Avoid these—if you can!"

I heard a high-pitched, soprano scream. It wasn't Mom, though. It was Marcus, covering his head as he yelled. Mrs. Jones began to thrust her hands upward, intending to shoot the bolts at the two ravens flapping in a desperate attempt to get out of range. Instead, she suddenly and quite without warning fell forward, collapsing to her knees with a sickening crack. One of the two blue bundles of energy bounced off onto the surface of the tar pits, where it buzzed harmlessly among the slowly puckering bubbles. The other escaped her palm, rolled along her arm, and affixed itself to her chest, stunning her into silence as she shuddered and jerked from the voltage. I blinked, astonished, to see Jen standing behind the slumping form of Mrs. Jones, the scythe in her hand. "Oh my God," I said, my jaw scraping the ground. "Did you . . . slice her?"

"What? Oh my gosh, Sam! Ew! As if!" Jen made an icky-poo face. "I knocked out the back of her knees with the handle, silly!"

"I thought you were unconscious! Or worse!"

Before I could avoid it, Jen reached out and gave me an affectionate rap on the forehead. "Hello! Anyone home? It's called 'playing dead.' It's so easy that a dog can do it. So why not me?"

Behind me, an exhausted and frightened Marcus Grant began to blubber. "Jen. Baby. Come help Marc out of his ropes. There's a good girl." The look that Jen gave me and my mother could best be described as dubious. "C'mon," he begged. "Do it for old time's sake, huh? Please? I'm begging you." Jen sighed, and then as if she'd never been kidnapped or nearly decapitated, bounced over and began to untie the agent's binds.

"This is where I need help," I told my mother. It had to be done now. Mrs. Jones had stopped shuddering from the electrical shock. Though she was dazed and weaving on her knees, she blinked slowly and looked around the cavern for the ravens that still flew above. "Hang on *hard*," I urged.

I knew she had a thousand questions to ask, but trusting me, she only nodded. Then she leaned forward and embraced me as tightly as only a mother can. I closed my eyes, tried to take a deep breath, and concentrated on the things around me—the good things.

I thought about Jen, patiently unfastening the bonds of a man she knew for a fact had sold her out.

I thought about my mother, who'd endured so much for my sake that afternoon, yet who clung to me as if I was the one who needed solace, instead of the other way around.

I thought about my father, lying mere feet away, unconscious or maybe even dead, who'd marveled at how little my mother had changed in twenty years. Who had sprung into action the moment he thought she might be in danger.

I thought about Ginger, who didn't like me, but who did what she could to protect me because she cared for her superior.

And I thought of Cor, and of his soft touch and even softer smiles. I thought about the warmth of his hands, and the way my body felt against his when we slept together at night. I thought of him soaring with wings spread, gliding on unseen currents of the air. I thought of his race's blood, flowing in mine. He was my lover. He was my Kin.

"Samantha?" I heard my mother say. Her voice was distant and soft, as if she were across the cavern. I couldn't even feel her touch, now, though I trusted it was there. "Are you doing that?"

"Hang on to me," I urged her. I didn't feel my mouth move, but the words came out, sounding equally far away.

"Oh my gosh," I heard Jen say. "Where is that *thing* coming from?"

"Get hold of Jen," the far-away me said. "And Mr. Grant." Cor and Ginger could take care of themselves, I knew. In that distance I heard the sound of some commotion; it sounded like Jen was yelling at someone, but I couldn't make out the particulars. I didn't want to try. I might lose the sensation, or let it get out of my control. Even in my drifting state, I knew that would be a bad thing.

Another sound joined the mix. At first it rumbled like a

subway train, deep underground. The vibrations continued, though, growing louder and more confusing. If they were loud to my ears, as distantly removed as I felt, I knew they had to be deafening to everyone else. A shriek filled the air, but it hadn't issued from any human or Peri lungs. It was the howl of a tempest, of winds stronger than any I'd heard, mournful and hungry. If I were to open my eyes, I would find the ground shaking beneath my knees.

"Samantha." I heard Cor's voice in my head, calm, firm. "Let go."

"Now?" I heard myself asking, grateful for some direction.

"Now," he replied. I sensed him standing nearby. "We're all here. Just let go."

I opened my eyes to an inferno. Heat roasted my face, causing me to throw up a hand to shield myself from the blazing vision that emanated from a translucent half-globe spreading into our cavern. If we were Hell-adjacent, as Jeroboam had said, then the mirage of raging fire and lava that was bulging through from another world had to be Hell itself. The tumult assaulting our ears was of a collective anguish, a keening of countless souls that left me without any hope or will of my own. I wanted to let go of my mother and clap my hands over my ears, though I knew I couldn't drown out the horror. If I'd thought I'd known the meaning of despair before, I was wrong. Any woes I'd had were mere pimples on prom night, compared to the vast and empty gulf of want and pain opening before us.

Even Mrs. Jones, disoriented, hoodless, bleeding, and trying to get her bearings as she stood, held up her hands against the terrible heat and clamor. "What—?" I heard her cry, turning away her face.

"Marc!" yelled Jen. "Get back here!"

When I turned, the agent had yanked himself from Jen's grasp. Attempting to run from the vision of Hell protruding into our dimension, he'd stumbled out into the tar. I saw him gasp, astonished, as the viscous goo clutched at his feet. It was far stickier than he'd imagined. He wrenched himself around, hands out, appealing without words for our aid. Already he regretted his flight. My mother continued to clutch Jen by the ankle, so she couldn't hare after him.

Without warning, the mirage vanished. It seemed to expand outward—and then caved in. It disappeared with a final whirlwind of noise and chaos. The burning sensation and the tumult vanished, leaving my skin cold and shivering and my ears ringing. But I was alive, and thanks to the chain of connections that had held us here, still sitting on the bridge of rock where I'd started. My mother's arm was around my waist. Jen sprawled nearby, still reaching toward the tar. Cor stood behind me, his hands resting on my shoulder. We were all okay.

Not far away, with the body of the fallen owl, crouched Ginger. Her hands explored the bird's feathers. Cor let go of me and ran around the stinking tar lapping at his feet to where she knelt. "He's got a broken wing," Ginger called over.

"And probably a concussion," said Cor, sliding the owl away from the tar. "But I'm pretty sure he'll be all right."

After all that she'd been through, my mother didn't have a thing to say. Instead, she stared at the owl carefully while rubbing my back. "Do you know," she finally murmured. "I honestly thought I heard . . ." She let the thought trail off. I felt her shaking her head. "Poor owl," she said instead, much to my relief. "Listen to me, worrying about the bird when we've all been through so much. But these things always seem so much harder on the poor, innocent animals, don't they?" She sighed, then started to rise, apparently so she could go help Ginger with Jeroboam. "At least, they do to me."

"Where's Marc?" Jen had managed to rise to her feet again. She peered out into the darkness and the tar, where moments before her employer had been struggling. Other than some deep marks in the black mess where his legs had begun to sink, there was no sign of the man. Even the marks had begun to disappear, as the tar slowly began to fill itself in.

Cor looked at me from where my mother was kneeling by my father's bird form. We both knew that when it had snapped back, the bubble I'd drawn from the adjacent world had taken with it the only two individuals not anchored to each other: Mrs. Jones and Hollywood's most recognizable manager. Exactly what was *Variety* going to say about that? If only he hadn't scrambled off on his own.

Before I could even assimilate the enormity of what I'd done, Mom let out a yelp. "It's him!" she said, pointing toward the tunnel from where I'd originally seen her emerge. When I turned, Azimuth stood in its entrance, his trademark hair hanging over his shoulders as if he'd just flat-ironed it to perfection. Sometime since I'd last seen him, he'd managed to change clothing as well. Gone was the muscle-wear; instead he'd donned a pair of black jeans and a leather jacket straight out of a road-show production of *Grease*. "It's that awful man!" When I stood up, ready to charge at him and kill him, she clutched at my leg. "He has a gun!"

"Only to ensure my safe getaway, madam, I assure you," he replied in cultured tones.

"Azimuth," I growled, aware of the pistol in his right hand. "All of this was your doing."

"Indeed," he agreed, bowing his head. "And I must thank you, Samantha, and your friends for your assistance in delivering me from a most unpleasant foe."

"Foe?" Ginger had stood up and was on the alert, ready to spring into the air at Cor's notice. "She was your *ally*."

"No," I said. The pieces were falling into place. "Azimuth didn't want us hurt. He only wanted to ensure we'd follow him here. He knew that kidnapping Jen and delivering her to the two people in the world who wished her ill would do the trick. Getting my mother in the bargain was a stroke of luck, wasn't it?" Again, he bowed, acceding to the question. "What was she to you—Mrs. Jones?" From the corner of my eyes, I could see Cor moving slowly toward him, inch by inch. I hoped he could evade Azimuth's notice.

"My relationship to her was similar to yours, Samantha. We were adversaries. I told you that once I'd identified an adversary, I moved to neutralize them. In this case, I couldn't have done it without your help." He nodded at Cor, and then once for every member of our party. "And yours. And yours. And yours. And his. Poor creature," he said, inclining his head in the direction where Jeroboam lay.

"You *used us*?"

"Just as you used me. It was a mutually beneficial arrangement."

"But we didn't know about it!" I growled.

"Details." He gestured with the barrel of the gun. "Besides, is not the enemy of your enemy your friend?"

"Not always," I said, trying to keep his attention on me.

It didn't work. With lightning-swift reflexes, Azimuth pointed the gun at Cor, causing him to leap back with his arms up. "A pity you don't see it that way. Corydonais, my respects to your dame and to your great-dame, if you please. And a word of advice?" He smiled as he backed into the tunnel. "Keep a close eye on your woman, you lucky man. If you're not careful, someone might snatch her away." He nodded at me and winked with a smile that I could only describe as saucy. Then, with a rustle of leather, he was gone.

"I'm on him!" yelled Ginger. She ran three steps, then was aloft, flapping her wings furiously as she disappeared into the darkness.

Cor turned to me, hands on his hips. "Are you in danger of being snatched away?" he wanted to know.

I shook my head, laughing and weary. "Oh, Cor." When he opened his arms to me, I ran over and fell in them. His lips met mine in a kiss. "Not a chance in hell," I whispered, once I'd tasted him. "Not a chance."

"Samantha." My mother's voice cut through the happy reunion. Limping from a broken heel, she stood up from Jeroboam's form, walked over to where I stood, tapped me on the shoulder, and spoke in a low and confidential voice. "Samantha! Is it my imagination, or did your young friend Ginger turn into a bird?"

"Baby Suri," I corrected, flicking him on the nose. "But you get an A for effort."

He had just leaned in for a kiss when I heard a knock at the door downstairs. "Nooooo!" he complained when I began to scoot across the sheets.

"Yes!" I called over my shoulder. "I've been waiting for this all week!" I slipped into some shorts and a pullover that had been conveniently lying beside the bed, then padded from the room.

"Waiting for your present from *him*?" Cor followed, his only concession to modesty being the narrow black slacks he'd folded over a chair. "Your other man? My rival?"

"Oo, yes, Lord Rufus Smedley, indeed I mean the swain for whom I swoon," I said over my shoulder, reaching the bottom of the stairwell and beginning to cross the living room. "My paramour. My toy boy. My tenderoni."

"It was okay when I was joking about it." Cor followed, his hands thrust deep into his pockets. "But you seem to have put a little too much thought in your synonyms."

Leaning against my doorway was a manila envelope, sealed, which fell into the room the moment I pulled open the knob. I scooped it up with a little thrill and began opening it without even closing the door again. As I'd expected, there were a number of formal documents inside, organized, clearly marked, and ready to be signed. Though I'd looked forward to getting them, simply holding the papers in my hand made me a little sad.

My grief must have showed. "That's it, then?" Cor rested his butt on the table we used for dining, letting his bare feet dangle. I nodded. "Everything's in order?"

"Looks like it."

Still, I didn't do anything. After a very long silence, Cor cleared his throat and said, in the manner of someone broaching a difficult topic, "He wants to see more of you, you know. Your sire." In a kinder voice he amended, "Your father."

I nodded, unable to say anything. "I know."

"He's well known among the philosophers, Ginger tells me. Her dame is a philosopher."

"Really," I said, finding that interesting. "You wouldn't know it." I studied the legal documents in my hands for a moment more, gnawing at the back of my knuckles.

"Beecham signed his cast."

"I'll see him again. I just need a little time. You know? Last week was so . . ."

"Weird."

"I was going to say compressed. But weird, too." I could hold on to these papers and mope, or I could give them to their rightful recipient. "Okay. Let's do this." I slipped on a pair of sandals I kept by the back door. From a basket of folded laundry sitting on the sofa, Cor grabbed a black T-shirt and pulled it on, following in his bare feet.

Birds strutted across the lawn on either side of the sidewalk. They didn't bother to fly away when we passed. Nor did the peacock who had taken up roosting in the old firewood bin, though it did strut from the enclosure, fan out its fancy feathers, and greet us with a glottal cry. I gave him a wave as I climbed the steps to my mother's back porch, rapped on the door, and let myself in. "Mom?"

"In here!" she called from the living room. When Cor and I wandered in, we were greeted by the unexpected sight of my mother in a housecoat with her feet propped up on the coffee table, toes separated by eight fluffy cotton balls. Landemann sat on the floor beside her, shades on, mustache expressively mournful as we caught him brandishing a brush laden with deep pink nail polish. "Tuesday is pedicure day!" she trilled, petting a contented Ragdoll cat that had settled on her stomach. "Don't stop," she ordered Landemann. Seeming embarrassed, he applied a little more polish to her big toenail, then puffed out his cheeks to blow.

"Delivery for you," I said, holding out the envelope as I cleared a space on the sofa beside her.

She leaned over and took it. "I didn't hear the mail. What is it?"

I grabbed her hand. "It's an official document for the dissolution of your marriage to . . . to Dad," I said, letting it all out. "Like you asked, remember? Girls' night out, way back when?"

Her mouth pursed. "Oh." I waited for her to say something else. Anything else. She remained silent as she looked over the papers, flipping through every page. When I'd become convinced that I shouldn't have come, she suddenly leaned over to the pile of books on the table nearby, plucked a ballpoint pen from within one of them, and began signing where Azimuth had placed the sticky tabs. "You saw him then, did you?"

"I did." I would never tell her that she had, too.

"And how was he?"

"Good enough."

"Remarried, I suppose," she said, with a sniff. "Another family?"

I shook my head. "Alone," I told her, quite truthfully.

Mom flipped to the final page of the documents and gave the last of her signatures a fillip before handing the bundle back to me. "Well. I think that's a shame. No one should have to spend a life alone. Should they, Mr. Landemann?" A particular tension had filled the room during the signing. Landemann still sat on the floor, motionless, as he stared at my mother with expectancy. At her question, his eyebrows shot into the air, hovering above his sunglasses like unidentified furry objects. "Yes, Mr. Landemann," said Mom, her face beaming with genuine happiness. "I can now marry you."

I was nearly thrown from the sofa when Landemann bounded to his feet, arms outstretched, to lunge at his beloved. Cor and I, along with several cats, fled the general vicinity. My mother's muffled voice cried out, "Mr. Landemann! Mind the polish!"

Once we were back outside and our giggles had subsided, Cor asked put his arm around me. "How legal are those documents your friend cooked up?"

"I guess as legal as a divorce can be when one of the people has forged documents and isn't human," I replied. "Legal enough. Azimuth owed us. Still owes us. It was the least he could do. Do you hate him?"

"I'm not happy with him. He put us both in danger, unnecessarily."

"But he also helped."

Cor conceded the point. "That's why I'm letting Ginger burn off some energy trying to track him down, but that's all the manpower I'm putting into it." He hugged me close, waiting until we'd gotten down the porch steps before speaking again. "You know," he said, suddenly changing course so that instead of running the gauntlet of ravens, we were taking the side path around my mother's bungalow that led to the canals, "I told you once, very long ago, that I'm not like your father."

"I know." As we squeezed through the narrow gateway that led to the canal-side walk, I could hear my mother whooping it up through the closed living room window. Her celebration made me grin a little. "I don't think you are."

"Can I prove it to you?"

"How?"

Cor took my left hand between his. With a fluid motion, he began to lower himself to a single knee. "If I promise to you that in twenty years' time, I'll still be around, will you, Samantha Dorringer . . ."

My heart froze. Once before I'd wondered if this moment could ever be coming, and here it was. "No, no, no!" I cried, yanking away my hand. "No!" I shouted back at him as I tripped down the path to the canal walk. One of the arched bridges lay nearby. I ran to the top of it, gripped the rail, and waited for him.

When he caught up, confusion and hurt colored his face. "Don't you want to—?"

"Poor Cor!" I said, grabbing him by the cheeks and searing a kiss onto his lips. I'd confused him.

"I wanted to ask—"

"No."

"I thought you wanted—"

"No!"

"But don't you want to m—?"

"Yes!" I said, laughing once more. "But don't ask me that question! Not today! Not even this week!" I'd confused him so much that he was afraid to say anything more. His eyes were wide and astonished; his lips worked slightly, then sputtered to a stop. "It's Mom's day today," I explained. "And Landemann's. Let's not eclipse that. Let it be all theirs." Finally he saw the light. Redness began to recede from his face. He stroked his chin, understanding why I'd stopped him. "Besides, sweetheart. When you ask—if you ask again—I want to be sure you're doing it because you mean it. Not because you're carried away by the emotion of someone else's special news."

He nodded, then took my hand. Slowly and deliberately we strolled over the peak of the bridge down to the far end of the canal. It was one of those effortlessly brilliant Californian afternoons, when the sun warmed the waters below, reflecting in ripples across the pink and white houses to either side. "Don't you think I meant it?" he asked, squinting at me.

"Oh, I know you do." I had no doubts. That was why he'd thrilled me so, setting my insides humming. "Are you going to feel the same way in a few weeks? Enough to ask me again?"

At a turn in the canal, near one of the handmade docks poking out into the waters, he stopped and turned. "Don't you know by now that I will?"

I already knew my answer, but I thought about it for a

moment. For most of my life I believed in only what I could see with my own eyes. I should have known better. I couldn't see his love for me. I couldn't reach out and touch it, or poke it, or put it in a bag and stick it in my pocket. Yet invisible as it was, I carried it with me everywhere, just as beside it I carried the boundless, buoyant love I had him. "I do," I told him, my heart glad and light and giddy. "We'll take that leap together, when it's time."

For a moment I worried when his face didn't change. Then I saw it—the slightest quiver at the corners of his eyes. I'd lit a smile inside him that burned slowly and steadily, igniting from the inside and consuming its way out, reaching the lips and exposing his teeth until at last he was whooping with the happiest laughter I'd ever heard. Without warning, he roared once again and danced over. Seemingly without effort, he scooped me off the ground and lifted me into his arms. "Wagh!" I'm afraid I said, disoriented when he whirled me around. "What're you doing?"

"Celebrating!" he cried. Kicking off his sandals, he navigated our way to the pier and jumped into the water. It was only mere inches deep at that point, but the impact jarred me from his arms. I found my own bare legs flopping down into the wet canal. Quickly I searched for footing in the mud. His pants were soaked. Gleeful as a kid, he leaned down and splashed some water in my direction. I shrieked, but it was too late; the spray had gotten my shorts and pullover wet. "To Landemann and Barbara!" he yelled.

Screw being soaked. Cor's mood was infectious. "To Mom and Landemann!" I yelled back, leaning down to push a wave in his direction.

As we chased each other around the mucky depths, one of Mom's neighbors poked a curious head from her deck. The woman shook her head at us, tsked, and went back to watering her plants. She didn't even seem to notice when, from her railing, and from the roofs and lawns around us, a mass of jet-black ravens rose to the skies as one. They swooped and circled the heavens in an elaborate dance, almost seeming to celebrate with us.

Although their wings filled the air with noise, neither one of us could hear it over our laughter. We were happy and exhausted as children. Both of us had stepped into the same river, and I trusted that in its waters, we would walk together for all time to come.

ELISSA WILDS

He says it was foretold, an inescapable way to bring them together. All Laurell Pittman knows is that ungovernable need surges through her body whenever the Axiom is near. Who is this godlike stranger who appears out of nowhere to steal her away from home? If she believes his claim, she is destined to conceive a very special child…and he is the appointed father. As he fights off demons trying to prevent their child's birth and patiently teaches her to use her own undiscovered powers, she finds her heart going out to this Balancer who is equally at home with good and evil, teetering on the edge of temptation, eternally caught …

BETWEEN LIGHT AND DARK

ISBN 13: 978-0-505-52791-2

◻ **YES!**

Sign me up for the Love Spell Book Club and send my
FREE BOOKS! If I choose to stay in the club, I will pay only
$8.50* each month, a savings of $6.48!

NAME: _____

ADDRESS: _____

TELEPHONE: _____

EMAIL: _____

◻ I want to pay by credit card.

◻ **VISA**   ◻ **MasterCard.**   ◻ **DISCOVER**

ACCOUNT #: _____

EXPIRATION DATE: _____

SIGNATURE: _____

Mail this page along with $2.00 shipping and handling to:
Love Spell Book Club
PO Box 6640
Wayne, PA 19087
Or fax (must include credit card information) to:
610-995-9274
You can also sign up online at **www.dorchesterpub.com**.

*Plus $2.00 for shipping. Offer open to residents of the U.S. and Canada only. Canadian
residents please call 1-800-481-9191 for pricing information.
If under 18, a parent or guardian must sign. Terms, prices and conditions subject to
change. Subscription subject to acceptance. Dorchester Publishing reserves the right to
reject any order or cancel any subscription.